THE SILENCED

THE SILENCED

JAMES DeVITA

LAURA GERINGER BOOKS
An Imprint of HarperCollins *Publishers*

Eos is an imprint of HarperCollins Publishers.

The Silenced
Copyright © 2007 by James DeVita
All rights reserved. Printed in the United States of America.
No part of this book may be used or reproduced in any manner whatsoever without
written permission except in the case of brief quotations embodied in critical articles
and reviews. For information address HarperCollins Children's Books, a division of
HarperCollins Publishers, 1350 Avenue of the Americas, New York, NY 10019.
www.harperteen.com

Library of Congress Cataloging-in-Publication Data
DeVita, James.
The silenced / by James DeVita. — 1st ed.
    p. cm.
"Laura Geringer Books."
Summary: Consigned to a prison-like youth training facility because of her parents'
political activities, Marena organizes a resistance movement to combat the restrictive
policies of the ruling Zero Tolerance party.
ISBN-10: 0-06-078462-8 (trade bdg.) — ISBN-13: 978-0-06-078462-1 (trade bdg.)
ISBN-10: 0-06-078464-4 (lib. bdg.) — ISBN-13: 978-0-06-078464-5 (lib. bdg.)
[1. Fantasy.] I. Title.
PZ7.D49827Sil 2007
[Fic]—dc22   2006019380
                                                                          CIP
                                                                           AC

Typography by Neil Swaab
1 2 3 4 5 6 7 8 9 10
❖
First Edition

*This story was inspired by,
and is dedicated to, Sophie Scholl*

1

Marena hurried down the street, past the long stretch of identical home units, the winter air needling her awake. Outside the open perimeter gate a green YTF bus sat huffing its exhaust into the chilly morning. Marena quickened her pace, trying to zipper her coat between strides. An electric bell buzzed, and the tall gate shuddered, creaked, and began to inch its way closed. She broke into a run, waving her journey permit over her head and shouting at the blank-faced Stof in the guardhouse, "I'm here! I'm here!" He didn't stop the gate. "Hold up. I'm right here!"

The thin doors of the bus closed, and its hulking frame clunked into gear. Marena sprinted the last few steps, scooted sideways through the gate, and held her permit up for the Stof to see.

He stared at her with dead eyes and waved her through.

The bus braked to a stop, the doors flapped open, and Marena climbed up the thick rubber steps. She pressed her hand into the digiprint, which flashed blue. The driver let her pass, and she headed down the aisle.

Sitting in the front seats to her left were a couple of nukes—newly culled kids whose parents had recently been convicted of crimes against the state. Marena knew what a joke the cullings were. All the big legal words—inherited guilt, associative responsibility, the Filial Internment Act—were just a bunch of lies made up by the Zero Tolerance Party. It was how the ZTs made it legal to arrest anyone for anything at all: wrong color, wrong religion, wrong ideas.

There were two nukes this month, and Marena nodded to them as she passed. A frightened-looking girl, about fourteen, clutching a clear plastic book bag, nodded back. The other, an older boy, looked at Marena quickly and then stared front again. Redheaded, thin and freckled, he looked like he was trying to act cool, but Marena noticed his foot tapping nervously beneath the seat in front of him. She would have liked to sit with them and tell them it really wasn't that bad, that they'd get used to things after a few months; she'd have liked to tell them which students at the youth training facility were safe and which were listeners, or who the nice instructors of public enlightenment were, or how to sneak out after curf and scavenge without getting caught, but she knew she couldn't take the chance. It was so hard to know whom to trust that it was easier not to trust anyone.

Marena continued down the aisle. To her right, the JJ-Girls—Jennifer, Heather, and Michele—stopped comparing the latest jewelry they'd scrounged and looked up. Marena turned her back to Jennifer's whispered insults and walked past her. Behind Jennifer, Franky "Pug-face" Poyer stuck his ugly puss into the aisle. Marena pushed by him and smiled at Dex, who was in the back row, saving her a seat. Dex had been a part of her relocation group after they'd been culled from their homes and assigned to the Spring Valley Re-Dap Community.

Marena flopped beside Dex, barely keeping the required foot of distance between them. They touched hands quickly.

"Hey," Dex whispered, ignoring the no-talking rule. Like ventriloquists, he and almost everyone at the YTF had learned to talk while barely moving their lips.

"Hey," Marena whispered back, staring at the ceiling.

"What's up?"

"Nothing. Just my dad being a jerk again."

The bus pulled away from the compound and gathered speed, skimming silently along what had once been country roads winding through the lush farmland of Spring Valley. The farms were dead now, and the roads were flat black asphalt, cutting straight across the barren fields.

Dex turned to Marena. "You get in okay last night?"

"Yeah. What about you?"

"Yeah."

She wriggled out of her coat, leaning into Dex longer than she should have. He pressed back, and she knew he too was enjoying the stolen moment of closeness.

"Wake me when we're there," he whispered.

Marena smiled, wondering if he felt as safe as she did when they were together. She twisted around and looked out the back window, watching the vast tracts of ruined cropland spill out behind the bus. Whatever had once thrived in the rich soil of Spring Valley was long dead. Weeds, wilted dark from the coming cold, blanketed the wasteland, and a black frost glinted under the early-morning sun.

Marena squinted at the odd beauty of it, wondering why the sun would even choose to rise on such a place as this. She tried to count the shadowy lines of old furrows ghosted beneath the weeds, but they flickered by too fast. A tree, overlooked somehow in the ravagings, still stood in one field. Scattered around its trunk lay most of its leaves, blazing in autumn reds and crimson-yellows. They looked almost fake, they were so beautiful, like someone had dumped out a box of paper cutouts. A few early flecks of snow flitted down.

A faint image came to Marena, something she'd seen before. . . . *White, something white.* Just a glimpse, then gone. *A snowman?* she thought. No, no, it was moving. *Clouds?* She turned front, keeping an eye on the bus driver, and slid down in her seat. She snuck her hand into a hidden seam of her coat and eased out a small stapling of scrap paper she'd stolen from art class.

Dex saw the paper and shook his head. He hadn't been sleeping at all.

Marena tapped her eyebrow twice, signaling Dex to keep watch and then leaned over as if to tie her shoe. She slid out the small stub of a pencil she'd hidden in the cuff of her pants and, staying low behind the seat back, started to write, but the image was no longer there. She looked out the window again. Sometimes she had to trick her memories into showing themselves, cold-shoulder them a little.

It came again.

The doorbell's ringing. It won't stop. Footsteps on the porch. My mother walking toward the front door. They're getting into the house. They have no faces . . . white heads . . . masked—

It's okay, it's okay.

It's kids. It's just kids. There's laughter, my mother's laugh. The little kids are dressed in white, dressed up like silly ghosts, holes cut out for eyes, goofy mouths drawn in Magic Marker. It's just kids.

Marena laid her small binding of paper against her knee, pressed it flat, and wrote:

I remember her arm above me holding open
the screen door. Her dress—a tiny-flower

*print, yellow and blue. I remember the
smell of cold and the wind. Outside, the
sound of dried leaves blowing. It was a
holiday we used to have . . . where kids
played dress-up. I had candy in my hand
that I passed out to the children. Then
they left, and my mother took me back*
*inside to the living room. I knelt at the
coffee table. It had a thick glass top
and—*

A different memory, an uninvited one that Marena
knew well, cut in.

*glass flashing white . . . bright, blinding white . . .
explosions . . . no sound . . . blood everywhere.*

She closed her eyes and tried to chase the images
away.

Still she saw the blood.

She focused on the first memory again: on her
mother, the dress, the flower print. *Keep writing*, she
told herself, trying to picture her mother's face, but all
that she could see was her hair. She concentrated on
her mother's hair . . .

Beautiful hair, dark and long, pooling out on the glass top of our coffee table when she wrote. But on this day, the holiday, she wasn't writing. She was playing with me, cutting shapes out of sheets of orange paper. I had my own scissors too—blue-handled and blunted.

Marena put the pencil down and let the memory wash over her: her mother unwrapping a new package of construction paper, clear plastic, the glint and crackle of cellophane, white glue on their fingers. She could smell the glue. She could hear the hollow *flup-flup* of the thick sheets of colored paper as her mother fanned them in the air. She could even feel the soft crunch the scissors made as she cut out crooked silhouettes of cats and bats and—

"Hey," Dex said, tapping Marena. "Put that away. We're here."

The memory vanished at his touch.

Marena hid her paper inside her coat and stuffed the pencil stub back into her cuff. She felt better. Recalling things that had happened made her feel good, like she'd accomplished something. It was one thing the ZTs couldn't get their hands on. They had tried to erase everything or twist it into something it wasn't. But they couldn't touch what she kept inside her. Whatever Marena could remember was hers. *Every thing of beauty*, she thought, calling to mind her mother's words, *every memory of something good, is a form of resistance.*

The bus idled in place within the gates of the YTF, waiting for the security sweep. A pair of black jackboots clacked by, a Stof inspecting the underside of the bus with a mirror attached to the end of a long silver shaft. Marena pressed her forehead against the cold window and couldn't help thinking how as a little girl she'd heard of things like this happening to other people in other countries. She'd felt so safe then, so sorry for those poor people in all those faraway places. *Do they feel sorry for us now?* she wondered. *Is there a faraway little girl somewhere thinking, Those poor people, or is she thinking, Those people, now they know?*

An electronic buzzer screeched the all-clear signal, and the bus eased through the security gate.

2

The bus began its tedious crawl from the gate to the front doors of the youth training facility, slowly rumbling over the hundreds of sensors embedded in the pavement. A vehicle moving faster than six miles an hour would trigger the pressure-sensitive cylinders into a field of steel spikes.

Marena sat back as the bus bumped toward the YTF, a converted high school bordered on all sides by a tall chain-link fence. The baseball diamond and football field had been removed—scraped flat and blacktopped over. Only the aluminum bleachers remained, looking out over a parking lot of utility vehicles, military transports, and spooring drones in neat rows. Marena stared at the empty grandstands, imagining the cheers that once might have come from them, the boys and girls who might have run the fields, the proud parents and cheerleaders, the school bands and pom-poms.

The bus hissed to a stop in front of the building: gray-green brick, many windowed, and L-shaped—an ugly reminder. Youth training facilities were one of the first things Marena's mother had fought against.

Three banks of massive steel doors clanked open and locked into position. A small detachment of state officers, stiff and synchronized, filed out, creating a uniformed corridor at the entrance.

Marena stepped off the bus and fell into line behind Dex. Like everyone else, she laced her fingers together and placed her hands on top of her head as she walked between the two lines of Stofs into the YTF. Mr. Farr hovered near the metal detector, tapping his pen against the clipboard that he always carried. Marena stepped through. *Jerk*, she thought, smiling at him.

Dex whispered, "See you second period," and disappeared into the crowd of students. Marena waved her ID card over her locker sensor, and the door clicked open. She tossed in her coat and backpack, grabbed her Commemorator, and headed to homeroom.

"Two-two two-four-three," Marena said into the roll

recorder as she walked through the doorway. She took her seat, placed her Commemorator in the center of her desk, and opened it to today's date.

One of the nukes, the skinny redheaded kid she'd seen on the bus, was in her homeroom. He was sitting in the front row near the door, twisting in his chair and looking around. Marena saw that he didn't have his Commemorator with him, and she tried to get his attention. She waved at him a few times until she finally caught his eye. He looked scared, like he'd been caught doing something. Marena pointed to the open book on her desk. He didn't understand. She held her Commemorator up and tapped its cover. He looked at her for the briefest of moments, then bolted out of the room, nearly knocking over Jennifer as she was coming in. Jennifer sat behind Marena, clicking her nails together and smelling of hair spray. Marena leaned forward to get as far away from her as she could.

Miss Goeff strode into the classroom. She snatched up a piece of chalk and wrote "Thursday is Remembrance Day" on the blackboard, then sat and opened the big red book that stayed on the left-hand corner of every IPE's desk in the YTF.

The new kid came running back into the classroom and made it to his seat just as the warning bell sounded. The door closed by itself and locked. Marena stood with the rest of the class and held her hand across her chest. They were required to hold their right hands over their hearts, but as soon as Miss Goeff turned to face the state flag, Marena switched them.

A single musical note chimed out of the intercom. Marena moved her lips instead of singing the state anthem.

> *Let our flag fly freely,*
> *Let us cherish freedom won,*
> *Let hand join hand and heart join heart,*
> *For out of many, one.*

Miss Goeff flipped through the big red book till she found the right page. "This, the new morning of the state calendar, third day of the tenth month."

Marena bowed her head along with the others.

"Grant us, our leaders," Miss Goeff recited, solemn and monotone, "the continuation of social harmony and safety for this, our glorious state."

The class responded in unison. "Grant us this."

"We pray for our leaders in the Protectorate, our instructors of public enlightenment, and all those who honorably serve the state. We pray for our students, that they may learn the ways of productive citizenship and embrace the doctrines of the Zero Tolerance Party, which welcomes them if only they believe."

"If only we believe," the class responded.

"Please be seated," Miss Goeff said. "Row three will read today."

Row three stood up with Commemorators in hand. The girl in the first seat began.

"'We believe that the intermingling and tolerance of different religions, foreign cultures, or personal beliefs of the individual dilute the national character and moral foundation of our state.'"

"This we believe," Marena echoed with the rest of the class, not believing. She had to say these words with the others. Miss Goeff always watched the responsories closely.

The girl sat, and the boy behind her read. "'We believe that the right to say and think anything one wants, regardless of the harmful effects on a community, is an abomination, and therefore a threat to the safety that we ourselves presently enjoy.'"

"This we believe," the class repeated.

The boy sat, and the next student read. "'We commemorate and honor the lives lost in the Great

Millennium War and pray for the safety of those who continue the battle against unbelievers within our midst. We humbly give thanks to the moral courage of the Zero Tolerance Party for saving us in our time of need.'"

"For this we offer grateful thanks."

Miss Goeff repeated the last response to herself. She paused and then looked at the class. "Who would like to read today?"

About two thirds of the class raised their hands, some quickly and others sneaking them up after holding out for as long as they dared. Marena and a few others didn't raise their hands at all, even though their small act of resistance would be recorded and reported. Miss Goeff made some notations in a book and then looked up at the new kid, who hadn't raised his hand.

"Mr. Eric," she said, "we welcome you."

The boy stiffened straight in his chair.

"Please take the honor of reading today's recounting. Page one hundred twelve."

The boy stood and tossed his head back, trying to fling a thin curtain of red hair from his eyes. It fell back into place, and he pushed it away. He held his Commemorator in front of him, and Marena noticed for the first time how pale his arms were, white and spindly.

Miss Goeff waited. "Mr. Eric."

The boy stared at the pages in front of him and then sat down and closed the book on his desk. Marena watched him closely. Not volunteering to read was one thing, refusing was quite another.

"Mr. Eric," Miss Goeff said again. "I suggest that you not begin your term here with an act of disobedience."

The boy clenched his hands together. His freckled cheeks flushed, and he wouldn't look at Miss Goeff. Something had happened to him, Marena thought, something recently. He had that look on his face. His hatred hadn't settled yet.

"Very well," Miss Goeff said, and waved her hand over the convocater on her desk. The classroom door clicked open immediately, and the Stof stationed outside stepped in. Eric rose and eyed the Stof, who gestured to him to leave the room. The door closed and locked behind them, and Miss Goeff looked back at the class. "Now then, who would like to read today's recounting?"

Jennifer Simmons leaned into Marena from behind. "You do it," she whispered. Marena ignored her, and Jennifer poked a finger into Marena's back. "Do it! You haven't read in a week."

Miss Goeff looked toward Marena's desk. "Miss Jennifer," she said, "thank you for volunteering. Page one hundred twelve."

"C'mon, Miss Goeff, I just read last—"

Miss Goeff's hand hovered near the convocater.

Jennifer stood. "'A Recounting from the Book of Valor.'"

"Let us never forget," everyone responded.

"'And thus it was,'" Jennifer said quickly, her voice flat, "'that he, the Great General, our benevolent and caring leader, did defeat the traitors who rose—'"

Miss Goeff stopped her. "Louder and slower, Miss Jennifer, or you will begin again."

Marena couldn't help smiling to herself as Jennifer sighed and read properly.

"'. . . our benevolent and caring leader, did defeat the traitors who rose against the state. Yes, let it be known that it was he who in his wrath, his sword of justice shining like so many suns, did lead our glorious soldiers into battle, swiftly striking down the unbelievers in their early bloom. And know ye all, that it was he, our Great Leader, who did cleanse the land for the faithful and has mercifully, and tirelessly, labored to bring the lost and misguided back into the fold.'"

Jennifer turned the page of her Commemorator, her bracelets clinking.

"'And forget ye not,'" she continued, "'that it was he alone who did cause the Great Wall of the Northern Escarpments to be built across the breadth of our land, the concrete embodiment of his moral certainty, under which we stand, beyond which we shall never tread, and through which the unbelievers shall never pass.'"

Jennifer closed the book and dropped it on her desk. "'A Recounting from the Book of Valor.'"

Marena could feel Jennifer's eyes burning into her.

"Thank you, Miss Jennifer," Miss Goeff said. "Please be seated."

Miss Goeff leaned sideways in her chair and twisted slightly, pointing to the words she'd written on the blackboard. "Thursday is Remembrance Day. We'll be having a guest speaker. There will also be representatives here from PRIDE, the junior organization for state security." Miss Goeff looked out at the class. "Can anyone tell me what PRIDE stands for?"

Jeremy Sykes stood quickly. "Punish Resisters: Identify, Denounce, and Expel."

"Thank you. And don't forget this week is the end

of the grace period for Electoral Mandate Ninety Sixty-six. Make sure you've turned in any writing implements or paper still in your possession. Any questions? Very good then. All rise."

The class stood and bowed their heads as Miss Goeff led the closing salutation.

"Our state forever, once awakened, never to sleep again."

Marena mouthed the words along with the rest of the class and waited for the bell.

3

Marena couldn't draw very well, but she didn't care. Neither did Mrs. Crowley, her art instructor. "It's the act of drawing," she'd told Marena at the beginning of the year. "It's what you learn while you draw that's important." The last instructor only allowed drawing with the compugraphs embedded in each desktop, but Mrs. Crowley regularly brought in real sketch paper and colored pencils for them to use. The drawings had to be shredded at the end of each class, but still, it was so much better than dragging a metal pen over a computer screen that self-corrected colors.

Mrs. Crowley strolled down the aisles and peeked over shoulders as the class quietly sketched. She pointed out something in Dex's drawing as she passed him. He sat on the other side of the room. Marena and Dex had decided to sit apart from each other in the classes they shared. They didn't want to be too obvious—displaying signs of affection toward the opposite sex, public or private, was forbidden—but they did whatever they could get away with. The ZTs couldn't watch everyone all the time.

Mrs. Crowley stopped by Marena's desk and leaned in. She patted Marena's shoulder. "Good job," she said, and kept moving down the aisle. Marena knew the pat on her shoulder meant *I see you. I'm glad you're here.* Mrs. Crowley really looked at people when she talked to them. She was one of the few instructors of public enlightenment who did. Marena had always sensed something different about her. Not every IPE was in the party by choice.

Mrs. Crowley never used the big red book when she taught. It was always on her desk, as required, but she never opened it, and in her classroom, art was everywhere: watercolor still lifes, shoe box–size installation art, paper mobiles, landscape prints, pastel portraits, and etchings. A new rainbow-colored wheel was drawn on the blackboard in chalk; prisms and sculptures stood in every available space; and long, wavy sheets of paint-splattered abstracts hung from the ceiling. The room was different from every-thing else at the YTF, just as Mrs. Crowley was. Marena often wondered how she had managed to get so much of her art past the ZT censors.

Mrs. Crowley walked the aisles a little more quickly than usual, leaning into every other student or so, whispering to one, pointing something out to another. She seemed nervous today. Maybe it was because of EM 9066. Mrs. Crowley had hinted earlier that week that she thought the mandate was ridiculous, but of course she couldn't come right out and say it.

Mrs. Crowley went over to the door. She looked out its window quickly, then walked back and stood in front of her desk. "All right," she said to the class, "let's listen up." The class fidgeted. "Listen up, please."

Marena stopped drawing.

Then Mrs. Crowley deliberately shoved aside the big red book positioned on the corner of her desk and sat where it used to be. Groans of mock disapproval rippled through the room, and someone imitated the sound of a siren. It wasn't permissible to treat the book with any form of disrespect, even for an IPE.

The class erupted with guilty laughter, sneaking quick peeks at the vidicam slowly sweeping the room.

Marena looked to the door, worried. Mrs. Crowley had pushed the limits of the YTF curriculum more than any other IPE she knew, but not lately, not since things had gotten stricter. More than once a Stof had shown up at the door, his blank eyes framed in the small rectangular window, and just stood there letting her know she was being watched.

Jeremy Sykes squirmed in his seat. "You shouldn't do that, Mrs. Crowley."

"Shut up, Sykes," Jennifer said.

"Do what?" Mrs. Crowley asked him.

"You know."

"No, I don't. Tell me."

"You know. The book."

"What book?" Mrs. Crowley asked, placing her hand on top of it. A few giggles escaped the class. Mrs. Crowley leaned to her side and slid the book a few inches toward the edge of the desk.

Heather cracked her gum and pointed a ring-filled finger at Mrs. Crowley. "You better watch it, Mrs. C."

"Watch what?" Mrs. Crowley asked, pushing the book a few more inches along the top of the desk. It hung half over the edge, then fell with a muffled clunk into the wastebasket below.

The class cringed and sat taller in their seats.

Marena held her breath.

No laughter this time. Nothing.

"Don't worry," Mrs. Crowley said, sneaking another look at the door. "I'm just trying to make a point." She leaned over the edge of the desk and stared down at the book. "You see"—she turned her head to the class and forced a smile—"there's no art in there." Then her smile faded. "All right," Mrs. Crowley said, hopping off the desk. "That's what we call a teachable moment. There used to be a lot more of them." She lifted the heavy book and placed it back on her desk, then walked to the blackboard and pointed to the chalked-in wheel of colors. "So who can tell me—"

At that moment the door swung open. Marena shot a look to it, expecting a Stof to come in, or maybe Mr. Farr, but it was Eric, the new kid who'd been removed from homeroom for refusing to read. A Stof was lingering in the hall behind him. Eric stepped in, and the door shut again.

"Mr. Eric," Mrs. Crowley said, after scrolling down to find his name on her desktop, "please come in."

The boy didn't move. He held his arms crossed in front of him, but Marena could see his wrists were blotchy red and beginning to darken with bruises. Mrs. Crowley seemed to notice them too and looked away quickly. "Take any seat you like," she said.

Dex gestured for Eric to take a seat next to him, but Eric walked to the chair farthest away and sat.

"Mr. Eric," Mrs. Crowley said, studying her computer screen, "I have instructions here to assign you a minder." The whole class raised their hands. "Thank you," Mrs. Crowley said, "but someone has already been selected."

Marena hoped she had been chosen. A minder could go to different classes, take a different bus home, sometimes even sleep at a different living unit for a while. All you had to do was show the nuke around for a couple of weeks till he had the rules down.

"Mr. Jeremy, please stand." Jeremy Sykes hurriedly tucked his shirt in as he stood. "You are to be Mr. Eric's minder for the next few weeks," Mrs. Crowley told him. "Please help him with any questions he may have."

Sure, Marena thought, *he'll help you right into the mentation center.* Sykes was ZT—Marena was sure of it—not just faking it to get by, the way a lot of people did. She'd seen extra things appear on his tray at lunchtime, and one day last month he was wearing a brand-new pair of sneakers—not the kind you could buy in the commissary. It was hardly a secret who was really ZT and who wasn't. But you couldn't do anything to people like him. If you threatened them, they'd have you or your family punished. If you beat them up, you could be arrested and sent to the Civil Justice Center.

Getting on the bus to go home that afternoon, Marena saw Eric sitting next to Sykes. As she passed by, she dropped her book bag, and when she leaned over to pick it up, she whispered softly into Eric's ear, "Sykes is a listener."

4

The front gate of the housing compound rolled shut and locked after Marena arrived home from the YTF. She'd cleared security, but Dex and two other students were stopped for a random search. The Stofs pinned them against the perimeter fence and checked their pockets, shoes, and book bags. Marena waited for Dex, but a Stof nudged her along. She walked away slowly until Dex caught up to her.

"That's the third time this week," she said to him.

"They're looking for something."

Marena knew he was right. Security had been getting stricter lately, but there'd been no explanation why. Dex walked Marena home and leaned against the fence in front of her unit. He looked at his watch. "You want to hit the Place?"

Marena glanced up and down the block. Two state officers were on patrol, walking the blocks of the compound. "Not too many Stofs today," she said.

"No."

"Give me five minutes."

"Meet you in the alley." Dex started away but stopped suddenly. "Hey, check it out."

"What?"

"The nuke."

Marena looked down the block and saw Jeremy Sykes trailing Eric into the Orph, a larger building where Dex lived. The Orph housed all the wards of the state, kids who had been orphaned by the ZTs.

"Great," Dex said. "I gotta put up with Sykes now."

"I warned him on the bus, the new kid, Eric. I warned him about Sykes."

"Yeah, I saw you saying something."

The screen door of Marena's unit slapped open. "Hey, Beaner!" Daniel called out. He hopped down the steps and jumped onto the swinging metal gate. "Dad says to come in. Hey, Dex."

"Hey."

Marena whispered to Dex as he walked away, "I'll be there."

"Be where?" Daniel asked.

Marena tickled him. "None of your business, nosy. What are you, practicing to be a listener?"

"Maybe," he said, twisting to get free of her. "Cut it out!" He grabbed his skateboard from the yard and kick-rolled into the street.

"I was kidding around," she called after him, and turned to see her father waiting just inside the front door. He watched her as she punched her code into the wall registry to record her arrival home. She looked up at him. "What?"

"What were you doing with that boy?" Marena walked past him. "I asked you a question," he said, following her to her bedroom. "What were you talking about?"

"Nothing."

"I've seen you with him before."

She tossed her book bag onto her bunk. "Yeah. And?"

"Don't be smart with me."

"He's a friend. I haven't seen any laws passed against that."

"There're laws against boyfriends."

"He's not my boyfriend!" Marena said, throwing open her closet door, digging around for a hat and gloves, wanting to get out of the stupid house and away from her father.

"Where are you going?" he asked.

"Out."

"You don't have homework?"

"No paper, no homework. We do it all in class now." She sidestepped past her father and squeezed down the narrow hallway.

"Stay near the unit," he called after her. "And don't miss curfew again."

She smacked open the front door and ran out.

"Where you going?" Daniel asked as she passed.

Marena ran down the long block of white housing units, scanning for Stofs, then made a quick right and ducked between two tightly spaced buildings. Halfway through, a tangle of barbed wire blocked her way. She pried back the loosened wires, as she'd done a hundred times before, and scooched through sideways. Inching her way toward the backs of the buildings, she looked out and then ran down the alley to the nearest Dumpster.

She hid behind the metal bin, tugging her gloves on tight, trying to forget her father. It was always the same with him. She squeezed in as far as she could behind the Dumpster and waited until she heard Dex's footsteps padding down the alley. He ducked low and crawled in next to her, kissing her as he caught his breath. "Hey," he said, "you ready?"

"Yeah, let's get out of here."

Dex scanned the alley and then dashed across to the perimeter fence. They worked their way through an opening cut into the chain links and sprinted across a stretch of low brush that led to the dead cornfield beyond. Then, running as fast as they could, they burrowed into the field, disappearing behind a thick wall of rotting stalks. Marena pushed into the deeper rows, following the shallow track of an old furrow north.

"We need to take another way next time," she whispered, stepping over fallen stalks. "This one's starting to get worn. They could track us." After heading north a few minutes, Marena cut through a thick strip of woods at the end of the cornfield. Dex followed closely, and when they emerged on the other side, Marena could almost touch the tall, razor-trimmed fence that surrounded the purging dump.

"Are we way off?" Dex asked.

Marena spied the metal pole that marked the way in. "No," she said. "It's just to the right."

Something dark scurried beneath the brush.

Marena quickly gripped the fence and pulled herself off the ground. Dex joined her, and they hung there till it was gone. Then, after jumping down, they squeezed under a small section of fence and scrambled up a steep hill of burned purgings. They maneuvered along the face of the pile, heading toward the Place.

Scattered around the vast dump were other purge piles: cars that had been confiscated, demolished, and stacked; batteries, gas tanks, rubber tires. By far the largest pile was the one that Dex and Marena were still climbing across: a tremendous mass of personal computers, cell phones, banned books, and newspapers that had been hauled in from around the state and burned. The melted plastics had fused together, mixing with ash to form what looked like a mountainous slag heap of garbage-encrusted lava.

A few months back, when they'd first found the dump, Marena had noticed a small, rectangular window beneath the main purge pile at just about ground level. They knocked out the glass, crawled through, and found themselves inside a dark stairwell. There was no way up—burned purgings blocked the steps—but they could go down. Walls and sections of ceiling had collapsed, but there were a few small rooms and a larger area that had survived. It was completely gutted, but the call numbers on the ranks of empty steel shelves made it clear that they were in the basement of what had once been a library. The books and everything else had been destroyed, but enough was left of the foundation to provide a space for Marena and Dex to escape to, a place to be alone with each other and speak freely.

"Look out!" Dex said, sliding a few feet down the side of the purge pile. He stopped just below a crumpled width of metal that hid the secret opening into the Place.

"Any drones out?" Marena asked, dragging it to the side.

Dex looked to the sky and listened. "Don't hear any."

Marena climbed in and dropped into the darkened stairwell.

5

Marena had forgotten to take a flashlight when she'd run out of her unit, so she waited in the stairwell for Dex to crawl in after her. He turned his flashlight on, and they made their way down the cluttered steps, along the hallway, and into a large common area.

"Your flashlight dead?" he asked.

"No. Forgot it."

Dex walked over to the far wall and knelt behind a couch that had half survived, its thick foam sticking out in spots, crumbly and yellowed. Behind it was a bank of car batteries he had scavenged. He attached two wires to one of them, and a string of colored plastics that crosshatched the ceiling flickered on and lit the room in a soft orangy-red glow.

Marena looked up. "We got two brake lights and a parking light out."

"I'll find some bulbs."

Marena took out the stapling of paper that she still had hidden in the seam of her coat and tore out the pages she had written earlier that day on the bus. She went into her room, the remains of a storage closet, and turned on a small tear-shaped lightbulb. There was a rust-pitted sink on the wall, opposite two rows of shelves she'd made out of cinder blocks and boards.

Marena collected paper, mostly from old grocery bags she'd scavenged from the rations office. She also used cardboard boxes, cutting them into squares and splitting them down the middle by peeling apart the two sides. Marena used everything she could think of to make paper: Old manila envelopes could be cut into two sheets, and so could file folders; one or two pages from old phone books were sometimes blank, and state-sanctioned reading material usually had two blank pages, one at the front and one in the back. All her paper was sorted according to size and color; each had its own feel, its own texture, its own smell. She also had a small stack of real eight-by-ten writing paper she had stolen sheet by sheet from the YTF. Paper had always been strictly rationed under the ZTs, but now that it was illegal, clean, uncrinkled paper, white on both sides, was like gold to her.

Marena grabbed the sink with both hands and yanked it toward her, shimmying it left and right, until it pulled a few inches away from the wall. She reached behind, into a ragged hole knocked into the cinder block, and pulled out a plastic bag. Squirreled away inside were assorted scraps of things she had written, a pen, three pencils, a picture of her little brother, a pocketknife from Dex, and a laminated bookmark of a white rose that her mother had given her. Marena took out the bookmark, wondering, as she always did, what the rose might have meant to her mother. She ran a finger over the smooth plastic, then kissed it and put it back.

At first Marena had written mostly about her mother. But lately she had begun writing about other things too, things she had started to recall about the war, and about her father, or about things she was beginning to feel and wished she could say out loud but wasn't allowed to. Writing gave her an odd kind of comfort. Just reading the words she'd put down seemed like a sort of resistance.

Marena took a small square of grocery-bag paper out of the plastic bag. She unfolded it and read something she had written about her mother.

She's reading to me, in the hallway. We're lying on our stomachs, on the carpet. I can't see her face, just her hands turning the pages. I want her to look at me so I can see her face again. She never looks at me. Her face is always turned away.

Marena closed her eyes. . . . It was always the same: a faceless figure lying beside her in the hallway in the house they had once owned. She could see everything else perfectly: the bright light in the hallway, her parents' bedroom, her poster-covered bedroom door, the wooden stairway down to the first floor, even the crayoned pictures tacked to the end of an old standing bookcase.

But she couldn't see her mother's face.

It puzzled her that some memories came to her so easily, as if there were a vidicam playing them inside her head, but others she could only feel, the way so many things about her father remained hidden to her, behind some locked door or just around a corner of her memory. She took the pencil out of her pant cuff, turned the square of paper over, and scribbled:

They don't want us to remember.

"Marena!" Dex yelled.

"Be right there!" she answered, scraping her pencil sharp against the concrete floor.

The ZTs keep taking things away, and the more they take, the more they hope we'll forget, so that one day there won't be any remembering. There will only be what they tell us. But we have to remember. And keep remembering. No matter what they do to us.

"Marena!"

"In a sec!"

Dex's room was down the hall, in what had been a small office. He collected whatever could be scrounged from up top: batteries and car lights—headlights, taillights—gallon cans of old paint, half-melted ballpoint pens, plastic bags, old rags, cans of gasoline siphoned from car wrecks, and just about anything else he could find.

Dex leaned into the doorway, watching Marena fold up her writing.

"What?" she asked him.

"Nothing."

She hated when he did that, stared at her like he was disappointed in her or something. *"What?"* she asked again.

"Just . . . you'd better be careful."

"I am careful."

"No, you're not."

"Don't worry about me."

"Fine," Dex said, and walked away.

Marena slipped the writings into the bag, shoved everything into the hole, then muscled the sink back into place and returned to the large room. She sprawled out on the moldy couch next to Dex and nestled into him, the tension she'd just felt between them melting away.

"Hey," Dex said, turning on his side to face her.

"Hey," Marena said, kissing him. He pulled her closer, and they held on to each other for a long, quiet moment. She felt her heart thud against his as he kissed her again.

"My dad was after me again today," Marena said, "when I got home."

"Yeah?"

"Yeah, you know, be on time, do this, do that. Watching us. He's always accusing me of something—" A snapshot of memory, one that had come to her before, clicked in Marena. H*er father somewhere . . . in a large room, a lot of people . . . staring at her.* Then it disappeared. "Sorry," she told Dex. "I keep remembering this thing about my dad."

Dex loosened his hold on Marena and sat up. Marena was instantly sorry she'd brought up her father. Dex always got a little weird when she talked about her parents, and she always felt guilty because she still had one. Dex never talked about his parents.

"I'm going to work on the back hall a bit," Dex said, pushing himself off the couch.

"Dex—"

"You want to help?"

Marena closed her eyes. "Sure," she said, and got up too.

She didn't want to work on the back hall at all, but she followed him anyway, navigating a path around jagged edges of ripped heating ducts, broken pipes, and half-burned beams. On the other side of the rubble, the remains of the hallway opened up. It was blocked by pieces of the ceiling and walls that had caved in. Dex had been clearing it a little at a time, trying to see if it led anywhere.

"I think the ceiling is pretty solid here," he said, shoring up a section of it with a large length of pipe.

"Can you see anything?" Marena asked.

Dex directed his flashlight into the crumble of cinder block and wallboard and peered into the tiny open spaces. "No." He laid his light down and began handing pieces of block back to Marena.

"You know," Marena said, "we should try to talk to that Eric kid before Sykes gets to him."

"Why, you think he's safe?"

"I'm not sure."

"He blew me off in art," Dex said. "I tried to get him to sit by me."

"Well, he's probably wondering if we're safe. He doesn't know."

"Maybe," Dex said, pulling free a mangled piece of ductwork.

Marena grabbed it from him and tossed it to the

side. "You know Sykes is going to try and get him to turn listener."

Dex tugged hard on a large piece of cinder block. "How do you know he's not one already?"

"I don't. I'm just saying—"

"Heads!" Dex said as the chunk of block broke free and rolled past him. It tumbled down the small hill of debris and smacked into the pipe bracing the ceiling. Marena saw it before it happened. "Dex!" She dodged left and fell backward just as a long stretch of dead fluorescent track lighting came crashing down, the tube-shaped bulbs bursting like clusters of mini-bombs around her. Dex aimed his flashlight at Marena. She screamed and shielded her eyes, frightened back to another time.

A blinding flash of honey-colored light brightened Marena's room, blasting the flower print of her window curtains into leafy silhouettes. In the eerie silence that followed, she dropped her crayon. Suddenly the room shook, and the window exploded in a shower of glass and wood that cut through the room, knocking Marena onto her back. She tried to stand, but a second blast knocked her down again. There was blood on her legs and feet, sooty smoke and snowflakes swirling around the room.

She screamed but couldn't hear herself. She couldn't hear anything. And then her mother was on hands and knees in front of her. Her hair was wet and red. There was red everywhere, running down her mother's arms. No face, just her hair, matted with blood—

"Marena?" Dex said, pulling her to her feet. "Marena!" He ran the flashlight over her. "Are you okay?"

"Get the light off me!"

"Did you get hurt?"

"Get it off me!"

Dex lowered the flashlight to his side. "All right, all right . . . it's off. . . ."

Marena's heart pounded wildly, the memory lingering with her.

Dex waited a long moment before speaking. "It's okay, Marena."

"Sorry," she said, "I—I just—"

Dex stepped in carefully and brushed some debris from her hair. "It's okay," he said again. Then he took her in his arms and made her look at him. "Marena, everything's okay."

She nodded silently, and the horrible images vanished.

6

In her room that night, Marena wrote down what she had remembered.

> *The day the war came, my mom had just come back from another demonstration. She'd been at the march on the Capitol. I was in my room coloring, and Dad was outside, shoveling the walk. We'd had an early snow. I could hear the marchers still chanting in the streets. The curtains in my room were closed, and I was sitting on the floor.*

Marena stopped writing and shut her eyes as if listening for a very small sound. Then it came again.

The light. The shattering glass. The blood. She wrote it all down, but there was more:

I am somewhere else now. An emergency room with many hurt people, everyone staring up at a TV on a shelf high in the corner. A reporter standing on a street corner, the picture shaky, LIVE FROM THE CAPITOL bannered in red graphics across the screen; the reporter pushing back wisps of hair from her face. In the distance, black smoke and flames surround the Capitol building. On the bottom of the screen, a ticker band of news runs nonstop: . . . GOVERNMENT TROOPS FIRE ON PROTESTERS . . . AUTHORITIES MAINTAIN TROOPS WERE ATTACKED FIRST . . . MORTAR SHELLS STRIKE FARMERS' MARKET AND SURROUNDINGS . . . DEATH TOLL HIGH . . . HEAVILY ARMED RESISTANCE GROUPS . . . REMAIN IN YOUR HOMES . . . MARTIAL LAW IN EFFECT . . . CIVIL DISOBEDIENCE DECLARED AN ACT OF WAR . . . REMAIN IN YOUR HOMES . . .

Then memories came in a rush: cars burning in the streets, the colored flags of the protesters, black smoke, smashed store windows, water hoses pummeling people into buildings, others clubbed by the police and dragged away. Thousands of protesters arrested. Some never heard of again—the "disappeared," they came to be called.

Marena wrote everything down, trying to find the right words, but how, she thought, how could she ever describe what it had been like to look out her window and see soldiers patrolling the sidewalks, their boot heels clacking along the cement, or what it felt like to have them walking into her house—into her bedroom, her bathroom, searching her drawers?

She tried as best she could to capture it, struggling with each sentence, wishing that she were more like her mother or that at least her mother could be there to help her write the things she felt, wishing simply that her mother were still there, but knowing it could never be, knowing that the world had changed forever and that she would never be there again.

7

A wail of sirens startled Marena awake the next morning. She sat bolt upright, breathing fast. Then her heart eased. It was just the alarm.

"Marena," her dad said, knocking on her door, "Marena!"

"I'm up!" she called out, and fell back into her pillow. She rolled over, smacked the alarm off, and lay there listening to the morning manifesto droning out of the loudspeakers that stood sentineled up and down the blocks of the housing compound. The ZT early show. Today's subject: collective responsibility, but then something else. Marena sat up on the edge of her bunk.

Please note and be advised.

Then she remembered.

Effective today: The personal possession of any form of paper or any material whatsoever, in existence now or to be invented in the future, upon which may be printed, written, imprinted, typed, or copied any manner of letters, words, tokens, signs, symbols, phrases, or pictographs forming any manifestation of a written communication in any language; or the possession of any recording implements whatsoever used to create these images, whether mechanical, manual, or electronic, in existence now or to be invented in the future, is from this moment forth and for all time forbidden. Said materials subject to immediate confiscation. Pursuant to Electoral Mandate Ninety Sixty-six.

The announcement was repeated. Then repeated again. It continued to drone over and over as Marena dragged herself out of her bunk and got dressed. She looked at herself in the mirror, reached for a pick, and stabbed it into her hair. It stuck in a clump of knotted frizz and wouldn't move. She grabbed the handle with both hands and remembered how her mother had once called her wiry curls tresses, and how she had thought she'd said "messes." Marena made a mental note so she could write it down later: *Mom used to call my hair tresses.*

The five-minute warning moaned over the loudspeakers like a birthing cow. Marena gathered her hair and choked it into a ponytail.

"Marena!" her father called from the kitchen.

"I know!" she said, tugging on her sneakers. She grabbed her coat and journey permit, hurried down the metal hallway, and stopped at Daniel's room to say good-bye.

"Leave me alone," he said from somewhere in his room. His voice sounded small and far away. Marena pushed open the heavy steel door and looked in. She heard a noise from under the bunk.

"What's up, D?" she asked. No answer. "C'mon, I'm going to miss the bus."

If she missed the bus, Marena knew, she'd have to call for a transport to come get her. That meant she'd get sent to mentation: a day of reevaluating commitments, restating YTF promises, video indoctrinations, and thought reports. She checked her watch, tossed her coat onto a chair, and dropped to the floor.

"Okay, I've got like four minutes."

She lifted the moon-and-stars blanket that hung off the side of Daniel's bunk. He was curled up tight and hugging Nightstar, a little stuffed horse, jet black except for a diamond patch of white on top of its head. It looked huge against his tiny frame. Marena flattened herself on the cold cement floor and scooched half under the bunk. Daniel curled up tighter.

"Go away."

"What's going on?"

"Daddy said to stay here."

"Under your bunk?"

"In my room."

"What'd you do?"

"Nothing."

"That sucks."

Daniel half smiled. "You can't say that. That's a bad word." He loosened his grip on Nightstar, and a quizzical look wandered across his face. "You're going to be late, you know."

Marena threw a glance to her watch. "No, I'm not," she said, and crabbed backward from under the bunk. "Get yourself dressed or *you'll* be late." She grabbed her coat and ran out of the room.

"I'm going!" she yelled to her father as she bolted down the hallway. She stopped at the end of the hall when he didn't answer. "Hey, Dad, I'm—"

He was standing at the sink and staring out the

back window the way he had done nearly every morning since Daniel had started junior indoctrination classes. Marena had no idea what her father did all day under house arrest. She imagined him sometimes, statuelike, gaze fixed out the window, dormant for the day until she or Daniel came home.

"Dad," Marena said.

He fumbled with something in the sink. "Just a sec."

"Why'd you tell Daniel to—" She stopped when she saw a thin wisp of smoke rising from in front of her father. "What is it?" Marena asked, rushing to the sink. He was burning papers again—or letters. "Dad, what are they?"

"Nothing," he said, waving the air in front of him. "Open the door."

"You said you had no more left!"

"Be quiet and get the door before the alarm goes off."

Marena ran to the door, propped it open, and hurried back. Her father doused the still-smoldering papers under the faucet and stuffed what was left of them into the garbage disposal.

"What were they, letters? Mom's letters?"

Her dad looked out the window and ran the disposal.

"Were they?"

He scoured the sink.

"I don't believe you!" Marena said. "You could've hidden them, Dad!"

"They'd find them."

"Why didn't you let me read them first!"

He looked at her with the same vacant stare he always put on and pointed to a box filled with loose-leaf paper, notepads, old letters, scrap paper, construction paper, pens, pencils, and paints, crayons, Daniel's watercolors and Magic Markers. "Everything has to be turned in today," he said. "Do you have anything else?"

"No."

"Nothing anywhere?"

"No!"

"All right." He turned back to the window. "You should go now."

Marena stared at him, wondering how many other things he'd been lying about. Every time she'd tell him something she'd remembered about her mother or about him, he'd just say he'd forgotten about it, huge things that nobody would ever forget.

She didn't believe a word he said anymore.

8

Marena didn't talk much on the ride to school. She sat slumped mostly, staring at the tin seat back, her foot resting on top of Dex's. The bus passed through security at the YTF and sat idling just inside the gates. Dex nudged her and pointed toward the building, crossed his middle finger over his index, and made a quick hooking motion through the air, their signal for a lockdown. *Again?* Marena thought.

The radio at the front of the bus buzzed a series of three dull hums. The driver took out his ID verification scanner, and they all held their cards aloft as he walked down the aisle scanning them. Marena handed hers over as he neared. He waved his scanner over it, studied a flash of colors on the tiny computer screen, then turned and walked away. He flapped open the bus doors and walked off.

Dex leaned into Marena and whispered, "I talked to him last night—the nuke, Eric."

"How'd you get him alone?"

"He locked Sykes in the bathroom."

"Eric did?"

Dex smiled and nodded.

"You think he's safe?" Marena asked.

"I'm pretty sure. They disappeared both his parents."

"What for?"

"I didn't ask."

Marena often wondered what it was like to have your parents disappeared, if it was worse than knowing they were dead. Most of the disappeared were probably dead anyway, but people never really knew. It must be worse thinking that they might be suffering somewhere, or that maybe one day they'd come back. At least Marena knew her mother was dead. She knew they couldn't hurt her anymore.

Dex sat taller in his seat when he saw the first few rows of kids standing and looking out the windshield. "Something's up," he said.

Marena ducked low and scooted past him. "I'll check it out." She made her way up the aisle to the front of the bus and pushed in between a few shoulders.

Jennifer pushed her back. "Do you mind?"

"I'm just trying to see what's going on."

"Go back to your blended boyfriend, hybrid."

"I'm sorry—like you're *pure*?"

"Purer than you." The other JJ-Girls around Jennifer laughed. "But then who isn't?"

Marena ignored her and stood on the edge of a seat, looking out the front windshield. Parked in front of the YTF was a long line of sleek limousines, polished to a dark olive-green glimmer. Front fenders flagged. Windows curtained.

Official state vehicles.

She wasn't particularly surprised to see them there. Remembrance Day was coming up, and that was a huge to-do every year. The ZTs had been laying down extra security the whole week. Marena tried to get closer to get a better look at the limos, but Jennifer shouldered into her, and Marena fell onto Franky Poyer.

He pushed her off and stood up. "Back of the bus, frizzhead."

"Drop dead," Marena said.

Poyer put his fat fingers on Marena's shoulder and shoved her backward.

Jennifer and the JJ-Girls laughed, and a flash of rage shot through Marena. She swung at Poyer as hard as she could. He grabbed her arm, and she tried to hit him, but he was too strong. She struggled with him as he walked her to the back of the bus.

"Back where you belong," she heard Jennifer say.

Out of the corner of her eye, Marena saw Dex striding up the aisle.

"Yeah," Poyer said, seeing him too, "and what's he gonna—"

Poyer barely got the last word out of his mouth when a fist came crashing into his face: Eric's. He'd leaped over Sykes and punched Poyer before Dex even got there. He kept punching him, his gangly body and skinny arms flailing, pummeling Poyer backward into his seat. The bus broke out into a chorus of quiet cheers, people standing on their seats and gawking. Poyer tried to fight back, but Eric was wild, his head swinging back and forth, his long red hair whipping around as he threw punch after punch at Poyer.

"Stof!" someone yelled. "Stof!"

Dex jumped in and pulled Eric away. "Eric, man! Stof!" Poyer swung at Dex, but Dex ducked it and shoved Poyer hard into the wall of the bus and held him there. Marena took hold of Eric and was pulling him away when Jennifer leaned over a seat and tried to stop her. Marena was about to go after her, but Dex grabbed Marena by her jacket.

"C'mon!" he said. "C'mon, enough!"

They all scrambled back to their seats—Poyer too, wiping the blood from his face. Dex and Marena ran to the back, and the whole bus settled in just as the Stof walked onto the bus. Nobody moved. They all seemed to be holding their breaths, waiting to see if he'd noticed anything. Then the driver returned and closed the doors. The bus shuddered into gear and lurched forward.

Marena looked at Dex. He shrugged, catching his breath. "Maybe he likes you."

"Who? Poyer?"

"No, the nuke."

"Yeah, right," Marena said, joking, but wondering if maybe Dex was right. She looked at Eric, who was staring out the window as if nothing at all had happened.

Marena straightened herself up as the bus bumped up to the front doors of the YTF. The building was still in lockdown. Through the school windows she could see the shadowy figures of Stofs searching the classrooms. Deeper inside, they'd be searching the lockers, closets, and desks and bringing in the dogs to secure the school. Marena checked her watch. The lockdown last month had taken almost an hour.

She wiped the window clear and read some of the posters that had been hung in the school windows for Remembrance Day. One was a picture of the Great Wall of the Northern Escarpments, with the words *Zero Tolerance* below it; another was the state flag with an eye in its center, the words *Be Watchful* scrolled across the top; still another was the silhouette of a hand reaching under a fence and a big circle with a line slash superimposed over it, meaning "no smuggling."

Marena had heard rumors of banned books and radios being smuggled into re-dap communities. Some people had even said that AYLR, the most active resistance group against the state, had ways of getting people past the Northern Escarpments, but Marena couldn't imagine anyone ever escaping. Spring Valley Re-Dap was in the heart of the Southern Zone. The housing compound might be easy enough to break out of, but it seemed impossible that anyone could ever get past the Scarps—the cement wall that spanned the length of the state, separating the Northern and Southern zones. Twenty feet high and crested with

razor wire, it angled inward, as if it had started to col-
lapse. It extended another twenty feet beneath the
earth, monitored by sensors that could detect any
movement underground. It was built right after the
war and helped put thousands of unemployed people
to work.

The ZTs told everyone that they had built the
Scarps to keep enemies of the state from getting in,
but everyone knew it had really been built to keep anyone in the Southern Zone from getting out.

The all-clear signal blared from the roof of the YTF.
The bus doors opened. Lockdown was over.

9

"This woman," the man said, wriggling out of his coat and dropping it over the back of a chair. "How long has she been an instructor here?" His large hand swiped a white handkerchief across his forehead.

Mr. Farr, serious and efficient, tapped his pen against a clipboard. "Two years." He pulled a file from under its metal clasp.

"The charges?"

"Public display of unsanctioned materials."

The man took up the file and flipped through it. He motioned to Farr's seat. "May I?" Farr stepped away, and the man sat in his chair. "And how long has this been going on?"

"About a year."

He looked up. "Little lag time in the reporting, no?"

Farr shifted awkwardly away from his own desk. "Her paperwork was always in order."

Nearly ten already, the man thought, and he still had a ton of work ahead of him: student profiles to wade through, his speech for tomorrow. Why hadn't this been handled before?

"I've documented everything," Farr said, laying another set of files on the desk.

"Yes," the man said, annoyed. He didn't like this Mr. Farr, didn't like the way he gripped his clipboard against his chest, or the way he tapped his pen, or the way everything he said was oiled with the sound of "it's not my fault." He didn't even like the way he dressed—what was he wearing anyway, a sweat suit?

Farr pointed at the folder on the desk. "There's a copy of one of her requests in the file."

"I see that. Thank you."

The man skimmed the request form, trying to ignore the fact that he was going to have to work with Mr. Farr and others like him. They were so transparent, so easy to spot, the ones who could barely mask their ignorance, the ones who had been unqualified for even the most menial of jobs before the war and now enjoyed positions of power. They were exactly what gave the ZT Party a bad name.

This guy had probably been a janitor or something before the war. How had he become a director of YTF security?

"Would you like to see photos of the materials?" Farr asked

"No, thank you."

"You can see there how all her paperwork came back approved."

"Yes, I see that." The man read through some more of the requisition forms. "And why now? Why is she such a problem now?"

"Well, sir, the New Initiative doesn't allow for such leniency any longer."

"It wasn't allowed before either."

"I, yes, I know," Farr said, "but . . . in the past—in the past we felt that there were many gray areas with regard to—"

"There is no such thing as gray, Mr. Farr. *Gray* is why I'm here."

"Yes, sir, I understand that," Farr said, laying a thick binder before the man and flipping it open, "but in the listings of acceptable and unacceptable visuals—if you'll look here—there's no mention of many of the works which she asked permission to use in class. So, in the absence of any—"

Why is this person still talking? the man thought. He stopped listening. Bored, he glanced out the window: snow. There was snow outside. Just a little. He watched a lone flake hurl itself against the glass and winced at the memory it brought with it. *Damn it,* he thought, *damn it.* The littlest thing could remind him. He willed it away—*Not now,* he told himself. *There's no time for this now*—but it was still there, right outside the window. *No.* He turned away from the window.

"Sir?" Mr. Farr asked.

"Yes?"

"Are you all right?"

"Am I—? Yes, yes," he said, rubbing the back of his neck. "Sorry. Please continue."

"As I said," Farr went on, "the new orders from ICCS no longer allow for these types of—"

The man tried to focus, but the memory was now tapping on the glass. He wouldn't turn around, though. *Stop it,* he thought, scolding himself, *just stop it and get back to work.* "This instructor," the man asked, cutting Farr off, "why hasn't she been removed?"

"She has promised to abide by the book. I spoke to her again just this morning."

"I asked why she hasn't been removed."

"Well," said Farr, "the parents have petitioned us to try another course. It's a very popular class, and they'd like us to allow her to—"

"Call a meeting with the parents. I'll respond to their petition." *Are they kidding me?* the man thought. *A petition?* This was just the kind of leniency that made the New Initiative necessary.

"The school windows," he said. "They're being seen to? They'll be finished today?"

"Yes, sir."

"Good." He was busy now, in action. He liked the feeling of purpose. It cleared his heart of other things and kept him looking ahead, not to the past. "And I want this instructor removed."

"Yes, well, we were going to, but—"

"Today. Now."

"Yes, sir . . ."

"What?"

"Well, there are no substitute instructors available yet."

Always something, the man thought, *always some excuse.* If these people were really committed to doing their jobs, if they wanted readaptive communities to work successfully and have their students integrated back into the community instead of winding up in a correction facility one day, then they could follow the damn rules.

"Remove the woman now," he told Farr. "I'll take her class."

10

"Good morning, class," Miss Goeff intoned in home-room. "This is the fourth day of the tenth month of the new state calendar." She looked directly at Jennifer and Marena. "Miss Marena, you will read. Let us all listen and reflect as we prepare ourselves for the coming Day of Remembrance."

Marena stood. She could feel Eric's eyes watching her, Jennifer's too, and she knew Jennifer was enjoying herself. But she had to read. Her father would kill her if she got another day of mentation or they took away any of her family's rations.

"Miss Marena?"

Marena opened her Commemorator and read. "'Forget ye not that it was on that day, the day that began the Great War, that the faithless enemies within our midst first did strike. But let it be known, and remembered, and shouted to the clouds, that they did slaughter naught but our innocence. For know ye also that on that day, thanks to our Great Leader and the Divine Providence that leads his every action, the true colors of the ZT government, phoenixlike, rose through the flames, unscorched, waving high with pride and righteousness. Our Great Leader, guardian of us all, in his generosity and holiness, remains unwavering in his commitment to our everlasting security, providing us with food and clothing and education—'"

Blah, blah, blah—gross! Marena thought as she finished the passage. *All lies. Lies, lies, lies.* She was so tired of pretending and being forced to say things she didn't believe. She glared at the words in her Commemorator. Her mother would never have stood up and read something like this.

Marena sat, and Heather stood to read the first of the responsories.

"For this we offer grateful thanks," the class said in unison when Heather had finished. Marena mumbled it too, her mind wandering. What would her mother have done? Marena had read some of her mother's articles and letters before her father had destroyed them. On a day like today her mother would never have kept silent.

"For this we offer grateful thanks."

Her mother would have stood up and told everyone how the Great War would never have happened in the first place if it hadn't been for the ZT Party. If they hadn't gained power by scaring everyone into believing that anyone who didn't think like them or look like them was "diluting the national character" of the country, if they hadn't convinced so many people that the state could survive only under their worldview, if they hadn't labeled everyone in the state who disagreed with them as traitors and attacked all the protesters or killed them or dragged them out of their homes—if they hadn't done all this, there never would have been a war!

"This we believe," the class responded. "Let us never forget."

Miss Goeff stood after the last reading was complete. "Very good then. All rise."

Marena stood with the rest of the class, ashamed that she wasn't her mother.

"Our state forever, once awakened, never to sleep again."

During second period Mrs. Crowley was acting strangely. She seemed distracted and had hardly even looked at Marena since the class had started. She walked to the blackboard and fumbled for a piece of chalk. "Okay, now, who will tell me what they think art is?"

No one volunteered. Marena almost raised her hand, but Mrs. Crowley sounded angry, and Marena didn't want to give the wrong answer. They weren't allowed to define art for themselves. Mrs. Crowley knew that. Marena was confused. She didn't know if Mrs. Crowley wanted a real answer or a ZT answer.

"Nobody?" Mrs. Crowley asked. "Okay then . . ." She wrote the word *ART* in fat letters on the board. "Who will tell me what they've been *told* art is?" she yelled suddenly. "You can do that, can't you?" Marena felt her throat clutch. Mrs. Crowley never yelled. "Oh, c'mon, guys!" she said, hurrying back to her desk. She grabbed up the big red book and slammed it in the center of the desk, startling Marena. "It's all in here, isn't it? So who'd like to come up and read it for me? You're all such good readers, aren't you?" She went back to the chalkboard, poised to write. "How about you!" she said, pointing to Jeremy Sykes. "Yes, *you*, Mr. Jeremy! You probably know this. Why don't you just recite it for me, and I'll—"

The classroom door unlocked and swung open.

Mrs. Crowley leaned against the blackboard and looked at the class. "I'll just be a minute," she said, and walked to the door.

Marena clenched her fists.

A Stof was in the hall. Uniform: dark green, meticulous, crisp. Tie: black. Cap: black, gold SO embroidered on the front. Boots: glistening. Jacket: waist length, buttoned, black, leather.

Mrs. Crowley paused in the doorway. "What?" she said to the Stof. "What is it now?"

The Stof gestured for her to leave the room.

Mrs. Crowley stared at the woman.

The Stof gestured again.

Mrs. Crowley stared another moment longer. Then she turned to the class and mustered a tight smile. She pushed a scraggly lock of hair behind her ear and looked at Marena. Yes, Marena was sure, she was looking straight at her. Then Mrs. Crowley took her coat and stepped into the hallway. She turned back briefly and said, "Keep drawing, okay?" and walked out.

The door closed and locked behind her.

As soon as it did, the JJ-Girls—Heather, Michele, and Jennifer—flocked to one another. They roosted on their desks behind Marena, cracking gum and jabbering.

Eric left his seat, Jeremy Sykes stayed where he was, and everyone else was talking about what had just happened. Dex sneaked over to the door and watched through the window. Eric joined him, tapping him on the back each time the vidicam swung their way. When it did, they both scampered out of its sight, then hurried back as soon as it had passed.

They're not going to do anything to her, Marena told herself, *they're not. Mrs. Crowley said to keep on drawing. She'll be back.* Marena wanted to finish before she came back. She wanted Mrs. Crowley to say "good job." She tried hard to tune everything out: the noise, the JJ-Girls at her back, her thoughts. She had become the queen of tuning things out, a regular magician. Most of the time.

She whirled around in her seat. "Could you please shut up!"

Michele stopped mid chew and glowered at Marena. Heather laughed. "How about no?" and Jennifer snapped her gum in Marena's face.

"Kiss off, reject."

Marena grabbed her things and moved to an empty desk in the back. She could have cracked Jennifer and Heather, right then, gone after both of them. Ugly thoughts were crowding in on her. *Finish the drawing,* she told herself, *just keep drawing.* She tried to complete the tree she'd been sketching but didn't like the color. She shaded it brown, added some yellow, and hated it even more. She tried to erase it, and it smudged all over the paper. She wished Mrs. Crowley were there to help her. She'd say, "Good job. Keep going. Just draw whatever you feel." Marena took out a fat black crayon and crushed it into her drawing, covering it, smearing it, darkening the page till there was no more tree at all.

Tree at night, she thought.

The siren sounded.

They all ran back to their seats and sat: feet flat on the floor, heels touching, hands folded, chins tucked, and eyes staring at a fixed point located approximately at the center top of their desks.

A long minute passed. No one moved.

The siren sounded only for body searches or purges. Lockers and desks had been purged that morning, and they'd been body searched two days ago.

What now? Marena wondered.

The classroom door clicked open.

It wasn't Mrs. Crowley.

11

The man in the doorway lumbered over to Mrs. Crowley's desk. His short-cropped hair was white; his face, fair skinned and chubby, was round like a baby's. He unbuttoned his jacket, placed his briefcase on the floor, and sat, staring at the class.

Usually when an instructor was pulled from class, a Stof was sent to watch them, or a substitute IPE, but Marena had never seen this man before.

One of the JJ-Girls snapped her gum.

The man at the desk cocked his head and listened hard.

The gum didn't snap again.

He gazed down across Mrs. Crowley's desk, a puzzled look on his face. He put his hand on the big red book and repositioned it half an inch to the left.

He glanced up at the ceiling, draped with colorful abstracts and fluttering mobiles, then slowly took in the whole room, studying the paintings and artwork pinned and tacked to every available space. He walked to the blackboard, roughly erased the word *art*, and found a piece of chalk.

Marena leaned out into the aisle and watched the letters creep across the board.

HELMSLEY GREENGRITCH

The man brushed the chalk from his hands and turned to the class. He gestured to the board behind him. "Everybody, please."

A few kids muttered his name.

Greengritch leaned across Mrs. Crowley's desk. It creaked under his weight. "That's *green*, like the color, *gritch*."

A giggle escaped from somewhere.

Greengritch's eyes died. He headed toward the laugh, quickly, down the row next to Marena, shimmying sideways to fit between the desks, right to where the JJ-Girls were. Marena swiveled around in her seat.

Greengritch pointed to the first girl he came to. "You. Who are you?"

"I'm—" Heather said, "I'm a JJ-Girl."

"A . . . JJ-Girl?" Greengritch asked.

Heather looked to Michele and Jennifer for support. Michele stared down at her desk, but Jennifer raised her ring-cluttered fingers and wagged her head from side to side, her dangly earrings tinkling like mini wind chimes. Heather did the same.

"We jingle-jangle," she said.

"I see," Greengritch said. "I may be mistaken, but aren't there regulations in the book concerning the wearing of jewelry?"

Heather faltered a bit. "Well, they—"

"Yes, yes, I know," Greengritch said. "It's not your fault. We've all been pretty lax around here. It's just another one of those silly rules that aren't enforced anymore, isn't that right?"

"Well, yeah," Heather said.

"Yes. I thought you'd say that." Greengritch put both hands on Heather's desk and leaned into her. His knuckles whitened. He tilted his pale, pudgy face to one side and spoke as if trying to explain something very wonderful and mysterious, almost in a whisper. "Now," he said, "do you really expect me to refer to you as a *JJ-Girl*?"

Heather sat up tall in her seat, her eyes darting

everywhere except at Greengritch. He hovered in close to her face. "Do you?"

"No."

"I didn't think so." He straightened and held his hand out, palm up.

Heather, not sure what to do, looked at her friends. Jennifer joined Michele now and stared down at her desk.

"The earrings," Greengritch said to Heather.

"But—"

Greengritch's hand flew at Heather's face. He grabbed one of her earrings and lifted. She stifled a scream and jumped out of her chair. Greengritch walked her around the desk and into the aisle. She scurried after, ear first, trying to keep up.

"I believe I asked you to remove your earrings."

"Okay. Okay!"

Greengritch let go, leaving his hand extended.

Heather fumbled with the earrings and slapped them into Greengritch's hand.

"Thank you," he said, noticing her other jewelry. "Tomorrow lose the rest." He looked at Jennifer. "You too." He strolled back up the aisle and dropped Heather's earrings into the garbage pail.

Fade him, Marena thought. *Erase him.*

Greengritch retrieved his briefcase from under the front desk and unlocked it. "I am here, people," he said, rummaging through it, "to change the way you think." He took out a bottle of water and a coffee cup. "Now, you may not like me. You may not like what I have to say." He filled the cup and took a quick sip. "I don't care. My job is not to be liked." He stared into the cup and swirled its contents slowly, as if the idea for whatever he was going to say next were forming somewhere at the bottom. "Now, I have a written assignment for all of you," he said. He reached into his briefcase and pulled out a small sheaf of white paper. "Yes, yes, no more *art* for today." He counted out some sheets, returned the rest, and carefully placed one sheet of paper on each desk. "These of course cannot leave the room. Put your name in the top right-hand corner."

He dropped a sheet on Marena's desk.

"Your assignment is to describe yourself to me— not your personality, not how you feel about yourself— but things you think are absolutely true about yourself. I want to know who you *think* you are. You have the rest of the period. Scheduled classes for today are canceled. We'll finish this and then take a break. Return to this room after lunch."

Marena fingered the blank sheet of paper that lay on her desk, wondering where they had taken Mrs. Crowley. She watched Greengritch turn his back to the classroom and stare at the blackboard. He erased his name and wrote:

WHO DO YOU THINK YOU ARE?

12

Greengritch collected the students' papers before sending the class to lunch. He flipped through them briefly, seeing plenty to work with, and locked them in his briefcase. Then he went to lunch himself.

He ran the class over in his mind as he walked down the long hall toward the faculty lounge. It had gone pretty well for a first intervention, he thought. The earrings had been a great opportunity. He'd scared them all a bit, not too much, but enough so that the word would spread. It helped to generate a little fear before he began to work on their perceptions of themselves and one another.

He stopped outside the long line of windows that spanned the cafeteria and watched the room. Only two Stofs were present, and no instructors. *Ridiculous,* he thought, making a mental note to fix that. He remembered himself on cafeteria duty when he was a young teacher, when the only real worries were whether or not the kindergartners had finished their milk. A time when the world was more innocent.

He had his work cut out for him, he thought, peering at the throng of students, some of them staring back. It wasn't their fault. He'd been telling party officials for the last few years that the schools were getting lax, rules weren't being enforced, intelligence gathering was poor, but instead of addressing any of these issues, the Protectorate passed another piece of legislation: the Preemptive Correction Act, which gave ICCS the right to use loyalty correction on juveniles.

It troubled Greengritch greatly.

He knew readaptation worked, but it took time. It was as much a science as loyalty correction. The little children were easy. It was the teenagers who were hard, those who still had memories of what the world had been like before. But that world was gone now. They had to learn how to live in this one.

Dex put his lunch tray down next to Marena. "See him out there?"

"Yeah," Marena said, watching Greengritch walk away from the cafeteria window. "Who do you think he is?"

"I don't know. Some creep substitute thinking he's somebody."

Maybe, Marena thought, but something about Greengritch disturbed her.

"Look," Dex said, tapping her tray. Eric was just coming away from the food dispenser and doing the YTF stare, scanning the cafeteria for the safest place to sit. He made eye contact with Marena for a brief moment and then sat at one of the empty metal tables.

Dex and Marena looked at each other. They picked up their trays and walked over.

"Hey," Dex said as they sat down across from Eric.

Eric looked up from his tray, then looked down again and kept eating.

"Thanks for this morning," Marena said, "you know, on the bus with Poyer."

Eric just kept eating, shoveling food into his mouth.

Marena looked at Dex, who started to get up. She waved him back into his seat. "Where'd you come from?" she asked Eric.

He flipped his hair out of his eyes and looked up,

still chewing. "What?"

"Where'd they bring you in from?"

"Central West. YTF up north by the Scarps." He pointed to the half-eaten protein patty on Marena's tray. "You gonna eat that?"

"Yeah."

Eric shrugged and looked around the cafeteria again. "Sucks about Mrs. Crowley. She seemed pretty cool."

"She is," Marena said. "Maybe she'll just do some redoc time."

Eric shook his head. "She's gone."

Marena knew he was right but didn't want to admit it.

"What'd they get your parents for?" Dex asked.

Eric shot back, "What they get *yours* for?"

They stared each other down for a short moment, neither answering.

"So," Marena said, "you know about Jeremy Sykes, right?"

Eric nearly spit out a bite of food. "Sykes is a friggin' idiot. He's about as smart as this fork. Poyer's even dumber. You shouldn't be taking any crap from guys like that."

"We have to be smart around here," Dex cut in.

"You throw someone like Sykes a beating, and you're in civie justice for three months, and if you've got family, they'll go after them too."

"There are other ways to get at them. Other things to do." Eric leaned across the table. "And not just to them."

"What are you talking about?" Marena asked.

Eric covered his mouth slightly with his fist and whispered, "Resist."

Marena was about to say something, but Dex kicked her foot under the table before she could. She understood the warning immediately and checked herself. This was dangerous stuff Eric was talking about. They didn't know him nearly well enough to trust him.

They all looked at one another for an uncomforttably long pause.

Eric guessed right at what they were thinking. "I'm not ZT," he said softly.

Dex kept staring at him. "How do you know *we're* not?"

"I don't."

They were silent again.

Eric ate the last few crumbs off his plate. "Why's he call himself Dex?" he asked Marena. "I checked his name out at the Orph. It's Andre."

"I don't like my name," Dex said.

"I don't like it either."

"Guys, chill, okay?" Marena said.

She tried to think of something safe to ask, but before she could, Dex questioned Eric further. "Where's Sykes? He's supposed to be with you."

"You know what?" Eric said, standing up. "You're right. I could be ZT, and so could you." He reached for his tray. "So, why don't both of you just leave me the hell alone?"

"Wait," Marena said, grabbing his hand. "Eric, just wait."

He jerked his hand away. "Look, you helped me out in homeroom the other day, warned me about Sykes—I figured you guys were cool."

"We are," Marena said. "Why were you sent here?"

Eric relaxed slightly and sat down. "They split up the whole YTF at Central West. Scattered us around the state. I was in civie justice almost a month—reeducation through labor, half rations. They're getting serious." He leaned into the table and spoke carefully. "The resistance is working. That's why they got this New Initiative going, and this Greengritch guy. They're trying to stop what's happening up north from happening down here."

"What's happening up north?" Dex asked.

Eric leaned in and whispered, "AYLR. They're growing bigger all the time. They're getting into the YTF systems. They're getting word outside the country."

"You know this?" Dex asked. "You've seen them?"

Marena waved Dex and Eric quiet. The JJ-Girls were jing-jangling toward them. "The one on the end," Marena said, pointing to Michele. "We think she's a listener—we know one of them is. Someone gets reported every time they're around."

The girls still wore their bracelets and rings, but they all were distinctly earringless. Eric leaned back and pushed off the floor with his feet, sliding his chair into their path.

"Nice ears," he said. "Watch what you use 'em for. You might lose 'em."

Michele said nothing, but Jennifer and Heather both chimed in.

"Scuzz."

"Twit."

"You think I'm kidding?" Eric asked. Jennifer flicked a red-polished middle finger at him. Eric kick slid his chair back to the table and grabbed a plastic knife. "Come here," he said, moving at the three of them. "I'll show you how I'm kidding."

"Cut it out," Dex said, stopping him. "You'll get us listed."

"Who cares?" Eric said, watching the girls hurry away. "You can't act scared around these creeps. They're like dogs. You let 'em know you're scared, and they keep coming after you."

Marena wanted to get back to their conversation about the resistance, but before she could, Jeremy Sykes ran up to the table. "Here," he said, dropping a book of ration chits on Eric's tray. "If you lose them again, you don't eat."

Eric smirked and showed Dex another book of ration chits he had hidden in his jacket.

Sykes pulled out a chair and sat. "Next time I can't help you," he told Eric. "I'm really not allowed to give you mine." He smiled at Marena. "Hey, you guys know each other?"

Marena stood to get away from Sykes when she saw a sudden rush of movement outside the cafeteria windows.

Eric turned in his chair. "What is it?"

"I don't know," she said, nodding toward the windows. "Something going on outside."

Dex stood too.

Stofs were coming toward the building.

Marena ran over and pulled up a set of blinds. Dex and Eric followed her, and a surge of chairs scraped the floor as the rest of the room stood up and crowded by the long run of windows.

"What are they carrying?" Eric asked.

"Ladders," Marena said.

The Stofs were holding ladders above their heads, two to each one, and placing them in front of the windows. Then some of the Stofs started climbing up as others ran back to their trucks.

"They going on the roof?" Eric asked.

"I can't see," Marena said.

The Stofs who had returned to the trucks were now running toward the building again, carrying gallon cans of paint. They walked the cans up the ladders. Marena could see only their feet now, a long row of black boots standing on ladder rungs. She and her friends pulled up the rest of the blinds and pushed their faces against the windows, trying to see what the Stofs were doing.

"Look!" someone yelled out.

All across the length of windows, at the same moment, thick dark-green paint oozed down the long panes of glass. Next, a dozen or so legs were visible as the crew stepped down a few rungs on the ladder.

Arms reached down, brushes and tools were pulled from the boxes and handed up. The Stofs windshield-wiped the gooey mess back and forth, covering every inch of window.

Dusk fell over the room.

The bell rang. Time for class.

13

Marena and Dex stepped out of the cafeteria and made their way back to Mrs. Crowley's room. The hallways had darkened. The overhead lights were on, but everything seemed dim. Marena glanced into the other classrooms. Every window had been painted.

"Well," Eric said, coming up from behind, "not much to look at anyway."

"Come on," Marena said. "We're going to be late."

Dex tapped her on the shoulder and pointed to the art room. Marena looked in, and her heart sank. Everything was gone: the artwork on the walls, on the doors, hanging from the ceiling, taped to the front of her desk—everything. Bare gray cinder block remained. Mrs. Crowley's desk was cleared of everything except the big red book. All the students' desks were gone. Only chairs remained, arranged in a large circle.

"Go on in," Mr. Greengritch said from the hallway. "Take a seat." The class funneled into the stark room and wandered around the circle of chairs. "Just sit," Greengritch said. "Make a choice."

Marena raised her hand.

"No questions now." He unlocked his briefcase, opened it, and took out the assignments they had written before lunch. "These are—" He noticed Marena's hand still up. "I said no questions now."

Her stomach tightened. "Where is Mrs. Crowley?"

Greengritch looked at her. "Was there something about what I just said that you didn't understand?"

"No, sir. I just—"

"You don't know who I am, do you?"

"I—no, sir."

He looked to the class. "Anybody?" No one answered. He dropped the handful of papers on an empty chair and sighed. He put his hands in his pockets and strolled about inside the circle of chairs. "All right then. To start with, can anyone tell me the name of the minister of youth and education?"

Marena had heard the name once. A long time ago. She couldn't remember it.

Greengritch prowled the circle, searching faces. "Actually, here's the real question. Can anyone tell me who the *new* minister is?"

Silence from the room.

"I'll give you a hint—you're looking at him."

Marena turned to Dex, who was already looking at her.

"Is everyone in awe? Or do you not know what to say?"

Jeremy Sykes put his hand up.

"They're alive," Greengritch said, dismissing Jeremy with something short of a wave. "That wasn't a real question. Put your hand down." He grabbed the papers off his chair, placed them underneath, and sat. "Anybody want to know why I'm here?" Nobody answered. "Not the most responsive group, are we? Well, to begin with, some instructors within this facility have been more preoccupied with their own theories concerning education than those sanctioned by the state. Everybody follow that?" Nods around the room. "Good. Now, it's not just the Crowleys who have been remiss but, more important, the leaders who have tolerated them." He paused. "Am I using words that are too big for you?" A few heads shook, Marena's included. "Liars. For those of you still stuck on *remiss*, it means 'lax, lazy, negligent in one's duty.'"

Marena knew what the word meant.

Greengritch leaned forward and clasped his hands together. "So here it is. I've come here to get this facility back in line with the readaptive guidelines developed by the state. This YTF has become lazy. So have the people who run it. We've been . . . *remiss*. That's about to change."

Greengritch stood again. "To begin with, this class, art, is no longer offered. Welcome to Zero Tolerance."

Marena started to object, but Greengritch cut her off immediately—"Quiet"—and took up the pile of papers from under his chair. "Now, who wants to read first?" he asked, looking right at Marena.

Dex stood up.

"All right," Greengritch said, thumbing through the papers in his hand. "A brave soul. Mr. Andre, yes?"

"Yeah."

"Okay," Greengritch said, stripping off his suit jacket. He pulled out Dex's paper and handed it to him. "Now," he said to the class, "this is what we call a teachable moment." He rolled up his shirtsleeves. "There used to be a lot more of them. All right, Mr.

Andre," Greengritch said. "Describe yourself to me."

"My name is Andre Ferrayo. I'm sixteen. I'm Cuban. I'm—"

"You're Cuban?" Greengritch interrupted. "What makes you say that?"

"What?"

"What makes you say you're Cuban?"

"Because my father came from Cuba."

"Oh," Greengritch said, as if he had just understood a huge concept for the first time. "So he came from Cuba. And where did the people in Cuba come from?"

"A long time ago they came from Spain."

"And where did the people in Spain come from?"

"They . . ." Dex shifted his weight and looked around the room. "I don't know."

"So you don't really know where your relatives came from, do you?"

"I know they—"

"You see, people," Greengritch said, turning to the class, "I'm not interested in what you think you might be. Or where you think your grandmother's mother's father might have come from. I'm not interested in your family tree! I'm interested in what you think *you* are."

"I'm Cuban."

"Prove it."

"Yo hablo español y mi padre—"

"Yo hablo español también. Does that make me Cuban? Look, if I were to cut you open and look inside you, am I going to see a little sign that says 'Cuban'? Is there a label inside you that says, 'Cuban. Machine wash. Tumble dry'? No, the answer is no. The only thing you know you are, the only thing that you can say with any certainty, is that you are alive and standing on this piece of earth, right here, right now. Isn't that right?"

Dex said nothing.

"Sit down," Greengritch said. "I can see this is going nowhere." He flung the rest of the assignments up in the air and turned to the class as the papers fluttered to the floor. "You see, people, you live like you're all so different and unique, like you're all so special. *Well, you're not!* Mommy and Daddy lied. And starting now, this facility will no longer tolerate any differences whatsoever." His voice was harsher now. "Look what you've regressed to! Look at this oh-so-tolerant, clique-driven class." He paced the circle, pointing at people. "There are the purer breds who think they're cool sitting together, and there are the weak ones, the mixed races, the foreign borns!" He moved faster now, his pudgy face pink and sweating. "You have to stop thinking about yourself and start thinking about the group!"

Greengritch kicked his chair out of the circle and strode to the blackboard. Next to the words WHO DO YOU THINK YOU ARE?, which were still chalked on the board from before lunch, he wrote ZERO TOLERANCE and tapped the chalk hard beneath the words. "You see, people, tolerance doesn't work! It doesn't work out in the world, and it doesn't work in here. So we're going to have a little ideology enforcement, okay? We're going to *recommit* ourselves to a state where no one ever has to worry about fitting in, because with Zero Tolerance there is no *in* to fit in*to*. *Everybody's* in. All there *is* is in!" He hustled outside the circle. "Okay, who's next? I can do this all day."

And he did.

Marena could barely keep up with what he was saying, he kept speaking so fast, asking questions and answering them himself, using big words, never stopping, hardly breathing. She looked at the wall clock to see how long he'd been talking. It was gone.

"Now, you may not like me," he said, running both hands through his thin, sweaty hair. "And I'm sorry.

I'd like to be liked by everyone, but I care enough about you to risk being hated. I'm here to help you. What am I here to help you with? Anybody?" He bounded to the blackboard again and underlined the words so hard that the chalk crumbled and snapped in two. "*Zero Tolerance*, people, *Zero Tolerance*!"

He walked back to the circle and leaned on a chair, rubbing his neck. "Is anyone starting to follow me? Anyone at all?"

The bell rang, and no one moved.

Greengritch dropped his head and stared at the floor. "Class dismissed."

Marena trailed the class as they jostled one another, pushing for the door. Last in the crowd, she stopped and looked back at Greengritch. He was still leaning on the chair and staring at the floor. A pock-marked ring of whitened scars was visible beneath his ear and across the back of his neck. Marena noticed the vidicam sweeping toward her, and without thinking, she darted her hand into Mr. Greengritch's open briefcase and stole a small clutch of paper.

14

Marena shoved the paper under her shirt and disappeared into the crush of students swarming down the hall. She maneuvered herself toward the nearest girls' bathroom, swiped her ID card through the scanner to unlock it, and ducked inside. Two girls were busying themselves at the mirror.

"*Yes?*" one of them asked.

Marena went into an empty stall and locked it. She pulled out the stolen paper from beneath her shirt and counted quickly. Seven. Seven sheets of pure white, baby-blue–lined paper. She folded them lengthwise and slipped them beneath the bra strap across her back, then hurried out into the hall.

There were a lot more Stofs than usual, standing silently at every corner. A tinge of fear stirred from someplace within Marena, and it troubled her. She was no longer afraid of IPEs who yelled and tried to intimidate, or of the Stofs who thought they could scare her by never smiling or speaking. She wasn't afraid of the humiliation of body searches or threats of confinement and mentation. She wasn't afraid of people who were mean and hateful. She'd seen so much that she was nearly numb to it. There simply weren't many things left to be afraid of. Why should she be frightened now? Nothing was really that different. Windows painted. A few more Stofs. Kids ran to their buses like always, wrestling on coats mid run. Bags dropped, boys teased, and lockers firecrackered shut. . . . Still, she had a bad feeling about Greengritch.

Eric came dodging out from the midst of a small crowd of kids and ran up beside Marena. He faced the lockers, pretending to open the one next to Marena's.

"What are you doing?" Marena asked.

"I just ditched Sykes."

Marena wanted to laugh, but she knew he could get in big trouble for ditching a minder. "You better be careful. There's Stofs all over."

"Yeah. They breed like maggots."

She opened her locker and grabbed her coat. "Sykes is going to be on the bus anyway. Why are you messing with him?"

"'Cause I can."

Marena put her coat on and noticed Dex at the far end of the hall, watching her. She waved him over. He hesitated at first but then came up to her. "Eric ditched Sykes," she told him.

"I'm just screwing with him," Eric said, bending over and sneaking out a Magic Marker from his sock. "He's going to be sorry he ever got assigned to me." Eric turned to the lockers and whispered to Marena, "Stay in front of me." Then he scribbled across a locker door:

ZTs SUCK

Dex wheeled on Eric, grabbed him by the neck, and pushed him up against the locker. Eric struggled to break free. His face reddened.

"Leave him alone, Dex!" Marena said, grabbing at his arms. "What are you doing?"

Eric pulled at Dex's wrists, his voice pinched and raspy. "Get the hell off—"

"*Stof!*" Dex said in a faint whisper, and let Eric go.

The Stof walked up. Dex leaned against the locker, hiding Eric's graffiti. The Stof eyed the three of them and then nodded toward the exit. "Yes, sir," Dex said. The Stof walked away, and they headed to the bus. Dex spoke quietly. "Start being more careful, Eric. He almost saw you."

Eric flipped the hair out of his face, looking embarrassed and pissed.

"I'm not kidding," Dex said to him. "He was right behind you."

"Okay! I didn't see him."

They walked a few more steps in silence. "You all right?" Dex asked.

"Yeah."

"You sure? Your face is kinda purple."

"Yeah, well, you almost tore my throat out, you maniac."

They pushed open the heavy doors of the YTF and ducked into a frigid wind. A thin dusting of snow skipped along the top of the sidewalk. The three of them trudged up the steps of their bus. Sykes was already in his seat. He gave Eric a nasty look.

"Hey, man," Eric said as he sat next to him, "I've been looking everywhere for you."

In the backseat Marena looked out the window and waited for the bus to leave. She couldn't believe Mrs. Crowley's class had been canceled. She fogged up the cool glass with her breath and tried to finger sketch a flower in the shape of her mother's white rose. Through it she saw the outside of the YTF—the windows, all but a few of them, painted over: dark-green rectangles set into cement.

She turned to Dex, who was staring off and quiet. "What's up?"

"Nothing."

"You mad about something?"

"No."

Marena heard a boy across the aisle say, "They're still here." She turned to see all the students on that side of the bus looking out their windows. Marena shimmied past Dex and looked too.

"What is it?" Dex asked, following after her.

Marena pointed across the parking lot.

Three dark-green limos were parked there. A shadow of a driver could be seen through the tinted windshield of each, and a fourth car had joined them. Not a limo. Almost like a station wagon, but bigger, long and boxy-looking. No flags on it, and a much darker green than the limos, almost black. Four Stofs in heavy coats surrounded it. Marena saw some movement in the backseat, then had a glimpse of someone's face through an opening in the curtains. Mrs. Crowley?

"Who do you think it is?" Dex asked.

"I don't know," Marena said, hoping she was wrong.

It was a long ride back to the housing division. Marena couldn't get Greengritch out of her head. Or Mrs. Crowley either. She stared out the window. Miles and miles of nothing but moldering fields and the occasional forgotten tree.

They passed under the towering metal sign that spanned the highway home:

SPRING VALLEY SOCIAL READAPTATION COMMUNITY

As they did, a scattering of memory came to Marena.

"For the deficients," my mother is saying over and over. "For the deficients." I don't understand. I want her to look at me again, and I don't want her to be so angry.

She's yelling now, papers in her hands, reading, shouting.

"It's just words," I say to her. "Mommy, it's just words." And she stops, everything stops, and somehow I know I've said something terribly wrong.

"It's never just words," she says. "Never."

15

"Thank you again," Greengritch said as Mr. Farr finished taking away the last box of his personal belongings. Farr, obviously not happy with having to give up his office, backed out of the room.

"Did we find a suitable building for the meeting?" Greengritch asked.

"Yes, sir."

"It's big enough and not too familiar?"

"Yes, sir."

"And the children? The T-shirts?"

"They'll be there."

"Thank you." Farr started to leave again, but Greengritch stopped him once more. "And print me out the names of anyone who signed the petition supporting Mrs. Crowley."

"It's in her file."

"I want every parent at the meeting. Not just the ones who signed the petition."

"Yes, sir."

"Has the Youth League arrived?"

"Not yet."

"Let me know as soon as they do. I need to talk to them before tomorrow."

"Yes, sir."

"Thank you. That's all."

Greengritch followed Farr to the door and closed it. He opened his briefcase and pulled out Mrs. Crowley's file and a stack of blank report forms: **Description of Offense, Recommended Correction to Be Imposed**. He sat behind Farr's desk and looked at his watch. Not enough time to eat before the meeting. He could try the cafeteria— *No*, he told himself, *do it now, get it done.*

He never really liked this part, the responsibility of having control over others' lives—unless of course there was absolutely no doubt that they were a threat to the security of the state. He had no problem sentencing those people. The problem was that it was getting much harder to tell who was truly an enemy of the state and who wasn't. Shortly after the war it was fairly obvious, but that was no longer true. And now, rather than working to prevent high-risk citizens from becoming "clear and present dangers" in the first place, which was the whole theory behind re-dap communities, ICCS had been pressuring Greengritch to send problem citizens, adults or children, straight to loyalty correction facilities.

"Zero Tolerance," the Leader had said. "Find the unalterables."

This didn't sit well with Greengritch, who didn't think anyone, especially a child, was unalterable. But he knew better than to let his own feelings stop him. He'd learned that lesson. He'd been against the early ZT crackdowns on protesters and dissidents before the war. He'd been so sure that he was right and the ZTs were wrong.

Fool.

No, he told himself, this was a new world now with new rules. Better to err on the side of caution, better the risk of one innocent person's being neutralized than another incident like the one that started the war, the one that hurt thousands of innocents. Greengritch stopped the next thought that wanted to come. *Keep working,* he told himself.

How big a risk was this Mrs. Crowley? She wasn't

doing anything that he wouldn't have done himself years ago as a teacher—push the rules a bit, give the kids something special—but he knew he couldn't permit it. Too many things were permissible now. The first priority of any government is the protection of its people. The early ZTs knew this. They saw the troubles coming. There were warning signs.

Why didn't we listen?

Greengritch considered Mrs. Crowley's file again, reading through it: "Artist . . . widowed in the war . . . R.P. Index: 63 percent . . . threat status: 0.03 . . ."

He took up his pen, let it hover over the section headed **Recommended Correction to Be Imposed**.

And made a choice.

16

"Let's meet later," Marena said to Dex as they got off the bus at the housing compound. Dex agreed and headed to the Orph, trailing Eric and Sykes at a distance. Marena walked down the block to her home unit. A few snowflakes blew across the pavement, swirling down the crisscrossing hatches of asphalt that made up the housing division. She tried to catch a few under her feet as she walked, but then she stopped and listened.

Something sounded different.

It was too quiet. Children should be out playing at this time of day.

Marena ran to her unit and pushed open the iron gate. It scraped a white arc across the pavement, the hinges bent downward from Daniel's daily gate swinging. She stepped over some of her brother's toys and hurried up the stairs.

"Daniel?" she called into the house.

She walked down the hallway and poked her head into the bedrooms, the bathroom—nothing. She went into the kitchen. Nothing. She looked around. Everything was neat. Orderly. No sign of a purging.

There'd been times before when Daniel and her dad had been gone when she came home, but she'd always been notified about it. She picked up the phone to call the housing authority but decided first to hide the paper she'd stolen. She hurried to her closet, pushed away a pile of shoes, and carefully pried back a section of the baseboard. Behind it was a narrow opening she'd cut into the drywall.

She heard knocking at the front door.

Marena took the paper from beneath her shirt and shoved it into the hole. She closed it quickly and ran to the living room. She was surprised to see Eric standing in the doorway.

"Hey," Marena said, "what are you doing here?"

"The Orph is empty. Everybody's gone. Dex said to meet here."

"Did you ditch Sykes again?" she asked, looking behind him.

"No. After school till curf is free time."

"It was twenty-four/seven when I had a minder."

He shrugged. "Well, it's not now."

Marena waved him in. "Close the door." She walked into the kitchen and looked again for signs of where her father might be. "Where is everyone?"

"I don't know," Eric said, glancing along the ceiling. He stepped closer and whispered, "Is this place LD'd?"

"No."

"That's cool," he said. "They had listening devices everywhere up in Central West."

"Dex coming over?"

"Said he was."

Marena picked up the phone. "Housing Authority," she said slowly and clearly. The phone recognized her voice and linked her to a recorded message that asked for her security codes.

"Unit five-nine-two-one," Marena said. "Family Regi two-two-two-one-nine-four-three."

After a moment another recorded voice spoke. "Family members of students are currently attending a YTF meeting at the Town Hall. All other inquiries, please stay on the line, and your call will be answered in the order it was received." It repeated itself,

"Family members of—" Marena hung up.

"Well?" Eric asked.

"They're at a meeting at the Town Hall."

"Where's that?"

"Not far from here. Just over the interstate."

Marena sat on the living-room couch. Eric looked around and then sat very close to her. "Got the unit to ourselves, huh?" Marena looked at him for an awkward moment. He looked right back at her, unembarrassed and silent. "I'm kidding," he finally said.

"I know," Marena answered, not sure. She liked Eric a lot, but not in that way. She didn't even know that much about him yet. "So how's it going for you here?" Marena asked, trying to get him talking about himself.

"It sucks here just like it did up at Central West." He threw the question back at her. "What about you?"

"Me?" she asked, loosening her ponytail. "I've been here a long time."

"Just you and your dad, right?"

"Yeah. They took my mom."

"Dex told me."

"And Daniel," Marena added quickly. "I've got a little brother, too, Daniel."

"Yeah?" Eric said. "I got a couple of brothers." He

pushed himself off the couch. "What do you say we go find Dex?"

"Where are they?" Marena asked. "Your brothers?"

"I don't know." He drew back the window curtain and peered out. "They split us up after they took my mom."

"What'd they take her for?"

He looked at Marena quickly. "What they take *yours* for?"

"High treason."

"You win," he said, and turned away again. "Can't beat that."

"Seriously, Eric. What'd she do?"

"Nothing." He let the window curtain fall closed. "Neither did my dad." Eric walked over and flopped on the couch. "He was a graphic artist." Marena sat up and pulled her legs beneath her. "Did a lot of digital art when computers were legal—freelance stuff, you know, websites, advertisements, whatever. Anyway, after the war one of the sites he'd built turned out to be some kind of an underground blog against the ZTs. My dad's name came up when they traced the site. They took him away, no bail, no lawyer, no trial date—"

"And . . . your mom?" Marena asked. "What did she . . . I mean, how'd they—"

"Mom went down to the justice center to try to find out what happened. I mean, she knew he wasn't involved in anything—he wasn't trying to help those guys—but no one would talk to her. No one would tell her where he was."

Eric paused for a second, as if trying to remember everything correctly.

"So . . . she started going down to the center every morning and staying on the steps. After a while she stopped asking where he was and just started holding this picture of my dad up over her head all day, you know, showing it to whoever walked by. My brothers and I, we'd go down after school to bring her home. After about a week there were like twenty, thirty people out there doing the same thing. All holding these pictures of people over their heads. One day we went to get her, she wasn't there. She never came home."

Marena waited to see if he had more to say. But he didn't. "I'm sorry," she said.

Eric hopped off the couch, restless. "Nothing to be sorry about. Like my dad used to say: Don't be sorry—*do* something about it." Eric walked in a wide circle around the living room. "What do you say we do something? Right now."

"Sure," Marena said, understanding exactly what

Eric was feeling. She grabbed her coat. "Let's go find Dex." They stepped out of the unit, and Dex was waiting just outside the front door.

"Hey, man," Eric said, slipping by him, "where you been?"

Marena pulled on her coat. "What are you doing standing there?"

"I just got here."

"You know everyone's at the Town Hall?"

"Yeah," he said, watching Eric, who was balancing surferlike on Daniel's skateboard.

"What do you think they're doing there?" Marena asked.

"I don't know."

She tapped his arm and lowered her voice. "Why don't we walk around the block and see?"

Dex snapped a look at her. *Walk around the block* was their code for sneaking out of the compound.

"What are you guys talking about?" Eric asked, skateboarding toward them.

"One sec," Marena said.

She and Dex walked to the middle of the street, where they could talk privately. "Look," Dex whispered, "we hardly know anything about him. We don't know he's safe."

"He is," Marena said. "Look, I'm not ready to show him the Place or anything, but he's okay." Dex barely nodded, and Marena called Eric over.

"What's up?" he asked, kicking the skateboard off behind him.

"You gotta promise not to tell anyone," Marena said.

"No one," Dex warned. "Not even somebody you think is safe."

"Yeah. Okay. I'm not stupid."

Dex scanned the street for Stofs. There were two on patrol about mid block, walking away from them. He pointed down the block. "See those two units?" he said to Eric. "There's a break in the barbed wire between them. Just enough to squeeze through. It's the only way to the alley behind them."

"We can sneak out of the compound back there," Marena said.

Dex grabbed a small football of Daniel's, and they started walking down the street together. Marena whispered to Eric. "At the end of the alley there's an opening in the fence. Once we get through it, there's plenty of cover in the cornfields."

"What about Stofs?"

"There's usually only two," Dex said, pointing to

the Stofs nearing the end of the block. "They each take one side of the street. Once they turn the corner up there, it takes them three and a half minutes to come around the block again."

"They don't patrol the alley?" Eric asked.

"No," Marena said. "We just have to make it back before curf."

"Keep walking," Dex said as they came up to the two units. He held up the football to Eric. "Go out." Eric jogged off a little, and Dex threw him the ball. Marena ran ahead, waving for the ball and watching the two Stofs, who were almost to the corner now. She caught Eric's pass and ran toward him.

"You up for it?" she asked, tossing the ball back.

Eric looked at his watch. "How far away is the Town Hall?"

"Ten, fifteen minutes," Dex said. "We've got plenty of time till curf." He ran up to Eric and grabbed the ball out of his hands. "What, didn't you guys do stuff like this up at Central West?"

"We would have if we'd had security as lame as yours."

"Cool then," Dex said. "Let's go."

Marena scouted the block. Only a few other kids were out. The Stofs had turned the corner.

"Stay behind me," she told Eric.

She waited for the right moment and then signaled to Dex, who lobbed her the football. Then he bolted between the two units and disappeared. "We'll go together," Marena told Eric. She checked up and down the block again and then sprinted after Dex, with Eric close at her heels. They skirted past the barbed-wire fencing and shuffled sideways down the tight passageway until they reached Dex.

"Wait," Dex said. He poked his head out and looked up and down the alley. "Okay."

They dashed across and crouched low when they hit the perimeter fence, then ran to the opening. Dex pushed his way through, and Eric and Marena stooped in after him. They all squatted in a tight circle. Marena took a woolen ski mask out of her coat. She twirled her hair into a wiry nest and shoved it under the cap. Dex took out his mask and looked to Eric. "You got one?"

"No."

"Take mine." Dex tossed it to Eric and took a bandanna from his jacket. He tied it over his nose and mouth and then pointed across the few feet of open ground that lay before the cover of the corn-field.

"Once we hit the corn, follow Marena. I'll stay behind you."

Marena grabbed the sides of Eric's ski mask, straightened it, and pulled the front down over his face. "It's not far if we cut over the interstate."

"I'm cool," Eric said.

It was still light out, but the sky was gray and darkening. "All right," Marena said, "let's go," and she was off and into the corn with both boys crunching close behind her. Masked, she headed west, moving faster, confident she couldn't be seen. Shriveled husks and bird-pecked cobs littered the muddy field below as they dodged their way among the rotting stalks.

"Hold up," Marena said when they finally reached the edge of the field. She got as low as she could and snuck out, peering down the interstate for any signs of transports or home-guard patrols. They stood still, listening for the thin whir of spooring drones above. Drones, the ZTs' unmanned tracking planes, had to be nearly overhead for their heat sensors to work, so if a person could stay far enough ahead of them or take cover, they weren't really that hard to elude.

Marena looked back at Eric. "Did you have drones up at Central West?"

"Yeah," he said. "Thermal imaging and a live video feed to security."

"Same here," Marena said, looking down the interstate again. She signaled that it was clear, and then the three of them sprinted across and leaped into a ditch that bordered the other side. Marena belly crawled up and poked her head out. No block wardens. No Stofs anywhere. "C'mon," she said. They crawled for a short way, then stood up and kept going.

"Piece of cake," Eric said, brushing mud from the front of his pants.

Across the interstate there were streets lined with old houses that had been taken over by the ZTs and were now used by instructors and party officials. There were also a few that still housed some residents of the past town, old people who for some reason hadn't been removed when it was taken over for a re-dap community. They lived as dark shadows behind closed curtains.

The streetlights overhead buzzed and fluttered on.

"Let's get off the street before we hit the IPE houses," Marena said.

The three of them ditched into the first backyard they came to. Quietly, they started hopping fences.

Marena kept an eye on Eric, making sure he stayed with them. She stopped in the last yard and called him over.

"That's it," she said, pointing into the next lot. "Town Hall. It used to be a church."

The building, now rotting and paint peeled, must have been beautiful once. Like one of those quaint small-town chapels surrounded by oak trees that Marena had seen on postcards years ago when there still were churches. Only this building's steeple had been torn off. What was left of its paint was a putrid mustard green, and there were no trees. The woods around it had been bulldozed to make a dirt parking lot.

"Limos," Marena said, nodding toward the cars parked in front of the hall. The dark car from the YTF was there too, along with two large gray buses with blacked-out windows.

"C'mon," Dex said. "Let's go around the back."

They hopped the last fence and ran across the parking lot. Ducking low and weaving their way between the parked vehicles, they ran to the back steps of the hall. There was a door there, but no windows. Marena gently pulled on the door.

"Locked."

"This way," Dex whispered, jumping off the steps. Marena placed her ear to the door, and felt the cold of the metal seeping through her woolen mask. She heard voices.

"Marena!" Eric said, coming back for her.

She followed him around to the side of the building. Dex was trying to pull himself up onto a window ledge. "I gotta find something to stand on." He jumped down and disappeared behind the dark of the building.

Marena and Eric looked around too.

"I don't see anything," Marena said. "Maybe you can—"

"Stofs!" Eric said. "Stofs!"

Marena and Eric dove to the ground. A thin carpet of dead leaves crackled as Marena rolled next to the building. A black-green limo cruised slowly down the street. Marena pressed herself against the cement foundation, craning her neck to keep an eye on the patrol. "Stay down!" she whispered to Eric. The limo slowed as it passed in front of the old church. Marena froze, not daring to breathe. Pulsing blue and white lights brightened the street in a flicker of slowly circling colors. A smaller blue-beamed spotlight swiveled from side to side, searching and poking its way through the parking lot.

"I can't find anything," Dex said, rounding the corner of the building. Marena and Eric waved frantically at him. "There's nothing but—"

Eric rolled out, grabbed Dex by the ankles, and pulled hard, dropping him to the ground. He covered Dex's mouth just as a shaft of blue light swept the area where he'd been standing. Dex nodded in understanding. The limo stopped. Its blue beam ran up the side of the building and swung back out to search the parking lot again. The patrol idled there for a short while, then drove away, the busy beams still probing from side to side.

"Whoa," Eric said as he sat up. "That was close."

"Yeah, thanks," Dex said, brushing himself off. He stood below the window. "Marena, come here. I'll lift you up." Marena grabbed his shoulders and put one foot into his hands. Eric steadied them both. "On three," Dex said, "one, two . . ." Dex straightened up and lifted Marena to the window ledge. Her fingers barely reached it. "Get on my shoulders," he told her.

"You sure?"

"Yeah!"

Dex leaned his back against the building for support. Marena placed a foot on each shoulder and pulled herself up to the window. The glass was tinted darkly, but she could still see through it. The room was packed, every seat filled. There were people in front of the window, blocking much of her view, but she could see parents and Stofs shoulder to shoulder along the walls on every side. Near the front of the room someone was speaking.

"Stop leaning!" Dex called up to her.

"Go left," she called down. "Left!"

"Left," Eric said to Dex. "She wants you to go—"

"I heard her!"

Dex staggered half a step and Marena strained to see through the huddle of backs and bumping elbows. The crowd blocking the window shifted, and an opening appeared. Someone was at the front of the room.

It was Mrs. Crowley.

A Stof stood on either side of her, and she was carrying the big red book, holding it in front of her with both hands. She was saying something, maybe yelling. Marena couldn't tell.

"What's going on?!" Eric asked.

Marena shushed him without taking her eyes off Mrs. Crowley.

"Hurry up!" Dex said.

She saw parents she knew and IPEs from the youth training facility. She saw all the eight-and-unders sitting on the floor, her little brother Daniel among them. Then, almost in unison, nearly everyone in the room raised his or her hand and held it aloft for a long moment. A question had been asked.

She saw her father then, his hand raised along with everyone else's, and Marena could swear he was looking right at her. But he wasn't. He was staring past her blankly. Marena remembered that vacant look from somewhere—

I was in a small cubicle. The glass was tinted dark green, but I could see a crowd of people watching the trial. My mother seemed so far away, all the way at the front of the big room. Her hair was gone. They'd cut off all her hair. I stood on tiptoes to see better and listened to the angry voices everywhere. Then I saw my father. He was staring at my mother, his face blank and empty, like a Stof's. The judge asked him questions, and every time, he pointed at my mother and said, "Yes," or "It was her," or "She did." There

were lawyers holding up articles my mother had writ-
ten, and my father was just nodding and saying yes,
over and over again. A Stof took my mother by the
arm and walked her to the front of a big table. The
judge read some long speech, big words: "propagat-
ing defeatist ideas . . . vulgarly defaming our Great
Leader . . ." He asked if she had anything to say. She
pulled free of the Stof and said, "Somebody had to
make a start. And one day soon you'll be standing
where I am." My father walked away then. He just
walked right past her without even looking at her. I
pounded on the glass and screamed for him, but he
wouldn't look at me. I knew he could hear me, I knew
he saw me through the glass, but he didn't stop. It
was like he was looking right through me—

Eric whacked Marena on the leg. "Marena!" He hit
her again, throwing himself flat against the building.
"Marena, someone's coming!"

"Don't move!" Eric called up.

There was noise from the front of the building.
Marena crouched below the windowsill. Too quickly,
though. Dex stumbled to the side, and Marena's feet
lost his shoulders. She hung from the ledge, toes
frantically searching the air. Eric grabbed her ankles

and guided her feet back onto Dex's shoulders. They all pressed as close to the building as they could. Marena shut her eyes and listened like a blind person. Boot heels on cement steps, three pairs—maybe four. Mrs. Crowley's voice. Car doors opening. A struggle. Doors slamming shut. Then the sound of a car driving away.

"Okay," Eric said, patting Marena's shoe. "It's okay. They're gone."

"Come on down!" Dex said. "I can't hold you anymore."

"In a second," Marena said. She stood up and looked in the window again.

Two eyes stared back at her.

An icy breath raced through Marena's body. A scream escaped from her mouth, and she fell.

"Look out!" Eric shouted. He tried to catch her but missed, and they all slammed against the side of the building. There was yelling inside now. Commotion. Faces at the window. Metal doors slamming open. The scrape of boots heels scuttling down steps.

"Get out of here!" Eric said, helping Dex to his feet.

Dex grabbed Marena's hand, pulled her up, and dragged her into a stumbling run. They ran as fast as they could, arms pumping, feet flying, boot heels thumping after them in the darkness.

"Split up!" Marena yelled, hoping that Eric would be able to find his way back.

He flew across the street, keeping just ahead of two beams of light bouncing after him. Dex took off toward the front of the building through the obstacle course of limos and transports. Marena ran back the way they'd come, leaping fences, her heart pounding, eyes burning. On the third leap, she lost her balance and fell hard, rising just in time to see flashlights closing in on her. There was nowhere in the yard to hide. She ran to the back of a darkened house and tried the door. Locked. Tried a window next to it. Locked. The Stofs were climbing the fence. Marena hugged the shadows of the house, trying to disappear. They were over the fence now. She threw herself against the building, pressing flat within the darkened doorframe, and fought to quiet her breathing until she heard the fence rattle as the Stofs continued into the next yard.

Marena waited. She leaned out from the shadow of the house and then took off at a run again, covering ground the Stofs had already been over. Scaling the last fence, she ran down the street and leaped into the ditch that lay before the interstate. She slid down into the shallow bottom of the trough, the memory of her father at the trial tumbling in after her.

She heard footsteps coming toward her at a run.

She rolled over, scrambled up the slope, and bolted across the interstate into the dark field beyond, fighting blindly through the stalks of dead corn that blocked her way.

A hand grabbed her from behind and pulled her backward. She screamed and flailed her arms wildly.

"Marena!" Eric said, covering her mouth. "Marena, it's me!" He pulled off his mask, breathing hard and staring at her. "Man, that was crazy! I almost got caught. What did you see?" he asked her. "In the window. Who was it?"

Marena caught her breath. "It was Greengritch," she said, looking around.

"Greengritch! Do you think—"

"Where's Dex? Did you see him?"

"I saw him cut through the parking lot. Then I lost him."

They both stared into the dark and listened for a moment.

"Should we wait?" Eric asked.

Marena looked at her watch.

"We should go," she said. "Dex knows what he's doing. He'll get home okay." She led Eric back to the housing compound, praying with each step that Dex was safe.

17

Anniversary of the Great Millennium War.

Marena made her way to the front gate of the compound. She'd snuck back in the night before just a few minutes ahead of the Stofs who had been checking the housing units. Her father arrived hours later, with Daniel asleep in his arms, saying only that he'd been at a meeting. Marena hadn't said anything to him about what she'd remembered of the trial. She hadn't told the boys either—she didn't trust the memory yet.

If it was true, what could she say?

The bus ride to the YTF was quiet.

Marena tried to talk to Dex about what had happened to him after they'd split up, but he was being even more cautious than usual. He didn't say much, only that he'd made it back, and it had been really close. She slid her hand into his. He held it low beneath the seat back but seemed lost in his own thoughts. Eric, a few seats up, kept whispering things into Jeremy Sykes' ear, trying to drive him crazy probably. Marena was relieved that she and Dex hadn't been picked up for questioning that morning. If Eric had been a listener, he surely would have reported them by now.

"Stof city, huh?" Eric said as they stepped off the bus at the YTF.

Thick white snowflakes were falling, only to be trampled into dark slush beneath the jackboots of marching Stofs. There were twice as many Stofs as usual. They patrolled the sidewalk, guarded every entrance. A transport of them was sitting in the parking lot.

"Keep moving," Mr. Farr said, herding everyone toward the open doors of the school. "No homeroom today. Don't stop at your lockers. Go straight to the auditorium for assembly. Single file. Arms' distance front and back."

Marena had never liked Mr. Farr. He used to teach physical education before he was made director of security. He was a puny, mean little man who wore crinkly nylon running suits and continually tapped his pen on the clipboard he always carried.

"Eyes front," he said, walking down the line.

Marena placed her hands on top of her head and shuffled into line. Farr weaved in and out, correcting distances between students. Marena turned around to look for Dex. Eric was right behind her.

"Eyes front, young lady," he whispered.

Farr stopped and turned. "Did you say something?"

"I'm sorry?" Eric said, feigning concern. "Could you repeat the request? I couldn't—" A Stof grabbed him by the back of the neck. Eric's mouth opened, and his shoulders scrunched up to his ears.

"You think we're kidding?" Farr said in his face. "You think this is some kind of joke?"

Dex appeared and started toward the Stof holding Eric.

"Get back!" Farr screamed. Four Stofs instantly surrounded Dex. "Back in line!" Dex stepped back. Farr signaled to the Stof holding Eric, who released him with a shove toward the doors. Marena tugged at Eric's coat, urging him toward the building. He followed her, cursing under his breath.

Marena didn't quite know what to make of what

had just happened. She'd never seen a Stof get so physical with a student before—at least in public. Stuff happened during mentation, but this was new.

"Things are different today, people!" Farr said, sounding eerily like Mr. Greengritch. "We are not what we were yesterday!" He signaled for the Stofs to back off. "Now, everybody, inside!" Farr stopped Dex and pulled him aside. "Not you."

Marena stayed, watching Mr. Farr question Dex and make notes on his clipboard. A Stof blocked her view and ushered her into the building. She went through security and waited for Dex.

"What'd he say?" Eric asked Dex after they let him in.

Dex didn't answer but went straight to his locker. He waved his ID in front of it, and the door sprang open.

"Bastards," he said.

It was empty. Marena ran to her locker and opened it. Everything had been purged. Even the pen marks on the inside of the locker had been scrubbed away, the sharp smell of cleaning fluid the only thing remaining. Other students opened their lockers too, and a grumble of protest began to rise.

"Absolutely no talking!" Farr called out, striding

down the hall. A line of Stofs followed him, shutting lockers. "Proceed directly to the auditorium."

Marena and the boys trudged up a short run of steps and were stopped by a traffic jam of bodies lingering at the top. Everyone was staring at the walls.

There were hundreds of posters everywhere. They covered the brick walls by the main office and the empty trophy cases. They hung on classroom doors and along the strips of plaster above the lockers, all the way down the hall as far as Marena could see. The crowd moved at a crawl, heads tilted back, shuffling slowly toward the auditorium.

Youth Led by Youth! read the first, a picture of three arms reaching into the center and clasping wrists. **We Are the Future!** was printed on the next, a picture of children embracing in a green, billowy field, rainbow-colored daisies, knee high, surrounding them. The last one showed a young girl lying on the floor, hands tucked under her chin, reading a huge red book. **The Future Is Yours** was written beneath her. **Join the State Youth League.**

The press of students shuffled to the auditorium. There was a hushed rumble coming from those already inside. The crowd bottlenecked at the end of the hall as they tried to cram their way in. Marena and the boys pushed through and flopped into the first seats they could find. They let their heads fall back and gazed up at the ceiling.

They didn't say anything for a while.

Eric leaned toward Marena. "I count twenty-one."

Hanging from the ceiling were twenty-one large red flags edged with golden tassels. At the top of each, embroidered in an arc of bright gold stitching, were the words *State Youth League*. Along the bottom, in an upward-turned arc, it read, "Youth Led by Youth." Between the two lines was the same picture Marena had just seen in the hall, three interlocking arms, each fist clenched around the wrist next to it. The stage was empty except for a podium that stood in front of an enormous blue curtain with the Zero Tolerance Party logo emblazoned on it: a large capital letter **Z**, red, superimposed atop a lowercase black **t**.

The auditorium doors closed. The lights dimmed.

Marena brushed Dex's hand as she sat higher in her seat.

"Showtime," Eric whispered.

The lights faded to black, and the auditorium immediately burst into whispery laughs and hootings but stopped dead when two spotlights snapped on, casting a huge circle of light onto the stage. A fanfare sounded, a curtain parted, and Mr. Greengritch stepped through. Stofs and most of the IPEs applauded as the spotlights followed him to the podium. His white hair shone brightly against the deep-blue curtain that fell closed behind him. His chubby pink cheeks looked chubbier and pinker. He waved the crowd quiet and whispered softly into the microphone, "We'll all stand, please."

The students in the auditorium shifted as a single mass and shuffled out of their seats. A tremendous state flag dropped down from the ceiling behind Greengritch: six silver stars in a field of four vertical stripes, alternating blue and black. Spotlights splashed beams of golden light, illuminating Mr. Greengritch, who lifted his arms straight out to his sides. Ten students Marena didn't recognize entered from either side of the stage. They were dressed exactly alike in Stof-green leather. Marching onto the stage in perfect unison, they flanked Mr. Greengritch. He bent into the microphone again. Very quietly, almost reverently, he whispered, "The anthem of our State Youth League."

Marena turned to Dex, who looked puzzled. She mouthed to Eric, "Youth League?" He shook his head and shrugged. Music filled the auditorium, and the chorus of students onstage began to sing. Like angels. Beautiful. Lyrical.

> *Close tight the ranks, O youth, and*
> *thrust our banners high!*
> *Unity! Defense! And might! Sing out our*
> *battle cry!*
> *Our fate with joy we face; with courage*
> *here we stand!*
> *We, the future keepers, the guardians of*
> *our land!*

Greengritch turned to the audience and leaned into the microphone. "Welcome to the future." He looked out and smiled. "Please join me in a moment of silence for those lost in the Millennium War." He bowed his head for a long minute, then looked up. "You may be seated."

The students onstage clasped hands behind their backs and stood at attention.

"The young people you see behind me," Greengritch said, "are proud members of the State Youth League, which until recently has been open only to faithfuls throughout the Southern Zone. These young men and women are graduates of YTF training programs just like this one. Through hard work and self-examination, they have successfully readapted themselves and have been reintegrated into the community. They are the chosen, selected because of the integrity of their convictions and their commitment to the ZT Party."

Eric nudged Marena. "Green uniforms. Brown noses."

"They are from all walks of life, from all parts of the Southern Zone, and they are here to serve as your mentors in the coming months." He looked back at the Youth League members. "In the words of our Leader, 'He who has the youth has the future.' You, the faithful, are the future of our great state." Greengritch turned back to the auditorium. "We are all so very proud of these young men and women. Let's thank them for being here."

Greengritch led the applause, and the Stofs and IPEs joined in.

"Today," he said, "is the anniversary of the first great test our nation ever faced. A test called the Millennium War. A test we as a nation failed because we weren't prepared. The ZT Party came to power in response to that failure, because it wasn't afraid to demand a standard of loyalty from all citizens. In doing so, we created a state where the faithful can live without fearing for their lives, their homes, or their families."

Applause from IPEs and Stofs.

"But now, in many communities to the north, antistate elements have been calling for the return of tolerance, calling for a return to the permissive, vulnerable ways of the past, to a time when people could say or do or think or write whatever they wanted without any accountability for their actions. They're trying to infect young people like you with these ideas and lure you down a very dangerous path, trying to make you forget the past. I have a simple response to these people: *Forgetting is not an option!* That's why we're sitting in these seats right now. That's why we *have* Remembrance Day—so that we *never, never* forget!"

The Stofs and IPEs applauded loudly.

"Yet that's exactly what these new resistance groups are asking the government to do! What kind of state would we be, what kind of *leaders* would we be, if we relented and changed policy every time some weakhearted minorities whined because they felt inconvenienced? Well, forgive us for protecting their very *lives*, but that's our job! The first priority of any government is the protection of its citizens. Nothing comes before that. We learned that lesson once, and we will never forget it!"

More applause now. Louder.

"There is no going back to the way we were!"

Greengritch stepped from behind the podium and walked along the stage.

"I'm here to help you," he continued, "but I need your help as well." He crouched down in a squat at the edge of the stage and pointed to a student in the front row. "I challenge you," he said, his voice quiet and intense. He pointed to another student a few rows back. "And I challenge you." He took in the entire breadth of the audience. "I challenge each and every one of you to help create a community where discipline and loyalty to the state are not a burden but an honor. Where the loss of a few personal freedoms is not an inconvenience but a great and noble sacrifice. Where students like you stop resisting the government and start taking an active *part* in it!"

Greengritch paced back and forth, his forehead glistening with sweat under the bright spotlights. Marena saw some students applauding now, joining in with the Stofs and IPEs.

"I believe in every one of you, and I know in my

heart that you're the only ones who can maintain the safety of this state into the future: not me, not your instructors, not the party officials—but *you*!" He was shouting now, more and more animated, passionate. He strode up and down the edge of the stage, arms raised, rallying the crowd. "I challenge you to create a state that doesn't need readaptation communities! You have a *right* to that, your children have a right to that, and you can make it happen!"

He took off his jacket and flung it over the podium.

"How?" he asked, letting the question hang in the air a moment. "Live as if the ZT Party were created for you . . . because it *was*! It's *yours*!" He stabbed at the air with his index finger. "And yours, and yours, and yours, and yours, and yours!" His voice grew louder still. "Don't dilute its power or *your* power! Don't let yourself be seduced by people promoting tolerance. Tolerance doesn't celebrate diversity! It doesn't foster respect for other cultures. It does just the opposite! It breeds racism, prejudice, a sense that you're different from the next person—and better! Zero Tolerance is the answer, people! *Don't resist it. Live it! With Zero Tolerance we can create a whole new world!*"

18

That night Daniel stood atop the kitchen counter, handing soups bowls to Marena. "The meeting we went to last night," he told her, "you know, at the Town Hall? Stofs were everywhere, and we stayed out late. You weren't allowed to go, but I was."

"I know."

"I was out past curf."

"You were asleep when you came home."

"I was still *out*."

Marena set the table, bothered by how excited Daniel was acting. "Why were all the eight-and-unders at the meeting?" she asked.

"Training," Daniel said, jumping to the floor. "We're in training."

"For what?"

"I don't know."

"But what did you do there?"

"Sorry, can't tell you."

Her father came into the kitchen. "That's enough, Daniel," he said. "Let's eat."

"Wait!" Daniel said, and rushed to his room.

Marena looked at her father. The images of him at her mother's trial wouldn't go away. She ladled soup into his bowl, wondering who he really was, wondering what she should say.

Daniel bopped into the kitchen wearing a green T-shirt. On its back, across his shoulders, were written the words *Junior Youth League* in thin black letters. A large number *5* was centered below it, and on the front his name was written in small script letters. "Look what I got today. I get to be trained just like you now. Don't have to wait till we're nine anymore."

"What's the Junior Youth League?" Marena asked.

"Special club for the eight-and-unders," Daniel said. "Mr. G is in charge of it."

An icy tingle trickled down Marena's back. "Who?"

"Helmsley Greengritch," her father said.

Marena's stomach fisted into a knot.

They ate in silence for a short while. Her father pushed the soup around his bowl. "The Protectorate," he said after a while, "has chosen a new minister of youth and education. You know this, right?"

"Yes," Marena said.

"He's in charge of redisciplining YTFs throughout the state." He looked at Marena. "They're going to be making a lot of changes. We'll need to be diligent in our support of state doctrine, the codes of conduct, reporting any infractions to the authorities . . . you understand?" Marena was hoping he wasn't meaning what he was saying. "Some of your instructors," he continued, "are going to be sent away for correction."

"Only the *deficient* ones!" Daniel blurted out, as if he'd just won a spelling bee.

"Daniel," her father said.

"Sorry. Forgot."

Her father hesitated, eyeing Daniel. "Mr. Greengritch and others have decided that some instructors are not effectively communicating state doctrine in the classroom. Mrs. Crowley was voted out at the meeting last night. The minister felt she wasn't beneficial to the group."

Marena felt her anger rising. Voted out? She had seen her father raise his hand— "Well, did you *say* anything at the meeting?" she asked, knowing the truth. "You know she was a good teacher. I've told you about her."

"I signed the petition, didn't I?"

"Besides that."

"It's done, so just forget about it."

"But why didn't you say anything?"

"I couldn't," he said. "Now drop it."

"Did you even try? Did you try to help her?"

"Did you hear what I just said? There was nothing I could do."

"God!" Marena yelled, pushing away from the table. "That's all you ever say, Dad, you know that? It makes me sick!" Her father stood quickly and followed her. "That's your answer to everything!" she yelled, backing away from him.

He grabbed her wrist and pulled her into the hallway. "Because it's true! Did you ever consider that? Did you!"

"Daddy!" Daniel cried. "Stop!"

"Stay in there!"

"Let go," Marena said. "You're hurting me."

"That's what you never seem to understand, Marena. All this righteous crap you want to go on about—sometimes there *is* nothing you can do!"

"And you should know, right? Just like there was

nothing you could do when they asked you about Mom at the trial. Is that what you're talking about?"

Her father's face went dead and cold.

Marena pulled her wrist free. "You think I don't know."

"Go to your room."

"You think I don't remember, but I do. I remember more all the time."

"I said go to your room. *Now!*"

Marena ran down the hallway, slammed her bedroom door, and locked it. She hated him right then more than she'd ever hated anyone. She paced her room, furious, wanting to do something, anything, to break something. She looked out her window into the darkened alley, wishing she could leap out and just run. She threw open her closet door and pried back the piece of baseboard, took out the paper she kept hidden there, grabbed a pencil, and wrote. And wrote. She wrote down everything she could remember.

There was a knock at her door. "Hey, Beaner," Daniel whispered, "open up."

"I'm busy."

"C'mon."

"Go to bed."

"Beaner . . ."

"No."

"I'll show you something else Mr. G gave me."

Marena stopped writing. She hid her papers and unlocked her bedroom door. "What is it?"

"Let me in first." Marena stepped back and let him in. "What are you doing?" he asked, sitting on her bed.

"None of your business. What did Mr. G give you?"

"Check it out," Daniel said. He fished out a laminated card, shaped like an octagon, that hung from a thin chain around his neck. "New ID card. It's really cool."

Marena sat next to him and read the odd-looking card. Olive green, bordered in black with dark-red lettering, it had his picture on it, his name and ID number, grade, age, all the same as before, but there was something new:

Threat Status/Father: 6.7
Threat Status/Mother: NEUTRALIZED
Familial Predisposition: Deviationism
Ethnicity: Immix
Racial Purity Index: 16%
Social Deficiency: Pediatric/No Known deficiencies to date

"Flip it," Daniel told Marena. "Look at the back." She did but saw nothing there. "You got to turn it."

Marena twisted the card slightly under the bedroom light. A hologram of three large letters ran across it: **DEV**.

19

Mr. Farr stayed late at the YTF. He hovered in his office doorway, pretending he wasn't listening to Mr. Greengritch's phone conversation. Greengritch gestured him in and pointed to a chair. On the other end of the phone, Mr. Blaine was pressing for more details of what had happened at the Town Hall meeting the night before.

"And the building was checked?" Blaine asked. "The grounds around it?"

"Everything was clean," Greengritch answered, thinking how young Blaine sounded for an ICCS officer. "They looked like kids to me."

"Yes, that would be the point, wouldn't it, Mr. Greengritch?"

"What I meant was—"

"You found no signs of sabotage or propaganda?"

"None."

"You ran a unit check?"

"Yes, sir," Greengritch said, tolerating the inane questions. "What I was trying to say before was that it could have been faithfuls from outside the re-dap. It could have been a prank."

There was a chilly pause at the other end of the phone.

"We don't tolerate pranks, Mr. Greengritch."

"Yes, sir. I know that."

Greengritch listened as Blaine launched into a minor tirade about the danger of mistaking a prank for actual activity by the resistance group called the Alliance of Youth for Liberty and Reunification. They'd recently been targeting YTFs for recruitment.

"Yes, but if it is AYLR," Greengritch said, "then we should—"

Blaine just kept talking. And Greengritch stopped listening.

If it had been kids from inside the re-dap, he thought, then there was a more serious breach of the rules in Spring Valley than he'd imagined. He'd have to do something about it right away. There were plans in motion, but he'd accelerate them. He had something radical in mind. A wake-up call. They'd been too easy on these kids. It was impossible to maintain security with this kind of tolerance, and it was the students who'd suffer. They were the ones who'd be sent to loyalty correction if they weren't reintegrated. These instructors lacked the will to stick to ZT convictions, and lack of will diluted the single most important element in the education of young citizens.

Fear.

It was one of the first things he'd noticed after arriving at the Spring Valley YTF, the lack of fear in the students. Greengritch believed religiously in fear. Fear begot responsibility and a sense of accountability. Fear was necessary for the smooth running of YTFs and, in a larger sense, for the survival of the state. Without fear, without a wariness of the dangers that always lie in wait, there came a cockiness, an arrogance—an invitation to disaster. Greengritch knew this better than anyone. His own loss had driven the lesson home time and time again.

Greengritch shifted in his seat, not really listening to Blaine on the other end of the phone. He placed a hand over the receiver and nodded to Mr. Farr.

"Yes, sir," Farr whispered.

"I want to meet with the instructors. Tonight."

"They've gone home already, sir."

"Call them back."

"Yes, sir," he said and started to leave.

"Mr. Farr."

"Sir?"

"Do me a favor, would you?"

"Yes, sir."

"Whatever that is you're wearing?"

Farr straightened his running suit.

"Don't be wearing it tomorrow."

20

All the students received new ID cards as they stepped off the bus at the YTF the next morning. Marena turned hers over in her hand and angled it in the gray morning light. Her hologram, like her brother's, was a large **DEV**. The rest of the information was identical to Daniel's except for the last line, which read:

Social Deficiency: Heterodoxy.

"Hetero what?" Eric asked, looking over her shoulder.

Marena shrugged. "I don't know." She waited to pass through security with the others. She had tried to talk to Dex about her father while they were on the bus, but a Stof patrolled up and down the aisle the whole time. Dex had promised to meet her in the alley after school so they could talk then.

"Keep moving," an IPE Marena had never seen before said. The woman, white-haired and solid-looking, dangled a sample ID card from its chain high in the air. "These are to be worn on the outside of your clothing. Clearly visible at all times."

Marena stepped through the metal detector inside the doors of the YTF. A Stof met her on the other side, took her ID card, and passed a scanner over it. He waited until it sounded a short chime and waved Marena on.

Mr. Greengritch was standing at the far end of the hall, waiting for the students to gather. He held a hand aloft until everyone saw him and the rustlings and whisperings quieted. When all was completely silent and still, he said, "There are no classes today."

The hall erupted in cheering.

"Quiet!" Mr. Farr said, wading through the crowd. He stood beside Mr. Greengritch. "There is still no talking! Quiet!"

Mr. Greengritch held his hand up until there was silence again.

"The smooth running of a YTF," he said, "or of any society for that matter, depends upon *rules* and, of course, upon those rules' being *obeyed*. The state, some time ago, after reviewing your backgrounds, chose to grant all of you an opportunity at readaptation. I shall do my part to make sure you succeed. And you will do yours." He put his hands in his pockets and paused. Then he looked toward the new IPE Marena had seen outside. "Miss Nadine."

"Boys report to the gymnasium," she said, "girls to the cafeteria. Line up on either side of the hall. Boys to the left. Girls to the right."

"Arms' distance apart," Farr said, walking down the center of the hall. He went to the end of the boys' line, which was forming, and Miss Nadine went to the opposite end of the girls' line. She blew a whistle, and the lines moved forward. Marena searched across the hall for Dex and Eric, but she'd lost them. The two lines moved in opposite directions, snaking down the hallway. Marena began to worry. Something didn't feel right.

Miss Nadine walked alongside the girls, leading them down the hall in silence, until they reached the cafeteria. "Inside," she said. "No talking."

Maybe it was nothing, Marena thought. Maybe they were just trying to scare them again. It would probably be a day of videotaped reindoctrination sessions, ideology correction, or ZT propaganda films.

The cafeteria was often used for such things.

She and the others marched inside. Marena squinted as she stepped through the doors. Everything was brighter, as if all the lights had been doubled in wattage. The girls wandered about, shielding their eyes from the glare. The stainless-steel lunch tables had been pushed up against the walls, leaving almost the whole expanse of the cafeteria floor wide open. All the chairs were gone, and on each table were several piles of clothes.

"Middle of the room," Miss Nadine said.

The girls huddled in a loose crowd in the center of the cafeteria. Everyone kept turning and jostling, unsure what to do. A group of Stofs entered. The circle of girls tightened inward. The Stofs lined up around the perimeter of the room and stood at attention, equal distance apart, arms behind their backs, staring straight ahead.

"Undress," Miss Nadine said.

There was a pause, a moment of uncertainty.

"Undress," she said again. "You will receive your uniforms now."

The girls milled about, confused.

"Place your clothes in a pile in the center of the room."

Marena looked around her, waiting for someone else to protest. She stepped out of the circle. "Can't we—"

"You will undress immediately or a state officer will do it for you." The Stofs around the perimeter of the room took a step forward and let their hands fall to their sides. Miss Nadine looked at Marena. "Jewelry and socks too."

Slowly, with furtive looks and bowed heads, the girls began to undress. Clothes fell to the floor.

"Hurry up," Miss Nadine said, walking around the group. "Nobody's looking at you. Leave any purses or book bags. They'll be documented and sent to you later. Keep nothing but your new ID."

This couldn't be happening, Marena thought. They couldn't make everyone—

"*Do it!*" Miss Nadine said, pointing a Stof in Marena's direction.

Marena stripped to her underwear and threw her clothes to the floor.

"Clothes in the center!"

She and the others gathered up their clothes and dropped them in the middle of the circle. They huddled together, shoulders touching bare shoulders, awkwardly twisting their bodies to help hide their near nakedness.

"You all know your ID numbers."

Marena, like everyone else, tried to cover herself with one hand as she listened.

"The first two numbers represent the state officer you will report to for your uniform."

Marena looked up and saw that the Stofs were holding neatly numbered signs.

"Keep in numerical order, and call out your number as you go."

The circle of girls split, anxious to be clothed again, and spilled across the room. Marena tiptoed over the cold tiled floor, hugging herself warm, and found her line. There were about half a dozen girls already there. Someone behind her called out, "Two-two two-four-two," then ran to the front and received her uniform. Marena stepped out next and ran up to the table. "Two-two two-four-three," she said, and the Stof handed her a uniform. She clutched it to her chest and ran to the center of the room. She sat on the floor, hurriedly pulled on ankle-high black socks, and kicked her legs into pressed green slacks. She threw on the khaki-colored shirt, buttoned it up, tucked it in, and snapped everything together. It all fit perfectly. She stepped into the tall black boots and crammed her hair under a black beret embroidered with the initials SYL. Then she picked up a cellophane-wrapped package. In it was a short black jacket. Leather. The thin pelt crinkled and squeaked as Marena unwrapped it. Its stench, a mingling of animal flesh and plastic, filled the room, and along with it, the hint of a memory came, the smell . . . that same stench . . . the thin creak of the leather—

"Quickly, please," Miss Nadine said.

Marena put the jacket on. It felt leaden and dull. She zipped it nearly to her neck.

Miss Nadine surveyed the group as the last few girls finished dressing. "Now give me five lines, size order, starting here." She traced an imaginary line on the floor with her foot.

The girls arranged themselves.

"Arms' distance, please."

Everyone touched fingers to backs in front of them and adjusted.

"Take off your berets."

A Stof stood in front of each line. Each was holding scissors and hair trimmers.

"No!" someone shouted out from the back of Marena's line. "No!" Everyone turned to look. It was Heather, one of the JJ-girls. "You can't do this!" Heather walked through the lines of girls. "They can't do this!"

The lines faltered, then broke apart. Everyone began to fall back into a sort of circle again. "Don't let them do this!" Then the Stofs stepped in, forcing the girls back into their lines. Two walked quickly over to Heather. "Get away from me!" she screamed. Each took an arm. "You can't do this! You can't— Get the hell off me!"

They bent Heather's arms behind her back.

"You're hurting me—"

They muzzled her. Quickly. Efficiently. Marena had never seen a muzzling. One Stof held Heather from behind as another strapped on the leather head restraint. He buckled it at the back of her head and looped a length of strap under her chin. Then he pulled it tight, sealing her mouth closed, and fastened the strap across the top of her head. Heather made a few muffled sounds of pain as her long hair was snagged and pulled up into the harness. Another padded strap went over her eyes and buckled just above her ear— it took only seconds—and she was quieted, almost calm, like a wild bird blanketed. The Stofs took her by the arms and walked her out of the cafeteria door. Her feet weren't touching the floor.

This isn't happening, Marena thought. *This can't be—*

"Form up," Miss Nadine said.

The girls obeyed and straightened their ranks.

Marena closed her eyes and clenched her fists tight, ashamed that she wasn't doing anything, wasn't saying anything. She heard the electric buzz of hair shears snapping on.

She took another step forward as the line shifted.

Her mind raced. What if they all fought back at the same time? Maybe everyone would do it if she began it, as they'd started to when Heather had spoken up. But would they? Would anyone follow her now? They might. But they might not. Then the Stofs would muzzle her and drag her away as they had done to Heather.

The line moved forward again.

But they couldn't muzzle everybody, Marena thought. They couldn't take everyone away.

She would do it. Her mother would, she knew her mother would. Marena looked up and down her line. She would do it.

Right now.

21

A gloved hand palmed the back of Marena's head and pushed it down, chin to chest. First scissors. Then shears. Clumps of matted hair fell around her feet, the hair she had once hated but now missed: her *messes*.

She wouldn't cry.

Marena strangled the beret in her hand and dug her knuckles deep into her legs, furious at herself. She hadn't screamed or resisted at all. She'd been afraid of being taken away, like Heather, or disappeared, like her mother and Mrs. Crowley. But she knew her mother would have risked it. She *had* risked it.

Shears scraped loudly behind Marena's ear as her head was tilted sideways.

She stared down at the leather boots of the Stof who was cutting her hair, identical to the ones she was now wearing. He pushed her head down harder. Marena struggled to breathe, her face pressed into the folds of her leather jacket. As she twisted away, a rapid battering of memories smacked at her—bits, pieces, sounds, smells—like images seen by lightning flash.

. . . boots . . . in my house . . . on the stairs . . . gloves, black gloves . . . in my bedroom . . . the smell, the stench of leather . . . gloved fingers, pulling, groping . . . my mother, against a wall . . . I can't breathe . . . hands on my face . . . on my mother—

The Stof lifted Marena's chin. With one last pass of the shears he buzzed away what was left of her bangs. He whisked the remains of wiry hair off her shoulders and gestured her to the side.

Marena lingered, willing the interrupted memory to continue, but the Stof nudged her away, and it was gone for good. Another Stof swept a large broom through the spot where she had been, and the next girl took her place.

"Line up by the door when you're done," Miss Nadine told everyone.

Marena got in line. The girl in front of her turned

around, and they stared at each other. Marena ran a hand across the back of her bristling scalp, put on her beret, and listened to the buzz and clip and muted weeping echo through the cafeteria, until the last girl was shorn.

"Follow me," Miss Nadine said, opening the cafeteria doors.

They followed, the tramp of new boots echoing through the halls. The girls in front of Marena all looked alike from behind: same clothes, same stride— like a flock of clipped birds, featherless and leather winged.

"Hats off," said Miss Nadine as they neared the gymnasium.

Marena removed her beret. Her scalp felt cold and raw.

"In."

The aluminum bleachers were pulled out on either side of the gym floor. The boys, their heads shaved, were on one side dressed in uniforms of the State Youth League. The line of girls slowed, turning their faces away from the boys' stares.

"Keep moving," Miss Nadine said, pointing at the empty set of bleachers across from the boys.

The file of girls crossed the gymnasium floor and

filled the bleachers. Marena looked across at the boys and scoured their faces for Eric or Dex, but she couldn't find them. Four members of the State Youth League entered with Mr. Farr. They were carrying cardboard boxes and went to either end of the bleachers.

"These are your new YTF manuals," Farr said as the Leaguers began handing out small red books. "Read them. Know them."

Marena grabbed the pile of books handed to her, took one, and passed the rest.

"Thanks to Mr. Greengritch, you have all been accepted into the State Youth League, the first time this honor has been bestowed on YTF students who have not completed the training."

A Stof opened a door, and Mr. Greengritch entered.

"We'll all stand," Mr. Farr said.

Marena stood along with everyone else as Greengritch walked down the center of the gymnasium floor, inspecting the students on either side.

"Yes," he said. "Yes. Much better. Please sit."

He paused, surveying the room. A long pause. Then he began slowly walking around the gym.

"Now, this doesn't have to be hard," he said. "In fact it shouldn't be. This is a great opportunity. Of course some of you may be upset that your clothes were taken away. Or that your hair was trimmed. But you know what? You'll get over it, because"—he pointed at the bleachers and screamed—*"you are not your clothes!"* He hammered out each word. *"You . . . are . . . not . . . your . . . hair!"*

He turned in a slow circle.

"I want you to ask yourselves something and really think about it. If I were to take away everything about you that you *think* is you, who would you be?" He let the question sit. "Because that's what I'm going to do. I'm going to kill whatever you think is you. There's no room for *you* anymore. There's only room for *us*."

Two youth leaguers, both not much older than Marena, stepped out from behind a line of Stofs. The boy, tall and slender with short-cropped hair, was wearing Stof-green sweatpants and a tight T-shirt to match. The girl wore the same, her hair pulled back in a short thick ponytail. Her body was tight, compact, and muscular. The two walked across the floor and joined Mr. Greengritch.

"Beginning now," Greengritch said, "you will be trained only in things that are useful to the state. Mr. Malcolm and Miss Elaine are your coaches. You don't have to believe in what they ask you to do, you don't have to like it, you just have to do it. Belief will catch up."

Greengritch shook hands with Mr. Malcolm and Miss Elaine and left the gymnasium. The metal doors swung shut behind him with a loud clank.

Mr. Malcolm turned to the boys, Miss Elaine to the girls. Mr. Malcolm spoke first, loud enough for everyone in the room to hear. "A physically superior individual is much more valuable to the state than what?"

The question drifted around the gymnasium. Miss Elaine walked the length of the girls' bleachers and answered it. "A physically superior individual is much more valuable to the state than an intellectual weakling."

"The finest member of the State Youth League is one who what?" Mr. Malcolm continued.

Miss Elaine picked up the cue. "The finest member of the State Youth League is one who possesses physical superiority and an undying belief in the worldview of Zero Tolerance."

"This alone is the supreme task of education," Mr. Malcolm said.

"This alone is the supreme task of good citizenship," Miss Elaine responded.

Mr. Malcolm gestured for both bleachers to stand.

"Everyone down to the gym floor. Hats on. Give me five lines."

The bleachers spilled out onto the gymnasium floor, and the students formed ranks.

"Arms' distance to the side and front," Miss Elaine said. She nodded to Mr. Malcolm when she was satisfied with the lines. He lifted his hand over his head, and music began to play.

"We begin with marching."

22

The room reeked of sweat. Marena had been marching around the gymnasium for almost two hours. Her legs ached. Her stomach was knotted with hunger.

"Again!" Mr. Malcolm called out from the far end of the gymnasium.

Anytime anyone made a mistake—a misstep, a sloppy halt, a not-sharp-enough turn—the whole group had to begin again.

"One person's mistake is everyone's mistake," Mr. Malcolm said. "Again!"

Miss Elaine kept time with two wooden batons that she tapped together. Stofs stood silent against the walls. No one was allowed to look at one another, or go to the bathroom, or talk.

"And again!"

They marched and marched and marched . . . until an annoying buzz sounded over the intercom.

Miss Elaine stopped tapping her batons. "Lunch."

A collective groan echoed through the room.

"Keep your lines," Mr. Malcolm said.

Miss Elaine whacked her batons together loudly, continuing the rhythmic beat. Two Stofs opened the doors, and the new, exhausted members of the State Youth League marched out of the gymnasium and down the long hall to the cafeteria.

"Eyes front," Miss Elaine said. She fell in step beside Marena. "Arms relaxed at your sides. Thumb and forefinger touching mid thigh."

Mr. Malcolm turned around and walked backward down the hall. "Physical training instills confidence. Confidence is the key to success, is it not, Miss Elaine?"

"It is, Mr. Malcolm."

"Confidence and what else, Miss Elaine?"

"Discipline, Mr. Malcolm."

"Discipline and what else, Miss Elaine?"

"Pride in the group, Mr. Malcolm."

"And more important?"

At that very moment Marena caught Miss Elaine's eyes, a brown so deep her pupils disappeared into them, almost the same as her own, she thought, almost the same as her mother's.

"And more important, Miss Elaine?" Malcolm asked again.

"Zero Tolerance, Mr. Malcolm!" She snapped at Marena, "Eyes front!"

Mr. Malcolm palmed the digiprint on the wall outside the cafeteria, and the doors swung open. Miss Elaine addressed the group in the hall. "You will be allowed to mingle and speak after the state anthem is sung." She marched the students in. A mixture of Stofs and Youth Leaguers were stationed around the room. "You are free to choose where you sit. Remain standing in front of your table."

Marena passed by the lunch tables, which had all been put back in place—except for two that were set near the front of the room apart from the others.

"Eleven students to a table," Mr. Malcolm called out.

"Eleven," Miss Elaine repeated.

Marena picked a table. Dex and Eric joined her, with Sykes not far behind. They stood on the other side, facing her.

"Hats off," Miss Elaine said.

Marena took off her hat, feeling ugly and naked.

Dex stared at her nearly bald scalp, then averted his eyes. A dark shadow was all that was left of his hair. A tinge of bright red was scraped in a thin line above his ear: blood from a hasty pass of the shears. Eric's sloppy bangs were now only an auburn-tinted fringe of stubble. His scalp, oddly shaped and bumpy, looked scrawny, like the rest of him.

The Stofs began to serve lunch. Marena looked down. It nearly took her breath away.

The plates were heaped with food.

Real food. Like nothing she had ever seen at the YTF before. A mountain of rice, a heap of carrots, with an actual pat of butter sitting on it, grilled chicken smothered in some kind of sauce, and a huge round cookie for dessert. The only foods ever rationed before had been cardboardlike protein patties, never anything like this. Dex pointed to the plates and whispered something to Marena. She couldn't make out what he was trying to say. She shook her head slightly to signal that she didn't understand. He started to speak again, but Miss Elaine tapped her wooden baton on one of the tables.

"The state anthem will be sung at the beginning of every day, before lunch, and at the end of every day," she said. "Healthy mind, body, *and* spirit." She signaled to a Leaguer, who unfurled a large flag of state. "Together, please," Miss Elaine said.

Music filled the cafeteria. One by one, table by table, they began to sing. Marena moved her lips and said nothing.

> Let our flag fly freely,
> Let us cherish freedom won,
> Let hand join hand and heart join heart,
> For out of many, one.

She felt nauseous and angry again. She wanted to jump onto the table, refuse to eat, refuse to sit down—anything. The impulse was there, fluttering in the pit of her stomach, the desire to *do* something.

The anthem ended.

"At my signal," Mr. Malcolm said, looking at his watch, "you will have twenty minutes to eat."

Across the table Dex and Eric were whispering to each other. Marena couldn't make out what they were saying. Dex looked at Marena and spoke a little louder.

"There's only ten," he said. "Only ten."

Marena heard him but didn't know what he meant. Dex pointed at the plate in front of him. "There are only—"

"Begin!" Mr. Malcolm said.

Immediately the silence of the cafeteria erupted into a riot of noise as students grappled for their food. In that flash of a moment Marena realized what Dex had been trying to tell her. At each table there were only ten plates of food.

And eleven students.

Chaos followed. Ugly fend-for-yourself chaos. Students screamed and hit one another. Boys shoved girls, girls punched boys. Food flew as students clawed it with their bare hands. All the decorum, all the discipline they had been practicing that day had disintegrated in an instant.

Mr. Malcolm and Miss Elaine, together with the Stofs and other Leaguers in the room, remained calm and still. They never said a word. They just stood there, observing.

The initial fury of the moment subsided as the victors settled in to eat. They hovered over their plates, covering them with one hand and shoveling in food with the other. The room fell into a dull murmur of voices and ravenous chewing.

At each table stood one student without food, looking lost. Marena was one of them. She hadn't even tried to grab a plate. It had all happened so fast.

"Marena," Eric said, "c'mon, you can have some of mine."

"No," Miss Elaine said, stopping Marena with her baton. "No."

Mr. Malcolm spoke. "All those without food go to the tables in the front and take a seat."

"What's the big deal?" Eric said. "Why can't she—"

Marena stopped him with a shake of her head. She turned away and walked to the tables at the front of the room. So did the others like her. When they were all seated, three Stofs came out of the kitchen doors with trays of food. A plate was put in front of Marena.

On it was a single crusty protein patty.

23

After lunch Marena was assigned to a group of twenty girls and sent to a classroom, home economics and parenting. Mornings from now on were to be devoted to theories of Zero Tolerance and physical education. School was to end at two o'clock, and there would be mandatory after-school participation in competitive sports programs until five o'clock: swimming for the girls and wrestling for the boys.

Before the last bell the students were given winter coats to wear over their leather jackets—black Windbreakers with thick zip-in linings, dark-green ribbing at the wrists and waists, and the letters *YTF* arched in gray across the backs. They were also assigned bus seats. On the ride home Marena wasn't anywhere near Dex. She was stuck all the way in the front, sitting beside Franky Poyer. A Stof again patrolled the aisle and enforced the no-talking rule.

There were more Stofs than usual milling about the front gate when the bus arrived at the housing compound. They weaved in and out among the students, following some of them home. Marena passed close to Dex. "The Place," she whispered, "after midnight. Bring Eric."

He hesitated but then nodded and headed to the Orph. Eric was walking toward Marena quickly, shoving something up the sleeve of his coat. "I stole Sykes's ration book again," he said, glancing over his shoulder. "He's freaking out on the bus trying to find it."

"We're going to meet tonight. Dex'll tell you about it."

"Okay," Eric said, looking a little baffled. "You're kind of crazy, but okay."

A Stof started in their direction.

Marena walked away, and the Stof followed her to her unit. She stopped and turned to him. "Found it," she said. Expressionless, he walked away.

Daniel was waiting outside, swinging on the gate. "Wow!" he said, looking at her new coat and uniform. He jumped off and circled her. "Wow! I want one."

"No, you don't." She bent down and kissed him. "Where's Dad?"

"Ah!" Daniel screamed, swiping off her beret. "Oh, wow, you're bald! You don't have any— Hey, Dad! Daddy!" He ran up the steps. "Marena's bald! She cut off all her hair!" Marena followed him inside. Daniel leaped as high as he could, trying to touch her head. "Wow, let me feel it!" She knelt down in the living room, and Daniel rasped his little-boy fingers back and forth over her stubble. "Wow," he said again. "Wow."

"You need to enlarge your vocabulary."

Her father entered from the kitchen and stopped mid step, wincing as he saw her sheared head and ZT colors. A small sound escaped him, a sound Marena thought was going to be a scream of anger, but he stifled it and pushed it back down.

Maybe he'll say something now, she thought. *Maybe now he'll do something.*

"They did it to everyone," Marena said. She took off her heavy coat, and again the sickly smell of new leather filled her with disgust. She ripped off the jacket and flung it on the floor. "How can they do this? Why isn't anyone saying anything?"

A rage seemed to be building in her father. Maybe

now he'd finally stand up for her.

"They cut off our hair, Dad! Look at me! They made us take our clothes off and change in front of Stofs. They muzzled Heather and took her away."

"What's a muzzle?" Daniel asked.

"Nothing," his father said.

"You see what they're doing, Dad!" Marena pleaded with him. "You've seen it before. You have no right not to do something about it!"

The concern on her father's face vanished. He picked up the jacket Marena had thrown on the floor and folded it. "I'm sorry, Marena. There's nothing we can do." His voice was measured and cold. "Not now."

Marena slapped the jacket out of his hands. "Not now?" she yelled. "When, Dad? When are you going to say something!" Daniel backed away.

Her father picked up the jacket and carefully folded it again.

"I don't believe you!" Marena cried.

"I'm sorry. We have to wait. It's not time to—"

"How long are we going to wait, Dad? Until they come for me, too? Or Daniel?"

"Marena, you don't understand—"

"No, *you're* the one who doesn't understand! I'm

not like you, okay?" She grabbed the leather coat out of his hands. "I'm not going to stand around, pretending things are going to get better, until they come and drag me away like they did to Mom!" She opened the front door and threw the leather jacket outside. "I'm not!"

"Stop fighting!" Daniel screamed from the hallway.

Her father pushed past Marena and ran out the front door. He ducked low, looking left and right, grabbed the jacket, and hurried back in. He slammed the front door, and a shutter flash of memory jolted Marena.

. . . my father outside the front door . . . Stofs . . . a rush of footsteps . . . Mother on the floor . . .

He thrust the jacket at her. "Put this away and don't—"

"Just leave me alone!" she cried, desperately trying to hold on to the new memory that had shown itself. She ran to her bedroom and slammed her door. Leaning against it, she slid to the floor, dropped her head into her hands, and tried to remember everything she could of the night they'd come for her mother. She'd always been able to recall some things about that night, but her father—her father had never been part of the memory. He hadn't been there that night.

Nothing else came to her, just the vague feeling that her father had been lying again.

Marena started to kick off her jackboots when she noticed neat piles of clothes stacked on her bed: two Stof-green uniforms, exactly like the one she was wearing. She hurled the uniforms against the wall. Had they been in here? Had they touched her bed? Gone through her drawers? Her heart panicked, and she rushed to her dresser. She pulled out the second drawer and checked beneath it to see if her mother's article was still taped to the bottom. It was. She slammed it shut, grabbed one of the uniforms, and pushed open her bedroom door. "Dad!" she yelled. "Dad!"

Daniel was sitting in the hall. Marena stepped past him. "Dad?" He appeared at the top of the hallway, and she held up the uniform. "Where'd these come from?"

"They were here today. There are no exemptions from the new dress protocols. We have to keep them clean and pressed. And we have to trim your hair every two weeks."

Marena, speechless, returned to her room. She tore off her uniform, put on kneeless jeans, and pulled on an old sweatshirt. Sitting on the end of her bunk, she ran her fingers over her scalp and covered her face. The faint smell of leather lingered on her hands.

. . . hands on my face . . . gloved hands . . . my mother . . . in the hallway—

"Damn it!" she said, not wanting to remember any more.

There was a tap at her door.

"Go away!" Marena said. She pulled the loose neck of her sweatshirt up over her face and lay back in her bunk. The door opened, and Daniel came in.

"You crying?" he asked.

Marena let the sweatshirt slide below her eyes. *"No."*

"Oh." He joined her on the bed, and Marena turned toward the wall. Daniel touched her shoulder. "Your head doesn't really look that bad, you know. Well, it kind of does, but it's kind of cool too."

"Thanks."

"Just wanted to tell you."

"Got it."

"Okay."

"I'm just tired, D."

"Okay. I'm going to go play," he said, and left the room.

"Close the door."

Marena scooted off the bunk and went over to her dresser again. She pulled out the same drawer and lay on the floor beneath it, staring up at the faded article. It was one of the only things she had left of her mother, that and the white rose bookmark. Every photo of her, everything she'd owned, had been confiscated and destroyed. Marena read her mother's words, hoping to hear her voice again.

> *I saw the ZTs for what they were, what they*
> *were capable of, and because of that, I had*
> *no right to be silent. I had no right not to*
> *do something.*

But even her mother's words couldn't ward off the sickening memory:

. . . gloved hands over my mother's face . . .
holding her down, pressing her against the wall. Out-
side . . . through the open front door . . . I see him . . .
he's there . . . my father is there . . . watching—

The image of her father again. On the sidewalk.
Could he really have been there?

The bedroom door opened. Marena quickly closed
her dresser drawer as her father came in with the
leather jacket.

"Marena," he said, "I know you think—"

"Where were you the night they came for Mom?"

He was taken aback by the question. "I've told you
that before."

"Where were you?"

"At work. At the Capitol."

"You weren't outside the house? On the sidewalk?"

"No."

He was lying. "Did you tell them, Dad? Did you tell
the ZTs where she was? The same way you testified
against her? Did you turn her in?"

"No. No, I—"

"Oh, God, Daddy, what did you do?"

He faltered, looking as if he were about to say

something, but then his face hardened again. "That's enough of this."

"Please, don't lie to me, Daddy. Please!"

He walked out of her room. "I said that's enough! I wasn't there." And he slammed the door.

24

The light in her father's room was still on.

Marena could hardly stand being in the same house with him anymore. He was everything she hated. Not only had he testified against her mother, but he was why she'd been arrested in the first place. That had to be the only reason he was still alive. He'd turned her in. He'd led them to her! How could he live with himself every day? How could he bear to look at her or Daniel?

Sitting on the floor of her closet, a penlight between her teeth, Marena pressed flat another scrap of paper and kept writing.

My mother never would have married him if
she'd known what he could do. She would

have hated everything about him. She always told me what a good man he was, how he had stood up for people when he was a lawyer, people nobody else would stick up for, how he fought the ZT judges and sued the state. She was so proud of him all the time. How could she be fooled like that? Why couldn't she see what he really was?

It was almost midnight when Marena peeked out into the hallway again. The light in her father's room was finally off. She put her coat on and stuffed the pages she'd just written beneath her shirt. She waited another five minutes, then eased open her bedroom window and snuck out, letting herself fall quietly to the alley a few feet below. She ducked through the cut flap in the perimeter fence and zigzagged across the ruined cornfield, running as hard as she could, swiping and punching at stalks along the way. Inside the Place, Dex and Eric, bundled up, were waiting for her in the stairwell.

Dex cupped a flashlight to his watch. "You're late."

"I had to wait for my father to fall asleep."

"This place is pretty great," Eric said.

Dex started down the steps. "There's a lot more. This is just the stairwell."

Marena pulled the papers from her shirt.

"You better be careful with those," Dex said.

"With what?" Eric asked.

"Nothing," Marena said, walking into her room.

"C'mon," Dex said to Eric. "I'll show you around."

Marena wrestled the sink away from the wall and hid her writings behind it. She put Dex's pocketknife in her coat. Then she took out the bookmark her mother had given her and turned it over in her hands, wondering if there were some small chance that her father was telling the truth. She didn't know what to believe anymore. She pocketed the bookmark and shoved the sink back into place. *He's a coward now, whether he was then or not.*

"Very cool," Eric said, falling backward onto the couch and staring at the ceiling. The overhead lights turned the room dark crimson. "Taillights . . . great idea. How'd you guys ever find this place?"

Marena dragged over a milk crate and sat on it, facing Eric. "Take off your jacket."

Eric's face went blank. He looked at Dex, then back to Marena.

"C'mon, Eric," Dex said. "Just do it."

Eric took off his jacket and threw it at Marena. "Hurry up, it's freezing."

"Get up," Dex said. Eric stood, and Dex patted him down, checking his pants and his hat. Dex found a fat black Magic Marker and tossed it to Marena. She took off the cap, put it on again, and tossed it back.

"Sorry," Marena said, handing Eric his jacket. "You'd do the same thing."

"Maybe I should."

"Go ahead."

Eric waved her off and pulled his jacket on. "Next time you might want to check for listening devices *before* you bring someone here."

"Nobody else is *ever* coming here!" Marena snapped at him. "You tell no one about this place, you understand?"

"I was just saying— Chill already! What are you getting so pissed about?"

"Nothing, I— Just forget it." Marena stood and walked away. So much had happened to her in one day, she felt like she'd been beaten up. Everything just made her angrier. "I'm sorry." She started to speak and stopped, not sure how to bring up what she wanted to talk about. "Listen, Eric," she said, "what you were saying the other day, in the cafeteria . . . Did you ever actually resist? I mean, did you know anybody in the resistance?"

Eric shifted, uneasy. "Why?"

"I just want to know. I want to know how they work, what they do. Did you ever meet with them?"

"No," Eric said, "but they were around."

"How do you know?" Dex asked.

"I told you we did stuff up at Central West. They were the ones who asked us to."

Marena stepped closer. "How? You said you never met them."

"I didn't. They usually—" Eric stopped himself from saying anything more and got up from the couch. "Why are you guys asking me all this stuff?"

"Why?" Marena yelled. She ripped off her wool hat and pointed to her raw scalp. "This is why!" Eric backed away from her. "Mrs. Crowley is why! Heather is why! *My mother* is why!"

"All right, Marena!" Dex said, pulling her aside.

She yanked away from him. "If there's a resistance, I want to *see* them, I want to *meet* them!"

"Relax!" Dex yelled at her. "Look, Eric, is there any way to contact them?"

"No. They contact you."

"Great," Marena said. "And you've never met with them?"

"They don't meet with anyone."

"Then how do you know they even exist!"

"I've seen their messages, Marena! I've seen things they've done." Eric sat on the edge of the couch. "All right, look, they work in these small groups called cells. They put you together with maybe one, two other people at the most, usually by a note or something, just to get you to meet each other, make sure everybody's safe. Then later—you never know when—you'll get another message telling you to do something."

"Who's leaving these messages?" Dex asked.

"I don't know, you never meet them. That way, if someone gets caught, the whole thing doesn't go down. Some people say they're faithfuls who turned against the ZTs. They could be IPEs, Stofs, even students or parents you think are ZT. There could be like fifty people around you in the resistance, and you'd never know it."

"I don't get it," Dex said, pacing the room. "How do they know who to contact? If they put you together with the wrong person, you'll just get turned in."

"They don't approach just anyone," Eric said.

"They must have people who watch us or know us, study our files or something."

"And they contacted you?" Dex asked.

"Yeah. A note in my bunk."

"What did it say?" Marena asked.

"To resist. Resist in any way I could, whatever I could think of. It had a list of things to do: graffiti, flooding bathrooms, turning your back on Stofs when they walk by, breaking windows, slashing tires, putting rotten food in IPEs' desks—anything to make things hard for them. They told me to make copies of the list and give them to people I could trust or just leave them places, you know, where people could find them."

"We could do things like that," Marena said, excited by the ideas. "We could do that right now."

"Yeah, *we could*," Dex said, "but we're not going to."

"What are you talking about?" Marena said.

"We should try to contact them first before we—"

"Why?" Marena said, irritated with Dex. "Who cares about them? God, I am so tired of waiting for somebody else to come and help us! When are *we* going to do something?"

"Marena," Dex said, "if you get caught at this kind of stuff, it's not like you'll get mentation or redoc anymore. They disappear people for this now."

"They're disappearing people anyway! It could be you next, or Eric, or me. Then what? Can't you see this is exactly why the ZTs are still in power? They make people like you and me too scared to do anything!"

"I'm not scared. I'm just trying to be careful. You have to watch what you're— We have to be really careful about what we're saying here."

"God, you sound like my father now."

"You're not going to help anything if you get caught!"

"Well, nothing's going to change if we sit around waiting for somebody else to do something . . . because nobody's coming! The faithfuls aren't going to help us. They don't care what's going on here—or they don't know, or don't *want* to know." Marena walked around the room, muttering angrily to herself. "People deserve whatever government they're willing to tolerate. My mother said that a thousand times, and it's exactly what's going on, it's exactly what we're doing! All we ever do is complain!" she yelled, kicking a milk crate against the wall. "We never *do* anything!"

She sat on a pile of cinder blocks near the back hallway and took her mother's bookmark, the white rose, out of her coat pocket. She knew she should be doing something. That was the feeling that was driving her crazy. That was why she felt so frustrated and angry and ashamed, because in her heart she knew she had a responsibility to do something. It wasn't a choice—she *had* to. Her mother had felt the same thing, Marena was sure of it.

Marena looked again at the white rose and prayed to hear her mother's voice—

And she did.

"Screw the resistance," Marena said, walking past the boys. "I'm starting my own."

25

Helmsley Greengritch couldn't sleep.

He pushed back the curtain of his front window and looked out into the night. He thought he had heard something, in the street, something like the voices of children playing. But there was nothing there. That sound existed only in his memory, and he knew it. Sometimes it was just so real.

He went into the kitchen and put the teakettle on the stove. It had been a long day. Mr. Blaine had called again, wanting him to step up the listener recruitments and keep pursuing whoever it was who had infiltrated the Town Hall meeting; ICCS had sent word that it wanted students for loyalty correction, and he'd argued for over an hour to be given more time; and he'd read through so many student files that they were all beginning to seem the same.

Greengritch folded his arms and leaned against the kitchen counter, watching the blue flames flicker beneath the teakettle. He took out his wallet and opened it to the small school photo of his son and felt the familiar pull of emptiness tugging at him, the same emptiness that had overwhelmed his wife before she'd left him—or he'd left her. He couldn't really remember. It was the only thing between them after their son had been killed, a hollow nothingness.

The spitty whistle of the teakettle roused him. Greengritch put away the photo and carefully poured his tea.

His son's image wouldn't leave his mind. Stirring his tea, Greengritch was once again struck by the beauty of the child, the innocence. This feeling had been coming over him more and more lately. Usually when recalling some small, everyday memory of his son. And he would remember in those moments, as he was remembering right now, the one obsessive prayer that had always come to him when he used to look at his son: *Take me. Please, don't take my child, take me.* Of whom he was asking this he wasn't sure. He had never believed much in spiritual things, but that hadn't stopped him from praying, attempting to strike some kind of a bargain.

A sudden tightening rose in Greengritch's chest and throat. He chased away the thoughts of his son and closed his eyes, angry at himself for having remembered. He no longer believed that his heart's prayers had ever been heard, all those hundreds, if not thousands, of times he'd repeated, *Take me.* Nobody had been listening. As much as he mourned the loss of his son, he mourned just as deeply the loss of something greater to believe in. Both had been killed on the same day.

Greengritch stretched out on the sofa and heard a Stof cruiser driving down the street in front of his house. He looked at his watch—nearly two A.M.— closed his eyes, and, as he did every night, tried to forget.

26

"Hurry up!" Eric said as loudly as he dared. He was running up to Marena after having finished painting the front door of the Town Hall. "Let's go."

Marena checked her watch: nearly two A.M. "I'm almost done!" she whispered. She stooped low and slopped another paint stroke across the black asphalt street as fast as she could.

"Eric," Dex said, "help her!" Dex kept lookout as Eric sponged out a huge circle to go around the letters that Marena was drawing. They had scrounged up over two gallons of white paint from among their scavengings and poured them into plastic detergent bottles that Marena had cut in half. There were no paintbrushes, so they'd ripped out large pieces of foam from the old couch and used them as sponges.

Marena was in the middle of the street right in front of one of the IPEs' houses. She dipped her foam into what was left of her paint and sponged out the last swipe of the *T* she had drawn. Eric was almost finished with the circle around it.

"I'm out of paint," she said. Eric held his out to her, and she soaked up another thick slop.

"I think I see lights!" Dex yelled from the shadows.

Marena quickly turned and looked down the block. She didn't see anything. She ran up to the edge of the circle that Eric had painted, and then, stepping carefully over the wet paint, she began drawing a large slash from one side of the circle to the other, running right through the letters *ZT*.

"Car!" Dex yelled.

Eric started away. "Come on, Marena. Leave it!"

"I can finish it. Get off the street!"

Eric ran to join Dex at the side of an IPE's house. Marena hurried, the sponge running out of paint. She dabbed and squeezed and slapped it against the asphalt, then tossed it into a yard and ran to join the boys.

They huddled close to the building and watched a Stof patrol cruise down the street. No lights, no sirens. The three of them tried to keep quiet but couldn't help letting out a whispered laugh as the cruiser drove over the graffiti they'd drawn on the street. The Stofs must not have seen it at all. The cruiser flopped out white tire prints every foot or two all the way down the street.

Dex pulled clean rags out of his pocket. "Let's clean up."

"Wait," Marena said. She dipped her sponge once more into Eric's paint, looked around, and ran back out to the street. Then, remembering her mother's words, *"Every thing of beauty—every memory of something good—is a form of resistance,"* she painted a large white rose in the center of the street.

"Marena!" Dex said. "Let's go!"

She ran back, and Eric opened the glass jar of gasoline they'd brought along. They each took rags and cleaned paint off themselves and one another, then ditched everything and raced toward home, hopping over fences as they ran.

"Man!" Eric said mid sprint. "I wonder who they'll think did it."

Dex ran alongside him. "They'll probably think it's AYLR."

"Well, that sucks," Eric said. "They shouldn't get credit."

Marena hopped the last fence. "It doesn't matter who gets credit," she said, but then thought differently. "Hold up," she said, stopping before the interstate. "Eric's right. We should have a name, let them know there's more than one group against them."

She didn't need to think. She'd known all along what the name should be. It had been with her always, waiting for her to find the courage to use it.

Marena held her hand out to Eric. "You still got that Magic Marker?"

"Yeah," he said, giving it to her.

Dex looked around nervously. "C'mon, Marena! We have to get back."

Marena ran out to a stop sign on the corner and, on tiptoes, wrote across the word *stop*,

You will NEVER STOP us!
The WHITE ROSE will NOT BE SILENT!

27

Second period. The gymnasium. Miss Elaine.

"Higher!"

Marena strained to keep her knees up as Miss Elaine marched alongside and screamed in her face, "Lift them higher!" It had been almost two weeks since the graffiti night, and not a word had been said about it by the ZTs. "You're a bunch of weaklings!" Miss Elaine yelled.

Marena thought for sure there would have been a lockdown and purging at the YTF or assemblies with ideology enforcers, but nothing had been said.

"This isn't that hard, Miss Marena! Push yourself!"

Marena's khaki shorts and T-shirt were darkened through with sweat, and the cotton rim of her hat itched. Miss Elaine had been singling her out and riding her about one thing or another almost every day for the past few weeks—ever since the day Marena had made eye contact with her in the hall.

"Hit it with your knees!" Miss Elaine said, stopping at times to hold her baton waist high above reluctant legs. Marena had started out well in the marching, and over the past few days she'd felt herself getting stronger, but her thighs were burning now. Miss Elaine walked backward beside Marena, studying her steps. "Unacceptable!" She pulled Marena from the line and made her march alone. "Everyone else stop!" she said, pointing her baton at Marena. "You all see this? Is this acceptable to the group?"

"*No!*" the class responded.

"Then everybody to the end of the gym and start over!"

The whole class moaned in protest.

"Why do *we* have to do it again?" Jennifer complained. "She's the one who—"

"Quiet!" Miss Elaine said, addressing everyone. "One person's weakness is the group's weakness. Now line up."

"This is bullshit," Jennifer muttered.

Miss Elaine heard her. "You just earned yourself twenty laps."

"For what?"

"Forty."

Jennifer swallowed whatever she was about to say next. She shot Marena a look and walked to the end of the gym.

"You will learn to succeed as a group," said Miss Elaine, "or you will not succeed at all!"

The class closed ranks.

"Again!"

They marched across the gym. Again.

Miss Elaine leaned into Marena. "Unacceptable!" She tapped each of Marena's knees with her baton. "Higher!" The muscles in Marena's legs were on fire now, her feet barely rising off the floor. "Higher!" Marena clenched her fists and tried to lift her legs. Her arms trembled and swung wildly at her sides. She dropped her head back and tried to fight the pain. "Focus front!" Miss Elaine said. "Not on the ceiling." Marena opened her mouth wide to breathe. "Stop showing me how much it hurts," Miss Elaine yelled. "I'm not interested in your exhibiting to the world how hard you're working!"

Marena's legs gave out, and she fell to the floor.

"That's enough!" Miss Elaine yelled to the class. "Take a break." She looked down at Marena. "You're weak."

Marena's calves and thighs throbbed. She limped over to the bleachers, sat down, and wiped her face with the bottom of her T-shirt. The other girls, scattered about the gym, were bent over, hands on knees, sweating and panting. Jennifer, gasping for breath, glared at Marena.

Miss Elaine jotted notes on a clipboard. "You're all weak."

A line formed at the water fountain and Marena fell in behind the others. The girl at the front of the line banged on the fountain. "This doesn't work," she said. "It's not on or something."

"I know," said Miss Elaine. She motioned to two Youth Leaguers sitting in the bleachers. They carried over a large cooler and placed it at Miss Elaine's feet. The girls migrated toward it.

Miss Elaine waited till they had formed a large semicircle around her. "Sit," she said. "Sit and stretch out." She looked at her stopwatch. "Now, I'm going to be asking you to do a lot of hard things in this class. Things your bodies aren't used to doing. But you'll get stronger." She walked among the girls. "I'm going to push you to the point where you can't go any further, and then I'm going to push you some more." She pointed her baton at Marena. "And I promise you, you can go further than you think. I promise you, the point where you think you can't go on is not where your body *has* to stop but where your mind *tells* you to stop. It's not weakness. It's fear. Fear makes you weak." She tapped the cooler with her baton. "Who's thirsty?"

Every hand shot up.

"Give me one line. Facing me down the center of the floor."

The girls hesitated. Some stood. Some inched toward the cooler.

"Now!" Miss Elaine said, slapping her baton against the top of the cooler.

They lined up.

"Even it up." Miss Elaine faced the line. "There are ten bottles of water in this cooler," she said. "There are sixteen of you."

Marena wanted to strangle her. Right there. There was only the one Stof, the two other Leaguers and Miss Elaine. The thought galloped through her head of rallying the girls—all of them—of leaping on Miss Elaine and the others and pummeling them senseless, of grabbing her by the back of her stubby ponytail, squishing her face into the gym floor, and yelling in her ear, *"Unacceptable!"* But then what? What would happen to her after that? No. Dex was right. Be careful. Be smart and play their game.

"Feet shoulder width apart," Miss Elaine said, using one of the Leaguers to demonstrate. "Hands behind your head. Elbows up and back in a horizontal line with your ears. Chest open." Miss Elaine tapped the Leaguer, who fell out of the stance and retreated to the bleachers.

"Now the rest of you," she said, waiting for them to take the position.

Marena adjusted her elbows.

"Pick a point of focus on the wall in front of you," Miss Elaine continued. "When I tell you, go to tiptoes and hold that position. Last ten left standing get a drink." She quickly surveyed the line one more time. "Go!"

Marena shot up to her tiptoes. She stumbled back slightly, found her center, and steadied herself, flushed with anger. Her legs, still tender from marching, began burning immediately. She fought through the pain and willed her body to balance, to stay still, to focus, to—

No, a voice in her head suddenly said. *What are you doing? What are you doing, Marena?* She let her arms fall away from her head and listened. *You don't have to do this.* She lowered her heels, looked at Miss Elaine, and sat.

Miss Elaine pointed her baton at her. "One down."

Marena watched the staggering line of her classmates grunt and struggle to stay up. Two dropped to their feet at the same time.

"Two. Three," Miss Elaine said, strolling behind the girls who had given up.

The line loosened, swaying back and forth as determined girls tried to steady themselves.

"Four."

Miss Elaine crouched down and inspected feet. One girl's heels just barely touched the floor.

"Five!"

Another girl gave up with a little chirp and fell to her knees.

"And there's six," Miss Elaine said. "Good work, the rest of you. Go get your drinks."

The ten winners ran to the cooler. Marena and the girls who hadn't made it stayed where they were and watched the others drink. Jennifer twisted open a bottle of water, took a long guzzle, and gave

Marena another look of disgust.

Miss Elaine came over. "You five," she said, excluding Marena. "You tried your best. Go get a drink. There's enough for everyone in the cooler." They ran over to the other girls before Miss Elaine finished her sentence. "You," she said, pointing to Marena, "laps." She turned back to the girls. "Everyone else, in the bleachers and watch—except you," she added, singling out Jennifer. "You owe me forty. Join her."

Jennifer slammed down her water bottle and started slowly jogging around the gym. Marena remained sitting on the floor. Miss Elaine looked over to a Stof, who took a step forward.

"I'm going," Marena said, standing up. "I'm going."

"Till I tell you to stop."

28

Helmsley Greengritch watched through the windows of the boys' gymnasium door. He'd canceled marching for the day and ordered them to wrestle. It was having a good effect—tiring them out, venting aggression— and he wanted to speed up the process. The boys, in shorts and shirtless, were paired off across the mat, slapping and pushing at each other, half circling one way, then backtracking the other. Greengritch folded his arms and watched, unable to remember a time when he was that young or strong. He could feel the heat from the room and the smell of youth seep from between the gym doors. Red cheeked and angry, the boys grappled each other to the floor, limbs wrenched into impossible positions, faces smashed against sweaty mats.

Only a few weeks and they were already stronger. Their natural abilities at this age had only to be tapped along with their anger. *Like greyhounds,* the Leader had said, *give me greyhounds.* Greengritch wasn't so sure about that, but he did know enough to keep the young busy. Give them more to do than there was time to do it in, and you solved half the problem of resistance. Take away the opportunity, take away the crime. That was his idea of preemptive measures, not loyalty correction.

Greengritch checked his watch, remembering he had a video conference in ten minutes with ICCS. He had to bring it up-to-date on the investigation into the graffiti found on the Town Hall and the street in front of his house two weeks ago. There'd been no other acts of protest since then, and Greengritch was hoping it had just been an isolated incident.

He walked farther down the hall to the girls' gym and looked in the window. They were sitting in the bleachers, taking a break, he guessed. All except two girls running laps.

The girls were getting stronger too, between their marching and swim team. Miss Elaine was pushing them hard. Greengritch was happy with her and the group of Youth Leaguers he'd brought in as mentors. They were strong, smart, and energetic, not just mindless zealots, as was often the case. Miss Elaine had asked to study all the girls' files so she could get an idea of who might be most likely to resist. It was a smart move, Greengritch thought. Each student had different needs depending on her past, and Miss Elaine could be as hard or as easy on them as she saw fit. She was ruthless, from what Greengritch could tell, a quality he admired.

His secretary, Mrs. Benson, came up behind him. "Excuse me, sir," she said. "Mr. Blaine from ICCS is on the monitor."

"Spread out," Miss Elaine said after Marena and Jennifer had finished running their laps. The girls emptied out of the bleachers and sprawled around the gym. Marena bent at the waist to breathe a moment and then joined the others, sitting as far away from Jennifer as she could. "Take your hats off and stretch out." Miss Elaine gestured to a Leaguer, who flipped down a long row of wall switches, darkening the gym. The hall lights streamed in through the windowed doors. "Lie back. Close your eyes."

Marena did as she was told. Her throat was so dry she could barely swallow. Her heart raced and pounded through her back, straight into the floor. But she felt good. Even that little bit of defiance had felt good.

"Deep breaths," Miss Elaine said, walking in and out around the bodies lying across the gym. "Nice deep breaths." Her sneakered footsteps squeaked by Marena's ear. "Now I want you to think of lengthening your body. You're being pulled from your heels and the top of your head." She spoke quietly. "Good, good. Now feel your body sinking into the floor, you're melting into the floor."

Her steps sounded far away. They stopped.

"Very good." She whispered gently. Rhythmically. "You have three minutes now. Three minutes to think about the day ahead. Three minutes to let go of what's past. Three minutes to embrace what is to come. You have three minutes, beginning now."

Marena's breathing eased. Her heart slowed and found itself again, her mind wandering off with the lullaby of Miss Elaine's words . . . half asleep, half not . . .

The minutes passed.

Strange, quiet-time minutes. Preschool nap-time minutes . . . soft and fuzzy . . .

A song drifted into her head.

. . . *"Mommy comes back, she always comes back, she always comes back to you, to you—"* Her father used to sing it to Marena whenever her mother had gone somewhere . . . *"Mommy comes back, she always comes back, she always comes back to you. . . ."*

"Okay," Miss Elaine said. "I'm going to turn the lights back on."

The room brightened. It pulled Marena back to the present, where she didn't want to be.

"Very good," Miss Elaine said. "You all did good work today."

Marena sat up and stretched. Miss Elaine looked at her as she passed and handed her a bottle of water.

"You're all going to be pretty sore tomorrow," she said. "Make sure you get some rest." She sat on the bleachers and wrote more notes on her clipboard. "You have fifteen minutes to shower and change. Then line up in the hall for lunch."

The gym emptied into the locker room. Angrier than ever, Marena squeezed the bottle of water in her hand. Miss Elaine had been riding her for weeks, nothing was ever good enough, and now she gave her the water anyway, like a doggy treat. As if Marena were some disobedient puppy that had finally learned its lesson. Miss Elaine noticed Marena staring at her.

"Yes?" she asked.

Marena took a step toward Miss Elaine, twisted open the water bottle, and drank a long guzzle. *Another time,* she thought as she left the gym, *another time.*

Marena joined the other girls in the locker room, trying to bring back the soft thoughts of her parents. She peeled off her wet clothes, wrapped a towel around herself, and started toward the showers. Jennifer was on her way out. She walked in front of Marena.

"I get in any more trouble 'cause of you, you're going to wish you were disappeared." She pushed past Marena. "Just like your crossbreeding mother."

Marena spun around and hurled the water bottle at Jennifer. She started after her just as Miss Elaine walked into the locker room. "Who's talking in here?" she said. No one answered. "Whose is this?" Miss Elaine asked, pointing to the water bottle that had just missed Jennifer's face.

"Mine," Marena said. "I dropped it."

"Well, pick it up." She walked to her office at the far end of the locker room. "Everyone, finish and get in line for lunch."

Marena showered, so furious her hands trembled. How dare Jennifer mention her mother, she thought, *how dare she!* Something wild and ugly inside Marena felt like it had been slapped awake and was clawing to get out. She kept it caged and kicked her locker shut, then marched with the others to lunch, her eyes fixed on Jennifer.

At the front of the cafeteria, Mr. Malcolm and Miss Elaine watched everyone choose his or her place. Marena followed Jennifer to her table and stood directly across from her.

"Eleven to a table," Mr. Malcolm said.

Eleven people, ten plates, and there was Jennifer. Marena struggled to control the thing she felt rising from her stomach.

"Together, please," Mr. Malcolm said. He stood beside the flag of state and led the singing of the anthem. "At my signal," he said, "you will take your plates."

Jennifer cocked her head and smiled.

And Marena exploded. She ran to the other side of the table.

"Begin!" Mr. Malcolm yelled.

Marena lunged at Jennifer, grabbed her by the back of her collar, whipped her around hard, and flung her away from the table. She stumbled backward, flailing her arms to keep from falling as Marena moved toward the plate of food. Then Jennifer jumped her from behind, wrapped a leather-jacketed arm around Marena's neck, and wrestled her to the ground.

Marena struggled to break free, but Jennifer bore down, twisting Marena's face into the folds of her leather jacket. Marena couldn't breathe.

And then a memory rushed at her.

. . . car doors thudding shut . . . footsteps on the sidewalk . . . pounding at the front door . . . voices yelling . . . boots clumping, hurrying up the stairs. People in our house . . . coming into my room . . . I try to run to my mom, but someone's right behind me . . . he grabs me and lifts me off the floor. I try to kick him but he covers my mouth . . . leather gloves, grabbing me . . . I can't breathe, I'm suffocating. A howl from the hallway then . . . my mother screaming, fighting her way into my room. More people rushing in, dragging my mother into the hallway . . .

Jennifer clamped down tighter on Marena's neck.

. . . my mother's standing between two Stofs in the hallway. She's breathing hard and holding her bathrobe closed, saying something, trying to say something to me, but a gloved hand grabs her face and throws her backward. Two Stofs twist her arms behind her back and handcuff her; another holds her head against the wall. She's staring at me. Her eyes are fixed on mine. Just look at me, *she's trying to say.* I can tell. Just keep looking at me.

And then they hit her.

Again and again.

And the whole time they're hitting her, she just keeps looking at me. I have to do something to help her. I want to do something, but I can't. I can't move, I can't do anything, I can't breathe . . .

A sound, a howl from somewhere unknown, retched out of Marena then. She twisted her head sideways and bit into Jennifer's hand till she felt the flesh give way. Jennifer reeled backward, screaming, and fell to her knees. Marena followed her, swinging insanely, slamming kicks into her body. Jennifer crumpled to the floor and the room disappeared. All

Marena saw was this leathered thing that needed to be destroyed writhing on the ground. She swung her leg back and kicked again. The thing on the floor screamed and tried to crawl away. Marena grabbed a chair and flung it with a wild shriek. She grabbed another—

Dex slammed into Marena and tackled her to the floor. She struggled in his grasp, swinging blindly. "Enough!" he screamed. "Marena, enough! It's me!"

Miss Elaine moved in at a crouch. She grabbed Jennifer by a leg and dragged her out of striking distance, leaving a thin smear of blood along the tiled floor.

"Hey!" Dex said. "Marena!" He grabbed her face with both his hands. "Marena!"

It stopped then. Once she looked into Dex's eyes, whatever had been loosed in her left as quickly as it had come. She rose to her knees to catch her breath as the last of the memory played out.

. . . they're dragging my mother down the stairs. I watch from the landing. And then I see him . . . clearly, without any doubt . . . behind a line of Stofs outside on the sidewalk . . . I see my father . . . watching—

"Marena," Dex said again. "Marena?"

She kept her eyes locked on him, and slowly the world returned. The cafeteria soft-blurred back into focus. People were standing on chairs. No one was eating. Two Stofs were helping Jennifer out of the cafeteria.

"All right," Mr. Malcolm said. "Excitement's over. Get back to your lunch."

People took their seats. Conversations started again. The room returned to seminormal.

"Come on," Dex said to Marena. He walked her back to the table.

"Man, are you all right?" Eric said, pulling up a chair. "You really lost it."

Marena nodded, not quite sure of what had just happened. A rush of nausea flew at her, and she remembered again the image of her father. Marena felt a swell of emotion fighting its way from deep inside her. She tried to force it back down.

"It's okay, Marena," Dex said, taking her hand.

At his touch, Marena let go and wept. She hid her face in her hands and tried to stifle the sobs. The people next to her were moving away, and she felt the eyes of everyone in the cafeteria on her, but she couldn't stop her tears, any more than she could stop what had been done to her mother.

Miss Elaine placed a tray of food in front of Marena. "That's what happens if you hold on to things, Miss Marena. You need to let them go. Stop resisting. Eat now, you've earned it."

Marena stood slowly. She picked up her tray of food and walked to the front of the room. Miss Elaine stared at her, holding Marena's gaze just as her mother had done so long ago.

Marena stared right back. And dumped her tray into the garbage pail.

29

Greengritch hadn't been able to give ICCS much information during the videoconference, and Mr. Blaine hadn't been very happy about it. The graffiti and slogans painted on the streets held no real clues. They were generic rantings used by many groups. The paint was ordinary store-bought ceiling white, not available anywhere in the re-dap, so it must have come from outside the community. So far the Spring Valley incidents were fairly harmless. Graffiti was the weapon of the weak.

Could there be a new resistance group this far into the Southern Zone? Greengritch wondered.

Maybe. But groups like AYLR sometimes took different names to give the impression there was a larger resistance than there actually was—a simple tactic that was often effective, since it could draw troops and manpower away from where the real trouble was. AYLR was growing more powerful in the north, recruiting whole counties into the resistance. Somehow it was traveling through the border crossings and finding ways to communicate. It could certainly be behind all this.

Greengritch took a bite of his sandwich and studied a photograph taken of the defaced stop sign. The White Rose wasn't on any of the lists of known resistance groups. He'd cross-referenced the name with all active organizations and come up with nothing. This group definitely had a knowledge of the area. It had targeted the street in front of his house and the door of the Town Hall.

Town Hall, Greengritch thought. Mr. Farr had said the building hadn't been used in a long time. The Crowley vote was the only thing that had happened there recently when the masked intruders had appeared. Was there a connection?

Greengritch finished his sandwich and took some notes. He looked again at the photos. The White Rose? An odd symbol for a resistance group. Was it a non-violent movement? Or was it run by women, like WAR, Women Against Readaptation? In the early years many of those women had died at the fences, trying to get their children out.

"White Rose," Greengritch spoke into the computer. "Antistate groups over the past twenty-five years." The computer cross-referenced his request. Nothing of interest appeared on the screen.

"White Rose," he said again. "No parameters."

The computer did a quick general search, and Greengritch read through a long list of flower shops and gardening groups, a paper company, a hotel—"Scroll down"—restaurants, and a day-care center. "Scroll down."

"The White Rose. A Story of Resistance."

Greengritch sat up straighter. "Select third entry."

A single-page website came up. It was nothing, a horticultural society with an essay on a new strain of disease-resistant white roses.

"Return to last search," he told the computer, and then instructed it to scroll through a dozen more pages of listings, but he found nothing.

Greengritch stood to get some distance from the photos scattered on his desk. He didn't know what to think. Could it be mothers again? But they all were accounted for the night of the Town Hall meeting. He paced the room for a short moment, then waved his hand over the convocater. Mr. Farr appeared at his door.

"Yes, sir?"

"I want to see the files on all the parents—wait." Greengritch reconsidered. "Just the files of the parents who signed the petition in support of Mrs. Crowley. Call ICCS and have them send down their court files, too."

"Yes, sir. Anything else?"

"Yes. Purge the compound and LD all the units."

"When would you like it done, sir?"

"Now."

30

Marena couldn't shake the image of her father standing outside their house the night her mother was taken. He had lied to her over and over again. There was no doubt in her mind now that he'd been there.

As soon as Marena stepped off the bus in front of the housing compound, Stofs tossed her and the other students up against the fence. Her body stiffened as she held on to the cold chain links, waiting to be searched. She could see parents and children forming a line down the middle of the main street, hands on top of their heads.

A full purging.

Stofs worked their way down the street, searching and scanning everyone. In the front yards were piles of furniture and clothes. The doors to all the units were open, and Stofs walked in and out, their shadowy figures passing back and forth behind windows. Marena prayed they wouldn't find her mother's article, or the hiding spot in her closet. Even from the front gate, she could hear the low, rumbly sound of things being overturned or broken.

Marena braced herself and gripped the fence tighter as a Stof kicked her legs apart and searched her. She spotted Daniel in the compound, his little hands balanced atop his head. Her father, standing behind him, was looking in her direction. Marena watched him, squeezing the metal fence till her fingers burned.

The purging lasted almost an hour. The gridded searchlights around the compound snapped on as it grew darker and colder. Finally, a voice came over the loudspeakers—"Return to your units. Security check is complete. Return to your units"—and the front gate automatically rolled open.

Marena spotted Eric, who was headed toward the Orph, with Sykes following a step behind. Dex fell in beside her and they walked together as close as they could, letting their hands touch every step or two. Marena hadn't had a chance to tell him anything of what she'd remembered in the cafeteria. They walked in silence, surveying the ransacked units on either side of the street.

"I need to talk to you," Marena said as they neared her unit. "Let's hit the Place tonight."

Dex looked at her, puzzled. "Not after a purging," he whispered. "It's way too soon."

"Yeah," Marena said, distracted by thoughts of her father. He was in the front yard of their unit cleaning up. "Okay. Later."

"Let me check in and we can meet in the street." He looked at his watch. "We've got a little time before curf."

"Okay."

Dex took Marena's hand, blocking her from a Stof passing by. "Marena, whatever's happening, don't go off and do something. They'll be watching."

"They're always watching."

He held her hand tighter. "No, *really*, Marena." He sounded worried.

"Have you heard anything?" she asked. "Are they planning something?"

"No," he said. "No, I just—I just want you to be careful."

"I will," she said.

"All right." After a moment Dex dropped her hand and headed toward the Orph.

Marena turned toward her father, who had been eyeing her and Dex. A surge of anger shot through her at the sight of him. It was there in a flash, like the crack of a funny bone. She pushed open the gate.

"Hey, Beaner," Daniel said, picking up his clothes from the front yard.

Her father gathered up couch cushions. "It's a mess inside," he said. "But we were clean. They didn't find anything."

Marena ignored him and walked up the steps of the unit.

"Marena?" her father said.

She felt her face flush hot.

"Marena, get out here and help—"

"You can go to hell!" she yelled from the doorway. "You're a liar! You lied to me! You turned her in! You stood and watched—"

Her father, trying to quiet her, pushed her into the unit and shut the door.

"You stood there and watched while they beat her! And you did nothing!"

He grabbed her by the shoulders. "What are you talking about?"

Marena struggled to break free. *"You coward!"*

"Marena!"

"I saw everything! I remember everything!"

"No. No, you—whatever you think you remember, you're wrong."

"Stop saying that! Stop making me think I'm crazy. I was there! I *saw* you!"

"Marena—"

"Swear that you weren't there! Swear on Daniel's life that you didn't let them take her!"

Her father was silent.

"Swear it!"

Marena watched as something fierce within her father seemed suddenly to crumble and die.

"I was there," he said.

Marena began to cry. "Damn you, damn you—"

"Marena, you don't—"

"Why?" she said. *"Why?"*

"Be quiet. Daniel will hear you."

"I don't care who hears me! I hate you! I hate you!" She threw open the front door and ran out. Her father, close behind, grabbed her arm. "Let me go!"

"Be *quiet*!"

Daniel sat down, clutching his football.

"It's all right, Daniel," her father said. "We're

just—we're having a talk. I'm going for a walk with Marena. You stay here.

"Walk with me," he said, pulling Marena down the block. She tried to wrench free of him, but he squeezed her arm tighter. "If you cut it out, I'll tell you what happened."

"Just tell me the truth, Dad!" Marena pleaded. "I just want someone to tell me the truth!"

"Look straight ahead and keep walking." Her father let go of her arm and took a few steps in silence. "You're never to repeat what I'm going to tell you, do you understand?"

Marena, forcing herself silent, nodded.

He spoke slowly, not looking at her. "Your mother and I," he said, "were both working against the ZTs before we were caught—you know that, yes?—right after the war, when they began the cullings."

"Yes," Marena said. The sound of her father's voice seemed different, not vague or dismissive, as it usually was, but precise and focused.

"They had no real evidence against me, but they'd tracked your mom down through the electronic imaging she used for some of her articles. The borders were closed, the safe houses had all been destroyed. They froze our bank accounts. Then they started marching into homes and taking people away." He looked over at Marena. "And their children too. They were taking away the children."

He paused for a second as if considering whether to say whatever was next.

"Nobody knew where the children were being taken. But they were never found." He looked at her intently. "Do you understand what I'm saying, Marena?"

She nodded, disgusted at the thought.

"The ZTs didn't want the children coming back when they were old enough to fight."

They neared the end of the block and waited for two patrolling Stofs to turn the corner. Then her father continued. "The children who disappeared were from families where both parents had been convicted of crimes against the state."

Her father looked at her, hard. Then he spoke softly. "Your mother asked me to turn her in."

Marena stared at him.

"Keep looking straight ahead." They continued walking. "We knew we both were going to be arrested, but they had a lot more evidence against your mom, all her writings, and she thought—we both thought— if the party believed I betrayed her, and only she was convicted, then there might be a chance they wouldn't come for you and Daniel."

He stopped at the end of the block and walked up to the perimeter fence.

"I turned state's evidence against her. I testified against her. I knew what they'd be looking for and what they'd want to hear. I denounced her as a traitor—" He took a breath, staring through the chain links of the fence. "I said that she had led me down the wrong path, and that I regretted her being the mother of my children—"

His voice cracked, and Marena didn't know what to do. She'd never seen her father cry before.

"She did everything I told her to do," he went on, angry, as if he didn't deserve weeping. "She memorized what to say at the trial. We practiced it, and it went exactly as we planned." He started getting louder. "I mean, I was a lawyer, for God's sake! I went through it over and over!"

"Dad," Marena said, trying to quiet him.

"I told her there were still laws on the books and not to worry, there was a good chance at a jail sentence, and she believed me, she did it all perfectly! But they just threw everything out! All the laws, all the statutes! It wasn't even a trial!"

"Dad!" Marena said. "Daddy, stop!" She grabbed his arm. The parents in the yards of two nearby units were watching. Her father started toward them.

"What?" he yelled at them. "What are you looking at!"

Marena tugged him away—"Daddy, let's go"—and began pulling him back to their unit.

He seemed to remember where he was and lowered his voice. "We never imagined," he said, "never thought anything like this could happen, not in this country."

They walked in silence for a step or two.

"Why didn't you tell me?" Marena asked.

"I was glad when you didn't remember. It was safer. If they'd found out what your mother and I did, they could've come for you and Daniel. They still can."

"I never would have said anything."

"They can make you talk, Marena. They can make anyone talk." He waved to Daniel, who was still at the far end of the block, holding fast to his football. "It doesn't matter now anyway," he continued. "They can make anyone they want disappear. That's why you just have to try to survive this, just make the best of it and stay out of trouble. Don't give them any excuses to—"

He stopped and looked at her. "Don't you understand, Marena? If they take you away, if they take Daniel, then your mother died for nothing."

31

The block was nearly empty now. Curf was approaching. It was getting colder and smelled like snow. Marena stayed in the center of the street and watched her father walk back into the house. The truth hadn't been what she'd expected. She'd been so sure about him, so sure that she was right, but she knew now that she'd seen only what she *thought* was the truth. What else, she wondered, did she think was true, but wasn't?

Marena watched Daniel toss his football against a fence and wait for it to wobble back to him. He smiled when he noticed her, and she was suddenly taken with an overwhelming sense of shame, not of her father but of herself: for being able to see Daniel's smile when her mother couldn't, for getting to see it *because* her mother couldn't, and of somehow owing it to her to . . . *what?*

To sit around and waste away? Is that what her mother would have wanted? Is that what she had died for?

Two Stofs turned the corner and headed up the block. Daniel grabbed his football and held it firmly under his arm till they passed, then started playing again. Marena's body tightened as the Stofs approached, but she didn't turn away from them. She didn't hurry to the side of the road to avoid their glares. She felt the same ugly thing rising in her again, the same rage that had loosed itself on Jennifer. The Stofs glanced at her briefly, then completely ignored her and walked off.

Their indifference enraged her even more. How could she possibly continue to keep silent? She could understand now the choices her father had made, but that didn't mean that she had to make the same ones. She was more like her mother than she was like him. She saw that now. She could feel it in every inch of her body. If her mother were alive today, they would be fighting side by side. Her mother would expect her to resist.

But how could she ever put Daniel in danger?

Marena walked to the curb and sat. She hugged her legs and rested her chin on her knees. It seemed to her that no matter what she did, she would be betraying her mother.

"Hey," Dex said, from across the street. He pulled his wool cap over his ears. "I didn't know if you'd still be out. It's almost curf."

Marena looked up and forced a smile.

"Catch!" Daniel yelled as he let fly his football at Dex. It missed its target completely and rolled clumsily down the street. "Come on, Dex!" Daniel called out, running after the ball. "Go out!"

"How about later, D? I want to talk to your sister, okay?"

"Aw, man." Daniel kicked the ball at them.

"Go in and help Dad," Marena said. "It's almost time for dinner."

Daniel trudged past her and into the house.

Marena was happy Dex was there. She wanted him to put his arm around her, hold her hand, anything—who cared if they got caught? She followed Dex with her eyes as he came toward her, hoping he could see in them what she needed, but he kept the required foot of distance between them as he sat next to her on the curb.

Marena leaned forward, restless and angry. Not at

Dex, just angry. So many things were tangled up in her mind. She felt her eyes begin to well up and looked away. She and Dex were quiet for a long moment. As the patrolling Stofs turned the corner and disappeared, Dex moved a little closer. Then, carefully, making sure the street was safe, he placed his hand on the small of her back. It nearly made Marena cry. She hugged her knees tighter and rocked gently.

"Marena, what's the matter?"

She looked up, wanting so badly to tell him everything.

"Is it about this afternoon?" he asked. "What happened with Jennifer?"

She shook her head. "No."

"Then what?"

So many thoughts and feelings were crammed into Marena's heart, and she didn't know what do with them: listen to what her father had said or listen to what she knew her mother would say. She wished she could explain everything to Dex and he could just tell her what to do.

Dex ran his hand up her back. "Marena . . ."

She closed her eyes. Then she stood quickly and looked to the end of the block, to see if the Stofs were coming back around the corner yet. "C'mon," she said to Dex, and headed down the street. They hurried, scouting the block, and then ducked between the two units that led to the alley. Squeezing past the barbed-wire barrier, they grabbed hold of each other and pressed against the wall, stealing what quick kisses they could—until Marena crouched to the ground and drew Dex down to her.

"You can't ever tell anybody."

"Tell what? What's going on?"

"No one. Not even Eric. Promise me."

"I won't say anything."

Marena inched closer and told Dex all of it: what her mother had done to save her, how wrong she'd been about her dad, how confused she was, how angry, how she couldn't keep silent, especially now, how she wanted to do more, and how she desperately wanted his help. And Dex listened, he listened closely, taking in every word that Marena spoke. She felt better just for having said it, as if finally being able to say everything that she was thinking was in itself another act of resistance.

When she finished, Dex stood up and stared off.

Marena hoped he'd tell her what she wanted to hear. She knew in her heart what she wanted to do, what she *needed* to do, but she wanted to hear it from someone she trusted, someone who knew her well and maybe even loved her, if that word could even be used anymore. It felt illegal just to think it. But she thought that he did, maybe he did. She knew she loved him.

"What should I do, Dex?"

She waited, hoping he was thinking of how to answer her, but when she stood, he took a step away.

"They took your mom and dad, Dex. How did you even survive after that? What did you do?"

"C'mon," he said, heading back between the units. "We're going to miss curf."

Marena followed him, starting to get angry. "You know, I just told you everything, Dex. You could at least say something. Anything. I just want you to talk to me!" He kept walking. "What's going on with you, Dex? You've been acting weird ever since—"

"They didn't take my mom and dad," he said, barely above a whisper.

"What do you mean?"

"My parents are ZT."

32

"I wish they were dead," Dex said, walking Marena back to her unit, "both of them."

They stopped as two Stofs rounded the corner again. Dex picked up Daniel's football and tossed it up and down, putting some distance between Marena and himself. One of the Stofs eyed them as they passed, tapping his watch.

"I know," Dex said to him.

Marena, still stunned by what Dex had said, waited till the Stofs were a safe distance away. "If your parents are ZT," she asked, "why are you here in a re-dap?"

"Because they sent me here, that's why." He fidgeted with the football as he spoke. "My mother never wanted me to begin with; the ZTs just gave her an excuse to get rid of me."

It still made no sense to Marena.

"My real dad was in the country illegally after they revoked labor visas. He ran off right before the war, when they started deporting foreign-borns. Never said a word. One day he was just gone. Anyway, like a year later my mom married my stepfather, a registered ZT prick. I didn't really care or even know what it all meant, not till my racial purity scan came in under eighteen percent. They tagged me a deficient, even though I was born here, 'diluting the national character' of the country."

Dex acted like he didn't care about what he was saying, like none of it mattered in the least, but Marena could hear the hurt and anger in every word.

"That's what they told my mother, anyway. And she didn't disagree with them. She told them they should find my father and let him take me. She didn't even—"

The screen door of Marena's unit flung open, and Daniel stuck his head out. "Dad says you've got to come in!"

"All right," Marena said, waving him back inside.

Dex tucked the football under his arm and stepped a little closer to Marena. His voice dropped.

"Do you have any idea," he said, "what it's like to hear about how brave your mother was and about everything she did for you? What she gave up for you? You want to know what my mother did? When they came for me? She served them coffee. My stepfather signed the papers in front of me. My mother even took her name away—not that I wanted it. Ferrayo is my real father's name." Dex shook his head slowly and looked away. "What kind of mother would do that?"

He took the football from under his arm, sprinted a few steps, and hurled it down the block with all his might. The curf siren sounded while it was still tumbling down the street. Dex watched it till it stopped rolling, then turned back to Marena. His eyes were liquid, and his face was flushed.

Marena started toward him, but he jogged backward as she got closer. "You want to know how to survive after that? You want to know what I do?" he asked, fighting through something that was trembling in his voice.

Marena nodded.

"Anything," he said. "Absolutely anything at all."

33

Marena's face and toes were numb by the time she hopped over the last fence. She pushed up the sleeve of her coat—one fifty-five A.M.—pulled her ski mask down tighter, and took off again, staying just inside the ragged line of trees that edged the parking lot of the Town Hall.

She worked her way around to the other side of the building, where the woods deepened. Dead leaves and branches crackled underfoot as she picked her way through, stepping over fallen limbs and ducking under low-grown branches. The YTF wasn't too far off, but soon the woods would end, and there would be almost no cover, just a long stretch of open road. Marena rested a moment, breathing hard, and peered out through the thinning trees. The road that led to the

YTF shone black under the hazy moonlight. Open fields, barren and dark, lay off to both sides. Marena knew she'd have to get off the main road as fast as she could.

She took off at a dead run and was on the highway in seconds, her sneakers thudding softly against the pavement. She leaped off the road as soon as she was able to and raced along the drainage ditch. She ran hard, suddenly aware of how strong she felt, and the thought struck her then that Miss Elaine had actually trained her for this. The weeks and weeks of marching and swimming and physical conditioning had made her much stronger. She enjoyed the idea and ran harder.

Her body warmed, and the cold air sharpened her sight. She passed the Spring Valley sign that spanned the highway, then the lone tree that stood silhouetted in the middle of the field to her right, and she kept running until she reached the end of the drainage ditch. There Marena stood atop a large corrugated pipe that ran under the perimeter fence of the YTF.

She checked her watch again—two-fourteen.

She climbed up the steep bank of the ditch and paused at the fence. The dark outline of the YTF sprawled out before her. The silver-poled streetlamps in the parking lot were on. So were a few lights on top of the building. Marena studied the grounds for any movement, her heart beginning to quicken. She followed the fence away from the road a few more feet, climbed up its full height with ease, and leaped to the ground on the other side. She took another quick look around, then ran to the parking lot and hid between the buses parked there. Everything was dark and silent.

Marena squatted and leaned against a bus tire. She fumbled nervously with her pocket knife, unable to open it with her gloves on. She gripped the blade with her teeth, pulled it out, and rammed the knife into the tire. It bounced off, hardly making a mark. She struck again and again—infuriated by each missed blow—till finally the blade sank deep into the thick rubber. Marena gripped the handle and leaned back, pulling hard. The knife popped out suddenly, and a loud hiss of air frightened her to the ground. The hissing faded to a whisper as she watched the bus slowly tilt in her direction.

A thrill of satisfaction thrummed through her. She ran to the back of the bus, her heart pounding steadily now, and slashed the tires on both sides. Sweating, she raced to the next bus, avoiding the scattered pools of light thrown by streetlamps, and did the same—and to the next, and to the next. She flattened the tires of all six buses and tried to break into the last one to slash the seats. She slammed into the doors, straining to pry open the double flaps, but they were locked shut.

Marena spied the row of spooring drones parked at the back end of the lot.

She rushed over and attacked them. Their smaller tires gave way easily beneath her violent thrusts, and the miniplanes sank quickly, their thin wings clinking to the pavement.

Marena turned back and ran at a half crouch along the row of buses. She stopped at the side of the last bus, and in tall, angry letters, she carved, and scraped, and scratched into the sickly green paint,

THE WHITE ROSE WILL NOT BE SILENT!

34

Marena lay in her bunk for a long while the next morning, watching the dawn light creep into her room. She wasn't sure whether it was from trashing the buses or feeling closer to Dex, or because her father had finally told her the truth, but she felt strangely relaxed and strong.

She rolled over and hugged her pillow, envisioning what might be happening right now at the YTF: Stofs finding the buses—God, she'd love to see their faces—and Greengritch. She imagined him gawking and angry, examining the scratch marks she'd etched into the side of the bus.

Marena went into the bathroom and showered quickly, then wiped a clear circle into the steamed mirror. She ran a hand over her bristly scalp, tracing the contour of her skull, the slight indentations, the ridges, a scar she didn't remember. She had an ugly head, she thought, bumpy and fish-belly pale. She looked into her own dark eyes, and her mother stared back. She had her mother's eyes.

The bathroom door flew open, startling Marena, and for a flick of an instant she thought they'd come for her. "It's called *knocking*," she said to Daniel, sidestepping past him. He lifted the toilet seat and said nothing.

Marena went back to her bedroom and put on her uniform and the rancid leather jacket. She'd play their game, she thought, play the good little citizen. She checked her room: window locked, shoes clean, pocketknife hidden in the closet. She remembered her mother's bookmark in her other coat and hid that behind the baseboard too. There was no evidence, she assured herself. Everything would be okay.

She said good-bye to her father, and he answered with a real good-bye for the first time in years. Marena felt guilty about it. She could see the change in him, a sort of relief in the fact that they now shared something and no longer had to live with this huge lie between them. But now there was a bigger lie than ever, only this time it was Marena's, and she was the one protecting him. Her mother had given up her life for her and Daniel, but Marena knew that in a way, so had her father.

"Be careful," he said as Marena grabbed her coat.

"I am, Dad."

"Did you hear the sirens this morning?"

"No. I didn't hear anything."

Her father looked out the front window. "There's something going on."

Marena bundled up and left the unit. She expected to be turned back at the gate because there were no buses, but there, idling under thickening flurries, was a huge black military transport. She continued through security, feigning surprise, and climbed on board. A Stof was patrolling up and down the aisle, tapping seat backs and keeping everyone silent. Marena edged by him and spotted Dex. He softened at her look but acted kind of neutral, the way he often did. She'd always known that there were things that were too painful for him to remember or talk about. She understood him a little better now, and she felt a deeper kind of closeness to him. Eric climbed up the steps with two other students and grinned hard at Marena. She couldn't wait to tell them both what she'd done.

The transport stopped sharply as it pulled up before

the front gate of the YTF. Marena and the other students squeezed up against the windows and watched the small army of Stofs at work in the parking lot. She reveled in what she saw. Tires lay strewn about, being changed or carried away. The spooring drones had disappeared, and gray-uniformed men were snapping photos. Mr. Greengritch, arms folded, was there, watching it all. Marena saw him gesture hurriedly to some Stofs as the transport pulled in. They carried over a large blue tarp and held it up in front of Marena's scratched message, but it was too late. Some kids on the bus had seen it. She heard them whispering the name White Rose as the Stof tapped their seats for silence. Eric threw a glance at Marena. She smiled at him, and he nearly laughed out loud. Marena couldn't wait to see Dex's face—he'd know right away she had done it—but he had turned away. She tried to get his attention, but he wouldn't look at her.

A blast of cold air bolted down the aisle as the double doors of the transport flapped open. Marena stood and shuffled out with everyone else. She stepped off the transport and waited for Dex, but two Stofs took her by the arms and hauled her toward the building.

"What are you—"

"No talking," Mr. Farr said, joining them. Horrible thoughts raced through Marena's mind as she was hustled into the YTF and down the long hall to the mentation center. Farr led her inside and closed the door.

"Give me your ID card," he said.

What could they know? Marena thought. *How could they know?* She handed over her card. Farr looked at it, then handed it back to her. "Please read to me what it says next to 'social deficiency.'"

"'Heta-heterodoxy.'"

"Can you tell me what that means?"

"No."

"I'm sorry?"

"I don't know what it means."

Farr pointed to a table along the wall with a large book on it. "Look it up."

A fleeting thought made Marena glance around for some way to escape, but just as quickly she knew it was useless. She flipped open the dictionary to the *H*'s: *heterodactyl, heterodox, heterodoxy.* "The quality of being heterodox."

"Look up the base word," Farr said. "*Heterodox.* Read it aloud."

Marena read slowly, unsure of what Farr was after. "'Heterodox: diverging from accepted political policy; holding another or differing opinion from the party line.'"

"Keep reading, there's more."

"'Deviant, aberrant, divergent. Departing from what is prescribed or expected.'"

"Thank you. Sit down." Farr put his hands in his pockets and paced in front of Marena. "Some trouble at your home unit yesterday afternoon?"

Marena had no idea what he was talking about.

"Well?" Farr asked.

Marena looked at him, wondering what this had to do with the buses.

"An argument with your father? About his actions in support of the ZT Party?"

Marena's mind flashed to the day before, and the talk with her father. *How could they—?* She didn't know what to tell Farr. "I don't remember."

Farr took up a file from the side shelf and flipped it open. "I have a report here that might refresh your memory—your words, I believe. I quote: 'You turned her in. You coward. I saw everything. I remember everything.'" Farr looked at her.

Marena's stomach instantly tightened. *How could*

they know that? Had her father lied to her again? Had he reported her?

"It will be worse if you lie," Farr said. He handed her the transcript.

There on the paper was the conversation she'd had with her father, word for word. It couldn't have been her dad, she thought. No, either someone else had been in their unit, taping them, or they'd been picked up by listening devices. She read more of the transcript, and her heart settled when she saw that it ended when she and her father had walked out the door. There was nothing in it about what they had said on the street. They'd been recorded, though, she was sure of it. The words were too precise. Somebody had LD'd their unit.

"Do you wish to confess anything?" Farr asked, watching her closely.

"I—I had an argument with my dad, that's all," she said. "I was upset."

"What your father did took an act of courage. By defaming him, you defame the party."

"Yes, sir."

"And how do you feel about what you said?"

Marena knew how to answer. *Confessional in tone*, she reminded herself. "I—I missed my mom. And I—"

"She was a traitor."

"She was my mother," Marena shot back, but quickly checked herself, "and . . . sometimes I get upset and say things I shouldn't—"

"Was she a traitor?"

Marena thought at that moment that she'd rather be beaten, she'd rather be muzzled and taken away, than say what she knew he wanted her to say. Farr started toward the convocater.

"Yes," Marena said, barely audible.

"I'm sorry," Farr said. "I didn't hear you."

"My mother was a traitor."

"Remember that. Never let personal attachments cloud your judgment." Farr folded his arms. "Now listen to me closely. In the past, denouncing others for actions in support of the party was treated as a minor infraction. It is not treated that way any longer. Nor is openly stating views and opinions contrary to the ZT worldview or criticizing its leaders. Do you understand this?"

"Yes."

Farr took the transcript from Marena's hands. "I intend to make examples of those who do not abide by these rules. Unfortunately you were influenced at a very impressionable age by the misguided beliefs of your birth mother, a traitor who filled your mind with warped views and lies." He put the paper back in her file and closed it. "You know this to be true, yes?"

Marena forced a nod.

"Despite these and your own personal failings, the ZT Party is compassionate toward individual circumstances."

"Yes, sir."

"You will work on this?"

"Yes, sir."

Farr waited a moment. "That will be all," he said.

Marena rushed out of the room and ran straight into the girls' bathroom, feeling like she had to throw up. Her arms shook as she gripped the sink with both hands. She tried to breathe and wondered, staring down into the drip-rusted porcelain, if she could kill someone like Farr if given the chance. She wanted to destroy him and everyone like him. She looked up at the dented metal mirror—

There was a note taped to it.

Marena backed up immediately, checking stalls and looking around for listeners. She walked toward it again . . . carefully.

STUDENTS OF THE
SPRING VALLEY RE-DAP!

The Alliance of Youth for Liberty and Reunification calls on you to put an end to the ZT Regime!

The northern cities are fighting back!
The ZTs can stay in power only if you are afraid.
Do nothing and

YOU COULD BE NEXT!

Think for yourself. Do what you know is right!

RESIST!

WE ARE HERE
AYLR

The purge siren blared, loud and incessant. Marena opened the door to the bathroom. The halls were aswarm with students, many of them holding papers in their hands, reading them, or passing them on to someone else. Stofs were pushing through the crowd, snatching papers, shoving students against the lockers. Marena was pulled out of the girls' room and thrust up against the wall with the others.

"Quiet!" Mr. Farr said, marching down the middle of the hall, a clutch of papers in his hands. "Everyone, quiet!" The siren echoed through the hallways.

"Who gave you this?" Farr asked a frightened girl.

"No one—it was in my locker."

Farr collected handfuls of leaflets from the Stofs. "If any of you are ever caught reading seditious material like this, or discussing it, or reading *anything* that has not been officially sanctioned by the party, you will be severely punished."

"We didn't know it was unsanctioned," someone said. "They were in our lockers—"

"Silence!" Farr yelled. "Is that understood?"

"Yes, sir."

"Everyone get to class!"

Farr gathered still more leaflets from the Stofs. Marena started toward class, searching the hallway for Dex, who always walked with her to ZT theory. She didn't see him anywhere. Eric ran up and grabbed her arm. He hurried her aside, eyes beaming.

"AYLR's here!" he said, barely able to contain himself. "I knew they'd come!"

35

Helmsley Greengritch spun his chair toward the window and held the leaflet up to the light. He turned the paper over in his hands.

"Computer printer," he said. "An old one, but they've got printers."

"Yes," said Mr. Farr.

Greengritch let out a weary sigh. This was the last thing he needed now. He had four other YTFs to get up to speed with the new state initiative, and Blaine at ICCS was breathing down his neck about this new group, the White Rose. The recent vandalism showed an escalation in its attacks, and Greengritch was thinking that it might be a larger organization than he'd first thought, perhaps even working with AYLR, which had now surfaced as well. He dropped his hands into his lap and watched a few fat snowflakes flutter into the windowpane.

"How many?" he asked over his shoulder.

"They're still turning up," Farr said, tapping a pen against his ever-present clipboard. He handed a thick sheaf of the leaflets to Greengritch. "We'll find the traitors responsible for this. If they are in the student body, we will identify them, denounce them, and punish them."

"Yes, yes, I'm sure you will, thank you," Greengritch said, annoyed at the mere sound of Farr's voice. He spun back around into his cluttered desk. "Where were they found?"

"Most of them were slipped into locker vents. But they were also found in the bathrooms and the auditorium."

"AYLR is in the school," Greengritch said to himself. "They could be students or IPEs . . . or an aberrant state officer—there's usually one or two per hundred. It could be one person, or ten." He looked to Farr. "Was there any activity like this before I arrived here?"

"No, sir. Nothing organized."

"AYLR is known for infiltrating training facilities, and ICCS wants it stopped before it gathers any momentum."

"We need to make an example of someone," Farr said.

Greengritch stared at him.

"And who would that be, Mr. Farr?"

"Anyone, sir. It doesn't really matter."

"You may leave," Greengritch said.

"Sir, I only—"

His glare silenced Farr, who gathered his papers and left the office.

Greengritch breathed easier with Farr out of the room. The man represented the very thing Greengritch had been trying to deny was happening around him, the thing he was beginning to believe was rotting away the core of the ZT Party, the same thing his wife had said would happen. Mr. Farr did everything he was told with diligence, was committed to the cause, a faithful party member, would turn his own mother in if he had to, but Greengritch knew that deep down the man enjoyed what he was doing too much; he'd stopped serving the party and begun serving himself.

Greengritch looked at both sides of the leaflet. There'd been nothing recorded on the school security tapes. How did they get in the building? Unless they were in the building already. A janitor or maintenance worker maybe?

He made some room on his desk, pushing the stacks of students' folders he'd been studying to the outer edges. He read the words on the paper again.

Think for yourself. Do what you know is right!

A small light on the intercom flashed green, and an automated voice said, "Line three."

"Pick up," he said.

Mrs. Benson came on. "Sorry to disturb you, Mr. Greengritch."

"Yes?"

"The Inner Council of Civic Security. Line two."

"The director again?"

"Yes, sir."

"Line two," he told the intercom, and waited a brief moment.

"Mr. Greengritch?"

"Yes, Madam Director."

"Any progress?"

"We're still in the early stages of the investigation. We're assuming there's some coordination between the two groups, and we're trying to verify the link. We're analyzing the paper and ink used for the leaflets, and—"

"I'm sending Mr. Blaine down to you," the director said. "He's to be given complete authority in the investigation. The resistance will not gain a stronghold in your YTF, is that understood, sir?"

"Yes, Madam Director."

She hung up.

Greengritch leaned back and rubbed an ache at the base of his neck. He started for the convocater but then just yelled, "Farr!"

The door opened. "Yes, sir?"

"Have you heard anything from your listeners?"

"No, sir."

"Offer more incentives," Greengritch said. "Allegiance credits, something special, journey permits for off-property, food rations." A second thought struck him. "And don't implement any new security measures. We'll let whoever's doing this think we can't catch them. They'll get overconfident and make a mistake." Greengritch looked at Farr and waited for him to leave. He didn't. "That's all."

"Yes, sir," Farr said, and strutted out looking purposeful.

Greengritch read the leaflet again and felt his anger rise. Whoever wrote these words couldn't possibly conceive of the immensity of trying to protect a state and its people. They couldn't possibly understand the complexities involved in preemptive correction. And he was certain that none of them could have lost someone close to them in the war, as he had, or they never could have written such words.

He continued studying the files of the students he'd been investigating and flipped open a thick binder to a picture of a woman. Somebody's parent. He skimmed the notes briefly: a writer before she'd been neutralized. A mother. Somebody's dead mother stared up at him, as if she were looking right through him, her dark eyes, bottomless, haunting and empty.

He'd seen eyes like those before. He'd seen them too many times.

Greengritch closed the binder and walked over to the window. It was snowing harder. He held his hand over the long, multigrilled heating vent, and the rush of hot air, the smell, reminded him of easier days, a lifetime ago . . . classrooms in winter, staying after school, grading papers, tutoring students—

A slushy snowball splattered head high against the window. It clung there for a short moment and then slid down the glass. Greengritch followed its path with his eyes, and a flurry of memories ambushed his thoughts.

The farmers' market ringed the Capitol building despite the demonstrators a few blocks away. Their chorusing chants were a weekend ritual now, barely noticeable above the scores of people at the market haggling prices and politics, unprepared for the early snow. Everywhere were cartons of apples, late-fall squashes, pumpkins, and spicy hot cider in paper cups. A "guys' day," his son used to call it. "We're going to have a guys' day without Mom."

Greengritch could feel a slow welling deep in his chest, and as quickly as the first images had broken through to his heart, the others came.

He felt a tiny snowball hit his back and turned to see his son, who had thrown it and was hurriedly stooping to make another, his eyes giddy with daring. It was his smile that Greengrich saw last. It happened then. Greengrich remembered the slight change in the sound of the protesters far off in the distance—they'd stopped chanting—and no sooner had that realization come than a deafening roar ripped through the market. He felt a blast of heat on the back of his neck, like a hot wind, but recalled only being flat on the pavement next and noticing with an odd curiosity that the snow beneath him had disappeared, melted away in a single flash. A horror rushed at him as he looked up. His son was no longer standing where he had been. Greengrich tried to stand, but his legs gave out beneath him, and only then did he feel the pain cutting into his back and neck. People were running now, sirens wailing. The flinty reek of sulfur was everywhere. Bloodied, Greengrich struggled to his feet. Take me, God, *was all he could think as he searched among the screaming crowd.* Please, take me and not my son.

Then he saw his son. For the briefest of moments Greengrich thought he was playing, lying back in the snow, arms out to his sides. But he wasn't moving. His eyes were closed. He wasn't moving at all.

Greengritch stared out his office window and waited for the memory to pass. He stared harder, through watery eyes, trying to focus on something, anything, until his heart eased.

Enough, he told himself.

The buses had been repaired, and batches of hurrying, hunch-shouldered students were clambering aboard. Greengritch focused on the business outside. IPEs assigned to each bus scanned the crowd, a state officer dutifully stopped an almost thrown snowball mid windup, and Mr. Farr patrolled the sidewalk, Ahab-like and eagle-eyed.

That's enough, Greengritch thought. *Get back to work.*

The buses pulled away, and Greengritch was himself again.

He returned to his desk and continued to study the files laid out in front of him.

He hoped it was adults behind the White Rose and the recent acts of resistance. He hoped he could find them quickly, before any of his students got involved. He prayed that ICCS wouldn't overreact and make him invoke the Loyalty Correction Act.

Not on children.

Marena flipped up the furred collar of her jacket and made her way to the buses waiting outside the YTF. She couldn't believe she'd made it through the day without getting caught. Nobody had even been questioned about the slashed tires. But she was worried about Dex. He hadn't been at ZT theory or lunch. She hadn't seen him all day.

Eric bolted out of the YTF doors and nearly fell as he slid to a stop in front of Marena. "Man! Everybody's talking about the White Rose! They're talking about AYLR and the White Rose both!"

Marena nodded toward Mr. Farr, patrolling the sidewalk. "Keep it down."

Eric made a face and pulled on his gloves. "You should've taken me with you last night. I'd have done some real damage."

She whispered, looking around. "Did you find out what happened to Dex?"

"He's okay. I saw him at wrestling. He was in mentation most of the day."

"What did he do?"

"Lost his Commemorator—on purpose. Hey, you going out again tonight?"

"No, no. It's way too soon."

"Yeah, well, they'd never expect it then, would they?"

Marena saw Dex coming out of the building. "Dex!" she yelled, starting toward him.

Eric grabbed her. "Hold on." He squatted down, scooped up a wet, mushy excuse of a snowball, and let it fly at Dex. Dex saw it coming, twisted quickly, and dodged out of the way. Marena started to laugh but cringed when she saw it sail past Dex's head and slam right into the window of Mr. Greengritch's office.

"Shit!" Eric muttered as he ducked and scampered onto the bus.

Marena followed him, turning to look for Dex, who waved her on. She walked to the bus and a snowball splashed off it to her left. She watched the beginning of a good snowball fight, but just then a whistle blew, and a Stof grabbed someone who was about to let another one fly. A few more whistles blew, Mr. Farr strutted into the middle, and that was the end of it.

Marena and the other students clambered up the steps of the bus, spanking at coats and slapping hats. Dex was last, quiet and uninterested in the snow that had settled on him. He smiled at Marena as he neared her and held his hand out low and to the side. She held hers up to meet his, and they touched fingertips as he passed. A surge of warmth tingled through her. Relieved that he was okay, she looked away, trying to hide her happiness.

As the bus doors flapped shut, Marena scooched closer to the window and cleared the fogged-up glass with a swipe of her forearm. She watched the YTF as the bus began to pull away. The Stofs and IPEs were slowly heading inside. A thrill of excitement pulsed through her when she saw Mr. Greengritch at his office window. He was looking out at the buses.

Good, she thought, wondering what he was thinking, what he was feeling, now that somebody had stood up to him. *Good.*

Marena slumped a little in her seat as the bus rumbled homeward. She soon felt the steady tug of sleep dragging her under with each bounce. It had been almost three-thirty when she'd snuck back into her bedroom that morning. But in spite of how tired she was and how anxious she'd been the whole day, she had never felt more alive in all her life. She wondered if it was anything like what her mother had once felt.

She had made a start, and it felt good, but Marena also knew she'd been lucky. They hadn't been expecting it. Next time would be different.

Wait, she thought, *let it sit awhile, and wait.*

She wasn't sure how hard the YTF would come down with security measures after today, she wasn't sure if the presence of AYLR was going to change anything or not, and she didn't even have an idea of what she would do next.

But she was sure of one thing: She wasn't about to stop.

She would be as careful as she could, she would do her best never to put her family in danger, but she would not go through life the way her father had. Her mother never would have wanted that. If her mother had died so that she and her brother might have a chance to live, then Marena knew in her heart that she had to act, she had to make her life worth living.

She would not be silenced.

36

Marena sat on the end of her bunk, folding and shaping a small piece of tissue paper and taping it to the end of another straightened paper clip. Nearly a week had passed with no further signs or actions from AYLR. Marena had hoped its leaflet was the beginning of something big, but there'd been nothing else since. She held the paper clip at arm's length and plucked at a few of the soft folds of tissue paper, pulling them out a little, tugging, until they resembled, as best she could, the tightly wound petals of a small white rose. She had been in her room since almost seven o'clock, and her fingers were beginning to feel raw.

Marena couldn't stop thinking about Dex. They were sneaking out to the Place that night, so at least she'd get to see him. They'd spent almost no time alone together since the night she'd trashed the buses. The one time they'd sneaked out to the Place, Dex had brought Eric along. Since Sykes was no longer Eric's minder, he could get around more freely. When Dex had planned to meet Marena in the alley, he had never shown. He'd explained the next day that he was being watched more closely at the Orph and trailed by Stofs whenever he was on the street. She prayed that he hadn't been listed because of anything she'd done. Marena knew she'd been too careless with the buses—Dex had told her so—but she wasn't being watched more closely. Why should he be?

Unless she *was* being watched and didn't know it.

Security hadn't really increased that much since the attacks on the YTF vehicles, but Marena didn't trust it. She didn't trust anything anymore. If they were watching Dex, they must be watching her. It frustrated her, but she had to think more like Dex and be more careful. She wracked her brain for things they could do to resist—busting water pipes in the locker rooms and flooding the gym, draining the oil pans of buses to make their engines seize up, writing leaflets like AYLR—but whatever it was going to be, Marena promised herself to plan it well and wait for the right time.

She promised Dex too, but he wanted to concentrate on trying to make contact with AYLR before they did anything else. They'd fought about it that last time they were at the Place, and Dex got so mad that he went to clear the back hallway and didn't talk to Marena or Eric for almost an hour. He yelled for them to join him, though, when he thought he'd found another room. Marena and Eric hadn't believed him at first, but he'd moved a huge pile of debris to reveal a large crack in the cinder-block wall. They could barely shine their flashlights through it, but it looked as if there were something on the other side. They hadn't been able to widen the hole enough to get in, so they were going back to see if they could finish breaking down the wall.

Thirty, Marena counted to herself as she finished another miniature white rose. She placed it with the others on her bed, straightened one of the last paper clips, and began again.

Her father had gone to sleep around eleven o'clock, but there was still almost an hour and a half before she could sneak out. He'd been quiet most of the week. They hadn't been able to talk openly about her mother or anything important, since they were sure that listening devices had been installed in their unit. Sometimes they talked outside, or her father would run the garbage disposal and dishwasher at the same time, and they could have a conversation in the quietest of whispers, but it was so much work to talk that they usually just kept silent. News of the AYLR leaflets and the trashing of the buses had spread through the compound. Her father warned her over and over not to get involved. Marena looked right at him and lied.

Thirty-eight, she counted, taping and folding the last of the tiny flowers and gathering them into a small pile in the center of her bed. She grabbed her YTF coat, undid the zippered lining, and carefully packed the tissue-paper roses behind it, spacing them out evenly so they wouldn't look lumpy through the coat. She bundled up, looked at the clock—twelve-fifteen A.M.—and waited another fifteen minutes to be safe. Then she slipped out her window into the alley and ran to the Dumpster, but the boys weren't there yet. She hid, waiting, and was just about to head home when she heard their footsteps skittering down the alley.

"Let's go," Dex said without stopping, and they sprinted through the fence, through the fields, all the way to the Place.

Eric was the first in, scampering over debris to the back hallway. When Marena caught up to him, he was lying atop a pile of rubble and peering into the ragged fissure that Dex had uncovered. "It's got to be another room."

"Let me see," Marena said, changing places with him. She shone a flashlight through the break in the cinder block and saw nothing but cobwebs and dust. "It's something, but I can't tell what."

Dex, a large length of pipe in his hand, motioned Marena back. "Look out." He climbed up, swung the pipe back waist high like a battering ram, and began bashing away at the wall.

"Hit it closer to the left there," Eric said. "To the left!"

Dex swung the pipe again and again and sent it crashing into the cement.

Marena turned away and shielded her face. "What do you think it is?"

"I don't know," Eric said. "Utility room or something." He directed Dex again. "If you really hit it, it'll probably go!"

Dex gave him a look and kept smashing away at the slowly widening hole.

"Hit it higher, up on top."

"Hey!" Dex yelled, pointing the pipe at Eric. "You want to do it?"

"All right. Get down."

"Fine," Dex said, handing Eric the pipe and switching places.

Eric smashed a strong blow near the very top of the opening, and three huge cinder blocks tumbled down the pile. "Heads!" he yelled as Dex and Marena dodged out of the way. "Told you." He knelt on the rubble, sweeping the air free of dust. "Gimme a light," he said, leaning into the opening. Marena handed him a flashlight, and he crawled all the way in.

"Come on," Marena heard him say softly.

Following the flashlight beam, Marena and Dex crawled into a small, partially destroyed room, its walls streaked black with soot. They stepped over tangles of wires, crushed chairs, and what looked like the remains of melted computers.

"Careful," Dex said, making his way in farther. "There's a lot of glass."

Marena tried to take his hand, but he wandered off to the left, exploring. She joined Eric at a metal table in the corner. On it was what looked like three computers nearly fused together as one molten mass—the monitors blown out, keyboards melted, and guts exposed. "It's a server room," Eric said, looking beneath the table. "Computer system for the library."

"Hey, check it out," Dex said, waving his flashlight at Marena.

Marena stepped around a clutter of debris and worked her way over to Dex. He was looking through a deep set of steel shelves filled with parts of old computers, the big clunky kind Marena remembered her grandparents having. Eric knelt down and started scavenging around too.

"There's all kinds of stuff in here," Eric said, pushing out a large box. "Pens, staplers, scissors, razor knives, rulers."

Marena noticed something metal and black near the back of the bottom shelf. She crawled in a little ways and dragged it toward her.

It was an antique typewriter.

She thought of her mother instantly. After the ZTs had confiscated computers, her mother had kept writing with an old hidden typewriter.

"What'd you find?" Eric asked, coming up behind her.

"It's a typewriter," she said. "I'll be right back. I want to see if it works." She scrambled to her room near the front of the Place, got a piece of paper, and ran back. Eric had cleared the table of the ruined computers and set the typewriter on it. He was playing with the keys, tapping them into the bare rubber roller.

Marena closed her eyes and listened. She remembered lying in bed as a child and hearing those same late-night tappings drifting through her house and how her mother had told her once that the taps were really coded messages she was sending, secret lullabies that only Marena could understand.

"What's the matter?" Eric asked her.

"Nothing," she said. "Dex, hold the light for me."

Marena stepped in front of him and rolled the sheet of paper into the typewriter. A chill skated through her as she remembered her mother doing the exact same thing years ago. She hit one of the keys. It hammered into the ribbon, but nothing appeared on the paper.

Dex swung the flashlight beam away. "It's dead. Leave it."

"No, wait," Marena said, remembering something else her mother used to do. "It's just the ribbon. The ink's dried up." She lifted the cover of the typewriter and spun the spool that held the ribbon. "Sometimes the ink is still good farther in." Marena spun the spool nearly to its center. She pushed the button that made capital letters and tapped the same key again. Then she pounded it. Nothing. "Damn it."

"What were you going to do with it anyway?" Dex asked.

"We could have written leaflets like AYLR," she said, "started like a chain letter and told people to copy it and pass it on."

"And give them to who?"

"No one. We could just leave them places." She unsnapped the spool of ribbon. "Maybe we could figure out a way to make some ink. Those pens back there—maybe we could get some ink out of them."

"It'd be a waste of time, Marena," Dex said. "How many could you type, anyway? And what good would it do? I mean—"

"Guys," Eric said. "Hey, guys, be quiet."

"What's up?" Dex asked.

"Quiet!"

Dex and Marena both stayed very still.

"What is it?" Dex whispered.

"I thought I heard something."

"Where?"

"Sh!" Eric said, backing up slowly. He ran the beam of his flashlight along the wall to his left, then slowly let the light drop lower, where it came to rest on four fluorescent-green eyes.

Marena screamed, and Eric dropped his flashlight.

There was a noise then, claws scampering over metal. Dex swung his flashlight across the room and caught the glare of the glowing eyes as they came toward him. "They're over there!" he called out. "C'mon!"

Eric and Marena stumbled toward Dex, and they bolted for the exit. Marena jumped out last, and the three of them ran as fast as they could out of the Place. They raced down the steep slope of the purge pile, scurried under the chain-link fence, and disappeared into the wasted fields, then sprinted side by side back to the compound.

"Hold up," Dex said, winded. "Hold up a sec."

They all stopped and caught their breaths. Marena, tears in her eyes, laughed at Eric. "Man, you were more scared than I was!"

"I don't like rats."

"They were way too big for rats," Dex said. "They were possums or something."

"What's a possum look like?" Marena asked.

"Like a huge rat!" Eric said.

The trio settled into a walk, teasing one another along the way. A few yards from the perimeter fence Eric stopped. "Drones are out," he said, crouching and quickening his pace.

Marena heard their low hum in the distance.

"They're over at the school," Dex said, looking at Marena. "Ever since you hit the buses, they've been out almost every night."

"Hey, Dex," Marena said, unable to forget her idea about writing leaflets, "what if we wrote out leaflets by hand—on my paper?"

"It would take forever," he said. "Besides, AYLR's already doing that, and the ZTs have handwriting analysis. They'd nail us in no time."

"What about doing them like creepy ransom notes?" Eric said. "You know? Cut out letters from magazines and stuff."

"And where do you think we're going to get magazines?" Dex said.

"Would you chill?" Eric said. "I'm just thinking out loud."

"Hey, guys, stop," Marena said. "I've got an idea." She was thinking of a project she'd once worked on in Mrs. Crowley's art class. She had most of the materials they'd need already. It would be risky, and she'd have to find a way to get into the YTF.

"What?" Dex asked her.

Marena looked at him, knowing he would think it was too dangerous. "I'll tell you later," she said. "Let's get home."

37

"You look tired," Marena's father said to her the next morning. "Are you feeling okay?"

"Yeah, I'm fine. Just couldn't sleep."

"Marena," her dad said. He tapped his ear and pointed to the ceiling. Marena nodded—he was talking for the benefit of the listening devices. "This stuff at the YTF—the vandalism, the White Rose, and AYLR—you don't want to get involved with any of those people, you understand?"

The question startled Marena, but she covered quickly. "No, I'd never do anything like that," she said. "I don't even know who they are."

"You'd report them if you did, right?"

Marena relaxed some when she saw her father nod, coaching her in what to say. "Of course I would," she said.

"All the parents have received warnings. Whoever's doing this will be severely punished when they're caught."

"They should be."

"Along with their families."

Her father suddenly looked very serious. Marena couldn't tell if he suspected her of being involved or not. "I know, Dad," she said. "I promise I'll report anything that I think is wrong."

He hesitated and then hugged her. She tensed slightly in his arms. "Okay," he said, releasing her. "I have to get Daniel ready."

Marena couldn't remember the last time her father had hugged her.

She left for school, anxious about the tiny roses lining the inside of her jacket and about her father. She'd have to be more careful about what she said and did around him.

As Marena stepped through security at the YTF, hands on top of her head, a sudden wave of fear hit her—*the metal detectors*. They had never picked up anything as small as paper clips before, when schoolwork had still been allowed, but then Marena had passed through with only one or two. She hesitated for a moment but knew it was too late. If she turned back now, it would just call attention to herself. What would happen if she *were* caught? She'd heard about jail time and brainwashing, reeducation through labor, but she really didn't know what happened to students who got arrested or where they were taken. Marena willed the thoughts away and stepped through the detector.

It was silent.

Relieved, she searched for Eric somewhere in the crowd of students. She'd lost him, but Dex was waiting for her down the hall. Marena waved her ID card in front of her locker sensor. Excited to show him the roses, she hung up her coat and whispered, "Any Stofs around?"

"One at the end of the hall, two by the front door."

Marena unzipped the lining of her coat and pulled out a large handful of the tissue-paper roses. Leaning over, as if tucking in her pant cuffs, she hid them along the inside of her boot.

"What are you doing!" Dex asked.

"Check it out," she said, palming one into his hand. "I made it. I got a bunch more."

"What are you going to do with them?"

"Scatter them," Marena whispered. She took out another handful and shoved them into her other boot.

"Marena . . ."

"What?"

"This is stupid—" She shot him an angry look. "I mean, it's stupid to risk getting caught. Right here in the YTF? I told you, we should wait. AYLR's going to—"

Marena slammed her locker shut. "You know, Dex," she said, fighting to keep her voice down, "I'm getting tired of you always telling me how everything I think of *won't* work. You want us to be more careful—that's great—but I'd appreciate it if once in a while you tried helping me instead of just telling me that every idea I have is stupid!"

"All right!" Dex whispered, glancing quickly up and down the hallway. He took his backpack off his shoulder and opened it. "Let me have them. I'll do it."

"No."

"Would you just give them to me? We're going to be late for homeroom."

"No! There's less chance of getting caught if it's just me." She snatched back the rose she'd put in his hand. "I'm being *careful*," she said, and walked away.

"Marena—"

In the darkened auditorium, during ZT theory, Marena pretended to listen to Greengritch as he launched into his daily speech. She tuned him out and searched the shadowy audience for Dex, starting to feel bad about the way she'd acted with him. She'd been getting frustrated with him more and more lately. He could go from being distant and quiet to being really close and sweet to being way too careful and even kind of cold. How could he just turn it on and off like that? She shouldn't have jumped down his throat, she thought. He'd only been trying to protect her as usual. They needed time to be alone, she was sure of it. They were better when they spent more time with each other.

A spotlight followed Mr. Greengritch as he paced the length of the auditorium stage, preaching about civic duties and the virtues of the ZT worldview. Marena leaned forward, as if to listen more closely, and slowly reached into her boot. She stayed there awhile, not moving. Then, as she sat back, she pulled a handful of roses into her lap and waited for Greengritch to finish.

Marena looked carefully left and right. No one was watching her.

When class ended, before the lights were turned on, Marena stood and let a few of the paper roses drop below her seat. She shoved the rest of them deep into her pockets and scuttled down the row sideways, letting a few more fall. On line to leave the auditorium, she dropped some on the floor beneath the surge of students pushing behind her, expecting any moment to be grabbed by the neck and pulled out of the line.

Out in the hall, Marena followed a group of girls into the bathroom so she wouldn't have to swipe her ID card to get in. She waited in a stall until they left, then hurriedly took the rest of the roses from her boots and filled her pockets. She put one on top of each toilet paper dispenser in the stalls, tossed a bunch onto the countertop, and ran out. During gym she managed to push the rest into the gridded front doors of a few of the girls' lockers. Her heart shuddered when Miss Elaine walked through on the way to her office, but Marena ducked into the showers before being seen. She stopped at her locker before lunch, sneaked out the last of the roses, and decided to scatter them on her way to swim practice later that afternoon. As she shut her locker, Eric and Dex came up on either side of her.

"C'mon," Dex said, leading her away.

"Look," Marena said, "I'm sorry about this morning. I—"

"Forget it."

The boys rushed her down the hall and pushed through the heavy doors of the first empty stairwell they came to. Eric stood at the door, keeping watch through its window.

"What's going on?" Marena asked.

"I talked to Eric, and he agrees. If you want to really start a resistance, then we have to start acting like one. You have to stop doing things without even telling us, going off on your own. You're going to get us all caught. We have to do this right."

Marena looked at Eric, who nodded.

"And we're going to start now," Dex told her. "We can't be seen together anymore."

"Yeah," said Eric. He looked back out the window, whispering over his shoulder, "We don't sit together at lunch, we don't even talk to each other."

"Eric's going to fake a fight with you or something," Dex said. "And I'll—"

"Stofs!" Eric said. They pushed through the doors and into the crowd of students heading toward the cafeteria. Marena had no time to think about what the boys had said. They hadn't even given her a chance to speak. As she walked through the doors of the lunchroom, Eric gave her a shove and, making sure he was heard, yelled, "Just stay away from me, you *reject*!" He kicked a chair at her and marched to a table as far away as possible.

Marena, not sure what to say, yelled back, lamely, "And what do you think *you* are?" She looked around at the other kids staring at her—and at Dex. "What do you think we *all* are?" She saw Miss Elaine and Mr. Malcolm listening and went to a table. Dex walked away and sat on the other side of the room.

Marena, angry, lip-synched the state anthem as it played. She didn't like the boys deciding things without her, telling her what to do. And she didn't like the idea of having to stay away from Dex any more than she already had to. They were barely able to see each other as it was.

A small army of Stofs brought out plates of food and set them on the tables. Again, there were eleven students to a table and only ten plates of food. Marena waited for the command to fight for lunch, wishing that she were sitting with Dex. When Mr. Malcolm gave the signal to begin, Marena didn't move.

She didn't know why. She hadn't thought about it. She hadn't planned it. She just stood there, fed up with always being told what to do and when to do it. She stepped back from the table, turned, and walked away.

Miss Elaine blocked her path. "Where do you think you're going?" Marena moved around her. "Answer me!" Miss Elaine said.

Marena walked to the table at the front of the cafeteria, where the losers, the rejects, ate. She sat down, folded her arms, and waited for her protein patty.

A Stof started toward her with a tray, but Miss Elaine stopped him. She tapped the table in front of Marena with her baton. "You will compete for your meal or you will not eat."

Marena said nothing.

Miss Elaine glared at her. *Screw you,* Marena thought, glaring back. Miss Elaine placed her baton under Marena's chin and lifted. Marena pushed her chin harder into the baton till it hurt. Whispers filled the cafeteria. The two locked eyes, and Marena watched the anger rising in Miss Elaine's face. She suddenly pulled her baton away and turned back to the cafeteria. "What's everyone looking at? Eat! Unless you want to join her!"

Marena folded her hands and stared down at the table.

"You have a choice, people!" Miss Elaine continued. "We always have a choice!" She walked behind

Marena. "But there are consequences to every choice."
Her voice dropped, soft and calm. "And guess what,
Miss Marena." She leaned over and whispered into
her ear. "You just made the wrong choice."

38

"There are some patterns to the puncture marks," said Mr. Blaine, the officer sent down from ICCS. He arranged the photos of the vandalized buses, each sealed in plastic, on Greengritch's desk. "The same implement was probably used on all the tires. The slash marks are identical."

Greengritch sat on the edge of the heating vent by the window and considered Blaine: thin to the point of gauntness and too young to have so little hair on his head or the sound of authority in his voice. He wondered how old he was.

"We want these groups stopped before they gather any momentum down here," Blaine said. He held up a clutch of white flowers made out of paper clips and tissue paper. "When were these found?"

"This morning."

Blaine unclicked his metal briefcase and retrieved a plastic bag. He placed the roselike flowers inside. "These acts of defiance are getting more brazen, Mr. Greengritch." He held up the plastic bag. "Symbolic gestures give a resistance movement credibility. It gives them an identity that people can rally behind."

"Yes, sir," Greengritch said, wondering why Blaine had bothered to come down to Spring Valley just to tell him things he already knew.

"We've found no history of this White Rose being active in any other region of the state," Blaine said. "They've originated here, in your YTF. And they will be stopped here." He picked up one of the AYLR letters. "These leaflets are authentic. The wordings match other seditious writings of AYLR. Somehow they got some of your students, or maybe an instructor, to distribute them."

He couldn't be more than twenty-five, Greengritch thought.

"Mr. Greengritch, are you paying attention?"

"Yes, sir."

"I'm a very busy man, Mr. Greengritch, and this is taking me away from important matters of state security."

"With all due respect, Mr. Blaine, these students are important matters of state security. The children here—"

"They are not children. If they're mentally and physically ready to fight against the state, then they're ready to fight *for* it. That's the law." Blaine began gathering the leaflets on the desktop. "The conversion age for national service has been lowered to fourteen."

Greengritch winced and wondered for the briefest of moments if he'd heard Blaine correctly.

"The state will be committing more troops to fight the growing resistance," Blaine said. "When needed, YTF detainees between the ages of fourteen and seventeen will be sent to loyalty correction centers, processed, and then used to fill the ranks."

Greengritch had been hearing rumors like this for a while now, but this was the first time anyone in authority had actually confirmed it. Some of the worst students had often been sent to correction facilities after graduation, but what Blaine had just said was absurd.

"First of all, Mr. Blaine," Greengritch said, trying to remain calm, "these are students, not detainees, and more important, what you're suggesting is not the function of a YTF."

Blaine, busy with his papers, didn't look up. "It's not a suggestion. It's an order."

Greengritch felt his face warm. "By law, Mr. Blaine, loyalty correction is to be imposed only on the unalterables. That's why I was sent here. That's why I took this job, to try to bring these students into the ZT worldview. And only"—Greengritch searched through his desk drawer as he spoke—"only as a last resort is loyalty correction to be applied." He pulled out the YTF protocol manual. "That's the law, Mr. Blaine. You don't have the authority to—"

"There are new laws, Mr. Greengritch," Blaine said. He took a large binder out of his briefcase and dropped it onto Greengritch's desk. "You'd be wise to familiarize yourself with them."

Greengritch flipped briefly through the thick reams of paper, shaking his head in disbelief. "Who approved this?"

"Emergency Council of the Protectorate. Look, Mr. Greengritch, this isn't that hard. Just keep these kids confined and physically fit until they're needed by the state. That's your job."

"That is not my job!" Greengritch said, slamming his hand on the desk. Blaine flinched upright. "My job is not to breed the next regiment of state officers.

YTFs were designed to guarantee students the right to reindoctrination—"

"The *right?*" Blaine said, meeting Greengritch head-on. A wormy vein thickened down the center of his forehead. "They'll have whatever rights the Protectorate chooses to grant them! They're lucky we didn't neutralize every one of them right after the war!" His face flushed as he took a breath and calmed himself. "I don't know if you've noticed it or not, Mr. Greengritch, but we're still at war. We've never *not* been at war. It's just gone underground. And it's not going away any time soon." He hurried to put on his coat. "If we let this kind of defiance go unpunished, we'll have another Millennium War on our hands in a heartbeat. I would think you'd understand that."

The accusation stung. "I lost a child in the war, Mr. Blaine. Don't—"

"I lost a father."

Both men were silent.

"Your orders are clear, Mr. Greengritch." Blaine's voice dropped low and cold. "Unless you're questioning the authority of the Protectorate on this matter? Are you questioning the authority of the Protectorate, Mr. Greengritch?"

Greengritch knew the game and how far he could

push it. "No," he said, a mingling of disgust and shame gnawing at him. "No."

"Good," Blaine said. "There are party officials who will hold you personally responsible if these acts of resistance continue. Don't forget that." He clicked his briefcase closed. "I need to finish my paperwork now. Is there an office I can use?"

"Yes," Greengritch said, walking him to the door. He pointed to a desk in the main office next to his secretary. "Mrs. Benson will get you anything you need."

"I'll be in touch," Blaine said, holding out his hand. "You have some work to do, Mr. Greengritch. Handle this."

Greengritch made himself shake Blaine's hand. It felt thin and weak, like a child's. He could have crushed it with a gentle squeeze.

39

After school Marena waited in the girls' bathroom for the halls to empty before going to swim practice. She had the last of her roses in the pocket of her coat. She'd locked herself into a stall and waited as long as she dared. When all was quiet, she walked out into the hall. It was empty except for the echoey steps of a few students hurrying to swimming or wrestling. She walked slowly, looking for a place to scatter the last of her roses.

In the classrooms? she thought. *Here in the hall?* But the main office was so close. She walked by it slowly. Mrs. Benson was on the phone. An officer was busy at another desk.

Do it, a voice inside her said as she passed the office, *drop them right here. Right under their noses.*

Marena looked up and down the hall.

No one around.

The vidicam was pointed away from her.

Drop them right at their door. Hurry up!

She pulled the last of the roses from her pocket and, running back a few steps, put them right at—

The office door opened.

Marena froze. An officer, thin and balding, stood in the doorway, staring at her. She crunched the roses under the waistband of her jacket and didn't breathe.

"In or out?" the officer said, then swung his brief-case to the side and maneuvered around her. Marena closed her eyes—*stupid, stupid!*—and nearly collapsed with relief when she heard his heels click down the hall. She opened her eyes, and Mrs. Benson was standing in the doorway, her gaze riveted on two roses that had fallen from beneath Marena's jacket.

"Yes?" Mr. Greengritch said.

Mrs. Benson poked her head into his office. "Student to see you, Mr. Greengritch."

He leaned back in his chair and spun toward the window. "Not now," he said, still bothered by his meeting with Blaine.

"She said she needed to see you."

"Let Mr. Farr handle it. I'm busy."

"She has some of those flowers that were found today, sir."

Greengritch sat up. "Send her in." He pulled his chair into the desk and waited a short moment. There was a tentative knock on the door. "Come in."

A student entered and stood at attention in the doorway.

"All the way in, please. And close the door."

She shut the door, her back nearly against it. She was dressed well, her uniform neat and trim, hands to her side and chin slightly raised. She took a step forward and held out a fistful of the handmade flowers. "I found these," she said.

Greengritch got up from his desk and walked over to her. She held her hand out farther. It was shaking slightly. He looked into her eyes, incredibly dark eyes, nearly black. They were familiar-looking and distracted him until she turned away to avoid his stare.

"I wasn't sure who to give them to," the girl said.

Greengritch took them from her. "Where did you find them?"

"In the girls' bathroom."

"All of them?"

"Yes."

"When?"

"Just now. On my way to swim practice."

"In the bathroom?"

"Yes, in the—on the sink, the counter."

Greengritch looked at the flowers again. "Do you know what these represent?"

"No."

"Then why did you think they needed to be turned in?" Greengritch watched her closely. She was lying.

"I mean, I . . ." The girl continued, stumbling. She dropped her gaze to the floor. "I . . ."

"Tell me the truth."

"Well . . . I've heard, you know, other kids were talking."

"About what?"

"This—these people called the White Rose."

"What about them?"

"Nothing. I—I just heard someone when I was in the bathroom. She said it was the White Rose who messed up the buses and stuff."

Greengritch placed the flowers on his desk. He had a fleeting thought to try to catch Mr. Blaine. "Okay," he said to the girl. He pulled a chair over for her. "Sit down, please." She sat, and Greengritch sat too. He'd spoken to this girl before, he was sure of it. "What's your name?"

"Marena."

He remembered now. Her file was right behind him with about thirty other potential sympathizers. She'd been in the art teacher's class, the woman he'd had removed. Greengritch waited and said nothing. He could tell a lot from how people sat through his silences.

The girl's hands fidgeted slightly in her lap.

He waited till she was a little more uncomfortable, then asked, "So, you found these just this morning?"

"No . . . only a little while ago."

"In the girls' bathroom."

"Yes."

"And you decided to turn them in."

"Yes."

"Why?"

"I—I was . . ."

"Yes?" Greengritch asked.

"I . . . heard that . . . I was . . ." she said, stumbling over words again.

"What?" Greengritch suddenly said with force, wanting to frighten her into a mistake.

"I—I was told that you could get allegiance

credits for turning things in or reporting information about . . . infractions. Mr. Farr made an announcement the other day, and I was wondering if . . ."

"What?"

"I was wondering if my father could be allowed to go to the swim meet next month."

Greengritch paused and watched her closely. "He's a house arrest?"

"Yes."

She was looking right at him, not avoiding his glare. His suspicions eased. He had felt she was there for some other reason, and now he was sure of it. "You know," he said, "you should be here because this is the right thing to do, not to get special treatment or rewards."

"Yes, sir, I know that. I just thought that—"

"You should turn in something like this because you know in your heart that it's an act of loyalty . . . and . . ." Greengritch faltered for a moment, and the strangest thing happened to him. As he said these words, he realized that he didn't believe them. "And," he continued, "it is an . . . act of loyalty, isn't it?"

The girl nodded. "Yes, sir."

Stop it, he told himself, and dismissed the thought.

He pulled the girl's file. "You've been doing well," he said. He skimmed through her progress reports. "Miss Elaine speaks highly of you. Did you know that?" The girl seemed surprised. "Well, she does. She says here . . . you've been doing exemplary work in gym class and swimming." He dropped the file on the desk. "Describe for me the finest member of the State Youth League."

"The finest member of the State Youth League is one who possesses physical superiority and an undying belief in the worldview of Zero Tolerance."

"Good," Greengritch said, watching her closely, but the thought came at him again. He didn't believe the ideas behind the words this girl had just recited either. He put his hand out. "Very good." The girl shook his hand—harder, it struck Greengritch, than Mr. Blaine had. "I appreciate your loyalty to the state and the hard work you've been doing," he said, feeling mechanical and fake. He spoke into the phone. "Mrs. Benson?"

"Yes, Mr. Greengritch?"

"Please have this student fill out an allegiance credit form."

"Yes, sir."

Greengritch smiled at the girl. "Thank you for your help." He opened the door. "Just over there," he said, pointing to a small room off the main office. "Fill out the form, and I'll consider your request. Mrs. Benson will write you a late pass for swimming."

Greengritch returned to his desk confused and deeply troubled.

Marena watched Greengritch's huge frame lumber back to his office. As soon as he shut the door, her shoulders dropped and her breathing deepened. God, she'd thought she'd been caught. *How could I be so stupid?* She hadn't known what to do when Mrs. Benson saw her at the doorway. She'd simply thrust the flowers out, and the words "I found these" came blurting out of her mouth.

"Here you are," Mrs. Benson said, holding out a pencil and some forms. "You'll need to fill them out in triplicate and return them to me." She pointed to the door of another room. "You can sit in there."

Marena opened the door to what looked like a miniconference room: a large oval table in the middle, a small blackboard on the wall to the right, state flag standing in the corner. No vidicams. A bank of windows that weren't painted green—

No vidicams.

Marena's mind immediately leaped to the idea

she'd been thinking about, her next act of resistance. It scared her to think she might actually be able to do it. She knew she'd probably never have this opportunity again, to be in a room at the YTF without a vidicam in it, and if there had been one, it would have recorded right then how, as Marena approached the table, she dropped her pencil, kicked it on purpose to the far side of the room, chased after it—out of Mrs. Benson's view for the shortest of moments—and unlocked a window.

Then she sat down at the table and filled out her allegiance credit form.

In triplicate.

40

Miss Elaine was ruthless at swim practice. She battered Marena with exercises. *"Again!"* she yelled as Marena swam up to the edge of the pool.

Exhausted, Marena tucked and rolled underwater and kicked into another lap. *"Faster!"* Miss Elaine said, walking the side of the pool and following Marena's every stroke. "Reach and pull! Reach and pull!"

Marena struggled to breathe, her legs sinking deeper and deeper with each lap, until she was barely dragging herself through the water.

"Again!"

Marena stopped in the middle of the pool.

"I can't."

"Out!"

Marena waded over to the side and pulled herself out.

"Starting position."

Marena crouched and tried to lift her arms.

"Chin up. Arms higher. Bend your legs."

She deepened her crouch, and her thighs began to burn.

"Everybody else!" Miss Elaine yelled to the rest of the team. "You're finished." They got out of the water and stood in small shivering groups, watching Marena. Miss Elaine squatted down close to her as she struggled to hold the position. "What seems to be the problem, Miss Marena?" she asked. "This should be easy for you. You're so tough, right? You don't—*Lift your head up!*—you don't need to eat when everybody else eats or drink when we drink, isn't that right?" Marena tried to focus on the pattern of blue squares on the tiled wall. "You're stronger than the rest of us, aren't you? Better than the rest of us? You're so *different*, aren't you!" Marena's legs shook violently now. Her whole body trembled. "Is that it, Miss Marena? *Is that what's going on here?*"

Marena's thighs buckled beneath her, and she collapsed into a puddled mess at the side of the pool. "I'm disappointed," Miss Elaine said. "You'd been doing well, and now this. Selfish. Still thinking only about yourself."

Marena sat up.

"You will do as instructed from now on," said Miss Elaine. "You will behave in the cafeteria like everyone else, and you will eat like everyone else. Is that clear?"

Marena looked across the pool at her teammates staring at her, at Jennifer and Michele staring at her.

"Do you understand me, Miss Marena?"

Marena looked up at Miss Elaine . . . and nodded.

At home that night Marena sat in the kitchen, unable to eat dinner, still sick to her stomach, and shivering slightly. Her father asked Daniel to go to his room. Then he turned on the dishwasher and ran the water in the sink to mask their voices from the listening devices. He sat close beside Marena and spoke in less than a whisper.

"What happened today?"

"Nothing."

"Marena, tell me."

She looked at him, wishing she could confide in him, wishing he could help her, but she knew it would be too dangerous for him—and for Daniel. Instead she explained what had happened in the cafeteria and how she'd refused to fight for her food, and how Miss Elaine had drilled her at swim practice.

"Marena," he said, dropping his look to the table, "this is exactly what I talked to you about. This kind of thing just calls attention to yourself. It accomplishes nothing. They'll list you and then keep watching for any little thing you do."

"Maybe," Marena said, "but it feels right. Even if it doesn't do anything, I know it's right." She looked straight at him. "Somebody had to make a start."

Marena knew her mother's words had registered with her father by the sudden surprise in his eyes. He stood, and the kindness vanished from his face.

"This family already has," he said.

"Dad, I didn't mean—"

"Nothing's going to—" He stopped himself, immediately upset, and forced his voice lower. "Nothing's going to change them, Marena, except for something stronger than they are, and we're not. Can you understand that? We're not!"

He leaned closer to her ear, whispering fiercely. "I used to do what I thought was right too. So did your mother. That's all she ever did, even when I told her to stop. And you know what? It got her killed. Saying what she thought got her killed. So stop holding her up like some kind of sacred martyr. She wasn't perfect, Marena. She made mistakes, she didn't think things through, she trusted too many people, and she'd still *be* here if she'd listened to me! I tried to get her to stop, but she wouldn't! She refused to stop!" He checked his anger as his voice started to shake. "But I'll be damned if I don't stop you."

He walked away and looked out the kitchen window.

Marena watched him, hurt by what he'd said, but she knew it wasn't only about her. It was about her mother. She was everywhere now, behind every word, every thought: at the kitchen table, in the bedrooms, and down the hall with Daniel. Ever since the day she and her father had talked, it seemed as if her mother had come into their lives again. Her absence filled the house.

Her father turned back to her. "I'm sorry," he said, the sound of apology completely gone from his voice. "But I'm not going to lose you or Daniel. And I don't care if you hate me for it. We're going to survive this. I don't care how long it takes." He whispered even lower. "This government won't last. They never do. Daniel still has a chance."

"And what about me, Dad?" Marena couldn't help asking. "What about my chance?"

* * *

Unable to sleep, Greengritch got out of bed for the second time that night. The house was too quiet. The emptiness always kept him awake. He made himself a cup of tea and wandered into the living room.

Sitting on the couch, he put his feet up on the coffee table, atop the files and evidence that he'd brought home to work on, and read through some of his notes. The conversation he'd had with Mr. Blaine troubled him deeply, and he couldn't get it off his mind. Indiscriminately sending students to loyalty correction? But what could he do about it? He couldn't change anything, not if the Protectorate had sanctioned it. Resisting would be useless. No, if he wanted to save these students, the best thing would be to destroy AYLR and this White Rose before any more of them got involved.

They needed to be stopped.

Curious, he thought, rereading one of the reports. There had been three separate acts by this White Rose group and only one by AYLR. Two fairly bold attacks by the White Rose and then . . . paper flowers in the girls' bathroom? What did they hope to accomplish by that? What were they trying to—?

Greengritch sat up as a thought struck him.

It's a girl. Or at least it had been a girl from their

group who had distributed the roses. He looked quickly through another file to make sure. *Yes.* The roses had been left in a number of places, but most of them were found in the girls' bathroom and the girls' locker room. Nothing in the boys'. He should be looking for a girl.

He didn't have all the files at home, but he knew he could get the records of the girls' parents from ICCS and cross-reference them with—

Greengritch heard what sounded like the muffled thud of a car door. He twisted back on the couch and pushed aside the curtains of the front window. Outside, idling beneath the streetlight in front of his house, headlights off, its windshield wipers methodically sweeping away a steady fall of snow, was a dark-green limousine.

41

Behind the Dumpster in the alley Marena and the boys knelt together to keep warm.

"Dex, I need you to get me some rubber, like from a tire or something," Marena said. "I'll do the stamp and the stencil. I was pretty good at them in art class. I remember there was a razor knife in those supplies we found in the back room of the Place. Eric, you can get that for me. And I need both of you to scavenge up whatever white paint you can find."

"Just slow down, would you?" Dex said. "Nobody's even agreed that we should do this."

"I have," Eric said. "Only I say, if we can get in, why don't we just trash the whole building, torch the thing? We've still got gasoline left."

"Yeah, and what if they just send us someplace worse?" Dex asked.

"Dex is right," Marena said. "Look, we want to let people like us know that they're not alone. We need to show them, and show the ZTs, that there are people who aren't afraid."

Dex leaned against the back wall. "And when are you thinking of doing this?"

"The night before the swim meet."

"Why wait?" Eric said. "Let's do it now."

"No, listen, the most important thing we can do is try to spread the resistance."

"And how do you intend to do that?" Dex asked.

"I want to paper the other YTF too. I'll do it while I'm at the swim meet." Marena waited for a reaction from Dex, but he said nothing. "Look," she said, "if I can get flyers into Valley West, the ZTs will think the White Rose is at both YTFs, and people there might pass them on. Who knows what could happen?"

Dex shook his head. "They're going to search you before you go in. And they won't allow bags."

"No, I'm allowed to have one," Marena said, "my swim bag. It has this plastic bottom that pulls up. I could get a lot of sheets under it."

"They could search there too. This is not smart,

Marena. It's way too dangerous."

"Oh, c'mon, Dex!" Eric said. "You're like an old lady."

"Screw you, Eric!"

Eric stood up. "You got a problem with me?"

"You're not the one putting your ass on the line like she is!"

"I do it a hell of a lot more than you do!"

"Both of you stop!" Marena said. "Stop it!"

"Look, enough with this discussion crap!" Eric said. "I'm tired of listening to the two of you fight. We're doing this, Dex, whether you're in or not. Right, Marena?"

"Yes," she said.

Dex looked at Marena. "I guess I don't have much of a choice then, do I?"

"Then we're on," she said. "All right, we'll meet again sometime before the swim meet. I don't know when. My dad's been watching me a lot. Till then we stay apart. We don't see each other. We wait."

"Okay," Eric said. "But right now I'm going to get my butt home before it freezes off." He headed down the alley. "C'mon, Dex."

"Go on. I'll catch up."

"Don't be pissed at me."

"I'm not. Go on."

"All right. Later," Eric said, and took off.

Dex took Marena's hand and pulled her up.

"I know," she said. "I'll be careful." She looked at him, his dark skin blushed with cold. "I promise. If I think it's too—"

Dex pulled her into him and kissed her hard. It surprised Marena at first, and she tensed at the suddenness, but gave in to it just as quickly and kissed him back deeper than she'd kissed him in a very long time. She hugged him to her body, pulling him in as close as she could. They kissed again, the tenderness nearly turning into a grapple as they clung to each other. They stumbled backward into the Dumpster, and Marena let out a breathless laugh.

"I love you, Dex," she said between kisses. Dex tried to look away, but Marena held him tighter. She pressed her forehead against his. "I love you. We can do this."

He pulled back, breathing hard, and looked at her.

"What is it?" Marena asked.

"Nothing," Dex said. "You're right . . . we can do this."

42

While Marena waited for the week of the swim meet, she worked at the stencil and the rubber stamp that she planned to use. She'd taken a large jigsaw puzzle box from Daniel's room, emptied it, pressed flat half of the box, and cut off its flaps. On the gray cardboard side she drew letters and, using the razor knife Eric had found, carefully cut them out as neatly as she could. She taped the stencil beneath her dresser drawer when she was done.

Dex had brought Marena a section of rubber from a tire off the purge pile for the stamp. This was much more difficult to make than the stencil. She managed to sketch a faint outline with a pen, and she worked on it in her room whenever she could. The rubber was harder than she'd thought, much harder. The razor knife broke, and she had to finish with her pocket-knife. She kept going at it night after night, hiding it from her dad, shaving and carving the tiniest of slices out of the rubber till her fingers blistered.

As the days at the YTF passed and winter deepened, little by little, the raised symbol she was carving began to take shape. She kept working at it—thinking of Dex, thinking of her mother and what she had sacrificed, thinking of breaking into the YTF—until the week of the swim meet finally arrived.

Marena sat on the floor of her room, finishing the rubber stamp, anxious to sneak out and meet the boys later that night. She prayed she'd be able to get out. Her father had been keeping a close eye on her, waiting for her at the door after school and checking in with her every night after curf. She hoped he wouldn't stay up late again. She'd hardly seen Dex at all lately, and she ached to be with him.

Marena cut a last shaving out of the stamp and smoothed the edges of the raised rose petals with an emery board. She held it closer to the light to get a better view when Daniel came bursting into her room.

"Lookit!" he yelped as Marena shoved the stamp under her bunk. "Lookit, Marena!" He leaped onto her bunk and monkey jumped till his head nearly banged into the ceiling. "Lookit! Just like you!" He pirouetted in midair, showing off his new outfit, a miniature Stof uniform. "And the hat! Look!" He took off his hat and Frisbeed it at Marena. She caught it and read the inscription on it: "Junior Youth League."

Daniel bounced off the bunk, his head shaved to the scalp. "It just came. We have to wear our uniforms all the time," he said, marching proudly around Marena's room.

Marena's father forced a smile as he leaned into the doorway. "I don't think they meant in the house, Daniel. C'mon, let's eat." Daniel marched into the kitchen, climbed up into his chair, and crossed his small black boots underneath him.

There was an uncomfortable silence as Marena and Daniel had a short staring contest. Their father finally broke in. "Marena, why don't you help with dinner?"

"Sure."

"I'm starving," Daniel said, hanging a fork off the tip of his nose.

"So, are you ready for the big meet?" her dad asked.

"Yeah," Marena said. "I'm going to compete in

freestyle and breaststroke. It's Friday at Valley West. They're going to bus us over."

"I've heard."

"I told you last week. I earned allegiance credits for you to come."

"You earned allegiance credits?" he asked, his face a little shocked.

Marena signaled with a tap of her lips and then her wrist that she'd tell him about it later. Her father nodded, and Marena served dinner. "So, you want to go?" she asked him.

"Of course."

"I'll come too," Daniel said. "I'll wear my uniform."

"Give me your plate, D." Daniel pushed his plate at Marena. "So, how's school going?" she asked.

"It's training, not school."

"Okay. How's training going?"

"It's just like yours. We learn just as much as you do now."

"Chew," Marena said. "Do they teach you that?"

"They train us same as you. Only it's easier for us because they don't have to get rid of the garbage in our brains like you guys."

Marena stopped eating. Daniel's remark hovered in the air.

"Could I have the milk?" her father asked, cutting into the pause.

"I'm sorry, Daniel," Marena said, ignoring her father. "What did you just say?"

"What?"

"The thing about our brains?"

"Oh, that, yeah. It's not your fault, don't worry. You can't help the garbage in your brain. It's because of Mommy." He held his glass out to his father. "Milk, please."

"Daniel," Marena said.

"Need to grow my bones."

"Daniel."

"Yeah, what?"

"What did you just say about Mom?"

Her father interrupted. "Marena, he only—"

"Daniel, what did you say about Mom?

"Mr. G knows all about people like her. Right, Daddy? She was sick. You know, sick in her brain. And you guys probably got it from her. She made lots of other people sick too—in their brains."

"That's enough, Daniel," her father said.

"Mr. G told me everything because I'm big enough now. My brain is clean, right, Daddy? Isn't that what Mr. G said? Isn't that why I—"

"Daniel, shut up!" her father screamed, slamming his fist into the table.

Instant tears from Daniel.

"I—I," Daniel said, crying. "I—"

"Just eat, please."

"All . . . I said . . . was—"

"Eat!"

Daniel bolted, sobbing. His small bootsteps faded down the hall.

Marena looked at her father. "You're going to let him believe that?"

Her father gestured toward the listening devices and spoke softly. "He—he doesn't know what he's saying. I'll explain it to him later. When he's older—"

"That's right," Marena said, recalling her father's words from an argument they'd had weeks earlier. "I forgot, *Daniel* still has a chance." She got up from the table. "A chance at *what*, Dad?"

She went to her brother's bedroom.

"Get out of here!" Daniel yelled.

"Daniel."

"No! Go away! I don't want to talk to you!"

Daniel was in his bunk, hugging his stuffed horse, NightStar, tight. "It's not my fault about your brains! So don't everyone get all mad at me."

"Daniel, forget it. It doesn't matter. I'm not mad."

"Well, I don't know why *he's* so mad. He didn't get mad when I said it before—when I came home."

"He's just tired. Just forget about it. Okay?"

"Everybody's so grouchy all the time," Daniel said. "Everybody's so mean."

"I'm sorry. You're right. Okay? We shouldn't take it out on you."

Marena sat on the bunk with Daniel, trying not to show her disgust for the little leather uniform he was wearing. "You want to get changed now?"

"No."

"Well, don't wear your boots on the bunk, okay?" Marena said, grabbing the heel of one. "Come on." He fell back with a groan as she stood and pulled off his little black jackboot. He held the other leg up, and she did the same. He stayed there, quiet and bootless, staring up at the ceiling. Marena lay down next to him. "Want to do something? Play something?"

"Nah."

"Want me to read you a book?" He didn't answer. "Earth to Daniel, want me to read you a book?"

"No."

"Aw, c'mon," she said, rolling away. She hopped off the bunk. "I said I was sorry. You can't stay mad."

"I said no."

Marena went to Daniel's shelf for one of his favorite books. They were all gone. "Where'd you put your books?"

"Nowhere."

"Well, they're not here."

"I *know*," he said. "They took 'em."

"Who did?"

"Stofs. This morning after you left."

"Why? They were all sanctioned."

"No more reading for eight-and-unders," he said, sounding proud. "No more books, no more reading. We don't have to do any of that now that we're in the Junior Youth League."

"They're not teaching you to read?"

"Nope," Daniel said, dangling NightStar above him by its two front legs. "No reading. No writing. We don't need any of that." He dropped his head to the side as if sharing a secret with Marena that he wasn't supposed to. "Our brains have everything they need. Reading, you know, is for inner-leckshul weaklings."

43

Greengritch had been reading for hours. Again he couldn't sleep, so he'd gotten up early and had been skimming old thought reports and reading transcripts recorded by listening devices. Once he was buried in his work, his doubts about the ZT party disappeared. He just needed to keep himself engaged and challenged. *Every system has its problems, its weaknesses,* he thought, and he should try to make a difference in those areas, not give up on the system itself.

A knock at the front door startled him.

He put his coffee down and peered out the window. Behind the limo that had been monitoring him for the last three weeks was a long black van. A bad feeling crept through Greengritch, and his doubts came rushing at him again. He slipped his gun out of its holster and held it low to his side as he approached the door and looked out the peephole.

Then he unlocked the door. "Mr. Farr," he said.

"Good morning, sir."

"I wasn't expecting you."

On the street behind Farr the back doors of the van swung open, and two officers leaped out. "The court files arrived from ICCS." The officers were carrying cardboard boxes up the snowy walkway. "Where would you like them?"

Greengritch's nerves settled. "In here is fine."

"May I?" Farr asked, stepping closer.

"Yes, yes, come on in."

Farr stomped his boots and walked in. He held a clipboard out for Greengritch to sign. "They're all classified."

"Yes, I know," Greengritch said. "Over there," he told the two officers as they came in. They stacked the boxes on his coffee table and went back to the van.

"Your request to see the trial transcripts was denied," Farr said, "but you can access them at ICCS." He referred to his notes. "There were nine students who met the profile you requested, all females who were in Mrs. Crowley's art class at one time or another this year and whose surviving parent signed the petition against her removal."

The officers carried in another armload of boxes.

Farr handed Greengritch a printout. "I've labeled each file with the familial predisposition of the student."

"Very good."

"Anything else, sir?"

"No, thank you," Greengritch said, walking Farr toward the door.

"Good morning, then."

Greengritch closed the door and watched through the peephole as Farr made his way down the snowy walkway and tapped on the driver's side of the limo. The window slid down silently. Farr handed in a piece of paper, said something, then pointed back at the house.

Greengritch locked his door and waited until the van drove away.

He made himself another cup of coffee and sat behind the small mountain of file boxes stacked on his table, each one neatly labeled.

Rajan C. Stevens	Professor of Literature	Neutralized
Angela L. Levinson	Writer	Neutralized

James L. Cabral	Writer	Neutralized
Marcos R. Huber	Professor of Philosophy	Neutralized
Colleen J. Williams	Professor of Anthropology	Neutralized
Lauren J. Mazur	Musician	Neutralized
Dylan C. Probst	Artist	Neutralized
Sophia M. Ventriti	Writer	Neutralized
Edward W. Kashani	Writer	Neutralized

44

The car lights that Dex had rigged up in the back server room of the Place were barely bright enough to see by. Marena had cleared the metal desk of its remnants of crushed and burned computer parts and smoothed out a stack of her paper made from grocery bags. "I need something like a sponge or rags to pour the paint onto—you know, to make sort of a big ink pad," she told Dex.

"I'll get something," he said, and headed toward the back hallway.

Eric brought in another stack of Marena's paper. "There's probably a couple of hundred at least," he said. "There's still some white paper, but you said to leave it, right?"

"Yeah. It won't print well on them." Marena took off her gloves and twisted open the plastic milk bottle of paint that Eric had scrounged up. "There's not much," she said.

"There's more," Eric said. "I stole it from the maintenance room at the Orph."

Dex came back with a plastic bucket and a large hunk of foam from the couch in the bottom of it. "How's this?"

"Perfect," Marena said, taking it and putting it on the table.

"You sure this is going to work?" Eric asked.

"It did in art class." She tilted the bottle, and the white paint, thick from the cold, poured slowly onto the yellow foam. Marena took a length of metal pipe and pushed into the foam, working it, helping it to absorb some of the paint. "The stamp doesn't need a lot. Too much and it'll smear."

Eric put a piece of cut grocery bag in front of her. "Try it."

Marena pushed the rubber stamp into the paint-soaked foam and then pressed it onto the piece of paper. She held it down for a short second and then lifted it off.

Eric smiled. "They're gonna be so pissed."

Marena thought it looked good, better than she'd imagined. She handed the stamp to Eric. "You try."

Eric pressed the stamp onto another piece of paper.

"Straight down," Marena coached him.

"Are you going to do all these?" Dex asked, pointing to her piles of paper.

"As many as we can." She tapped Eric on the shoulder. "You keep doing the stamp. Keep the rose sort of in the center of the paper so we have room on top for the stencil." Marena pulled the stencil out of her backpack and handed it to Dex. "I'll go get some more foam from the couch."

Marena crawled out the ragged opening in the wall of the server room and made her way down the hallway and to the couch. She tried to tear large chunks of foam from its seat cushions but kept losing her grip. She rubbed her hands together, hoping to get some feeling back into her numbed fingers, and tried again.

"What's the matter?" Dex asked, startling her for a moment.

"Nothing," she said. "Just cold. I can't feel my fingers."

Dex pressed in close behind her, and she felt the warmth of his body against her back. He reached around her, took her hands in his, and hugged her tightly. She leaned back into him and stole a long, quiet kiss.

"Marena," Dex whispered. His hushed voice stirred something inside her, and she turned to face him. He looked troubled and worried again. "Marena . . ."

"What, Dex? What is it?"

"I—"

"Hey!" Eric called from the hallway. "Are you guys going to help or what? I'm not staying back here by myself. Those rat things might come around again."

Dex looked at Marena. "I'll talk to you later," he said, and ripped out a few handfuls of foam from the couch cushions.

Eric had about a dozen papers stamped and lying around the server room to dry. "I'll hold the stencil," Marena told Dex, "and you paint it. Remember when we did it with Mrs. Crowley? Just a little paint and you have to kind of blot it straight on so—"

"I remember," Dex said, upending the milk bottle of paint onto a rip of foam.

Marena took one of the papers Eric had stamped and steadied the cardboard stencil above the white rose, feeling an odd sense of satisfaction that she was resisting by doing something that Mrs. Crowley had taught her. Dex patted the wet foam quickly across the words cut into the cardboard. Marena removed the stencil. It looked perfect. Above the stamp of the white rose, it read:

YOU HAVE NO RIGHT TO BE SILENT!

They kept stamping and stenciling. Marena held the stencil, Dex dabbed, and Eric stamped. A little assembly line of resistance. Soon the papers were lying everywhere around the room.

"We'll have to leave them here to dry," Marena said. "We'll get them later."

Dex capped his milk container of paint, and Eric wrapped a plastic bag over the bucket with the foam in it. They'd need them both for the YTF. Dex tore out some more chunks of foam from the couch. After cleaning themselves up, Marena filled a glass jar with gasoline and gathered some clean rags. She stored them with the paint, stamp, and stencil, ready for tomorrow night.

Marena checked her watch. "Let's get out of here."

As they pushed through to the last row of dead cornstalks near the housing division, they snapped off their flashlights and crouched low.

"Be at my window at two A.M. tomorrow," Marena said. "It shouldn't take more than a couple of hours. Then we can still get some sleep before the buses leave for the meet."

Dex groped for the opening in the perimeter fence and pulled it up for Eric to crawl through. "You sneak into the Orph first," he whispered to Eric. "I'll go to the back window and wait for your knock."

"All right." Eric looked left and right, then ran off.

Marena crawled through next and waited for Dex. After he stooped through, he kissed her quickly and took off, the muted thuds of his tennis shoes racing down the alley. Marena watched till he disappeared between two building units. She knew he cared for her deeply, even if he couldn't say the words.

Marena sprinted the last few unit lengths to her bedroom window, eased it open, and quietly crawled back in. The warmth of her room enveloped her immediately and felt good. As she undressed, she tripped on something in the darkness, then staggered into her bunk. She fell back and couldn't help letting out a little laugh as she rolled onto her side. Then she saw the dark outline of a figure silhouetted in her doorway. Marena kicked backward in her bed as a small flashlight blinked on.

"What are you doing up?" her father asked. He moved toward her, lowering his voice. "It's three in the morning." Marena tried to retrieve enough breath to speak, but it didn't come quick enough. He held the flashlight on her. "I asked you a question."

"I can't see with that in my face," she said, shielding her eyes.

"What were you doing?"

"Nothing. I just couldn't sleep."

"I heard banging around in here—" Her father stopped then and looked at her as if he'd seen something on her face. He leaned closer, then thrust a hand at her cheek, feeling it. "What have you been doing?" he asked in a furious whisper. He sat on the edge of the bunk and grabbed her hands. "Your hands are freezing. What the hell have you been doing?"

"I—" Marena couldn't think of anything. "I . . . nothing."

"Were you *out*? Out of the unit?"

"No!"

He swung his flashlight around the room: at the window, at her clothes left in a trail on the floor. "Damn it, Marena," he said, dropping his voice even lower. "If you don't tell me, I swear I'll—"

"I was with a boy."

A pause then. As if it were the last thing her father had ever expected to hear. "What?"

"A boy," Marena whispered again. "I was with a boy, okay?"

They moved closer to each other, nearly cheek to cheek, and argued in the smallest of hushed voices. "A boy?" he asked. "Who? Where?"

"Just—just at the window. I—he comes to the window. We just talk."

"At three in the morning? What were you talking about?"

"Nothing. We just—we were hanging out together."

"Who is it?"

"You don't know him."

"Is it that Dex kid?"

"No."

"Then who?"

"I'm not going to tell you. It's private. There are some private things left, you know."

"Don't start—" He began louder than he should have. He took a breath and started again. Less than a whisper now. "This kid's sneaking out of his unit? You know what they could do to him for that?"

"How else are we going to talk to each other?"

"Well, never again. You understand me?"

"We're not doing anything wrong, Dad. We just—"

"I said no. He's breaking about ten different laws by sneaking out."

"Then can I bring him here?" Marena asked, hoping he wouldn't call her bluff. "During the day?"

"No," he said immediately. "It's not allowed. You don't mess around with these people now, Marena. There are things going on. Things you don't know about."

"I know what's going on, Dad."

"No, you don't, Marena. You don't know everything!" he said, his lips close to her ear. "God, you are just like your—" He stopped himself and pushed off the bunk. "Think of Daniel. They could take him away because of what you do."

Marena hated her father again at that moment. He was the same as ever.

He started toward her door and stopped. "You're grounded for two weeks."

"Grounded?" Marena said, nearly laughing out loud.

"Shh!"

"My entire life is grounded!"

"Don't be smart. I'll keep you in *before* curf. You understand me? There's too much at stake." He snapped off his flashlight and walked away.

Marena listened as his bare feet padded down the hallway.

As soon as she heard his bedroom door close, she fell back in her bunk, breathless with relief that she'd lied her way out of being caught again. She stared at the ceiling, weary but not tired, and thought about what her father had said and had been saying again and again over the past weeks. Was what she was doing worth the risk? Would it change anything at all? She wasn't completely sure, but every time she asked herself that question, her heart answered yes.

Her mother had not been silent. But she had been silenced. And now that Marena had given the White Rose a voice, her mother would be heard again.

45

The pool at the YTF had never been used before Helmsley Greengritch arrived. It had been shrouded in a huge gray tarp, locked up in a dark room lined with long windows that looked out into the hall. Now the room was alive and colorful. The tarp was gone. The bright-turquoise chlorinated water sparkled, the white floor and wall tiles were scrubbed clean, and Marena loved it. After spending the entire day being so careful about what she said, what she did, and who she looked at, she felt fast and sleek in the water, unconfined.

She swam hard that afternoon, so hard that even Miss Elaine stayed off her back. With each stroke she rehearsed in her mind what she and the boys were going to do that night and the next day at the meet.

"You took almost two seconds off the hundred," Miss Elaine said as Marena pulled herself out of the water. "Do that tomorrow."

Marena nodded, catching her breath, and grabbed a towel.

"All right, everyone, listen up!" Miss Elaine called out. The girls gathered. "The bus will leave the housing compound at exactly seven o'clock tomorrow morning. Make sure you have your IDs, your journey permits, and all your swim gear. Do not be late. We should be back to Spring Valley around two. I want everyone in bed early tonight. Get some rest."

The buzzing beneath Marena's pillow frightened her awake at one forty-five in the morning. She groped for the muffled alarm clock and quickly turned it off, hoping it hadn't roused her father. She dressed quietly and peeked out into the hallway. Her father's door was half open, but the lights were out. She eased back into her bedroom, got her coat, and waited by the window, spiderwebbed with ice. It was black outside. The rotted fields beyond the perimeter fence seemed one large shadowy mass, and the hills of the valley, in the distance, a ragged curtain of dark.

She looked for the boys. *I can do this*, she told

herself over and over again, *I can do this.*

Eric's face suddenly appeared at the window. Marena grabbed her backpack. She dropped to the alley a few feet below, the frigid air stinging her face and throat.

"It's freezing tonight," Eric whispered.

Dex had an empty backpack too. "We're good to go."

They tugged on gloves, pulled their wool ski masks down, and took off quickly, trying to keep warm. Marena hoped her father wouldn't notice that she'd snuck out, but even if he did, what could he do? Turn her in?

They stopped by the Place and gathered up the White Rose flyers they'd printed. Marena took about fifty, pressed them flat, and put them into her backpack along with the stencil. Dex put the rest of them into his. Eric shoved the stamp and pieces of foam, the jar of gasoline and rags, into his backpack. He took the plastic-wrapped bucket for inking the stamp and handed the bottle of paint to Dex.

"We got everything?" Marena asked.

The boys said yes, and they hurried out again. Marena led the way over the interstate, running the same route she'd taken when she had trashed the buses. She stayed close to the woods around the Town Hall and then kept off the road, jogging down the drainage ditch until they stopped just outside the fence of the YTF.

"All right," Marena said. "All right—" Too busy to be afraid, she caught her breath. "We get over the fence and then make our way around to the back of the building. The room is just opposite Greengritch's office on the back side—"

"Drone!" Dex said, looking skyward.

Marena heard the hum too. She looked around for cover and dove into the large opening of corrugated pipe that tunneled belowground. She crawled forward over a puddle of slushy ice. The boys tumbled in after her, hunched over from their bulky backpacks.

It was pitch-black inside, but Marena managed to flick on her penlight.

"I'm getting soaked," Eric said, his voice shaking with cold.

They huddled together, waiting for the drone to pass. After a moment Dex leaned his head out and listened. "All right," he said. "It's gone."

They crawled back out, climbed up the side of the ditch, and scaled the tall fence, tossing some of their supplies down on the way over. "Let's get under one of the buses," Marena said, and took off for the parking lot, Dex and Eric right beside her. They slid under the first bus they came to and waited for the drone to return.

"There," Marena said, pointing to a small bank of windows at the back of the YTF. "The middle one. That's the one. You see it?"

"Here it comes," Dex said, listening to a faint whir above. "They're running short passes over the school."

As soon as the drone passed, Marena scrambled out and ran toward the window she'd unlocked weeks before. She fell against the short brick wall beneath the sill and prayed the window was still unlocked. Dex and Eric hit the wall right after her.

It's okay, she told herself. *We've got plenty of time.*

Marena crouched, trying to open the window. She pushed up on the pane, but her gloved fingers slid along the glass. "It won't go."

Eric stood and looked at the top of the window. "It's unlocked. I can see it." He knelt and took out a screwdriver, dug it under the sill, and pried up. The window moved—just the slightest bit—but it moved. He slid the screwdriver down to the other end and pried again. It rose just enough for Dex and Marena to get their fingers underneath.

Marena heard the hum of the drone returning. "Hurry up and get in!"

She pulled herself into the darkened room, knocking aside the venetian blinds. The boys handed in the bucket and container of paint and came tumbling in right behind. Marena leaped out of their way and pulled the window shut.

They were in.

Marena squatted low and surveyed what she could see of the room. She didn't know if her heart was pounding more from running or from fear, but it felt like it would burst through her coat. She snapped on her penlight. "Dex, give me your flyers."

Dex swung off his backpack and pulled out a fat stack of papers.

Marena held the penlight between her teeth and gave each of the boys a stack. "C'mon, we've got to fold these," she said. "They're too big to fit in the locker vents."

"What about the ones you've got?" Dex asked Marena.

"Those are for the swim meet."

They worked as fast as they could, pressing and folding flat sheet after sheet.

"We ready?" Eric asked when they finished.

Dex nodded, and Marena said, "Leave the paint here. We'll do the flyers first."

Marena crawled over, opened the door, and made her way through the main office, past Mr. Greengritch's room. She looked out into the front hallway, lit dimly with tiny green emergency lights, and watched the vidicam slowly sweep the area. As soon as she was completely out of its sight, she began counting silently to herself and kept counting till it returned.

"Twenty-four seconds," she told the boys. "I'll count out loud. We do as many lockers as we can. When you hear me say twenty, get into a doorway fast."

They lined up behind one another and waited for the vidicam to turn toward them. As soon as it swung the other way, Marena ran down the hall to the first stretch of lockers, calling out, "One one thousand! Two one thousand! Three—"

She shoved the folded papers into the thin vent slots at the top of each locker. She finished three, moved to the next, and completely scrunched the paper up, trying to cram it in.

"Ten one-thousand! Eleven—"

Slow down, she thought, *slow down!*

She made herself go more slowly and shoved a few

more in—the vidicam was coming back around—"nineteen one thousand! *Twenty!*"

She ducked into the nearest doorway, slamming deep into its shallow alcove, and heard the boys do the same. She waited, then stepped out again.

"One one thousand! Two one thousand! Three—"

Eric and Dex bolted out and continued down the hallway. Shoving and cramming, hiding and ducking, until they reached the end of the long run of lockers. Breathing hard and resting in an alcove at the end of the hall, Marena yelled, "I'm out!"

"I've still got some left!" Eric echoed down the darkened hall.

"I'm out too!" Dex said.

Marena poked her head into the hallway. The vidicam was away. She ran to where Eric was, calling for Dex to join them. He sprinted over and crammed into the same alcove, the three of them breathless and sweating.

"Give me what you've got left," she told Eric, turning her backpack toward him. "I know where we can put them." Eric shoved them in her backpack, and Marena said, "Now for the windows."

"I'll get the stuff," Eric said. He waited for the vidicam to pass, ran back to the main office, and quickly returned with the bucket, paint, and other supplies.

"All right," Marena said as they took out what they needed from Eric's backpack. "We'll start with this room and work our way down." Marena peeked through the window of the darkened classroom and was relieved to see that the vidicam inside the room was off. "Eric, stamp as many windows as you can and anything else you can find. We'll catch up to you."

Eric pushed open the door, penlight in his mouth, and ran toward the bank of windows, dabbing the rubber stamp into the paint-soaked foam inside his bucket on the way. He smacked the stamp into the first window he came to, pulled it away, and left a near-perfect image of a white rose against the green-painted glass. He ran down the row of windowpanes, dabbing and stamping one after the other, leaving an erratic line of white flowers printed behind him. Then he bolted out the door to the next classroom.

Marena and Dex followed behind Eric as fast as they could. The stencil took longer to do, and they quickly decided to do only every other window. Marena held the stencil above the roses that Eric had stamped, and Dex hastily blotted paint against it with the hunk of couch foam. She pulled the stencil away. The paint

dripped slightly on the slick glass, but it was still easy
to read against the dark-green background:

YOU HAVE NO RIGHT
TO BE SILENT!

Eric had nearly finished the other classroom by the
time Marena and Dex had gotten to it.

"What's taking you guys so long?" Eric asked.

"Just keep going!" Marena said. "Don't wait for
us!"

Eric thrust his bucket at Dex. "Give me some more
paint!" Dex poured some more in, and Eric took off
again. They worked furiously, Marena's heart flooding
with adrenaline as they raced from room to room,
stamping, stenciling, Eric hitting some of the desks
and lockers as he passed them. They ran from the last
classroom all the way down to the cafeteria, barely
scooting in before the hallway vidicam came their way
again. Once inside, they did every single green window
in the large room. Then Eric ran up and down the rows
of lunch tables, smacking the stamp onto each one of
them.

Marena's stencil, soaked through with paint, was nearly falling apart. She yelled to Eric, who was stamping roses wildly along the cafeteria walls. "Let's get out of here!" As they hurried out, Marena turned and ran her penlight across the long line of darkened windows, now whitened by the words and image that her mother had left her.

She wanted to do more.

"Dex," she said, taking the container of paint he had left, "get Eric and all our stuff out of here and start cleaning up."

"What are you doing?"

"I'll be right behind you."

"C'mon, Marena, that's enough!"

"Just go!"

Dex looked angry, but Marena didn't care. She ran down the hallway, splattering the last of the paint wherever she could—against the lockers and walls, on the classroom doors, up against the State Youth League posters—and poured the last of it out on the floor as she hurried back to join Dex and Eric. Then, before she climbed out the window again, she took a handful of flyers from her backpack, pushed open the door to Greengritch's office, and tossed them high in the air, scattering them across his desk and the floor of his room. She took another small batch and flung them across the main office as she headed to the window, then climbed out.

Once outside, they quickly regrouped, stripped off their paint-soaked gloves, and stuffed them and everything else—stencil, stamp, pieces of foam—into a plastic bag. Eric and Marena scrubbed their hands raw with the gasoline while Dex ran off and ditched the bag. The paint had soaked through their gloves in spots, and their shoes and clothes had splatters of white on them. They'd have to get rid of whatever couldn't be cleaned. Dex returned, and they helped one another rub away what paint they could. Then, half thrilled, half terrified, they flew across the YTF parking lot, scaled the fence, and ran back to the compound without saying another word the entire way. They just ran, faster, it felt to Marena, than she ever had in her life.

46

Mr. Greengritch drove to ICCS the morning of the Valley West swim meet. He didn't have to be at the YTF till late afternoon, so he took the time to get a look at the trial transcripts of the parents he was investigating. The files that ICCS had sent to his home had shown that each of the girls he was still looking at was a potential suspect, and all had an identical motive: At least one of their parents had been convicted of crimes against the state and neutralized. He had hoped the files would have evidence and details of the actual crimes, but there were none.

An ICCS officer met Greengritch in a small, secured room.

"These can't leave the premises," he said, handing

Mr. Greengritch the transcripts. He pressed his palm against the digiprint on the wall, and the door clicked open. "I'll come back for them in about an hour."

Greengritch waited for the door to lock again and quickly opened his briefcase. He took out the files of the few girls he hadn't eliminated, matched them with their parents' transcripts, and began reading.

If he could find which kids were behind this— soon—it was possible he could question them privately, pressure them, scare them into stopping. He knew ICCS would make an example of whomever he brought in as a suspect.

The transcripts began with legal preambles. Greengritch waded through one or two pages, then checked his watch. He'd never have enough time. He skipped to "Summary of Results of Investigations" and read through the short paragraph.

" . . . *unrepentant . . . irrefutable evidence . . .*"

He read another one, looking for anything that might help narrow down the number of suspects.

" . . . *irrefutable evidence . . .*"

Strange, he thought. He flipped the two transcripts over and checked the signatures; different judges, but their summaries were almost the same. He looked at a third transcript, and a fourth.

"unrepentant . . . irrefutable evidence provided . . ."

Different judges again, same words. He flipped through page after page of the transcripts, struggling to decipher the thick legal language, searching for what the "irrefutable evidence" actually was. He read and read.

" *. . . acting with intent to organize a conspiracy for the preparation of high treason."*
" *. . . acting with intent to influence the masses against the state."*
" *. . . acting with intent to weaken the will of the state in its right to self-determination."*

Each parent seemed to have been convicted of different crimes against the state, yet all had received the same punishments. He scoured the transcripts, looking for evidence.

" . . . their presence at the Capitol march being irrefutably confirmed by video surveillance."

The Capitol march. Where he'd lost his son.

Greengritch read through the same sections in the different transcripts and was baffled by the fact that each parent had been present at the march on the Capitol. The day the state troops had opened fire. The day his son and so many others had been killed.

Greengritch pushed away from the table. The marchers had fired first that day—the Great General, after he'd been elected leader of the Protectorate, had testified to it—but the protest organizers who were arrested denied it to their deaths. It had never been proved.

He paced for a short moment, then hurried back to the table and searched for the names of the defense lawyers. All the transcripts read the same.

" . . . the defendant knowingly and willfully waived right to counsel, and therefore one has been appointed through the generosity of the state."

It doesn't mean anything, Greengritch said to himself. *I must be wrong. I must be missing something.* He

sat back down and picked up another transcript, determined to read it through completely. A writer this time,
a woman. Her photo was familiar to him: those eyes
again, incredibly dark and bottomless, almost black.
Greengritch read through some of her writing samples.

We as a people deserve whatever gov-
ernment we are willing to tolerate.

He couldn't concentrate. His mind kept running
over the similarities of the trials. They had been desperate times, he told himself, when the trials had
taken place. The state had done the best it could.

He tried to read the woman's writings:

Every thing of beauty, every memory of
something good, is a form of resistance.

But his thoughts broke in again. These had been
wartime trials. There were bound to have been mis-
judgments, unfortunate mistakes, in the rush to restore
public safety.

He checked the dates.

Two of the trials had taken place three years after
the war.

Stop it, he told himself. He was losing track of why he was there in the first place. So what if a traitor's conviction was guaranteed? He deserved it.

If they were guilty, he couldn't help thinking, *if they all were guilty.* Could these people have been neutralized just for having been at the march? There was no evidence in the files that any other real crime had been committed.

Greengritch tried to chase the thoughts away. There would be no reason to neutralize the marchers. Why would the state need to do that?

Unless the marchers hadn't fired first, unless the ZTs were getting rid of anyone who might have known—

Greengritch dismissed the thought as he had dismissed all the other conspiracy theories that had circulated after the war: how there had been no weapons found on any of the marchers that day; how the ZT Party had planned the attack to provoke a war; how it had counted on the fear and chaos to follow, even manufactured some of it, so it could rewrite the laws and take control of the state—

No. That's ridiculous, Greengritch told himself again. He had seen the Great General. He'd heard him speak before the Assembly of Nations. He would never lie to those who served the state.

Greengritch fought to silence his doubts. He checked his watch and concentrated again on the woman's writing samples.

> *I saw the ZTs for what they were, what they were capable of, and because of that, I had no right to be silent. I had no right not to do something.*

The words struck him.

> *I had no right to be silent.*

He'd seen those words before. He read them again, then fumbled through his briefcase, took out his folder on the White Rose, and flipped through to the photographs of the street graffiti. He read the words scrawled across the stop sign.

"The White Rose will not be silent!"

He looked back at a sentence he'd read earlier and lingered on it.

> *Every thing of beauty . . . is a form of resistance.*

He remembered the roses dropped around the school.

Greengritch picked up the files of the YTF girls and pulled one of the photos, then pushed aside all the other transcripts on the table and placed the photo alongside that of the woman.

No one had to tell him that they were mother and daughter.

He remembered now where he'd seen the woman's incredibly dark eyes before: in the girl who'd met with him in his office and placed a rose in his hand.

The door clicked open.

Mr. Blaine walked in.

Greengritch had an impulse to grab the photos and hide them, but it was too late. "I saw your name in the registry," Blaine said. He leaned on the table and studied the pictures. "Find anything useful?"

Greengritch started to gather the photos. "Have you ever read the trial transcripts, Mr. Blaine?"

"No. Why?"

"Nothing—"

"Wait," Blaine said, stopping him. "I've seen this girl before." He held up Marena's photo. "As I was coming out of your office that day." Blaine flipped through the other evidence on the desk and stopped at the article Greengritch had left next to the photo of the stop sign.

Greengritch watched Blaine, overpowered by the feeling that what was about to happen was deeply wrong, and knowing that he wouldn't be able to do anything about it.

He stood there, ashamed of himself, hoping that Blaine wouldn't see the connection.

"It's her," Blaine said, looking up. "Good work, Greengritch."

47

"C'mon, Beaner, we're going to be late!" Daniel said, pounding on the bathroom door.

Marena threw some water on her face and looked in the mirror, barely able to keep her eyes open, her cheeks still pink from last night's cold.

"Marena!"

"I'll be right there!" She hurried back to her room and took out the extra flyers she'd hidden in her closet earlier that morning, dumped out her gym bag, and placed them beneath the hard plastic bottom. Then she threw everything else back in.

"Marena!" her father called down the hall again. "They're already at the gate!"

Snow was falling heavily outside. The swim team was assigned a single bus, and the line to get on it was crowded with parents and younger brothers and sisters who had been allowed to go. Marena, her father, and Daniel shuffled sideways down the aisle and found their assigned row while a Stof scanned IDs.

Daniel tried to squeeze past Marena. "I want the window."

She pushed him away. "Get out of here."

"Both of you stop," her father said. He put Daniel on the aisle. "Just sit down."

Marena closed her eyes, envisioning what it would be like that afternoon when the flyers and graffiti were found at the YTF. She jumped unexpectedly when someone tapped her shoulder.

A Stof stood in the aisle, his hand extended.

Marena froze, clutching her gym bag tightly.

"Marena," her father said, "your ID."

"Sorry," she said, handing it to the Stof. He scanned it and continued on.

Her father looked at her. "You nervous?" he asked.

"About what?"

"The meet."

"A little."

"You'll do great."

She turned away from him again, feeling that if she looked into his eyes, he'd be able to see that she was lying. Her father nudged her.

"Why are you so quiet? Are you still mad?"

"Mad?"

"About the other night."

"What'd she do now?" Daniel asked.

"Mind your own business," her father said.

"No," she told him. The bus grumbled to a start and pulled away. "No. Just forget it."

Marena stared at the perimeter fence, the chain links blurring faster and faster until they vanished. She leaned her head against the frigid window and watched the view become unfamiliar as the bus took them away from Spring Valley. The roads lengthened into long stretches of nothingness—open fields on either side, wide and barren and white. Marena closed her eyes and didn't open them again until she heard the hiss and squeal of the bus easing to a stop.

Valley West Youth Training Facility was identical to Spring Valley, down to the windows painted green. The gates opened, and the bus pulled ahead to the back of a large brick building. People gathered their bags and moved out into the aisle. The driver opened the doors, and Miss Elaine stepped in.

"Stay seated, please," she said. "The back door to the gymnasium is right over there. Girls, go straight to the locker rooms and change immediately. Families, proceed to the front of the building."

Marena held her bag and squeezed past Daniel and her father.

"Good luck," her father said.

Daniel whacked her on the arm. "Don't drown."

"Thanks."

She stepped into the aisle and was swept along with the rest of the team rushing forward. She lifted her bag over her head and followed the stream of girls out of the bus. As soon as feet touched snowy pavement, they all ran for the back door of the gymnasium.

Relieved that no one was searching anyone or inspecting bags, Marena sprinted through the back door and around the edge of the gymnasium floor, and joined the girls pushing and shoving their way into the locker room. Each scurried to claim a locker, then tugged on swimsuits and goggles.

Marena studied the room for places to scatter the flyers. The lockers that belonged to Valley West students were padlocked, and they were the tightly gridded kind, like small cages: too small to get the papers through the holes. There was a large glass-enclosed office on one end and communal showers.

"Hurry!" somebody whispered. "She's coming!"

Everyone shot her arms down to her sides and fixed her eyes front.

Miss Elaine came into the room.

"Good morning, Miss Elaine," the girls said.

"Shoulders back," she said, looking up and down the line. "Chins." They raised their chins a little higher. "Girls," Miss Elaine said when she finished her inspection, "losing is not an option." She opened a door at the far end of the locker room. "Line up in size order. We'll have ten minutes to warm up after Valley West has finished."

Marena fell into the line, and they all marched out to the pool. Chlorine fumes instantly made her eyes water as she passed into the echoey expanse of slippery floor and white-tiled walls. The air was thick and warm. Marena pulled her goggles over her eyes and reached around the back of her head to tighten them. She pulled, tighter still, when an idea came to her. She kept pulling, harder, till the thin strap of her goggles snapped with a rubber-band pop.

"Damn it," Marena said, pretending to be upset. "Miss Elaine," she called out, holding the goggles up over her head and flopping the broken straps back and forth. "Miss Elaine!"

Miss Elaine looked up from her clipboard and saw

the goggles. She tapped her watch and waved Marena off.

Marena headed back to the lockers. She pushed the door open, and as soon as she was inside, she checked the room to make sure nobody else was there. She hurried to her locker, pulled the flyers from her bag, and spun around. *Where?* she thought, racing through the locker room. *Showers, garbage pail*—the fear focused her—*locked office, bathroom?* Miss Elaine had seen her come back in; so had a few of the other girls. She'd only have time to stick them all in one place—

The paper towel dispenser.

Wide and silver, it was mounted on the bathroom wall and its long paper hand towels were about the same length as the folded sheets of paper. She could take a handful of the paper towels out, hide her flyers inside, and then shove them back in. They wouldn't be found for days.

Marena plunged her fingers up through the opening at the bottom of the dispenser. She yanked out a stack of paper towels, lost her grip, and they spilled out onto the countertop. She stacked them again, added the flyers, and tried to cram everything back into the opening, shoving the thick clutch of papers up, trying to work it in from end to end. *C'mon, c'mon!* She was taking too long, and she knew it. *Go in already!* She saw herself in the mirror, her eyes beginning to panic—

There was a blur then that Marena saw flash across the mirror to her right. Before she could turn, a hand seized her by the back of her neck and yanked her away from the dispenser. The paper towels and flyers flew from her hands, scattering across the counter and floor, and Marena, stunned, watched in horror as Miss Elaine grabbed one and unfolded it.

Miss Elaine had barely seen the words when her glare snapped to Marena. "It's you!" she spit through her teeth, rushing at Marena. Marena raised her arms, ready to fight. Miss Elaine grabbed her wrist and shoved her toward the counter. "Pick those up and give them to me. Hurry!"

Marena fell to her knees, hurrying, confused, gathering up the flyers that had fallen on the floor. Miss Elaine grabbed the few on top of the counter and crouched in front of Marena.

"Give them to me!" she said, snatching the flyers out of Marena's hands. "Stupid," she muttered to herself, then looked at Marena. "Half the room saw you come in here. What the hell were you thinking?"

Marena said nothing, but the dismay on her face must have registered, because Miss Elaine met her baffled stare. "I'm with AYLR," she said, shoving the flyers beneath her jacket. "We have to hurry."

Marena's world jolted to a stop.

"There's another one," Miss Elaine said, pointing to a paper beneath the counter. "C'mon!"

Marena, shocked quiet, reached under and grabbed it. Miss Elaine stood and ran to the end of the bathroom and leaned out, scanning the locker room left and right. She looked back at Marena, a fierceness in her voice now. "Hurry up!"

Marena handed her the leaflet.

Miss Elaine snatched it. "Are there any others?"

Marena didn't answer quickly enough.

"Are there any others!"

"No," she said, flustered. "No . . . sorry . . . that's it."

Miss Elaine buried the flyers deep in the bottom of a garbage pail. "C'mon, we have to get back in there." She inched open the locker room door. "The other team's still in the water. I'll go out first. When Valley West starts to get out of the pool, I'll blow the whistle, then you come out. Just get right in line with the other girls. All right?"

"Yes, but how—"

"Just listen for now," Miss Elaine said. "Somebody will contact you later." Marena started to ask another question, but Miss Elaine cut her off. "Not now!" She smoothed out her uniform and took a breath and looked like the old Miss Elaine again.

Then she turned and walked out of the locker room.

48

The shrill blast of Miss Elaine's whistle brought
Marena out of the locker room. She hustled as casually as she could across the puddled floor and lined up
with the other girls.

"Ten minutes," Miss Elaine said, ignoring her and
walking to the far end of the pool. "Let's go!" She took
out a stopwatch and flipped over her clipboard.

Marena, trying to stay focused, ran quickly to the
front of the line for warm-ups. At the edge of the pool,
she crept her toes out, crouched, and waited for the
whistle.

Miss Elaine, she thought, still unable to believe it.
Miss Elaine! If she was in the resistance, who else
might be? Her thoughts ran wild. AYLR had found her,
or she'd found them, or it was an accident—it didn't

matter. What else might she be able to do now that she'd made contact with them? Wait till she told Dex! Wait till Miss Elaine saw what she'd done at the YTF. Would the resistance give her things to do? How would they contact her?

The whistle blew.

Marena sprang off the edge of the pool. Like a cat, she pounced over the water. She was awake now, fully alive, strong and purposeful, the way she'd felt the night before inside the YTF. She heard the plunge of swimmers behind her, and she raced to the other side.

Miss Elaine was waiting there, clicking her stopwatch and jotting down times. Marena leaped out and ran small careful steps along the side of the pool, glancing around the room. On the other side of a glass wall were the visitors, arms stretching over their heads, waving silently. Marena spotted her dad. He was smiling and mouthing the words *Good luck.* Daniel was sitting on his shoulders, waving maniacally.

Someone nudged Marena from behind. She stepped to the edge of the pool again and crouched, waiting for the whistle. She peeked down the buoyed lane of water and saw Miss Elaine raising the whistle to her lips. Marena swung her arms back, and—

"*Out!*" a man's voice yelled. "*Out!* Everybody out!"

Miss Elaine started blowing her whistle, alarmlike now, again and again. She joined in with the command: "Everybody out! Let's go!"

A wave of terror pulsed through Marena with each screech of the whistle. She and the other girls flagged down their teammates who were still finishing laps. Slipping and scared, they huddled in a dripping group, sharing towels and frightened looks. At the far end of the pool an ICCS officer was talking to Miss Elaine. Marena wrapped a towel around herself, watching the muted conversation, trying to decipher what was going on. The crowd of visitors behind the windows had stopped waving. A gnawing fear shivered through Marena.

"Spring Valley, form up!" Miss Elaine yelled.

The locker-room doors slammed open, and the crack of boot heels against tiled floors echoed through the room as two officers came through, heading straight for Marena.

She ran, without thinking, her legs just sprang, and she ran. The other girls screamed as Marena headed for the doors on the far side of the room. She slipped on the wet floor, and before she could get to her feet again a leathered hand bent her arms behind her back and she felt the cold steel of handcuffs cutting into her wrists.

49

It wasn't hard to find the others.

Greengritch folded his arms and leaned against the bare wall as Blaine continued questioning the boy. This one was lying. They both knew it right away. Blaine had questioned him about the graffiti and the destruction of state property that had occurred at the YTF overnight and now about the flyers that had been discovered inside students' lockers and scattered throughout the main office, all attributed to the group calling itself the White Rose.

"Who smuggled you in the supplies to print the flyers?" Blaine asked again. "And the stencils for the graffiti?"

"I told you already, nobody!"

"Who contacted you first, the White Rose or AYLR?"

"I was never contacted by anyone. I don't know what you're talking about!"

"You don't?" Blaine said, hovering behind the boy. "And this girl never approached you to join the resistance?"

"No. I've never even seen these flyers you're talking about."

Greengritch had done what little he could for the boy and Marena. He'd explained to Blaine that much of what he'd discovered was circumstantial, but Blaine said that at least in the case of the girl, it was enough to convict her twice over. He knew she was a sure thing, so he was concentrating on the boy for now. What neither Greengritch nor Blaine knew, though, was how many other people were involved and how AYLR played into everything. Its one leaflet had been a warning, to let everyone know that it was there. Here was a chance to stop it before it could rally the people against the state. If these kids had any information, Blaine was determined to get it out of them.

"Was it AYLR who contacted you first?"

The boy dropped his head. "No, I told you, no, they never contacted me."

"How long have you been working for them?"

"Why do you keep asking me the same thing!"

Blaine had been at him off and on for nearly four hours. The boy had gone through playing dumb, playing tough, refusing to say anything, being angry, crying. There wasn't much left now. If he did have any information, he would give it up soon.

"So everything that you did," Blaine asked, "it was just you and your girlfriend?"

"No, I—she didn't do anything. I hardly even know her. You keep asking me the same stupid questions—"

In an instant the boy was sprawled on the floor, the chair kicked out from under him. "And I'm going to keep asking until you tell me the truth!" The boy staggered to his feet, eyes riveted on Blaine.

"Mr. Blaine," Greengritch said, stepping between them.

Blaine pushed Greengritch aside and screamed in the boy's face, "We know she printed the leaflets! We know you two were together all the time—in class, at the compound. We have video evidence! The only question is how much you were involved in these treasonous acts against the state. Now, you can either help yourself and tell me when AYLR joined forces with your White Rose and who your contacts are, or you can face the same charges that she does!"

"She didn't do anything!"

"Who gave you the materials to do the printings? The supplies! The paint!"

"Nobody. I told you a hundred times, nobody! We didn't print anything. We didn't stamp anything! We don't have paper, we don't have anything to even do what you're saying!"

Blaine paused and cocked his head slightly. He looked at Greengritch, then turned to the boy and spoke easily now. "How did you know a stamp was used?"

The boy froze. "I—"

Blaine slid a stool over and sat directly in front of him. "Explain that to me, would you?"

"I—I just thought—"

"You said you'd never seen the flyers. Why would you think a stamp was used?"

The boy gripped the sides of his chair, searching the room for words.

"I asked you a question!" Blaine screamed, grabbing the boy's neck.

"That's enough, Blaine!" Greengritch said.

Blaine dragged the boy off his chair and slammed him hard against the wall. "I want names!" Greengritch tried to pull him off, but Blaine twisted out of his grip and pushed the boy to the floor, yelling, "I want to know every single person involved in this! In the White Rose and in AYLR! Do you understand me!"

"There is nobody else, you sick bastard!" Eric screamed, spitting the words at Blaine. *"I did everything alone! It was me! It was only me!"*

50

Marena sat on a stool in the center of a small room, the outline of her swimsuit a dark shadow beneath the uniform they'd let her put on over it. She dropped her head into her hands and closed her eyes. It had all gone wrong. It had all gone so terribly wrong. *How had they found out? What would they do to her? What would they do to her father and Daniel? Where were Dex and Eric?*

There were no windows in the room. No clock. Just bare walls. The door had been left open, and across the hall Marena could see another room with its door closed. Once in a while a Stof would slow down and glance at her, but no one ever came in.

Marena stared down at the purple bruises beneath her handcuffs and saw her mother's hands.

She wondered if this was how they had looked before— Marena stopped the thought.

There was a noise in the hallway.

Then she stood, but a Stof appeared in the doorway, blocking her path. An officer entered the room across the hall, opening its door just wide enough for her to see a boy sitting in a chair. He turned and looked at Marena.

Oh, God, Eric.

Mr. Blaine stepped into Marena's room. "Friend of yours?" he asked, gesturing across the hall.

Marena backed away, hoping they hadn't caught Dex too. *How much do they know? What should she say?*

Blaine took off his coat and dropped it on a stool. "You know Eric, right?"

"Yes."

"Interesting," Blaine said. "He says he doesn't know you, says he's seen you around the YTF, in some of your classes, but that's it. So, who's lying?"

"No one," Marena said, trying to cover. "I meant that I know him from seeing him around the YTF and in class. That's all."

"You're both lying." He folded his arms. "You're lousy liars, you know that?" He looked at his watch and closed the door. "We know everything. We have your writings from behind the sink at"—he consulted his clipboard—"the *Place*, I believe you called it. We have the rubber stamp and stencil that you made." Blaine took out a small plastic bag from his pocket and tossed it to Marena. "Look familiar?" It was her pocketknife and her mother's bookmark, the one she'd hidden in her closet. "The knife matches the punctures in the bus tires. And that's a *white rose* on that bookmark, isn't it?"

Marena's mind was spinning. Her father wouldn't have said anything—or would he? Would he report her to save Daniel? How had they found everything so quickly?

"There are just a few details we'd like to clear up. And you can either give us the information we want or not. The outcome will be up to you." He picked up another stool, placed it against a wall, and sat. "If you cooperate, it might go better for you at the trial."

The word lingered with Marena. *Trial.*

"We have evidence enough. We know you're both responsible for destroying state property, and"— Blaine took out a piece of paper—"the more serious crime of printing seditious material against the state."

Marena stiffened at the sight of one of her flyers.

"Yes," Blaine said, "they were discovered at the YTF a few hours ago."

A lie flew out of her mouth. "I didn't do it. Somebody else must have put them there."

"Somebody else? Who, Eric?"

"Eric doesn't have anything to do with this."

Blaine stood and walked toward Marena. "Did you people really think you could get away with this?"

Marena found the wall with her back and pressed into it. "I—"

"How long have you been working with AYLR?"

"I—I'm not."

"When did they first contact you?"

"I don't know what you mean—"

"Who approached you to start a resistance?"

"No one."

"Does AYLR have a cell in the YTF? Is it somebody here? I want their names!"

"I don't know any! I did everything myself. I started it myself!"

Blaine spoke softly, his thin face taut and ferret-like. "I warn you not to play games with me. You think Mr. Greengritch is bad? He's nothing. He's a bluff, a lot of talk, a lot of words. I don't have time for talk, and I never bluff. You're going to tell me how many people are in your cell and who your contact is in AYLR."

"I swear to you, I don't know what you're talking about!"

"We know you were in the building! You unlocked the window in the main office."

"No, I didn't."

"You're lying, Marena! I saw you there. I was coming out of the office the day you turned in the roses to Mr. Greengritch. You unlocked the window, came back, and papered the YTF. Your muddy footprints and two other sets are all over the school. You stamped and stenciled the windows!" Blaine showed her the flyer again. "Did Eric contact AYLR?"

"No! I don't know anything about AYLR!" They must not have caught Dex yet, Marena thought, praying she was right. Blaine had said two other sets of footprints besides hers had been found, but he hadn't mentioned Dex at all. "I swear, Eric has nothing to do with any of this."

"Would you like to see him released?"

"Yes, he didn't do anything!"

"Then tell me who your contact is. Give me a name of somebody in AYLR."

"I told you, I don't know anyone."

"If you cooperate, I walk across that hallway right now and release Eric. He gets complete immunity. We'll put it in writing. No charges against him."

Marena searched her heart for what to do. Miss Elaine's name was hovering close to her lips. Blaine seemed interested only in AYLR. Why keep lying for it? He knew everything. He had evidence. Witnesses.

Blaine bore down heavily on his words. "I want a name."

Marena looked at the door as if she could see Eric through it, then turned back to Blaine. "I don't know anyone in AYLR. I did everything myself."

"Stop lying to me!"

"I printed the flyers! I painted the windows in the school! I was the only one who did anything!"

Blaine grabbed his coat off the stool. He punched his arms into the thick leather sleeves. "We have your father."

Marena's throat clenched tight.

"And your little brother."

"Mr. Blaine," Marena said, moving toward him, "they didn't do anything. They don't know anything about this. I swear to you—" Blaine opened the door. Marena's breath caught. She didn't want to cry, but she couldn't help it. "You have to believe me—"

He walked out and slammed the door.

Marena ran to it. "Please, Mr. Blaine!" she yelled. "Please!"

The door opened again, and Mr. Greengritch walked into the room. He came at her slowly.

"I don't know anything!" she said.

"Marena, there's not much time. You need to listen to me."

"Just leave me alone!"

"Marena, please."

"Get away!" she screamed. "I don't know anything about AYLR! I don't know any names! I printed the flyers! Nobody helped me!"

"Marena!" Greengritch yelled, scaring her silent. "Keep your mouth shut and sit down." He pointed to a stool. "Now."

Marena did as he said. Greengritch reached into his jacket. "I have a notebook here. And a pen." He handed them to her. "Now listen to me, and listen closely. They're going to bring you to trial, and when they find you guilty—because they will—you will be sentenced. I've been studying the new guidelines under the Loyalty Correction Act, and I think I can help you if you do as I say."

Marena believed nothing that was coming out of

his mouth. She looked at him with disgust. "You're a liar!"

"I'm not lying, Marena," he said. "This is all I can do for you, so pay attention." He glanced at the door, then back at Marena. "Anything you want to say in your defense you can write down." He gave her a look then, as if he were doing something he shouldn't.

Greengritch spoke slowly and deliberately. "Legally, I'm allowed to tell you that if, for some reason, you were perhaps not able to remember the names of your contacts in AYLR, or if, say, they never told you their names?" He nodded his head ever so slightly as if he were leading her, coaching her in what to do. "You would be allowed to write that down. And more important, if, for some reason, you were now to suddenly realize that you were . . . somehow . . . misled? The judge might take that into consideration."

Marena, unsure of what Greengritch wanted, locked eyes with him. He pulled up the other stool beside her and sat.

"The judge might take into account the fact that you are very young and impressionable. He might also take into account how you were influenced in your upbringing by people like your mother."

Marena's heart hardened.

"Do you understand me now?"

She could feel her mother in the room.

"You could," Greengritch said, "if you wanted to, make a formal statement that you no longer agree with your mother's philosophies." He pointed to the notepad, leading her strongly now, spelling it out for her. "You were not aware of what you were doing, you were confused, and you now regret having taken the wrong path. Write it down, Marena. Now."

Marena didn't know what to think anymore or whom to trust. Her father was right: Her mother hadn't changed anything. All she'd done was get herself killed. And here Marena was making the same mistake. The ZTs had all the power, all the strength. They could do whatever they wanted. What Marena and her mother had done made no difference, and nobody would remember it anyway. All they had accomplished was to hurt the people they loved. Maybe Greengritch was telling the truth. Maybe she could still salvage something of her life and her family's.

Marena took up the pen and opened the notepad. *They're just words,* she told herself. *They don't mean anything.* She thought for a moment.

Greengritch watched Marena quietly struggle to write with her handcuffs on. She took a long time.

Then she handed him the notebook. "Good, Marena,"
he told her. "Good."

He read her statement. It was surprisingly brief.

I'm not on the wrong path, Mr. Greengritch. You are.

51

Late that night Marena was transferred to the Center for Civil Justice to go before the Tribunal for State Security. She snapped awake the next morning at the buzzing of her cell door. It slid open, and a guard tossed in a jumpsuit. Marena got out of her clothes and pulled it on.

The guard took her down a long hallway lined with cell doors and up a flight of stairs. At the top the stairs spilled out into a tremendous lobby teeming with Stof-uniformed young people, most of them Marena's age but many of them younger. They carried armloads of file folders and large bound books. Their heads were shaved clean, and they gazed straight ahead, never looking left or right. It was absolutely quiet except for the echo of bootsteps clacking back and forth across the expanse of marble floor.

The sea of busy people parted without looking at Marena as she was marched through the lobby. The guard hustled her through a large stainless steel door, which quickly shut behind her. He let go of Marena's arm as they stepped inside.

The room was cavernous. Directly in front of Marena, Mr. Farr, Mr. Greengritch, and Mr. Blaine were sitting behind a long table in the center of the room, a large state flag hanging behind them. Stofs flanked the table, three to the right, three to the left, hands clasped behind them, expressionless. A uniformed boy, not more than nine or ten years old, sat at a table off to the side with a small computer in front of him.

On both sides of Marena were rows of folding chairs. Most were empty, but in one was her father, his handcuffed wrists resting on his lap. She could barely bring herself to look at him. He nodded a single quick nod to her and then looked front again.

To Marena's left were Mrs. Benson, Mr. Malcolm, Miss Elaine—

And *Dex*.

Dex, dressed in a Stof-green uniform of the ZT Party. Marena's heart shuddered. He sat upright and rigid, looking forward, not acknowledging Marena. She stared, unable to take her eyes off him.

"Dex?" she whispered. He started to look at her but stopped. "Dex?"

"Silence," Mr. Blaine said.

"Dex!"

"Silence her!"

Two Stofs immediately placed themselves on either side of Marena and pulled her to stand in front of the table. She twisted in their grasps, trying to look at Dex, but he refused to look her way.

"All stand," Mr. Blaine said. "The Honorable Raeleen Fresler presiding."

An older woman robed in dark green and gold walked out from behind the state flag. She carried a large file. "Be seated," she said, taking her place in the center of the table. She arranged her papers and addressed Marena.

"This tribunal has commenced."

The young boy's fingers flew across the computer keys. Marena, unable to grasp the horrible truth, kept trying to see Dex, to catch his eyes, but the Stofs forced her to face the judge.

"Prisoner two-two two-four-three," the judge said, "you stand before this court of the people accused of high treason: of acting with intent to organize a conspiracy against the state; acting with intent to influence the masses through the preparation and distribution of seditious writings; and acting with intent to weaken the will of the state in its right to self-determination, thereby giving aid to the enemy and constituting a clear and present danger. How do you plead?"

Her father suddenly rushed from his chair. "Marena, don't say anything!" he yelled. "She has a right to a lawyer! She has a right to counsel!"

"Silence that man," the judge said.

"She still has rights!" A swarm of Stofs leaped on her father, trying to wrestle him back to his chair. "The little of the constitution we have left says that she still has a right to—"

"You are in contempt, sir," the judge said.

"Please! I was a lawyer. Let me represent her!"

"Remove him."

"This isn't a trial! It's a sentencing! Why are you even pretending to—"

A Stof wrestled her father into a headlock and took him to the floor.

"Đad!" Marena cried as they dragged him out of the courtroom. "Daddy!" She tried to reach him, but she was pulled back by two Stofs and placed again in front of the judge.

"Damn you!" her father yelled, trying to break free. "Damn all of you! You'll answer for this one day! You'll—"

The large steel door closed him out, and the room fell silent again. Marena spun around, rage blackening her thoughts, and saw Dex standing half in the aisle.

"Look at me, Dex!" she screamed, wrenching free and running to him. He turned away, struggling not to look at her. She grabbed his head, forcing his face to hers. *"What are you doing!"* A Stof wrenched Marena's arms behind her back. *"What are you doing!"* A gloved hand clamped her mouth shut.

The judge, looking bored, waited for Marena to be brought before her again. "Next time," she said, "you will be muzzled."

The Stofs held Marena in place. She was so angry she could barely see.

"Now, if you are quite done," the judge said, "we shall proceed." She referred to her notes briefly. "Prisoner two-two two-four-three. The case against you is overwhelming. Besides a preponderance of physical evidence, we have irrefutable testimony from a newly recruited listener for the state." She opened a file folder and took out a sheet of paper. "Andre Ferrayo."

Dex took a step forward.

"Mr. Ferrayo," the judge continued, studying the paper she held and reading from it. "You were first questioned by the Protectorate the night of the Town Hall meeting when a . . . Jeremy Sykes reported you missing from your room at the housing compound. You were later taken into custody and questioned about the early acts of vandalism attributed to the group calling themselves the White Rose. Is that correct?"

Dex nodded.

"Yes or no, Mr. Ferrayo."

"Yes."

"Having confessed under questioning, you were then recruited as state's listener in exchange for immunity from these charges, and your sentence to loyalty correction was duly rescinded."

A stunned horror slowly grew within Marena.

"You were in no way forced," the judge said, "pressured, or threatened into this alliance. The arrangement was freely negotiated between yourself and the Protectorate, Special Branch, Youth Resistance Division. This is your signature, is it not?"

A Stof took a paper from the judge and showed it to Dex.

"Yes," he said. "It is."

"Let it be so entered," the judge said, and the young boy behind the computer tapped her words quickly onto the keyboard. "Mr. Ferrayo, is the information you are about to give accurate and truthful?"

"Yes."

"Speak up, please."

"Yes, it—the information is correct."

Marena listened in disbelief.

"Very well," the judge said. "Would you summarize for the court your role in the apprehension of prisoner two-two two-four-three?"

Dex pulled a paper from his jacket and stared at it.

"Mr. Ferrayo," the judge said, after a long silence, "your summary." Dex looked at the judge and at the people sitting to either side of her . . . and said nothing. "Mr. Ferrayo, your contract with the state will be voided without your present testimony. I shall not ask you again." The judge waited a moment longer and then gestured to the Stofs. "Guards."

"Just a second," Dex said. "I was—" He looked over the paper in his hand. "My notes . . ." The guards stepped back, and Dex read. "My primary objective in—"

"Louder."

"I was ordered by the Protectorate to gather information about AYLR—that was my primary objective—and, if I could, to make contact and try to join them. I—my goal was to infiltrate their organization and to identify any other people interested in joining them."

Marena let out a deep breath she hadn't known she was holding, and the Stofs gripped her arms tighter.

"The YTF staff and ICCS weren't told that I was a listener, so that I would have less chance of being discovered by anyone, and especially by"—Dex nervously looked around the room—"by the accused. To the extent that I . . ." He fumbled with the paper, and his voice trailed off. "I—I'm sorry, I—"

"Continue, Mr. Ferrayo," the judge said.

Dex stared at the paper shaking in his hands. Then he crumpled it and wheeled on Marena, a vicious, pained look in his eyes.

"I tried to make her stop! I tried to, but she wouldn't. She wouldn't stop! She didn't understand what you have to do to—to— I tried, but—" He spun back to the judge and stood at attention. "I never found out if she had any contact with AYLR, I never had any myself, I never saw them, I don't think she did either, she just— The White Rose just kept getting bigger and bigger, and she wanted to do more, and I couldn't stop her!" Dex slowed down and composed himself again. "After we broke into the YTF, the Protectorate ordered me to record everything that I knew about Maren—about two-two two-four-three's illegal activities." Dex took a file folder from the chair behind him and handed it to a Stof. "It's all in my report." Then he stepped back and clasped his hands behind his back.

Marena watched him, numbed. She didn't even recognize him any longer. She felt filthy and violated. How could he do this? She'd rather have died than do what he'd just done. How could she have been so wrong about him? He'd been lying to her for so long. Had anything he'd said been the truth? Or had he just used her, used her to save himself?

"Prisoner two-two two-four-three," the judge said, "have you anything to say on your own behalf?"

Marena looked at the tribunal sitting at the table in front of her: Greengritch, thumbing through a large binding of papers, uninterested; Mr. Farr, tapping his pen; and Blaine, sitting back with his arms crossed, looking righteous. They all disgusted her. They were the same kind of men her mother had faced.

The judge stood abruptly. "If you have anything to say, say it now."

Marena shook herself free from the Stofs and took a step closer to the judge. "Somebody had to make a start," she said. She looked at Dex and then back at the judge. "And one day soon you'll all be standing where I am."

The judge was silent for a moment. Then she gestured to the boy at the computer. "The court will enter the defendant's plea as guilty."

Marena tried with all her might not to let them see how much she was trembling inside. She pressed her arms against her sides and willed herself to be calm. She knew that what she had done was right, she *knew* it. And she would never deny it, because she wanted to be able to tell her mother that when they met again. No matter what happened, that was something no one would ever take from her.

The judge stood again. "Witnesses for the state."

Dex, Mrs. Benson, Mr. Malcolm, and Miss Elaine rose from their chairs.

"Because of the defendant's admission of guilt, your

testimony will not be required." Miss Elaine sat again with the others. Marena could tell she was struggling to appear unmoved. "We shall proceed directly to sentencing," the judge continued. "In the face of overwhelming evidence, a duly witnessed confession, and the defendant's appalling lack of remorse, the court has only one sentence open to it under the Loyalty Correction Act—"

"I wish to speak," Greengritch said, rising.

"Yes," the judge said, "what is it?"

He handed her a thick ream of papers. "Paragraph thirty-seven J—I've marked it." The judge read the paper. "I've been studying the new laws given to me by Mr. Blaine. The amendments made to the Loyalty Correction Act under the Emergency Council of the Protectorate clearly stipulate that in such offenses as this—'if an admission of guilt is freely given and recorded,' which it *was*—the only punishment open to the court is behavior modification. The level of alteration to be voted on by the tribunal after final statements from the guilty party. Neutralization is not an option."

Blaine glared at Greengritch.

The judge, studying the document, nodded reluctantly and then looked up at Marena.

"Do you wish to add anything before sentencing is determined?"

Marena suddenly felt terribly frightened. *Alteration . . . behavior modification.* She'd heard the words before, but what did they really mean? "I—I don't understand," she said.

Greengritch interrupted. "Would you like to express any remorse for your actions, Marena?" he asked, leading her again. "Could you tell the court any reasons why you might have done something like this? Were you perhaps influenced by anybody?"

Marena met Greengritch's eyes. She knew exactly what he wanted her to say, what he'd spelled out for her before the trial: how she'd been confused and taken the wrong path, how she'd been misled by her mother.

Greengritch nearly pleaded with her. "It could greatly affect your sentencing, Marena."

"This is your last chance," the judge said. "Do you have anything to say with regard to your crimes before we determine your sentence?"

Marena took a tortured moment to think, then spoke to Greengritch.

"What I said, and what I wrote, is what so many people are thinking, but they're afraid to say it." She turned to the judge. "I deny nothing. What I did was right."

"Clear the room," the judge said.

The Stofs opened the door in the back and ushered out everyone except those at the table. As she passed, Miss Elaine seemed desperately trying to say something with her eyes, but Marena looked away, not wanting to implicate her in any way. Dex, trailing the others, tried to keep half hidden behind a Stof.

Marena stepped into his path as he tried to pass her. The tears in his eyes meant nothing to her. They were shameful. He started to speak, and she smacked him across the face as hard as she could. Dex barely reacted as the Stofs descended on both of them, taking him out of the room and dragging Marena again before the judge.

The room quieted again as the guards returned and the door closed.

The members of the tribunal wrote down their votes and folded their papers in half.

A Stof walked the table and collected them. He handed them to the judge, who read them, paused at one longer than the others, and then looked at Marena.

"Prisoner two-two two-four-three. In the face of overwhelming evidence and a duly witnessed confession, the People's Tribunal, under the power granted by the Loyalty Correction Act, hereby sentences you to level A-three behavior modification. Sentence to be carried out immediately."

52

In his living room that night Greengritch watched through the window as a transport, loudspeakers mounted on its roof, broadcast the verdict over and over again down the streets of Spring Valley.

Just punishment for enemy of the state!

It drove slowly past his house, past the rims of snow plowed to either side of the street, past the limo still parked beneath the streetlight out front.

At a time of heroic struggle to maintain our safety from foes abroad and traitors within, this despicable criminal is guilty of giving aid to the enemy. She is guilty

of creating, writing, and distributing seditious material in an attempt to undermine the unity of the state.

It had been announced at the YTF and repeated in the evening manifesto at the housing compound.

The accused, having put in jeopardy the safety of our community, has by those actions voluntarily excluded herself from society henceforth.

Greengritch paced his small kitchen.

Her honor and right as a citizen is forfeited for all time. Sentence to be carried out immediately.

I'm not on the wrong path, Mr. Greengritch. You are. It repeated itself over and over again in his head. He had tried to do what he could for the girl. Within the law. *What law?* he asked himself. There was no law, only the will of the state. The courts no longer existed to administer justice, only to eradicate enemies. This girl, no older than his son would have been had he lived, was to be altered to A-3, and for what? For writing down what she thought? *They're just words,* he thought. *Even if she's misled, they're just words.* No. No, he was lying to himself again. *They're never just words. They alter thinking. My thinking?* No. Her words were childish, naive. *She's young and doesn't understand.* Things are complicated. Unpleasant actions are sometimes necessary for the continuance of the state.

Not able to untangle the knot in his mind, Greengritch poured himself a cup of coffee and walked over to the front window.

Again the verdict blared down the street.

Her honor and right as a citizen are forfeited for all time. Sentence to be carried out immediately.

He turned away from the window and sat on the couch. He was so tired, he wanted nothing more than just to sleep. He let his head fall back and stared at the bare walls of his empty house.

I'm not on the wrong path, Mr. Greengritch. You are.

53

The car reeked of shoe polish and leather.

Marena lay cramped in the back, on her side, her hands cuffed. Her mouth was dry, her tongue gritty and hard. There was no more crying now. Whatever tears she had were dried up, replaced with a kind of parching, helpless fear. She looked out at the night. The moon ran alongside the car for a while and then disappeared as the driver turned.

It was all happening so fast—trial, judge, sentencing, no good-byes. Where were her father and Daniel? Where was Eric? What was a correction facility, and what would they do to her there? She couldn't even think of Dex. The mere thought of what he'd done crushed her heart. She knew he hadn't wanted to become a listener, but he had, and willingly. How could he ever have done such a thing? Because it was easier, Marena thought. Doing the wrong thing is always easier.

The car bounced gently now, the highway humming, the streetlights flying by. A drowsiness overtook Marena. *Go to sleep and we'll get there faster,* her mother used to say. Marena knew that wherever they were taking her now wasn't a place she wanted to get to any faster. She fought to stay awake, trying to keep her eyes open—

It seemed only a moment of darkness, a mere blink, and then jarring brightness as the car lurched to a stop. Marena sat up groggy and unsure of where she was. The back door opened, an arm grabbed her, and the horror of what was actually happening came rushing in again. She stumbled out of the car, squinting into the heavy snow. Shadowy figures swinging flashlights walked back and forth in front of a massive chain-link fence topped with spiraling razor wire. It seemed to run on forever into the snowy darkness. Huge floodlights, dozens of them, rimmed the top, whitening the night.

Somewhere in front of Marena, chains rattled. A flurry of small green lights flashed, a high-pitched warning bell sounded, and the enormous fence yawned open. Marena was led in, and the gate closed behind her. To her right was an office. A guard walked her inside and sat with her on a long metal bench. Marena's eyes flitted nervously in every direction. Everything was metal: the chairs, the desk, cabinets on the walls.

A handsome officer walked into the room and startled Marena. A puppy the color of peanut butter bounded in after him, playfully swiping at his heels. Marena straightened up, not knowing what to expect. The tiny dog ran over, sniffed her feet, and then skittered to a water bowl in the corner, its nails clacking along the tiled floor.

The officer tossed his hat onto the desk and signed some papers, then handed them to the guard. "You can take those off now," he told the guard, who removed Marena's handcuffs.

"Two-two two-four-three, yes?" he asked Marena.

"Yes," Marena said just as the puppy came yelping and sliding into her ankles.

The young officer laughed. "He likes you." He sorted through some more documents, glancing occasionally at the puppy, who was pawing at Marena. "You can pet him."

Marena nervously leaned forward. The puppy nipped

and tugged at her sleeve, and leaped again and again, trying to lick her face. Despite everything, Marena managed a frightened smile at the little dog.

"Sorry," the officer said, shaking his head. "He likes to play." He put down the papers he was holding and looked at Marena closely. "I know you're frightened," he said. "But there's really nothing to be scared of here." His voice was kind and understanding. "It's basically a really intensive reindoctrination and an absolutely ridiculous amount of paperwork, but don't tell anyone I said that. You'll do fine. Okay?"

Marena felt the slightest glimmer of hope.

The officer took something from his desk drawer that looked like a miniature scanner and turned it on. He sorted the papers on his desk and then compared some of them with whatever was on the small screen of the scanner. "Good, most of your information is already entered," he said. "This won't take long." He talked to himself as he entered the rest of Marena's data, poking at the tiny instrument with the eraser end of a pencil: "Mother, none . . . father, Richard M., in custody . . . sibling, Daniel . . . heterodoxy . . ." Then he pushed a button on the side and waited, staring at the screen until something appeared.

"That's all I need," he said, walking to Marena with the scanner. He knelt in front of her, petting the puppy. "His name is Puppy. My little boy named him that—very original, don't you think?" He pushed the dog to his side and nodded to the guard.

The guard pulled Marena to her feet and stood behind her.

"What are you doing?" she said, panic rushing into her voice. She struggled under the guard's grip as he forced her arms behind her back. "What are you—" He wrapped one of his legs around her ankles and pinned Marena as the young officer unzipped the front of her coveralls.

"Please," Marena begged, a new terror creeping in. "Don't . . . please, don't—"

The officer touched the tip of the scanner to Marena's chest, and a searing pain cut through her heart. Her mouth opened to scream, but there was no breath, no air. She doubled over, pulling the guard with her, flailing her head back and forth.

The guard let her go.

Marena crumpled, limp, to the ground.

She lay there unmoving. The dark tiled floor, fogged and faded with each frantic breath she took. She couldn't hear clearly . . . voices above her somewhere, the puppy barking squeaky barks, tail thumping the floor.

Marena curled up as small as she could. She bent her head down, chin to her chest, and looked at the thin red line burned above her heart.

54

The guard helped Marena up and guided her back to the bench. She shook slightly as the officer knelt and examined the small red mark, which had already started to disappear from her chest.

"The insertion is painful, but it doesn't last," he said. He prodded the area, and Marena felt nothing, only a little numbness under his touch. "Cauterization deadens the nerves." He pushed a little harder. "It looks just fine." He stood and walked away. "You'll feel light-headed for a few minutes, though." He took what looked like a long black weapons detector from his desk.

Marena flinched suddenly when he pointed it at her.

"It's okay," he said, coming closer to her. "It won't

hurt you." He waved it over her heart and turned to look over his shoulder at a computer screen, where Marena saw her picture appear. "Let's see," he said, going over to the computer. He scrolled through page after page of information. "Looks like it's all there. You're done here."

Marena looked at her chest. There was nothing but a rosy blush mark now. She touched it, and it felt completely normal. "What did you do to me?"

"Nothing," he said. "It's just a small data chip. You're one of the very first. We've just introduced them." He sat at his desk and began filling out some papers. "No more digiprints, no more ID verificators. It's much more convenient for everyone. You walk through the doors of a bus, a school, or any building really, and we have everything we need without disturbing you." He stacked the papers against the countertop. "You just do as you're told here, and you'll be out in no time."

Marena nodded and stood slowly.

"You feeling okay?" the officer asked. "You should be fine by now."

"Yes," she said, surprised that she did.

"Excellent." He waved the guard over and handed him a file folder.

The guard led Marena down a long hallway. Then he passed her off to an older woman with short gray hair and a pale-blue uniform.

"I'm Miss Renée," the woman said, taking the file from the guard. "I'll be with you during your pre–loyalty correction process."

Marena's fear returned.

"This is just a prep," Miss Renée said. "So don't get yourself upset." She flipped through Marena's file. "I've seen hundreds come through, and they've all done just fine. Come with me."

They walked down a long white hall, the doors on either side marked with different colors and shapes: a red triangle, a blue square, a red square, a green circle.

"I know how scared you must be," Miss Renée said, her heels clicking along the marble floor. "But don't worry. If you cooperate, you'll be out before you know it." She stopped outside a room marked with a blue rectangle and unlocked it. "Come in, please."

Inside there was a bed, a small bathroom area with the door removed, and a chair.

"It's not much, but better than a cell, yes?" Miss Renée said. She looked at Marena's head. "First, a trim. Then some sleep. Come."

Marena followed her into the bathroom area. A thin black cord wormed out of the ceiling. Dangling from it were electric shears.

"Take your coat off and sit, please." Marena did as she was told. Miss Renée pulled the shears down and snapped them on. "We do follow the rules very closely here. Head down, please." Marena flinched as the shears touched her scalp. "It's okay," Miss Renée said. "Head down." Marena lowered her head again, and Miss Renée buzzed off the dark stubble of hair that had grown back. It rained into Marena's lap and down her neck. "Don't worry about the hair," Miss Renée said. She pointed the shears at a shower stall that had no curtain on it. "You can wash up after."

Marena's thoughts flip-flopped back and forth: the trial, Mr. Blaine, people screaming and threatening her. Now, people were being nice to her, smiling. *Be out in no time.*

"You can shower," Miss Renée said, snapping the shears back up into the ceiling. "I'll put a gown on your bed."

Marena ran the water cool across the palm of her hand. It wouldn't warm. The chilly water slid quickly off her bald scalp as she washed the hair from her neck and shoulders. She looked down at her chest where the data chip had been inserted. There was almost no mark at all now, just a faint pink shadow. She scrubbed at it hard. There was no pain, but she could feel the chip just beneath her skin, thin and round, like a small watch battery.

The water cut off.

"That's enough," Miss Renée said, twisting the faucet shut and holding out a towel. "Dry off in here, and then some sleep for you. You've got a big day tomorrow." She walked to the head of the bed and pulled the sheets down. "I'll be right back," she said, and left the room.

Marena put on the sheer gown and slipped into bed. Her whole body felt as if it were buzzing from lack of sleep. Frightening thoughts began to haunt her. Where were her father and Daniel? What had the ZTs done to Eric? And what would they do to her?

Miss Renée came in with two female Stofs, one pushing a cart. Marena thought it was food at first. "Something to help you sleep," Miss Renée said, retrieving a large needle from the cart.

Marena panicked and started out of the bed. The two Stofs rushed over and pushed her back down. "I don't want anything! Get off me!" One of them sat on her legs, and the other held her arm firmly in place.

"Don't be frightened, now," Miss Renée said, filling the syringe from a vial on the cart.

"What is it?" Marena said, struggling under the Stof. "What are you putting in me?"

One of them bore down on Marena, her cold hands gripping the sides of Marena's head, pinning her to the mattress. Miss Renée wiped something wet across the inside of Marena's arm.

"Little pinch here—"

Marena cringed at the lengthening sting of the needle sliding under her skin and the rush of warm fluid that followed it. Miss Renée patted her arm and looked at her watch. "Not long now," she said.

Marena felt it immediately. Her muscles went limp. Miss Renée, still staring down at her, went slowly out of focus. The ceiling blurred.

Then blackness.

55

"He will be punished too."

"But the boy didn't do anything."

"He did enough," Blaine said, placing Eric's folder in a large metal file cabinet. "The people need to be assured that anyone involved in treasonous activities—even those with the mere knowledge of it—will be tracked down and punished."

Greengritch walked away to keep from grabbing Blaine by his slender throat. He'd spent the afternoon at the Civil Justice Center trying to get Blaine to release Eric, or Marena's family, held under the Filial Internment Act, or at least to let him appeal Marena's sentence.

"It takes some students longer to readapt than others," Greengritch said.

Blaine fingered through some folders in his file cabinet. "We don't have time, Mr. Greengritch." He held out a map, and Greengritch took it. "Our informers tell us that two new breaches in the Scarps are currently under operation." Greengritch laid out the map, and Blaine leaned across it, running his finger along the long black line of the Northern Escarpments that cut the map in half. He tapped two highlighted sections circled in yellow. "The new tunnels," Blaine said. "They're under surveillance, and we'll be putting together a force to close them down." He pointed out a scattering of other marks circled in red. "These are new safe houses in operation to the north, in the countryside, in small towns, on farms, dozens of them, maybe hundreds. Antistate elements like this girl are infecting everyone."

Greengritch looked over the map briefly and handed it back. "Whether that's true or not, Mr. Blaine, we can't keep altering everyone who doesn't agree with state policy."

Blaine put the map back into his file cabinet. "Why not?"

"Because eventually there won't be anybody left with enough intelligence to *run* the state!" Blaine turned around, and Greengritch checked himself.

"Look, Mr. Blaine, some of these kids we're talking about are the brightest ones we have. They're the leaders. They think for themselves. We need to modify their worldview, not them. We have to get them to believe in what we're doing."

"I don't care what they believe," Blaine said, walking away from Greengritch. "These kids will be corrected and assigned civil positions until they're old enough to serve as state officers. Resistance will not be tolerated."

"Resistance!" Greengritch said, unable to restrain himself. He grabbed one of the flyers off Blaine's desk. "This is your so-called resistance? A kid throwing around some papers? Writing graffiti? This is why we're modifying children?"

Blaine shut the file drawer so violently that it banged into the wall behind it.

"Well, perhaps you'd like to tell all this to the Security Council yourself!" he screamed at Greengritch. "Yes? If you feel so strongly about this, why don't you explain it all to the Protectorate? And while you're at it, why don't you explain to them how this *so-called* resistance, as you like to call it, seems to be getting bigger and bigger under your watch; how they're recruiting kids—your kids—from some of the most secure areas of the state; how they're infiltrating our facilities and spewing their vicious propaganda everywhere; how these flyers are starting to show up in other YTFs and towns throughout the Southern Zone— yes, Mr. Greengritch, we obviously didn't get them all, because they're being *copied* somewhere—and how— now, this is what I'd really like you to explain to the Protectorate—how in God's name we ever allowed this *so-called* resistance to get to the point that we'd actually be here *discussing* it! Why don't you explain that to them?"

Greengritch said nothing.

"I'd be glad to let you, because I'm sure as hell not looking forward to it. And that's exactly what I have the privilege of doing right now." Blaine pulled on his coat. "You're going to be called to account for this, Mr. Greengritch. I promise you that." He swung open his office door and pushed past a Stof who'd been standing just outside.

"Yes?" Greengritch asked the Stof.

He held out a manila envelope.

"Thank you," Greengritch said. He broke the seal on the envelope. Inside were his orders. He sat on the leather bench in Blaine's office and read them. He read them again. He was to resign from the office of minister of public education and report to his living quarters immediately.

Greengritch leaned back against the wall. He lifted the leaflet still in his hand. His eyes came to rest on the white stenciled plea.

YOU HAVE NO RIGHT TO BE SILENT!

He felt old and spent, worn out, not from work— work was easy—but from trying to keep at bay the doubts that hounded him, the thoughts that burrowed ratlike into his mind, the same thoughts voiced by this girl, Marena. It had been so much easier in the early years, right after the war. He knew in his heart that what they had done then had been right, had been necessary, but what had happened since?

He leaned forward on the couch and tried to shake the thoughts from his head.

He took out his wallet and opened it to the picture of his son, forever nine, his boy, who used to wake laughing.

* * *

It was almost two hours later that Greengritch headed home. The snow had let up, and the streets were plowed, but still the driving was slow. As he eased up to the corner of his block, Greengritch noticed not one but three state vehicles parked in front of his house. He drove slowly past his street and turned down the next one. Stopping close to the corner, he got out and walked down the shoveled sidewalk already whitened again with a slick feathering of snow. He stopped about halfway down the block and followed a walkway between two houses that lay directly behind his. The curtains of his house were drawn, but all the lights were on, and he could make out shadowy figures moving about, four, five, six at least.

Greengritch returned to his car and sat there for a long minute or two.

Then he drove away.

56

The words sounded garbled, like listening under-water.

"Marena. Marena." A hand nudged her shoulder. "Wake up now."

Marena moved her head from side to side. "She's coming around," a voice above her said. She forced her eyes open as far as she could, squinting under the glare of the bright lights. "Keep your eyes closed," someone said. "You've been sleeping for a long time."

Marena didn't know where she was. It wasn't the room she had been in when they'd put her to sleep. A buzzer sounded, and a thick glass door swung open. Three or four people in light-green gowns entered.

Another group already in the room chatted among themselves as they headed toward the open door. They peeled off their gowns and thin rubber gloves and tossed them into a receptacle as they left.

Marena tried to speak, but her mouth wouldn't respond.

A voice from somewhere behind her said, "You're doing fine. Just try to relax."

Marena tried to turn and see what the woman was doing, but she couldn't move. Her arms and legs were strapped down.

Miss Renée appeared at her side.

"You've been heavily sedated," she said, snapping on green rubber gloves. She unwrapped a small square of gauze and wiped away drool that was spilling from Marena's mouth. "You'll be able to speak in a little while. Just try to relax." She disappeared behind Marena. "This might feel a little cold."

Marena heard Miss Renée doing something. The clink of a bowl. Tearing something open. "Just going to clean you up a bit here," she said, placing a hand on Marena's head. A cold, wet sponge slopped across Marena's scalp. She tried to resist, but Miss Renée held her head down and scrubbed till it hurt. She wiped it dry with a warm cloth and patted it.

"Almost done," she said.

Then something colder that smelled like iodine was being brushed on.

"There we go now," she said.

Marena tugged at the straps that buckled her down. She arched her back and twisted under the restraints. It was no use. She tried to speak again. "What—what—" Her words bottled up behind her tongue at first and then came pouring out. "What are you doing to me? Where am I? What are you doing?"

"She's lucid," Miss Renée said to someone.

Another woman, dressed in a green hospital gown and black hairnet, walked into Marena's view. She checked IDs on the crew that suddenly gathered at the foot of Marena's gurney. "You running the cognitive?" she asked one of them who was holding a large file folder.

"Yes."

"Any questions?"

"No."

"Good. Continue."

The woman in the hairnet walked away, and the one holding the file folder approached Marena. "Hi.

I'm Miss Diane. I'm going to be—"

"Get away from me!" Marena screamed, struggling under her restraints. "Get away from me! Where am I? What are you doing to me?" The scream turned to a plea, the plea to tears. "Please don't. Whatever it is, please don't do it."

"Calm down," Miss Diane said.

"Please, please don't—"

"If you don't calm down, we'll have to sedate you again, and that will delay the operation."

"What operation? What are you talking about!" Marena thrashed wildly under her restraints. "Let me go! Let me—"

"Dr. Frances!" Miss Diane called over her shoulder. She looked back at Marena. "Now, if you'll just try to calm down, the doctor will explain everything to you."

Dr. Frances, the woman in the green gown and hairnet, came back over to Marena.

"I'm sorry," Miss Diane said to the doctor. "She's still a little—"

"I'll talk to her," the doctor said.

Marena slammed her head against the gurney. "Let me go!"

The doctor clamped her hands on Marena's forehead

and pushed her head down into the gurney. "You're going to hurt yourself if you keep that up." Marena tried to fight back, but the doctor pressed down harder and waited. "Finished?" she asked.

Marena, exhausted, stopped resisting and let her body relax.

The doctor released her hold on Marena's head and turned to Miss Diane. "Be kind but firm." She put her hands in the front pockets of her gown and looked down at Marena. "I'm Dr. Frances. I know this all seems very scary, but believe me, this is an extremely simple procedure. After the prep, you'll be transferred to another facility for the operation. You'll be completely functional afterward and will lead a happy and productive life."

"What operation?" Marena asked, trying to control the panic pulling at every word. "What are you talking about!"

"This is Miss Diane," the doctor said. She gestured for Miss Diane to come closer. "She's going to ask you some questions. They're very important. You'll be asked them again during the operation, so you have to pay attention."

"Tell me what you're going to do to me!" Marena screamed.

Dr. Frances folded her arms. Her voice turned harsh and deadened. "Listen, young lady, you are here due to the kindness and leniency of the state. Most criminal elements like you are simply neutralized. You should be thankful. The A-three neurological alterations require a very simple surgery—"

"Oh, God—"

"Performed on the cerebral cortex . . ."

"No."

" . . . more specifically on the left parietal lobe. A minor incision and minimal cauterizing of brain tissue produces the required aphasia, alexia and agraphia demanded by the state, with no resulting paralysis—if you participate responsibly during the process."

"I don't . . ." Marena tried to speak. "Oh, God . . . I don't understand." She pleaded with the doctor. "What's going to happen to me?"

"Read the sentence of the court, please," Dr. Frances said to Miss Diane.

Miss Diane took a paper out of a file folder and read: "'For the preservation and security of the state and its citizens in this time of dire struggle, and in the face of overwhelming evidence, pursuant to article thirty-seven-J of the newly amended Loyalty

Correction Act, the State Tribunal has decreed that your physical and mental capabilities to read, write, and speak are to be forfeited for all time.'"

Dr. Frances leaned in. "Any other questions?"

57

It was particularly ironic, Greengritch thought, that the same neurological alteration that revolutionized the loyalty and efficiency of state officers was the very thing that was slowly revealing itself to be the cause of their most profound weakness.

Aside from the menial tasks of guarding, standing watch, or manual labor, none of the Stofs could truly make decisions for themselves. They could take orders and offer allegiance, but their communicative abilities were reduced to the limit of yes or no gestures. Any information that needed to be conveyed to them, or by them, had to be done with a simplified series of alarms, color-coded symbols, geometric shapes, or signal lights. They could patrol if told to patrol, arrest when told to arrest, and purge a house when so instructed, but if left to solve a problem or to act without a direct order, they were at a loss. The unforeseen side effect of their having been deprived of the ability to read, write, or speak was that over time they also lost the ability to think. Almost all those in the Protectorate denied this. They admitted that the procedure could be further refined but insisted that it was still a vital practice necessary to the security of the state. Greengritch knew better. He'd watched it mutate over the years. The ranks of the altered had lost their frame of reference, and what remained was blank. Nothing entered their minds but what was put there by the state.

They were empty of opinions. They had no points of view.

The good thing about this, from the standpoint of state security, was that Stofs no longer possessed the ability to question their superiors. The bad thing about this, from the standpoint of state security, was that Stofs no longer possessed the ability to question their superiors.

"They're being moved to loyalty correction," Greengritch told the two Stofs standing guard outside Blaine's office at the Civil Justice Center. "I'd like them cuffed and placed in the transport in front of the building. It's snowing again. Dress them warmly." One of the Stofs hesitated longer than Greengritch was comfortable with. "Today, please! I'd like to keep on schedule." The Stof stiffened and dutifully headed down the hall.

Greengritch slipped into Blaine's office and locked the door. He flipped through the file cabinet and took out the paperwork on Blaine's investigation of the northern resistance. He grabbed a handful of blank forms—transfer papers, release and confinement forms, Marena's correction orders and schedule; but most important, he took the map marking the safe houses to the north that Blaine had shown him earlier. Greengritch placed the papers in his briefcase and sat. He took a long breath and stared at the wall across from him.

Nothing. He felt nothing.

He waited for something to tell him to stop. Nothing came.

He took out the transfer papers and pressed them flat atop the briefcase in his lap. Then, carefully, he entered Marena's information and forged Mr. Blaine's signature. He stood and smoothed out his uniform, put on his overcoat, and walked as casually as he could into the hall.

A hint of nerves tingled through Greengritch as Judge Fresler passed through the lobby. Greengritch saluted. The judge returned the gesture, barely, and continued on.

Greengritch made his way down the hallway and saw Marena's father, Richard, being led away by one of the Stofs. He was handcuffed, and Daniel was asleep in his arms.

"Get them in the transport," Greengritch said.

The door to Eric's room was open, and Greengritch heard yelling from inside. He hurried over and saw Eric struggling with the Stof, one cuff on, one off.

"Get your friggin' hands off me!" Eric yelled.

"Enough!" Greengritch said, pushing Eric up against the wall. He screamed into Eric's reddening face, "I said enough!" Eric fought for a moment more, then loosened his grip on Greengritch's wrists. "Get me a muzzle!" Greengritch ordered over his shoulder to the Stof, who rushed out of the room. Greengritch quickly leaned in and whispered into Eric's ear, "Keep quiet. I'm going to try to get you out of here."

Eric's eyes fixed on Greengritch. "What—"

Greengritch tightened his grip. "Quiet! Give me your hands." Eric, uncertain, slowly raised his hands.

"C'mon!" Greengritch said, placing the other cuff on his wrist. "We don't have a lot of time. I'm going to try to get Marena."

"How?" Eric asked, shooting a look at the open door. "Where is she?"

The Stof came in the room with a muzzle.

"Give it to me," Greengritch said. He took the muzzle and looked into Eric's eyes, trying to reassure him as he strapped it over his head. Eric fought back as the gag was pulled tightly over his mouth. Then Greengritch pushed him roughly at the Stof.

The Stof hauled Eric out of the room. Greengritch took a moment, calmed himself, then walked out into the hall. Not too much farther and he'd have them out of the building. Daniel and his father were nowhere in sight. Greengritch hoped they were already in the transport. Stofs and ICCS officers passed by as he walked toward the huge glass doors of the building. He breathed a little easier when he saw Eric being led outside.

It was cold and dark and snowing much harder. The prisoners were already in the backseat of the transport.

"You," Greengritch said to one of the Stofs standing outside the car, "you drive." He pointed to the other. "You're dismissed." The Stof saluted and returned into the building.

The driver opened the passenger side door for Greengritch, then walked back around and hunched in behind the steering wheel, a small flurry of snow gusting in as the door slammed shut.

Through the metal-caged safety barrier separating the front and back seats, Richard asked, "Where are you taking us?"

"If you speak again," Greengritch said, "you and your son will be muzzled." He leaned over and lowered the heat, which was blasting. "Keys to their cuffs," he said, holding his hand out to the driver. The Stof gave over the keys, and Greengritch pocketed them. "Put your seat belt on," he told the Stof. "Roads are terrible."

The Stof obeyed.

Greengritch pressed backward in his seat, searching the pockets of his coat. "Hold on," he said. "Damn it. The transfer papers." He looked at the Stof. "On the file cabinet in Mr. Blaine's office. Get them, please."

The Stof undid his seat belt and walked back into the building.

Greengritch quickly spun around and fumbled with

the handcuff keys, trying to push them through the small openings of the grated safety cage. "Take them," he said to Richard, who stared at the keys in dismay. "Hurry up and take them! Unlock Eric first."

Greengritch slid over into the driver's seat, threw the car into gear, and sped away, watching in the rearview mirror as Eric wrestled off his muzzle and then uncuffed Marena's father.

"Eric," Greengritch said, "keep an eye behind us. Tell me if you see any transports." Eric spun around, knelt on the seat, and watched out the back window.

Barely awake, Daniel stirred. "Daddy?"

"It's okay, Daniel. Everything's okay."

Daniel rested his head on his father's shoulder. "Where are we going now?"

"Mr. Greengritch," Richard asked, "where are you taking us?"

"To get your daughter."

58

The massive floodlit gates of the Loyalty Correction
Center loomed above Greengritch. A young officer on
the other side squinted at him through the driving
snow.

"Just a minute, sir," the officer said, and stepped
back to examine Greengritch's ID.

Greengritch nodded to him, rubbing his hands
together for warmth, and glanced back at the car,
where Eric and Marena's family lay unseen in the
backseat. He double-checked the transfer orders he'd
stolen from Blaine's office and forged. They looked
authentic. But what if they didn't work? What if the
officer called to confirm?

The officer opened a small door in the gate. "This
way, sir," he said, leading Greengritch into the front

office. Brushing snow from his coat, Greengritch stopped and looked around, feigning surprise.

"Why isn't she here?" he asked.

The officer turned back to Greengritch. "Who, sir?"

"What do you mean, *who*? My transfer. She was to be ready when I got here."

"I'm . . . sorry, sir, I've received no such orders."

Greengritch took the forged papers from his coat. "ICCS order to have the prisoner transferred into my custody. You should have been informed of this."

The officer hustled to his computer. "Number, please."

"Two-two two-four-three," Greengritch said, knowing nothing would come up in Marena's files to indicate a transfer, so before that could happen, he pressed the lie further, berating the officer for not responding quickly enough. "What is the problem here!"

"Nothing, sir."

"You have her on record, don't you?"

"Yes, sir. I processed her when she arrived." The officer fumbled for the phone. "This is the front gate," he said. "We have an order here to transfer custody of—"

"Give it to me!" Greengritch said, grabbing the

phone out of his hands. "This is the minister of public education. You have a prisoner, two-two two-four-three. She has an A-three correction scheduled for today. . . . Yes." He listened closely, thumbing through Marena's other papers. "When? . . . Yes, thank you. . . . No, no, I'll meet them here."

Greengritch hung up, not sure what to do. Marena's ambulance was just about to leave the compound for the Neurosurgery Center. He looked out the window, scouting the grounds, trying to ignore the clawing knot in his stomach. There were too many Stofs around to try to take her here if anything went wrong.

"Some coffee, sir?" the officer said, trying to appease Greengritch.

"No, thank you."

"I'm very sorry about this—a missed entry, perhaps." He stood too close to Greengritch and looked out the window over his shoulder. "It's really coming down, huh?"

"Yes," Greengritch said, moving away.

"I can call up a transport if you're worried about driving. You don't want to get stuck in this."

"Thank you, but the ambulance is leaving now. I'm going to meet it here."

"Here, sir?"

"Yes."

"I'm sorry, sir, but transfers leave out the ambulance bay, the back gate." He turned back to his desk. "I'll get them on the radio."

Greengritch thought quickly, racing through what little options he had. Should he let him call? If he did, they might turn her over to him. *No, no, they might radio ICCS to confirm the orders.*

"No," he told the officer. "No, I have to go to Neuro anyway. I'll meet them there."

"I'll call ahead to play safe."

Greengritch's muscles tensed as he backed away. "Actually, I need to call," he said, taking out his cell phone. "Confirmation numbers are classified." He punched randomly at the buttons on his phone, keeping an eye on the officer to make sure he wasn't calling anyone. Forcing himself not to rush, Greengritch stopped at the door. "Where is the back gate?"

"Left at the end of the fence, sir, and down about half a mile."

"Thank you," Greengritch said.

He walked out of the office, pretending to talk on his phone, and hurried back to the car.

59

Greengritch drove slowly, craning over the steering wheel and wiping clear the fogged-up windshield. The back of the correction center was mostly dark. Only a few small lights flickered through the thickening snowfall. He drove past the back gate and continued down the road half a mile or so, then made a U-turn and faced the building.

"Stay down," Greengritch said, turning off the headlights.

He dug the map out of his briefcase and studied it again, found the small black square on it—the correction center, deep within the pine forests of the valley—and traced his finger along the road they were on: single-laned, one-way, no turnoffs. The ambulance had to come this way. "Richard," he said, "come up here. Eric, watch the gate."

"I can hardly see it," Eric said.

"Watch for lights."

Richard jumped out of the back door and quickly ducked into the passenger's seat.

"This is where we are," Greengritch said, flattening the map between them. "These areas here, to the north and west, are strongholds of the resistance." He pointed to a number of small squares circled in red. "These are all safe houses. The closest one is here, River Valley. We'll try for that. It's not far, just on the other side of—"

The high-pitched ping of the gate's warning bell began to sound.

Greengritch turned to the backseat, running through their plan once again. "All right, now Richard and I are going to go for the ambulance. Eric, you stay here with Daniel. If we get it, we'll pull up to the car, and you jump in. Okay?"

Eric and Daniel nodded quickly.

Greengritch folded the map and handed it to Richard. "If anything goes wrong, take the car and head north."

"I see lights!" Eric said.

Greengritch wiped the windshield clear again.

Flashing red safety lights blinked atop the gate as it began to roll open. Then a white ambulance appeared, nearly invisible in what was turning into a blizzard. Its headlights cut two snowy beams into the darkness as it bumped through the gate. Greengritch let the ambulance get a good distance away from the building. Then he snapped on his headlights, bringing the ambulance to a stop some five or six car lengths in front of them.

The driver waited a moment, then flashed his brights.

Greengritch unholstered his gun and slipped it into his coat pocket.

"Stay behind me," he told Richard, and pushed the door open.

Greengritch stepped out into the glare of the ambulance's headlights and walked quickly toward the vehicle, shielding his face from the biting snow. As he approached, he could see there was a Stof in the passenger side and an officer driving. He tapped his ID against the glass and gestured for the officer to roll the window down.

Looking puzzled, the officer obeyed. "Can I—"

In an instant the man was gasping for air and clutching at the large hand wrapped around his throat.

Greengritch dragged him half out the window, leveling his gun on the Stof, who was escaping out the passenger side.

"Stay where you are!" he screamed, but the Stof was gone. "Richard!" Greengritch yelled, struggling with the officer in his grasp. *"Richard!"*

The officer twisted under Greengritch's hold, swinging wildly. Greengritch pushed him back and brought his gun crashing against the side of the man's head. He crumpled to the ground as Greengritch rounded the back of the vehicle. The Stof who had escaped was running full out toward the correction center, with Richard on his heels.

"Stop him, Richard!" Greengritch called out.

Richard dove at the man's legs and brought him down in a tumble of snow. Greengritch ran as fast as he could. The Stof was on top of Richard and drawing his gun. Greengritch threw himself at the man, grabbed his wrist, and wrestled the gun out of his hands. He fought to keep the man pinned, but the Stof broke free and began running again for the building. In a moment he had disappeared into the blurry whiteness.

"Forget him!" Greengritch yelled, rising slowly, a stabbing pain in his neck and back. "Come on! Let's go!"

Richard helped Greengritch up, and they both ran to the ambulance.

Marena, in the back of the ambulance, struggled to free herself from the gurney when she heard voices yelling outside. "Help me!" she screamed, straining against her leather bindings. "I'm in here! I'm here!"

Suddenly the ambulance doors banged open in a flurry of snow and freezing air. Marena could barely comprehend the sight of Mr. Greengritch climbing in.

"It's okay," he said, winded, his face wet and pitted red with cold. "You're okay."

The front door of the ambulance thudded shut, and Marena turned to see her father in the driver's seat. Her heart felt as if it were going to burst.

"Dad? Daddy!"

The ambulance jerked into gear and took off.

"Is she all right?" Richard called out, his voice panicked.

"Yes!" Greengritch answered. He fumbled open the blade of a pocketknife that dangled from his key chain and slipped it beneath Marena's restraints.

"Thank you," she said as he cut her free. She knew there were better words for what she felt, but "thank you" was all that kept coming out of her mouth.

Greengritch just nodded and worked faster. "We're going to get you out of here."

"Daniel?" Marena asked. "Do you have Daniel?"

"Eric too," he said as the ambulance skidded to a stop. A second later Daniel came clambering in through the back doors and dove into Marena's arms.

"Hey, D," she whispered, crying more than he was. "Hey, buddy."

Eric jumped in and turned to pull the doors closed but stopped. "I see something!"

In the distance, spotlights were snapping on across the back of the correction building.

"Let's get out of here!" Greengritch said. "Go, Richard! Everybody's in! *Go!*"

"I'm trying!" Richard said, gunning the accelerator. The engine screamed as the tires spun helplessly for a frightening moment. Then they grabbed, and the ambulance sped off into the snowy darkness.

Greengritch crouched low, crawling through the small passageway that led to the front of the ambulance. After climbing painfully into the passenger seat, he unbuttoned his coat, barely able to breathe. "Everyone's okay," he said. "Your daughter's okay."

Richard, his eyes riveted on what he could see of the road, nodded quickly. "It's getting worse."

Greengritch looked through the windshield. There was nothing but a swirling blur of white in front of them. "What are we going to do?" Richard asked, slowing the ambulance. "I can't see the road."

Greengritch watched the compass mounted on the dashboard creep eastward as the road slowly curved. The resistance strongholds were to the north and west, on the other side of the woods to their left, and they were headed in the wrong direction.

"Cars!" Daniel suddenly cried out. He was banging on the back door of the ambulance. "I see cars!"

"They're coming!" Marena said.

Greengritch looked in the side-view mirror. Far behind them, in a haze of icy white, dim flashes of blue beams streaked the night sky.

Richard gripped the steering wheel tightly. "What do we do? I can't see anything!"

Greengritch thought quickly. He punched open the glove compartment, rifled through its contents, and smacked it closed. Then he searched the floor beneath him.

"What are you doing?" Richard asked.

"We're getting off the road," Greengritch said, looking behind the driver's seat. He found a flashlight and pocketed it.

"What are you talking about?" Richard said.

"If we can't see, neither can they. Now, pull off the road! Turn the lights off, and get as close to the trees as you can. Keep your foot off the brake!" Greengritch called to the back, "Everybody, hold on!"

"But we won't be able to get out of there!" Richard said.

"Do it!"

Richard killed the lights and pulled the steering wheel hard to his left. The ambulance went completely black and veered sideways. Greengritch held fast to the dashboard as the vehicle plummeted down a steep embankment. Its nose hit the bottom hard and then leveled off as Richard fought to steer toward the dark shadow of trees. He gunned the engine, pushing the vehicle as far as he could, until it shuddered violently and came to a thudding halt. He gunned the engine again, but nothing happened.

"Turn it off!" Greengritch told Richard. He did, and the ambulance went deathly quiet except for Daniel's cries and the soft sound of snowflakes pelting the vehicle. Greengritch spoke into the darkened cabin. "Everyone okay?"

"Yeah, I think . . ." Marena said. "We're fine."

"All right, just stay down." He tried to see out his window, but it was encrusted with frozen snow. "Eric, can you see anything out the back?"

"I can just about make them out . . . two transports. They're still a ways back from where we went off the road."

Greengritch knew there was nothing else to do.

Richard leaned close and whispered, "What do we do if they see us?"

Greengritch slipped out the gun he'd taken from the Stof and placed it in Richard's hand.

Then they waited in silence until the slow rumble of the approaching transports could be heard.

"Here they come," Eric said. His voice was shaky.

The noise grew louder and louder till it sounded as if the transports were right on top of them. Greengritch closed his eyes and saw the ambulance in his mind's eye. He imagined it—*willed* it—to be invisible in the whiteout, as if by thinking it hard enough, he could force it to happen, and then, slowly, very slowly, the noise began to grow fainter.

"They're passing us," Eric said. "They didn't see us!"

"Wait," Greengritch said, beginning to breathe

again. "Wait till they're out of sight."

A long moment passed, and then Marena came crawling up along the floor of the cabin. "What do we do now?" she asked.

"We get out of here," Greengritch said. He pointed to the compass mounted on the dashboard. "Richard, get something to break that off." Richard gripped the compass and began twisting it back and forth.

"Where are we going?" Marena asked.

Greengritch looked at Richard. "The woods."

After a quick moment Richard nodded. "Tell Daniel," he said to Marena. She crawled back, and Greengritch noticed that she was wearing nothing more than her hospital gown and slippers. He spied a coat draped over the back of the driver's seat and tossed it to her. "Marena," he called out, "take that, and find something for your feet."

Richard, yanking and pulling on the compass, swore loudly. Then he leaned to the side and kicked it twice. Hard. It snapped loose from its brackets and tumbled off the dashboard.

"All right," Greengritch said, taking the map and buttoning up. "Let's go."

He stepped out of the ambulance and looked down

the road where the transports had gone. He could see no sign of them. They too had disappeared into white. He held his head low in the frigid wind and trudged through the snow to the back of the ambulance.

Richard met him there, and they opened the back doors. Marena had a small piece of blanket swathed around one foot and was wrapping it tight with medical tape. Eric was busy cutting another piece with a pair of surgical scissors. Richard jumped in to help.

"Come on, Daniel," Greengritch said, reaching in. "I'll take you."

Richard, wrapping Marena's other foot, looked at Daniel. "It's okay, buddy. Go with Mr. Greengritch."

"Daddy!" he cried when Greengritch took him in his arms.

"It's okay," Richard said. "I'm right here." He wrapped a last rip of tape around Marena's ankle, grabbed what was left of the blanket, and jumped out. He threw it over Daniel and took him from Mr. Greengritch.

"Get into the trees!" Greengritch yelled above the wind. "It's not far!" He handed Eric the flashlight and sent him after Richard. Then he and Marena hurried to catch up. Only a few yards ahead, Eric was already disappearing from their view. Greengritch struggled to keep him in sight as they neared the darkened line of trees.

"I can't see him!" Marena said.

Greengritch squinted into the snow. "There!" he said as a glimmer of the flashlight began flicking on and off. A sudden roar of wind tried to push them back toward the road, but Greengritch bent into it and led Marena into the dense forest. As they stepped in, Greengritch looked back. The ambulance, the road, the cars that had passed them—all were invisible in the storm of white. He took Marena's hand and they pushed deeper into the woods.

A few yards in they caught up with Eric and Richard and gathered behind a small cluster of trees, sheltered from the wind. Breathing hard, Greengritch rested his back against a tree trunk and looked into the darkness that surrounded them on every side. Then he looked up, trying to see the sky through the thick weavings of pine boughs above. "I don't know if this storm will last long," he said, unfolding the map, "but let's hope it does."

"Which way?" Marena asked.

"Eric," Greengritch said, gesturing for the flashlight.

Eric muted the beam through his fingers and held it to the map. Richard, his hands shaking, stepped in and held out the compass. Marena picked up Daniel, and they all huddled around Mr. Greengritch, waiting for the thin white marks on the magnetic orb to point their way north.

60

They marched deeper into the dark woods, leaving the storm behind. The soft snow muffled their steps, the forest thickened and quieted, and the heavy canopy of boughs seemed to pull itself closed above them.

Little by little, the wind began to cease until there seemed to be no sound at all within the forest, and as Marena marched deeper and deeper in, she felt a growing sense of being sheltered and protected, as if the night, her mother, and the very trees themselves were conspiring with one another to hide her and keep her safe.

Daniel tripped but got up quickly without complaint and tried to keep up with everyone else. Marena watched him struggle to take bigger steps, and her heart ached for him. She walked up beside him and took his hand. "You doing okay, D?"

He nodded, keeping an eye on his father in front of him, and Marena knew he was scared. She squeezed his hand and led him through the quiet woods.

Marena watched Mr. Greengritch in the lead, huffing and tramping among the timbers. He was moving more slowly and seemed to be limping slightly. He looked completely different to her, as if another person had entered his clothes, so unlike the man who had walked into her classroom not long ago and strutted across onto the auditorium stage at the YTF, smaller somehow, his hair askew, his clothes disheveled and mud caked, as desperate to escape now as she was. But a question that she hadn't had time to think about before began to trouble her: Why was he helping them? Why was he even here?

Greengritch stopped suddenly.

"What is it?" Eric asked.

"Shh!" he said, checking the compass reading. He looked up again. "There's a light."

Marena quietly pressed forward. Through the thinning expanse of trees she felt the wind again. She knelt alongside Greengritch, who had crouched a few feet from the end of the forest.

The storm was waning, but beyond the trees, gusts of snow still blew sideways across an open field. Marena could make out what looked like a barn in the distance, a thick sliver of light escaping from its wide front door. A silo next to it cut a dark, spired silhouette against the gray night sky. Beyond the silo a flickering of lights skirted the horizon.

"Is it the house?" Richard asked.

Greengritch strained to see the map. "I think so. It looks like a farm on the map."

"What if we're wrong?" Marena asked. "What if they're ZT?"

"I'll go in alone," Greengritch said. "If they're ZT, I've got ID on me. I'll make up some reason why I'm there, try to feel them out, see if they know anything." He put the map in his coat. "We need to get out of the snow. Let's get into that barn first. Then I'll try the house."

"My feet are cold," Daniel whispered, trying not to cry.

"I'll take him," Eric said. He wrapped the blanket around Daniel and picked him up. "It's okay, D."

"Stay together," Greengritch said.

They approached the very edge of the wood.

Greengritch stopped. "Wait here." He tapped

Richard, and the two of them crept out of the woods and walked about ten feet across the field. They paused and looked around. Then Greengritch waved to Marena that all was clear.

"Let's go," she whispered to Eric. She bowed her head into the wind and hurried out of the woods.

Suddenly the whitened field exploded in a burst of snow. White figures leaped up from the ground, rushing at them, screaming, *"Down! Down! Everybody down!"* Ghostly shapes, black holes where their eyes should have been, came at them from every side. *"On the ground! Now! Everybody on the ground!"*

"Daddy!" Daniel cried. "Daddy!"

"Get back to the woods!" Richard screamed. "Get back—"

A vicious tackle silenced him. Greengritch raised his gun, but a swarm of figures appeared at his feet, dropping him instantly, and before Marena could react, she was knocked to the ground and struggling to breathe, a hand pinning her facedown in the snow.

19

"It's her?"

"Yes."

"You're sure."

"Yes."

"How'd they find her?"

"Movement sensors, north quad of the pines."

"The other targets?"

"We got them all."

"And it's true?"

"What?"

"About Greengritch."

"Yes. He had the map on him."

"Where is he?"

"Interrogation."

"I'll deal with him."

"That's why we called you in."

"And the safe houses?"

"We're on it."

"I want nothing left of them."

"They're being cleared as we speak."

"Not a single person. Nothing. Not a scrap."

"Understood."

"Good."

"What do you want done?"

"What?"

"With the girl and them."

"I want them taken out tonight."

"The boy too?"

"All of them. Except Greengritch."

"Yes."

"Put them in the tanker. Take them out to the Pine Barrens."

"Yes . . ."

"What?"

"*All* of them?"

"I already said."

"Yes."

"I'll do it myself."

"No, I can."

"Give me a gun. I'll do it. You have one?"

"Yes."

"Then give it to me."

"Where is she?"

"The room behind you."

"Give me the key."

Marena stumbled backward as she heard the key turning in the door. She groped in the darkness, trying to find a window, another door, something to fight with—anything—clawing at the empty walls.

The door opened, and Marena wheeled around, only to be blinded by the glare of flashlights.

Two masked figures stood like black shadows in the doorway.

One started toward her.

Marena wanted to scream then, scream so loudly that it would be heard for a thousand years, so loudly that her mother would hear her and come to her, but suddenly, at the thought of her mother, all the horror, all the fear seemed to go silent within her, and a frightening calm took over.

One of the hooded figures approached Marena, and her newfound peace changed to wonder when she saw who was standing in front of her. She'd seen those eyes before, incredibly deep and dark.

Miss Elaine pulled off her mask. "We have to get you out of the country tonight. I'll take you myself."

62

Miss Elaine paced the small room in the barn as Marena hurried into dry clothes. "I don't like him being here," Miss Elaine said.

"He could have been killed," Marena told her again. She dropped to the ground and pulled on a pair of hiking boots. "He helped at the trial too. You were there, you saw."

Miss Elaine adjusted the pistol in her belt and looked out the open door of the stall. "Something's not right about him."

"I'm telling you, we can trust him."

"Like you trusted Dex?" Marena winced as if hit. "The ZTs could have planned this whole thing. They've done it before, trying to track us, find our escape routes. How'd he find the safe house so easily?"

"I told you, he had a compass—and the map."

"Through the woods? In a blizzard?"

A woman ran into the doorway, and Marena couldn't help staring. Her jaw and the side of her head were badly deformed, sunken in and thinned. Her right eye was deadened and milky white. She jutted her chin oddly to the side and scripted a flurry of symbols in the air with her fingers.

"When?" Miss Elaine asked.

The woman signed another series of messages.

"Pull the tanker up to the barn. Get the others ready—"

The sound of fighting suddenly erupted outside the room. Marena ran out to see two people swathed in white plastic—T-shirts over their heads, holes cut out for eyes—dragging Mr. Greengritch across the barn. "Leave him alone!" her father was yelling, trying to stop them. "Get off him!" Eric and Daniel were yelling too. Guards were restraining everyone.

"Let him go!" Richard said to Miss Elaine. "He's with us!"

Greengritch, his hands bound, was forced in front of Miss Elaine. Stooped slightly and his head bowed, he looked exhausted and hurt. His face was badly bruised, and one of his eyes was nearly swollen shut.

He stared at her, a shattered look on his face, as if he didn't trust what he was seeing. "Miss *Elaine*?"

She looked at him. Cold and indifferent. "Take him into the house," she said to the men holding him. "And get the others into the tanker."

"Miss Elaine, please!" Marena cried. "Let him come with us!"

Daniel twisted free and ran at Greengritch. "Leave him alone! He didn't do anything! Just leave him alone!"

Miss Elaine waved the men off. "Do what I said."

"Oh, God, Miss Elaine!" Marena cried. "Wait! I swear to you—I swear on my mother, he's not one of them anymore. He's not!" She searched her mind, frantic, latching onto the only thing she could think of. "He had the map with him! The ZTs would have found every one of those safe houses if you hadn't seen that map and cleared them out. They would have caught everyone. He never would have brought it with him if he were still ZT!"

Miss Elaine paused.

Marena watched Greengritch, his arms pinioned behind his back, and an ugly thought began to gnaw at her. What if Miss Elaine were right about him? *No,* Marena thought, *no, she couldn't be.*

Miss Elaine stepped closer to Greengritch. She looked him over and spoke very quietly. "Why the sudden change of heart, Mr. Greengritch?"

Greengritch sighed. "It wasn't sudden."

"What was it then?"

"I told them everything already . . . I explained—"

"Come here, Jan," Miss Elaine said, gesturing to the mute woman. She came over, and Miss Elaine placed her in front of Mr. Greengritch. "This is my sister." The woman straightened her shoulders and looked at him, her chin raised, her head twitching in tiny uncontrollable jerks. "You only cut a few parts out of her brain," Miss Elaine said. "She was lucky, she escaped—not like the others you butchered when you started all this, the ones you blinded and paralyzed and stuck in old houses in re-daps so you could study them like they were animals. Not like the Stofs." She looked at Marena, who was understanding all of it now. "That's what you would have been if they'd corrected you, Marena. Did you know that? There's no such thing as being reintegrated anymore. There never really was. Isn't that right, Mr. Greengritch?"

"No. No, it's not," he said. "It wasn't always like that."

"Oh, no? When *wasn't* it like that, Mr. Green-gritch? You tell me, when *wasn't* it? When you dragged my parents out of their bed! My *mother*—and—" Miss Elaine struggled to keep speaking, fighting through feelings she couldn't stop. "My *father*—my broth—"

"No, no, we—" Greengritch said, dropping his head. "We—I tried to—"

"You tried to *what*!"

"To do what I could. You don't understand. The party wasn't always like this."

"Yes, it *was*, Mr. Greengritch!" Miss Elaine screamed. "You knew that from day one!" She stepped back and wrenched the gun from her belt. "Don't you say you didn't know what was going on! You knew! And you either took part in it or stood by and did nothing. Admit that much to me, Mr. Greengritch!" Her arms trembled as she aimed the gun at Greengritch. *"You look at me and tell me!"*

Mr. Greengritch lifted his eyes to Miss Elaine.

"Say it!"

"I did," he said. "I knew."

Miss Elaine looked ready to burst into tears, but she turned suddenly and strode away.

"Blindfold him," she said, shoving the gun back into her belt. She stopped and addressed the men holding Greengritch and the others. "No one says a word in front of him from here on. No one speaks anybody's name. He's to know nothing more than he already does." She took a walkie-talkie from her jacket and turned it on. "He'll go with us. Jan and I will take them out alone."

63

Everything was happening so fast that Marena just tried to stay out of the way.

Miss Elaine held the walkie-talkie close to her ear and gestured to one of the masked guards. "Put out the page in five minutes." He ran out, and she turned to Jan. "Get everyone in the tanker now."

Two other guards rushed over, ripping off their white camouflage. Marena saw that both men were fitted out underneath in the same kind of heavy gear: knee-length canvas jackets, light tan, with wide yellow fluorescent stripes on the sleeves, rubber boots, and thick pants with the same yellow stripes down each side.

They were firefighters or dressed like them.

Miss Elaine listened intently to a quiet voice on

her walkie-talkie. "ZTs are going to hit the Northern Zone as soon as the storm dies," she said to the guards. "Get the first responders. Do a second sweep of the safe houses. People are to clear out *now* and disappear into town."

The barn door swung open wide, blowing in a wintry gust of diesel exhaust and snow. A tremendous, boxy-looking truck idled outside, gleaming red in the snowstorm, large chrome valves protruding from its sides. Mr. Greengritch, who'd been held in the back of the building, was hustled out by two guards, a black hood tied over his head. Richard and Eric followed quickly. Daniel was helping Jan carry water bottles.

"About two minutes!" Miss Elaine called after them. "Let's go," she said to Marena, and hurried out to the truck, which dwarfed them both. Miss Elaine jumped up onto a short silver ladder bolted to the side of the tanker, tossed her walkie-talkie into the cab, and leaped back to the ground.

"Where'd you get this?" Marena asked.

"The resistance here is hidden in the volunteer fire department," Miss Elaine said, crawling under the tanker. "We use their trucks and com systems." She waved Marena down to join her and pointed to a metal door that hung open from the undercarriage. "This is a tanker—carries water. There's a hidden compartment built into the well."

A three-wheeled ATV roared to a stop at their feet. Miss Elaine crawled out and yelled above its loud engine, "Get this place cleared too! Electronics, weapons—everything. I want it all moved back into town!"

She unclipped a pager from her belt and showed it to Marena. "Fire and EMS systems get us past ZT checkpoints. We call in a fire or fake an accident, and dispatch sends us out." She pressed a button on the pager that screeched static. "They don't inspect emergency vehicles under way."

Jan appeared out of the snow and signed a quick series of messages. "Good," Miss Elaine told her. "Probably grounded by the weather." Jan scaled the ladder on the side of the tanker and jumped into the driver's seat. Miss Elaine turned back to Marena. "No drones out."

Suddenly a shrill beeping tone, loud and rapid, blared from Miss Elaine's pager. "That's us!" she said. "Go on, get in."

Marena crawled under the tanker and looked into the open hatch, barely able to make out the dark outlines of her father and the others already crammed into the small compartment. She climbed in, listening to the page as she pulled the heavy door shut behind her.

River Valley Fire, you're being requested for mutual aid at a structure fire in the Pine Barrens, Route Seventy-eight. Fire number E-Edward, sixteen fifty-two. Requesting one tanker. Again, River Valley Fire, you are being requested. . . ."

Not a word was spoken as the tanker rumbled off and traveled deeper and deeper into the northern woods. The small compartment was pitch-black and claustrophobic. The wail of sirens seeped in through the thick walls, and the water surrounding Marena and the others sloshed back and forth, smacking loudly against the walls. The ride was noisy, dark, and airless.

Marena wasn't really sure how to pray or what to pray. She thought that she might have known once, when she was little, but that seemed an unremembered time, something lost. Whenever she tried to pray now, the words just seemed to drain out of her. She reached into the dark and held on to Daniel's foot. And prayed anyway.

She prayed to remember how to pray and didn't stop until the tanker groaned, the air brakes hissed, and the truck skidded to a halt.

The door in the floor fell open. "Let's go," Miss Elaine called in.

Marena helped Eric hand Daniel down. Then they both tried to help Mr. Greengritch, who was having a difficult time moving out of the cramped space with his hood on.

"Can we take that off him now?" Marena called out to Miss Elaine.

"No!"

Marena's father helped, and the three of them managed to get Mr. Greengritch out from beneath the truck. When Marena finally emerged, Jan was already throwing the tanker back into gear, ready to pull away.

Miss Elaine gathered everyone around her. "This snow's letting up, so we have to move fast." She handed out flashlights to all except Greengritch. "Keep them off unless we need them." She turned her own off. "It's not far from here," she said, and disappeared off the side of the road.

Marena ran after Miss Elaine, stopping at the edge of a steep hill. Below her, as far as she could see, vast tracts of wooded land, like dark rivers, snaked through the whitened valley.

"Miss Elaine," Greengritch said as Eric guided him carefully through the snow.

She stopped and looked up at him. "What?"

"Where are we going?"

"Eric," she said, ignoring the question, "take him down the hill."

"They know about the two tunnels," Greengritch told her. "If you're going to the Scarps, they're marked on the map."

"I'd advise you to stop speaking, Mr. Greengritch."

"Look at the map," Greengritch said. "That's the first place they'll look for an escape."

"Eric, I said get him down the hill!"

Eric obeyed, tugging Greengritch farther down.

"He's telling the truth," Richard said to Miss Elaine. "They're on the map."

Miss Elaine spoke softly after Greengritch was far enough away. "Those are dummy tunnels—decoys. We leaked that intel weeks ago. Those tunnels are miles away from where we're going." She checked her watch again and took off down the hill.

Richard carried Daniel, and Marena stayed close to his side, helping her father maneuver down the slippery hillside till they reached the bottom. There they trudged across a few hundred feet of level ground till they reached the wood. The snow had nearly stopped, there was no wind, and the gray clouds had given way to wispy threads of white that no longer hid the stars.

"No sound now," Elaine whispered back as she disappeared into the trees.

She stopped a few feet in, flicked on a penlight, and pointed it at Greengritch's hood. "You can take it off," she told Eric, and began weaving her way through the trees.

They walked in complete silence.

Richard stumbled twice, nearly dropping Daniel, who could barely keep his head up. "Let me take him," Greengritch said. Daniel turned and looked at the man behind him, and let go. Greengritch winced as he caught him and then held him close, looking down at the little boy as if he didn't know what to do. Then he hugged Daniel tighter and started off again.

Now they needed no light. The moon rose and the dark of the wood began to lighten. Marena fell to the end of the line, watching the shadowy figures marching in front of her. They were all so different from the people she'd thought she knew just a short time ago.

Even Eric, silent and focused since the escape, seemed to have sensed what was needed of him and become another person.

Miss Elaine stopped and held up her hand. "We're here."

64

"You stay back," Miss Elaine told Greengritch. She nodded at Richard and Eric to make sure he did and then turned to Marena. "Come with me."

Marena and Miss Elaine crawled the last few feet to the edge of the forest. Beyond the line of trees, a sea of new-fallen snow, slate gray and silvery beneath the dim moonlight, spilled out in all directions.

Miss Elaine took a pair of binoculars from her coat and peered into the night.

Marena looked in the same direction, and there, across the frozen field, still some ways off, an enormous dark shadow, like a cresting tidal wave of black, seemed to rise along the entire breadth of the horizon. The Great Wall of the Northern Escarpments. It was massive, bigger than Marena had ever imagined.

Floodlights, spaced at equal distances along its top, scalloped it out of the blackness, and its spiraling razor-wire trim glinted east and west as far as she could see.

Miss Elaine steadied herself against a tree and scanned the dark wall through her binoculars. "Still too dark—I can't see."

"What?" Marena asked.

"The wall's built in sections," Miss Elaine whispered. "They're numbered. The tunnel is under eleven forty." She glanced back at Greengritch. "The ZTs clear-cut a hundred yards in front of the wall. You can't approach under cover, and you can't dig the tunnel into the tree line because of the old roots. The entrance is in the middle of the field, about fifty yards from the wall."

Miss Elaine trained her binoculars on the Scarps again. "They've got motion detectors on the wall and in the ground," she said. "Tunnels have to go thirty feet down to avoid them."

"Marena," Eric whispered, coming up behind her. He cocked his head and motioned to his ear. Marena looked around and listened too, but didn't hear anything.

"There we go," Miss Elaine said as the moon

showed itself again, "eleven thirty-eight."

"Quiet!" Eric called out. Everyone stood absolutely still. Marena strained to hear what he was listening to, but she heard nothing.

After a short silence, Miss Elaine looked skyward. A second or two later Marena heard them.

Spooring drones.

Miss Elaine stepped away, looking confused and panicked. "How could they— They couldn't possibly know to look here. They're out of range for thermal—" She whirled on Greengritch suddenly, drawing her gun. "They're tracking us! He's got something on him. I was right—the whole thing is a setup!"

Greengritch shook his head and backed away. "I— I don't. I swear to you, I don't!" He looked stunned as he stumbled backward through the snow, Miss Elaine chasing after him. A wave of horror chilled Marena as the truth hurtled at her.

"Stop! Stop! It's not him," she screamed, suddenly remembering the chip in her chest. *"It's me! They put something in me! It's me!"*

Miss Elaine lowered her gun.

"They did something to me at the correction center," Marena cried, slapping frantically at her heart. She pulled down the neck of her sweater. "They put—

they put some kind of chip in me, a computer chip or something. It was just an ID, they said. You can't see it anymore, but it's there. I can feel it. Oh, God, I'm so sorry. I didn't know . . ."

Miss Elaine ran to her and prodded at the small bulge beneath Marena's skin.

"Damn them," Greengritch said to himself.

"What?" Miss Elaine asked him. "What the hell is it!"

Greengritch examined it too. "I think it's a global positioning chip. There was talk of implanting them in infants, but—"

"I hear something, Daddy," Daniel said.

Everyone listened again. It was far away but distinct.

Dogs.

"What are we waiting for!" Eric said. "Let's get to the tunnel!"

"No!" Miss Elaine said. "The drones are locked on the chip. We'll lead them right to it."

"Get it out of me!" Marena said, horrified by what was happening. "I want it out of me!" She tore at the neck of her sweater and pulled at the chip beneath her skin, disgusted by the thought of it being inside her body. "Cut it out and leave it here!" she said. "The drones will stay locked on the chip." She knelt, grabbed a small branch, and snapped it in two. She held the sharp end like a knife. "Daddy, help me!" She reached for a handful of snow and held it to her chest. "Somebody help me!"

Miss Elaine tore the stick from her hands. "We're wasting time!" She said. "We have to try to make it back. We're too close to the tunnel."

"We can't make it back," Eric yelled. "They'll track us there too!"

"I'm not compromising the tunnel!"

"Listen to me," Greengritch said. "Everyone, just stop and listen! Do what Marena said. Get the chip out. It'll work. I can get the drones away from you."

"What are you talking about?" Miss Elaine asked.

"Get the chip out. I'll take it, and I'll lead them away."

As soon as Marena fully understood what Greengritch meant, she cried, "No! I'll do it. I'll go. It's my fault." Her father grabbed her, and she struggled with him. "It doesn't matter, Daddy, don't you see? They're either going to get one of us or everybody. Just let me go!"

"Marena," Greengritch said, stepping in front of her. "Marena, we don't have any time. Look—look at me. Let me do this. I need to do this."

"No, I can't, I can't—"

"There's nothing for me over there, Marena," he said, a quiet certainty in his voice. "Please let me do this."

"He already knows too much." Miss Elaine cut in. "When they pick him up, they'll make him talk. They can make him say anything. He knows that."

"That's true," Greengritch said, "but if you give me your gun, I can promise I won't be captured."

The silence that followed was almost unbearable.

Then came the hum of a spooring drone in the near distance.

Miss Elaine stared at Greengritch until something seemed to release its hold on her. She stepped over to him and handed him the gun.

59

Miss Elaine pressed a handful of snow to Marena's chest, trying to numb the area around the chip. Eric ripped the pocketknife off Greengritch's key chain and cleaned it in the snow.

"It's not very deep," Marena told her father, guiding his fingers. He traced the outline of the small shape beneath Marena's skin. Greengritch took hold of Marena's arms as she lay back in the snow.

"Do it fast," he said.

"Give me the knife," her father whispered to Eric, "and get Daniel out of here."

Marena held tightly to Mr. Greengritch's hand, and Miss Elaine steadied her flashlight. Marena felt nothing at first, just a dull poking at her chest. Then suddenly the knife cut deep, slicing into her skin. She slammed her head into the snow, trying not to scream, but a muffled sound burst from her. Greengritch threw his hand over her mouth and held her down.

"It's bleeding too much," her father said. "I can't see!"

Miss Elaine wiped the blood away, and her father cut again. Marena groaned, thrashing her head from side to side. Her father dropped the knife and kneaded the incision, fumbling with his thumbs, trying to squeeze the chip out. A wave of nausea filled Marena as she felt the thin metal chip slide out from beneath her skin.

"I got it," her father said. "I got it." He searched in the palm of his hand and then held up the bloodied chip between his fingers.

Miss Elaine handed Marena a torn piece of shirt. She held it to her chest and sat up just as they heard the tinny whirring of drones right above the treetops.

Greengritch wasted no time. He stood and took the chip from Richard and placed it in his pocket. The baying of the dogs could be heard clearly now. "We need to hurry," Greengritch said. "Give me a couple of flashlights."

Miss Elaine and Richard gave Greengritch their lights.

"Eric!" Richard called into the woods. "Come on back!"

"Mr. Greengritch," Marena said as he helped her to her feet.

He seemed about to say something, but he just looked at her. Then he heard Daniel, returning with Eric. He listened to the little boy's sound for a moment and limped away, fading into the graying wood.

"Come on," Miss Elaine said, leading them off. "We have to go."

Marena lingered on the spot where Greengritch had been and then took off at a run.

"Stay inside the tree line!" Miss Elaine said.

"Where's Mr. Greengritch?" Daniel asked, bouncing in his father's arms.

"He'll meet us later," his father said. "We need to be really quiet now, okay?"

Miss Elaine dodged through a long run of small trees. Then she cut to the right and stopped, peering through her binoculars in search of the number on the wall. "One more," she called out. "We're near it!"

The group ran as best as they could, trying to keep up, until Miss Elaine stopped again at a large tree and everyone stumbled in around her. She knelt and felt along the base of the tree, groping through the snow.

"C'mon!" she yelled at whatever she was looking for. "C'mon!" Then she took hold of something and lifted. It was a thick white rope looped around the trunk of the tree. She untied it, wrapped it around her hands, and leaned back, pulling hard. The rope tightened in front of her, running straight out toward the Scarps, ripping up through the field in a snowy zip that disappeared somewhere beyond view.

"Follow the rope," Miss Elaine said. "At the end of it is the tunnel entrance. Richard, go first with Daniel. When you get to the—"

Another drone buzzed toward them again, and everyone stopped to listen. It got louder and louder till it was right overhead, but it didn't circle. It kept going, passing them, heading off in another direction.

Heading toward Mr. Greengritch.

"Now!" Miss Elaine called out. *"Go! Go!"*

Marena burst out of the woods, straight into the night, not wanting to think or feel or know anything anymore, just wanting to run.

Helmsley Greengritch stayed just below the line of trees so he could move more quickly and cover a greater distance. He hurried across the wide expanse of snow, stomping through the occasional deeper drift, kicking up icy flakes that melted on his face. It felt good, and he pushed on farther and farther. With each step he put between himself and where he had been, a surprising sense of peace began to settle upon him. It had been so long since anything remotely like peace had visited him.

It silenced everything else.

Wandering farther from the trees, he angled down a slope that banked steeply to his left and followed it to the bottom, where it leveled off. He stopped for a brief moment, stirred by the terrible beauty of the stillness that surrounded him. There was absolutely nothing as far as he could see but an endless field of untouched snow, pure in its new fall.

He wondered what that might be like. To be pure.

Walking more slowly now, Greengritch enjoyed the quiet. He held his arms out to his sides, a flashlight in each hand, trying to make himself look like more than one person. The thought struck him then that he must look quite ridiculous, alone and trudging through the snow, and he couldn't help thinking of his son, smiling at him as he tramped along. Yes, his son was very near now.

Greengritch knew it as sure as he knew he breathed.

He wanted to see his son again.

His heart flooded completely at the thought, and he sat down right where he was, spread his arms open wide, and lay back into the soft snow. He rested there, the cold hugging him on all sides, staring up at the beautiful night sky. The black clouds above had thinned, and shimmering stars flitted in and out of them, playing hide-and-seek with the moon.

99

Marena made her way down the narrow ladder of the shaft leading to the tunnel. The others had gone before her, silent and careful. She watched Miss Elaine, a few rungs above, pull in the rope and drag the heavy covering back into place.

"Keep moving," Miss Elaine whispered, aiming her flashlight down the ladder.

Marena continued down, feeling for the rungs, but stopped suddenly when she heard the metallic shriek of engines somewhere far above. She hugged the rungs tightly, and listened: snowmobiles cutting through the quiet night in one long continuous scream. Then, abruptly, they stopped. In the silence that followed, only the baying of dogs could be heard, full throated and vicious.

Then a shot. Just a quick sound, a crack. Then nothing.

Marena clutched the sides of the ladder and pressed her forehead into the rung till it hurt.

Miss Elaine called down to her, softly but urgently, "We need to keep moving."

Marena nodded. She knew she had to go on. She let go, jumping to the bottom of the shaft, and squinted into the dimly lit tunnel burrowed into the wall. A few meager candles flickered along the floor beside thin railroadlike tracks.

Miss Elaine landed behind her. "No signal yet?"

"No. Did you hear anything else up top?"

Miss Elaine shook her head no.

They waited in nervous silence, Marena's thoughts returning again and again to Mr. Greengritch, until finally they heard a dull rapping coming from the tunnel.

"That's it," Miss Elaine said. "Pull it in."

Marena took hold of a rope and pulled the flat-wheeled cart through as fast as she could. Another rope trailed behind it the entire length of the tunnel. Miss Elaine picked up a pipe that lay near the entrance, took hold of the cart, and steadied it. "Headfirst and lie on your back," she told Marena, who crawled in and rolled over. Miss Elaine ducked in beside her. "Good luck, Marena," she said, and started backing out again.

"Wait!" Marena said, grasping at her, barely catching her hand. "Wait, you're coming, right? You're not staying here?"

Miss Elaine pulled away. "I'll make it back okay."

"Miss Elaine—"

She shook her head gently. "Tell people what's happening."

Miss Elaine tapped the pipe on the tracks, and immediately the rope behind Marena slapped the tunnel floor as its slack was drawn out. Marena fixed her eyes on Miss Elaine. The rope tightened, jerked, and pulled Marena into the darkness.

And Miss Elaine was gone.

Marena dropped her head back and held the edges of the cart as she was dragged and bumped through the narrow passageway. There was nothing now but the cold clay ceiling and seeping walls, which pressed in close on every side. Farther in, the candles had gone out, and Marena began to panic. She struggled to breathe in the murky air and tried not to think about where she was. She squeezed her eyes shut and remembered her mother.

Her mother was watching her.

Marena knew it as surely as she knew her heart beat.

She opened her eyes and looked fully into the darkness.

And was unafraid.

Finally, the cart bumped to a halt. Marena rolled off and could barely see the unknown hands reaching to help her.

"Follow me," someone whispered, and disappeared quickly up a ladder.

Looking up, all Marena could see was a ragged circle of sky, and there, in the center of it, hovering far overhead, were stars. A morning blue surrounded them. But still they glimmered brighter than any stars Marena had ever seen. She clambered up the last few steps, clutched a tangle of stubbed roots that jutted from the dirt, and pulled herself out.

The shadow of the Scarps rose up behind Marena as she raced across the icy field toward her father and Daniel.

She stopped suddenly and looked up. It was snowing. The sky was nearly cloudless, and yet from somewhere, like a million white rose petals let loose from above, it was snowing, magnificently.

AUTHOR'S NOTE

In the summer of 1942, leaflets calling for resistance against the Nazi regime began appearing around the city of Munich, Germany. They were found in the mail and left on trains and buses, in phone booths and theater lobbies, and in and around the university. Soon they began appearing in other cities around the country. The group responsible for these leaflets called itself the White Rose.

Sophie Scholl, her brother Hans, and their friends Christoph Probst, Alexander Schmorell, Willie Graf, and Professor Kurt Huber were the driving forces behind the White Rose. Their acts of resistance against the oppressive and barbarous acts of their government were once described as ". . . heroism unsurpassed in European history."

Anyone familiar with the details of Sophie Scholl's life and the actions of the White Rose will recognize in *The Silenced* scenarios that mirror actual events that took place: The real White Rose's primary form of resistance was the printing of leaflets, by the tens of thousands, which they ran off one sheet at a time on an old mimeograph machine and then secretly distributed around the country; they stenciled antigovernment graffiti around the university and adjacent streets; they tried to link up with other universities to spread their form of resistance, and were successful. Some of the words I gave Marena to say in her trial scene and elsewhere are the same, or paraphrasings, of things Sophie Scholl actually said. Smaller details also made their way into the book: Sophie loved swimming and nature; her writings are filled with images of flowers, trees, and wind, and constant references to the moon and stars; she loved art and drawing, particularly sketching, and unlike Marena was very good at it. She was also an accomplished and deeply thoughtful writer, as her diary entries and letters show.

I first read about Sophie Scholl by accident. In 1993, I was walking past a bulletin board in a university, and I noticed a newspaper clipping announcing a seminar on the White Rose. The article said something about college students being arrested for passing out leaflets during World War II. That image never left me. How could people be arrested merely for writing what they thought on a piece of paper? How could one of the most terrifying regimes ever to exist in history be so threatened by what a young girl and her friends had written that it would mobilize forces against them? I was struck by the power of the written word and by those brave enough to use it.

I was also struck by the fact that Sophie and her friends did not have to do what they did. They were racially and ethnically acceptable to the regime. They were in no immediate physical danger. They could have just kept quiet and survived. But they did not. They saw students and teachers disappearing from the university, friends next door who were suddenly gone one day. They saw the marches in the streets and the book burnings; they were in the youth organizations and saw them for what they were. Hans and the other boys brought back from the front news of atrocities being committed against civilians and prisoners and ethnic populations, and with the full knowledge of the risks they were taking, Sophie and her friends refused to be silent. What was particularly horrific about this dark time in our history was the extent to which young people collaborated with the authorities. Yet here were young people who refused to do that and who fought against one of the most powerful regimes on Earth with no greater weapons than their words.

I think of myself and what I was concerned with at the age of twenty-one, and I'm embarrassed. Sophie Scholl shamed me—in a very positive way. Since learning about her, I have been unable to ignore the fact that every time I do nothing when I see an injustice, it is me *choosing* to do nothing. It is not that I can't do anything to help, it is that I choose not to. Sophie Scholl will not let me forget that.

There is a line Sophie wrote that I have always remembered: "The world has widened for me." This book, over the course of six years, has also widened for me. The early drafts were quite literal retellings of the events that happened during Sophie's life and times, slightly veiled yet still too overt. But as the book grew, with each new revision, it moved further away from actual events and became more and more fictionalized. Marena began to demand a story of her own, as if she were distancing herself from the real events, and she became more like a fictional daughter of the White Rose, silenced under yet another totalitarian regime; this horrible nightmare was happening again.

As this transformation evolved through the next series of revisions, it freed me to be influenced by many other sources and contemporary events—and unfortunately, the resources were all too plentiful. Intolerance and oppression abound in every corner of the globe. Indeed, every time I opened a newspaper, I found present-day words, phrases, and ideas from all over the world that made their way into the book: *thought reports, associative responsibility, readaptation, education through labor, the disappeared, inner councils, loyalty correction* (invented from the actual phrases *loyalty oaths* and *nationality correction*), *re-indoctrination, closing borders, foreign borns, imbedded data chips* (already in existence), *walls between nations*, and many other such instances. The parallels are everywhere.

On February 22, 1943, Sophie Scholl, aged 21, Hans Scholl, 24, and Christoph Probst, 23, were sentenced to death and executed. Alexander Schmorell, Willie Graf, and Professor Kurt Huber were executed on July 13, 1943. Many others involved were subsequently executed or imprisoned. They were triumphant in their deaths. The leaflets of the White Rose were eventually copied and smuggled out of the country, and near the end of the war Allied planes dropped them by the millions over Germany and occupied countries. It is said that people wept when they read them.

The story I wrote ends with hope, because for me that is what Sophie Scholl and the White Rose left to the world. If such people as they exist, then there is always hope.

SELECTED BIBLIOGRAPHY

Dumbach, Annette E., and Jud Newborn. *Shattering the German Night: The Story of the White Rose.* Boston: Little, Brown, 1986.

Hanser, Richard. *A Noble Treason: The Revolt of the Munich Students Against Hitler.* New York: Putnam, 1979.

Kaplan, Robert D. *Balkan Ghosts: A Journey Through History.* New York: Picador, 2005.

Krüger, Horst. *A Crack in the Wall: Growing Up Under Hitler.* Translated by Ruth Hein. New York: Fromm International, 1982.

Scholl, Hans. *At the Heart of the White Rose: Letters and Diaries of Hans and Sophie Scholl.* Edited by Inge Jens. Translated by J. Maxwell Brownjohn. Preface by Richard Gilman. New York: Harper & Row, 1987.

Scholl, Inge. *The White Rose: Munich, 1942–1943.* With an introduction by Dorothee Sölle. Translated by Arthur R. Schultz. Middletown, Ct.: Wesleyan University Press, 1983.

Vinke, Hermann. *The Short Life of Sophie Scholl.* With an
    interview with Ilse Aichinger. Translated by Hedwig
    Pachter. New York: Harper & Row, 1984.

FILM

The White Rose. (Original German title: *Die Weisse Rose.*)
    Directed by Michael Verhoeven. 1982.
Sophie Scholl—The Final Day. Directed by Marc
    Rothemund. 2005.

ACKNOWLEDGMENTS

I would like to express my sincere thanks to Laura Geringer, my publisher, and to my editor, Jill Santopolo, for taking on this book and seeing it through its many revisions. Their suggestions and criticisms, and the rigor with which they apply them, have greatly helped to shape not only the book but also me as a writer. Similar thanks to my agent, Noel Silverman, for his integrity and frankness as always.

Special thanks to Stephanie Breiby for being an insightful reader and critic of early versions of the manuscript. The same to Sara Young and Sarah Day, who also waded through reams of paper they'd find dropped on their desks or thrust into their mailboxes; a heartfelt appreciation to my children, Gale and Sophia, for understanding and respecting the times their dad disappeared into the garage for hours (and for bringing him the occasional breakfast there); and a nod to Isaac Ernst for his lending me the use of *The Place*.

During the last few years that I worked on this book, I was generously supported in part by a literature fellowship from the National Endowment for the Arts. I am deeply grateful for that honor.

And above all, I must thank my wife, Brenda, for her challenging criticisms (particularly in the times when it is difficult to say them to me), and for her tireless encouragement through the inevitable periods of disappointment and self-doubt. She's the person you want in your corner.

All the people acknowledged above have been, and continue to be in one way or another, my teachers. I treasure teachers. They hold the bar firmly, and high, and I thank them for that.